Age of Quintessence

Vortex Crucible

Vista Townsend

AGE OF QUINTESSENCE: VORTEX CRUCIBLE

Cover designed by Vista Townsend. Contributors who own
copyright to some images are David Carillet, Harris Shiffman, and
Microstocker2. Used with permission.

Print Edition 2018   ISBN 978-1-7325597-0-7

First Edition

Printed in the United States of America

Books By Vista Townsend

Science Fiction

Age of Quintessence series
Synthetic Genesis
Shadow Legacy
Vortex Crucible

Fantasy

Salt Legacy series
Masters of Souls

Historical Fiction

Jagged Road To Sainthood

Dedication

To my family. Thanks for your support over the many years.

Prologue

Over seven hundred years ago Emperor Anayasipi, using both diplomacy and war, united the entire galaxy with its diverse sentients under one government. His son Kalyuga inherited a fragile empire where ancient races feuded with each other and insurgents threatened the secession of entire sectors.

When geneticist Layla Rangan created a new species of clone warriors, the quintessences were heralded as the miraculous force to hold the Basanti Empire together. Their loyalty was to the Emperor, their master who paid for their births and training. They owed no allegiance to individual governments or political groups. The perfect weapon the Galactic Senate could wield against all who opposed them.

But the Galactic Senate was fractured from its conception, with species harboring hate for each other. At the core of the conflict was the Coalition of Human Advancement which attracted extremists who believed it was the destiny of humans to rule all others. The Ediethean High Council, whose ancestors had first formed a pact with humans when the Basanti Empire was only a loose alliance of a few planets, stood up against the Coalition.

Many highly populated Core planets took sides, backing either the Coalition or the Ediethean High Council. With their allies, the edietheans managed to cut the government funding for the quintessence project by half. The Coalition plotted retaliation.

Other species living far away on the Rim of the galaxy cared nothing about the problems of the *civilized* Core planets. Sensing the Basanti Empire weakening, entire sectors declared themselves independent. The Galactic Senate responded by sending warships to deal with the uprisings, leaving themselves exposed to their own inter backbiting.

Naysayers claimed the Age of Quintessence was finally ending, triggering the collapse of the Basanti Empire.

Part I

"I refused, and I did right in refusing, to create a companion for the first creature. He showed unparalleled malignity and selfishness in evil; he destroyed my friends."

—From *Frankenstein* by Mary Shelley

Chapter One

A large military shuttlecraft flew above the rolling purple hills of farmland on the planet Tamaris, the ripen crops waiting to be harvested. A gentle mountain slope came into view. Along its sides grew twisted trees with red tipped leaves. A town nested near a dammed stream which generated electricity for the community. Just beyond the river, a large building protruded out of the mountain, the entrance to an underground research complex.

The pilot slowed the craft as he banked towards a landing pad. The box-shaped ship hovered over the tarmac as its wheels lowered. Loud clanging announced that the craft had settled, and then the hatch opened. Out stepped ten men dressed in the dark blue uniforms of the Republic of Maris.

Using her large tail for balance, a lab technician hopped across the landing pad to greet the visitors. Her long hair was twisted into a dozen braids embedded with fake jewels. The temarer slowed as she neared, her worried eyes studying the ten identical human-like faces which watched her with expressionless faces.

Quintessences here, at her lab. Why? What could the foeditas horribilis want? Trying to appear calmer than she felt, the technician held up the three fingers of her right hand in greeting. "Welcome, soldiers, to Keyteen Research Labs. I am Tee'ta. How can I aid you?"

The one with a lieutenant badge on his uniform stepped forward and returned the three finger greeting. "We have been sent on urgent business. I must speak with your director immediately."

"Of course. Follow me."

Tee'ta led the squad indoors, passing two security guards. In the elevator which carried them deeper below ground, she kept glancing at the soldiers, feeling both awe and trepidation. On newsfeeds, reports showed that a company of quintessences had been sent by the Basanti Empire to aid the Republic of Maris in its ongoing war against its neighboring enemy the Union Islands Nation. It was said quintessences could heal from mortal wounds by biting others and sucking away their victims' life force. She would love to observe that first hand—as long as it was an enemy dying and not herself.

The soldiers were nearly two feet taller than Tee'ta. Their brown hair almost brushed the roof of the long hallway. When they reached the doorway to a busy lab, they had to duck to enter. The technicians all froze and stared at the newcomers, their snouts quivering in concern.

Tee'ta said, "Director Lee'zez, these visitors wish to speak with you."

The director stepped forward, frowning that his work was being interrupted. "What message do you have that can't be sent by telecoms?"

A quintessence looked down at the director. "I am Lieutenant Joseph. General Zii't orders that this complex be evacuated immediately."

Lee'zez stood tall, his tail pointing straight up in rage. "This is a civilian company. He cannot order an evacuation."

"Nevertheless, he did so. He is concerned that your lab will fall into enemy hands. You have one hour to gather what you wish. Our ship will fly you and your staff back to Camp Iceshard."

"I refuse. We are right in the middle of a major project. We are nowhere near the frontline of that despicable war. I will not bow to a tyrant. He does not have authority here. "

Joseph kept his voice calm, but he was losing patience. Time was being wasted. "It is the Republic of Maris who pays the majority of your budget and your research is used by the government. You will comply, now."

"No. I will talk with the general myself." Lee'zez hopped over to a computer monitor to contact the military.

The other temarers stared at their leader, admiring his tenacious to stand up against a foeditas horribilis, yet they glanced in concern at the lieutenant, worried about what he would do. Joseph did not disappoint them. He walked over to a different monitor and entered in a high level security code. The large words *self-destruct* flashed across the red screen.

Tee'ta gasped in shock. "Director! Director, he's about to…"

The warning came too late. Suddenly sirens screamed throughout the building and red lights began to flash. A computerize voice came over the intercom. "Self-destruct in sixty minutes."

Lee'zez bounded over to Joseph and screamed, "How do you have access to our computers? Who gave you the codes? Turn it off, now!"

With a stern face, Joseph responded, "Like I said, you have one hour to evacuate. If you wish to make a backup of any files, do so now."

Temarers panicked and begin hopping about, grabbing random objects. Several of the quintessences left the room to aid researchers in other labs.

Lee'zez stood in front of Joseph, his snout quivering in rage, his hands clenched into fists. "You are destroying everything! We have worked years on this. How dare you!"

"I am saving your life. Your people need your leadership now. Tell them we have a ship to fly them to safety."

"To go to a military base or a prison? We are free civilians who can't be treated like this."

Tee'ta grabbed Joseph's arm. "Our families are in town. When this base blows, it will endanger their lives."

"I suggest you warn them then. I will send several of my birthmates to help." Joseph gave commands into his high tech e-band.

As Tee'ta turned to leave, Lee'zez called out, "I need you here to help backup the files."

"My children are more important than my job." She bounded out of the lab, and two quintessences followed her down the hallway.

Lee'zez began barking orders to subordinates who scrambled to monitors. Joseph found the controls to the intercom and announced that a ship waited to transport the staff. He was worried. They had been ordered to evacuate a company, not a town. The shuttle could only hold a hundred and fifty. Joseph glanced at several of his birthmates. As their eyes met, he knew they also shared his concern. But what could they do?

As the timer ticked down, temarers raced about carrying computers and small machines. The hallways began to clear as researchers headed above ground. Only two technicians remained with Lee'zez who complained every twenty seconds that there was not enough time to back up everything.

Once the timer reached fifteen minutes, Joseph said, "My squad reports that the rest of the base is clear. It's time to go."

"We have not even touched the archives yet."

"Your lives are more important than those files. Let's go."

It took several more minutes before he reached the elevator with the three temarers. As they walked into the bright sunshine of the outdoors, the sirens still howled. The shuttle was being boarded by anxious temarers, some with children in tow.

Seeing the lieutenant, Tee'ta called out, "They say there may not be enough room for all of us." Two youngsters clung to her legs, looking in fear at the quintessences.

A male wearing a dirty mechanic outfit said, "I told you we should have drove. We will get out of here much faster."

"But the road will be full of vehicles now."

Joseph reassured the couple. "We will find room for you, even if you have to sit in the aisles." Louder to the whole group, he yelled, "Move faster. Time is almost up."

Finally the shuttle lifted into the sky with only a few minutes to spare. Joseph stood in the cockpit behind the two temarer pilots for there were no seats left. Neither was there room for walking as the aisles were crowded too.

"We are overloaded," complained one of the pilots. "We may not have enough fuel to get back to Camp Iceshard."

"Then we set down at a commercial spaceport to refuel. And we let off any who wish to leave. I only need the director and his upper staff."

The pilot shrugged. "You're the boss."

Purple fields covering gentle hills filled the viewscreen. Joseph glanced at his e-band. One minute left. Suddenly he heard screams of horror from behind the cockpit door. He opened the metal door to see passengers staring wide-eyed out the windows to the east. Some pointed while others covered the faces of children. Yells, screams, and curses filled the air.

Unable to walk more than a foot into the room, Joseph glanced at his birthmates who looked equally puzzled. Joseph bent downward, trying to see out the windows. What frightened them? All he could see were dark, black clouds sweeping outward from a central column. Surely they were not afraid of a whirlwind that was miles away. A distant boom sounded from the west. The laboratory exploded, sending fire and rocks high into the air, but the ship was already several miles away from its danger zone. The passengers barely took notice. It was the fast moving clouds to the east that terrified them.

Seeing Joseph's mystified look, Tee'ta said, "They…they set off a cobalt bomb. The people on the ground…."

"We're all dead, all of us!" shouted another temarer. "The Islanders have won."

"My family is down there," screamed another. "We must land. I must get to them."

Lee'zez raised his voice loudly. "Stop the panic. There is nothing we can do for any of them. We must focus on preserving our work. The weapons we design can still end this war."

"We have already lost! Our world is gone!"

Joseph looked again at the dark clouds which had become a huge, volatile wall racing across the terrain, destroying everything it touched. Cobalt bombs had been outlawed by the Galactic Senate centuries ago, but that had not stopped the Islanders from developing the technology. The detonation must have been a hundred or more miles away, but the blast wave would soon hit the ship. He turned back to the pilots.

"Fly us up into the stratosphere."

"We don't have enough fuel…"

"And we don't have enough time to outfly that blast wave. Get us into space, now." Joseph did not raise his voice, but the intensity of his eyes was enough.

The pilots angled the ship upward, climbing steeply. As they passed into the stratosphere, the craft trembled then leveled out. The pilots cut the lights and other unneeded systems to save power as they put the ship into low orbit. They were seventeen miles above the planet with a panoramic view of its surface. Joseph watched with the other passengers as radioactive clouds spread across the midsection of the continent. Large cities in the impacted zones disappeared under the black clouds. Millions of temarers were dying below them while they hung in the peaceful silence of space.

Joseph and his birthmates forced their emotions under control and kept their faces stoic. The temarers cried, cursed, jumped about, or sat in mute shock. They plotted revenge, swore ancestral oaths, and ranted about the end of the world.

For a long time neither the pilots nor Joseph spoke. Finally one responded to voices on his headset. Then he said out loud, "Camp Iceshard says we are cleared for landing. The clouds did not reach that far north."

"Do we have enough fuel?"

The pilot's snout winkled nervously. "If we drop out of orbit with the right timing, I think we can. But if we are short, there will be no second chance. All commercial spaceports are closed."

"Do your best. Have you heard from my other squads?" Six other squads of birthmates had been sent out to various complexes around the Maris continent to pick up personnel. As lieutenant, Joseph oversaw the entire Company C5-20453.

"I'll ask." The pilot talked for a few minutes into the headset then said, "News is spotty. At least two squads made it back before the blast. Two or three are in orbit like us. Not sure about the others."

Joseph forced himself to relax. There was nothing he could do for his missing birthmates, at least not now. Yet he still worried. Out of the one hundred infants who had grown up together, thirteen had already died during the thirty-two years they have served of their bondage after graduating from Essence Institute. Usually it was just one at a time, often from explosions or gunshots. Four years ago a crash in an enemy military zone had killed three but two others managed to survival by feeding on the enemy that tried to loot the craft.

Every death was painful to the surviving birthmates. They were a family that relied intensely on each other. To outsiders, quintessences were just clones to be used as pawns for politicians. If one died, he could be easily replaced by a thousand more. But to quintessences, each individual was important. No bond was greater than that of birthmates.

The pilots triple checked their calculations. At just the right moment, they turned the engines to full speed and dropped out of orbit. The ship shook as it reentered the troposphere. They flew north, bypassing the radioactive clouds. The computer beeped a low fuel warning as they slowed for the descent to Camp Iceshard. The engines sputtered dangerously as the ship finally settled onto the landing pad.

Joseph waited until all the passengers were off before he left. His squad escorted the passengers to the main building where Major Lo'is greeted the newcomers. He then separated Lee'zez, Tee'ta, and other high-level personnel from the others, telling them they were needed for an important meeting. The other refugees were sent to a barracks. After seeing them settled, Joseph sought out his other birthmates.

He did not have to go far. Four of his sergeants waited for him near the concrete barracks which served as their home for the last year, ever since they had been assigned to this planet.

Philip was the first to speak. "Tom's squad has not returned yet. All others are here. The evacuation went smoothly, overall."

"Have they been able to track Tom's ship?"

The sergeants glanced at each other uneasily. "They were the closest to the detonation and disappeared from radar."

"I see." The grief Joseph felt was raw, acute. Ten birthmates dead. Ten more who would never know the taste of freedom when their bond years were completed.

"We have not told the others yet. We were waiting for you."

Joseph nodded then entered the barracks. The concrete walls were painted a dull brown, the floor dark green. Beside fifty bunkbeds were a hundred footlockers holding the few possessions of the quintessences. But only eighty-seven beds had been in use. Now ten less would be needed.

All the birthmates looked towards Joseph. Those who had been sitting on their mattresses stood up. Joseph swallowed, unable to speak for several minutes. One glance at Joseph's face was enough for them to know their missing comrades were not coming back. Still, they stood motionless, waiting.

Finally, Joseph was able to contain his emotions enough to speak. "Today we lost Tom and his entire squad. We honor their sacrifices. The temarers have also suffered a great lost today. Be thankful for the ones we were able to save."

With that, he turned to his bunkbed and sat on the thin mattress, staring across at the next bed. It had been Tom's.

The other quintessences began moving about the room. Few talked. Their faces showed little emotion. If a stranger had entered the barracks, he would not have known they were in mourning. Their grief was beyond words. Occasionally a quintessence would bite a birthmate in the back of the head where neck and skull met. Using the epulo appendage located under their tongue, they would connect with the brains of their friends, sharing memories of the dead. It was the quintessence way of truly expressing oneself. And it was a closely guarded secret. Outsiders only knew the epulo was used when quintessence feed on others to heal or kill.

The next day General Zii't called Joseph to a high security meeting. Top officers sat around a circular table on which a hologram of the planet rotated. The continent of Maris took up nearly a fourth of the planet. Islands of various sizes were scattered across the vast ocean. As Major Lo'is recapped yesterday's events, the mid-section of the continent turned red.

"This is now the uninhabited zone. Anyone who did not die outright will die from radiation poisoning within the next few days." The major clenched his three fingers into a fist. "Total causalities is three and a half million."

The officers muttered angrily, several calling for retaliation. Their tails swished back and forth as they ranted. Joseph listened quietly.

General Zii't waited until their anger had been vented before he spoke. "Our President agrees we must react quickly before another bomb is used. Last night he authorized Operation Fireburn. We will take out their King and his lords."

Joseph spoke for the first time. "I thought it had been decided that Operation Fireburn would have too many military and civilian causalities. That is why it has not been considered practical."

"Over three million of my countrymen are dead, Lieutenant. And another of those horrific bombs could be set off at any moment. They thought fear would pacify us. They were wrong. We are no longer concerned about protecting their civilians. You are authorized to kill as many as needed to reach King Oct'tis. Is that clear?"

"Yes, sir."

The general looked over his eager officers. "Our navy sets sail in two days. It will take nearly two week to reach their capitol. Prepare your troops."

Joseph waited until the others left then approached the general. "Sir, my birthmates are in mourning. As you know, we lost ten yesterday. I asked that we may skip this mission to have time to grieve."

Zii't wrinkled his snout in disgust. "Grieve? We all grieve. Many of my officers lost family and friends yesterday. Has your kind turned into a flock of weeping younglings? Can your unit function?"

"We function, but when there is a large numbers of deaths of birthmates, C models are sometimes affected by the berserker symptom. Putting them into battle so soon could trigger that."

"Thank you for reporting your concerns, Lieutenant. As we already predict a high level of civilian causalities, perhaps berserking quintessences is what we need. Prepare your solders. Dismissed."

Two weeks later Joseph stood in front of his birthmates. All were dressed in heavy body armor. They were on the deck of a huge battleship which plowed through the ocean towards the capitol city of the United Islands Nation. They waited for the last of the aircraft to be fueled. The sun would soon disappear behind the horizon, and then they would be plunged into darkness—the last sunset some of them would ever see.

Joseph looked each of his birthmates in the eyes, wondering how many of them would still be alive tomorrow. He tried giving a final motivational speech but it fell flat. This was not their war. They had little concern about which government ruled Tamaris. During the forty years of their lives, they had fought in countless battles for various rulers across many planets. Bonded quintessences fought because they were ordered to do so. Disobedience meant death.

Once they were dismissed to board assigned aircraft, Philip paused beside Joseph. "Be careful, brother."

"I always am."

"You cautioned us about not losing control. To stay vigilant about each other's behavior. But you are the one who shares the least. We mourn collectively, but you mourn alone."

Grief briefly clouded Joseph's eyes. "It is my orders the others followed to their deaths. Their lives are my responsibility."

"And you follow the orders of superiors. We do not blame you for our birthmates' deaths. Do not blame yourself."

Joseph nodded then headed to his aircraft where his squad waited. As he strapped himself into his seat, he was once again the stoic warrior.

Hours later Joseph stood beside the open hatch looking down at the capitol island city below him. Wind whipped violently at the straps of his backpack. Several aircraft flew ahead of them. Suddenly the night sky was lit up by missiles firing from the ground at the aircraft.

"Brace for impact," yelled Joseph just before their craft lurched violently sideways. Fire sputtered from an engine. The aircraft would not last much longer, but they were still too far from their target. "We jump now. Go, go."

One by one his birthmates leaped through the open hatch. Joseph followed, feeling the wind rushing pass. The city of Ruymach lay below him. Just a week ago it had been a beautiful, tropical paradise with elegant buildings surrounded by tall, silvery green trees. For the last four days, the island city had been besieged with wave upon wave of Maris aircraft dropping bombs upon the city. The Republic held nothing back. Every available aircraft and naval vessel had been sent for this final battle. Now smoke rose from half collapsed buildings, fires burning uncontrollably in several sections of the city.

At the center of Ruymach was an ancient volcano upon which kings of long ago had built a grand palace. Over the centuries, the underground lava tubes had been turned into a fortified bunker. That was where King Oct'tis would be now. Hiding while his once magnificent city was pulverized into ruins. At least, that was what General Zii't hoped.

Seeing the ground rushing closer, Joseph pulled the cord of his parachute. He felt it catch in the wind, jerking him briefly upward. He navigated towards a quiet street in a well-to-do residential area. Shots fired somewhere in the distance but he was not the target. One of his birthmates jerked in pain as he flew over a rooftop. Joseph pulled out his laser gun and aimed at the two assailants on the building. He hit one and the other ducked behind a railing. Then Joseph was out of range. He barely had time to tuck away his gun before touching down.

He quickly took off his backpack and gathered his squad. Only Jack was injured with a deep burn to a leg. Joseph sent four of his squad into the nearby home while the rest hid behind an expensive garage. Soon his birthmates returned with one of the assailants, an angry Islander who swore oaths against their parents.

"We have no parents," said Joseph.

He pulled the temarer over to Jack who rested against the garage wall. Jack bit the Islander at the base of the neck. The temarer's body trembled, his tail flopping about. Then he went limp. Jack broke contact, and the lifeless body fell to the ground. The burn was gone, replaced with pinkish, recently healed skin.

"He had two sports cars," said Jack, a grin briefly flirting across his face. "I suggest we use them to make up for lost time."

They dragged the body into the garage and used his fingerprints to open the security locks on the cars. Soon they were racing through the damaged city in the sleek cars, dodging debris and ignoring traffic signs. They slowed down once they began climbing up the steep mountainside of the volcano. They pulled into a parking lot of an upscale resort hotel built into a cliff face overlooking the city below.

From the lobby of the hotel, several Maris soldiers pointed guns at the newcomers. Recognizing the quintessences, they lowered their weapons.

"You're late, Lieutenant," called out the temarer Captain Isin'at.

"We had to bail early," answered Joseph, leading his squad into the lobby. "Did you find the entrance?"

"Yes, it's here. Philip's team is setting the charges now."

Joseph and his squad followed several soldiers through the opulent building with plush furniture and thick carpets. The quintessences had to stoop to enter

17

doorways. They passed gift shops and entered a restaurant. The storeroom of the kitchen was built inside an ancient lava tube. A secret passage led deeper into the mountain.

Philip's entire squad greeted their birthmates. The other squads would be meeting up at several other entrances. The plan was for them to assault the underground fortress from four different entrances.

"Are you late so I would have to set the charges instead of you?" jested Philip.

"I did not want to interrupt a master blaster." Joseph allowed a faint smile to form, relieved his brother had not lost his sense of humor.

Quintessences and temarers pulled back to the safety of the kitchen before the detonator blew. Then they carefully treaded through the dust and rubble to the remains of the twisted steel door. Beyond was a well-lit teal hallway. The floor was tiled with marble. Joseph's squad took the lead, followed by Philip's group. Behind followed several dozen Maris soldiers.

Joseph had barely entered the passageway beyond the door before laser bolts hit the wall beside him. He ducked down and returned fire with his setting on stun, but the assailants were hidden behind overturned furniture. Their enemy had prepared for them by barricading the underground passageways with choke points. The battle would be long and bloody.

Several quintessences rushed down the hallway, taking hits as they ran. Joseph stayed on the floor firing at Islanders who raised their heads up to shoot his birthmates. Jack and Todd leaped over the desks, firing shots.

"Clear," came Jack's voice.

Philip's squad advanced down the hallway to deal with the next choke point while Joseph and Jack pulled the unconscious Islanders to their injured brothers for healing. The two squads repeated the pattern of one group attacking while another healed as they worked deeper into the fortress. The Maris soldiers followed, protecting their flanks from surprise attacks from behind.

With gun out, Joseph rounded a corner and found himself face to face with another quintessence. For a brief moment he thought the other was from one of his birthmate's squads. But the model was a C2, not a C5 like Joseph. The newcomer had black hair, instead of brown, and was young, only a recent graduate from Essence Institute. He wore the green and gold uniforms of the Islanders.

Joseph and the C2 stared at each other in surprise, neither firing their weapons. Quintessences fought each other in training exercises, but not on actual battlefields. Their entire species viewed themselves as a collective hive society who lived for the whole. It was stated in their Code of Conduct which they learned as toddlers as soon as they began talking.

Several of Joseph's squad came around the corner. Seeing that he was outnumbered, the C2 held up his hands in surrender and handed over his gun.

"On the floor, now," said Joseph.

The other sat on the floor, saying nothing. Joseph met his birthmate's eyes. They were just as shocked as him at the sudden appearance of a quintessence fighting for their opponents. Philip led his squad down the hallway, pausing to deal with shots coming from a well-stocked library. Seeing they needed help, Joseph's group joined them.

Joseph remained by the prisoner. "What is your company? How many are there?"

"I am from Company C2-30689. There are ninety-eight of us."

"All are in this fortress?"

"Yes."

"Where?"

"I cannot tell you that, Lieutenant, as we fight on opposite sides."

The Maris soldiers turned the corner and stared at the C2 on the floor. Their lieutenant complained, "The filthy Islanders have their own leeches? How could the Basanti Empire double cross us like that?"

Joseph pulled out a plastic band to cuff the C2.

"We don't have time to deal with prisoners," said Captain Isin'at.

He pointed his gun at the head of the C2 and pulled the trigger. The C2 slumped over, a smoking hole exposing his skull and brain tissue.

"That was unnecessary," barked Joseph.

"Wouldn't want him to break loose and feed on us later. Let's go."

Joseph obeyed, keeping his face blank, but inside he boiled with rage. He viewed killing a surrendered quintessence as murder. Bonded quintessences were required to always obey authority, but he was sorely tempted to kill Isin'at.

He entered the large library which had a second floor balcony. Several dead Islanders lay around the room along with two C2's. Near an overturned shelf of books lay a still C5 in a pool of blood.

"Jack's dead," said Philip, wearing a shirt with a charred hole revealing pinkish flesh from a recent healing.

Joseph nodded, forcing his emotions away. He must only focus on the mission. Nothing else. "The C2 prisoner is too."

Isin'at frowned as he looked over the messy room. "The barbarians. They still use paper for books. We'll burn these later."

They continued down hallways and stairs. The rooms become more extravagant, with statues, expensive decorations, and potted trees. And the fighting more furious. Four more birthmates died before they reached the heart of the mountain, along with half of the Isin'at soldiers. Joseph kept his emotions in check until he fired point blank into the face of a young C2, killing the clone a second before the other would have killed him.

Joseph stared in horror as he watched the C2 fall to the tiled floor. In the heat of battle, he had forgot to change the setting of a gun he grabbed off a dead Islander after his own weapon has ran out of charge. *Quintessences should not be fighting quintessences. This is madness.*

His body trembled and his vision turned red. Breath became ragged. Joseph wanted to kill, to slaughter. Not just Islanders but the Maris soldiers too. He hated all of them for forcing him to fight his own brethren. He pointed his weapon at the nearest temarer.

"Joseph? Joseph, snap out of it. Brother, we need you."

His name seem to come from a great distance. Joseph stood, breathing hard, not knowing where he was or what he was doing. All he knew was he wanted to kill those short, hopping mammals like they were vermin.

"Lieutenant Joseph! Lower your gun, now!"

Hearing a direct command, Joseph blinked, slowly becoming aware again. He stood in an art gallery, his gun pointed at Captain Isin'at. He wanted to fire. The captain deserved death for murdering the young C2.

Philip stepped in front of him. "Remember your own orders, brother. You commanded us not to go berserk. That includes you."

"You are right." Joseph lowered his weapon, allowing his breathing to return to normal. By the time he had himself back under control, the room was empty except for Philip.

"Ready, brother? We must be near the king."

"Yes." Joseph rejoined his squad which was now down to seven members.

The hallway opened to a balcony overlooking a large atrium. A three story waterfall splashed into a flowery basin. The blue painted roof, full-size trees, and bright lights created the illusion of being outdoors. Hearing footsteps below, the quintessences ducked behind the railing and peeked over. A squad of their own birthmates marched pass below. Jacob called out a greeting and they stopped to salute. Two of their members were missing.

Joseph led his group down the broad stairs. He was only half way down when the steps exploded, sending him flying through the air and hitting the floor hard. He tried to stand but his body refused to obey. Pain throbbed through him. Dimly he watched as birthmates jumped down from the balcony, several rushing to the side of fallen comrades. *How many dead this time?* he wondered as darkness claimed him.

He awoke to his name being called and felt a warm neck pressed against his mouth. Instinctively he bit, pulling the Islander's life energy into himself. At the

20

same time, he probed the other's mind, seeking info about the fortress's defenses. He broke contact and a birthmate rolled the dead Islander off him. Joseph gingerly stood, checking his body. His body armor had protected his chest, but his pants and shirt were ripped and covered in drying blood. Most likely he had broken a few bones, but they had mended, at least he hoped so. He felt weak and needed a second feeding.

Around him, birthmates attended the injured who feed on captives. Near Joseph's shoe was a severed arm of a birthmate. Further away lay a headless body.

"How many dead this time?"

"Three," said Philip. "You were almost the fourth."

Only four remained of Joseph's squad, including himself. So many of his brothers dead. Yet their task was still uncompleted. Joseph refused to allow grief to come. He would mourn for his brothers later.

Captain Isin'at and his troop entered through a side passageway. They had taken the long way around to avoid the ruined stairs. He barely glanced at the dead bodies and bloody floor of the atrium.

"Keep moving. We have to be near the barbarian king now." Isin'at avoided eye contact with Joseph as he directed soldiers down another hallway. He had not forgotten that Joseph had pulled a weapon on him earlier.

Several gunfights later, they stood in front of the lavish royal suite. Joseph had been able to feed again, and his body was now fully mended. Several birthmates took turns kicking the ornamented double doors, but they was braced from within.

"Time for another explosion," said Philip, pulling out a detonator.

"No need," came a quintessence voice from behind the door. "We surrender."

"We accept," said Joseph. "Lay down your weapons and open the door."

"It's a trap," said Isin'at, flashing his pointed teeth in contempt. "King Oct'tis is too prideful to surrender."

"They are quintessence. I trust them." More than he did the temarers.

Scrapping sounds came from inside as furniture was moved, and then the doors opened. Joseph stepped into the large room along with several of his birthmates. Twenty young C2's stood silently along the walls of a lavish living room. Several high-level Islanders nervously sat in plush couches. On a table was a pile of guns.

Seeing there was no ambush, Isin'at hopped in. "Where is King Oct'tis?"

Several C2's pointed towards a door. No one spoke. Isin'at frowned, sensing something amiss. He motioned for the C5's to investigate. Joseph walked to the door and turned the golden knob. It opened smoothly. He stepped in then froze. The room was a study with desks, shelves of books, and couches. On a table were vials containing green liquid. On the floor lay over a dozen dead temarers, one wearing a crown of golden vines. Stretched out on a couch were the bodies of two children, their braided hair bedecked in jewels. Their mother, adorned in a flowery gown, lay on the floor beside them, an empty glass by her lifeless hand.

"Well, is he in there?" demanded Isin'at from the other room.

"Yes," said Joseph. "The whole royal family."

"Arrest them!"

An Islander officer spoke for the first time. "You can't touch them. They are beyond your evil grasp."

Isin'at hopped to the door and looked in. Rage came over his face. "Suicide! How dare he!"

"Our royalty will not be paraded around like toys for your amusement."

"Your king was a coward."

"He was far braver than you, mogul. I wish I had his same courage."

"Then join him!"

The captain pulled his gun and moved to the officer. He shot the Islander in the head, leaving a burning hole in the skull. Then he moved to the next one and fired again. After he finished killing the Islanders, his fury was still not satiated. He turned towards the nearest C2.

Joseph stepped in front of him. "They have surrendered and are not high ranking officers."

"Out of my way, now." A dangerous tone was in Isin'at's voice.

"They are property of the Basanti Empire and must be returned for a new assignment."

Isin'at pointed his gun at Joseph's face. "Get out of my way now, leech."

"No." Joseph stared at the muzzle but refused to move. He would not allow another quintessence to die needlessly.

Philip pulled his own weapon and pointed it at Isin'at. His birthmates copied him. Maris soldiers focused their gun's sights on various quintessences.

"The war is over," said Joseph. "There needs to be no more bloodshed. Let me take away the prisoners. You have your victory."

The captain scanned the room, noting there were far more quintessences than temarers. If there was a shootout, his men would lose. He lowered his weapon. "Take them. But if they kill any of my soldiers, I will take their blood price out on you."

Joseph led the prisoners out of the room and down several hallways. Then he paused to have them cuffed. They remained quiet, subdued. Most of their birthmates were dead. Joseph studied their young, stoic faces. They had not experienced nearly as many battles as he had. Maybe that was why his birthmates had won today. If up against veterans, the battle could have easily gone the other way.

22

Skirmishes were still taking place in other areas of the fortress. Joseph sent his birthmates off in groups of four, taking a prisoner with them. Whenever they ran into Islander soldiers, they informed them that King Oct'tis was dead and the war over. Quintessences stopped fighting immediately, but some of the Islanders continue to put up a struggle. Eventually the fortress was secured and the city of Ruymach under Maris control.

Mid-afternoon General Zii't and Major Lo'is marched through the city with their army behind them. Isin'at met them at the palace, bragging about his many accomplishments. Joseph and his birthmates stood at attention nearby. After formalities were over, Isin'at pulled Zii't to the side to speak privately. A few minutes later the two hopped over to Joseph.

The general sternly looked up at the quintessence. "Captain Isin'at reports that you threatened to shoot him and disobeyed a direct order. Is that correct?"

"Yes, sir."

"What is the penalty for those crimes?"

"I am to appear before the Five at Essence who decide the fate of quintessences who break the Code."

"You will be shipped off with the prisoners this afternoon. Report to the brig on my flag ship."

Isin'at grinned as he bounced away beside the general. Joseph turned and looked over his forty-six birthmates—all that have survived the battle. Over half the company was dead under his watch. His brothers gone. He swallowed, overcome with emotion. His birthmates broke formation and surrounded him, saying their goodbyes. They all knew that death was the punishment for disobeying an officer.

Philip said, "They ought to be promoting you, not sentencing you to death. We won the war for them."

Joseph took off his lieutenant's badge and handed it to Philip. "Take care of our brothers."

Philip stared at the bronze badge for a moment, then reluctantly took it. "I cannot replace you."

"We have dropped below the fifty percent death rate which means your new assignments will be low-level missions until your bond years are completed. I expect each of you to enjoy your hard earned freedom. Live happily for me."

Several of his brothers murmured replies. Others nodded silently. They could not express their grief verbally, but Joseph knew he was loved by his birthmates.

He took a deep breath to steady himself then gave his final command. "I need an escort to prison."

Chapter Two

The large, circular room was disorienting. Everything was painted white including the floor, walls, and computers monitors which hung from thin rods. There were no chairs. Joseph stood in the middle of the Chamber of Five, answering questions. He spoke matter-of-factly, not hiding or embellishing details.

Though they were called the Five, only four elderly quintessences stood by their computer monitors. Recently the fifth had died and the spot was yet to be filled. Near the concave wall, several guards wearing dark purple uniforms watched the proceedings in silence.

"Thank you for your report," said Director Caden who oversaw Essence Institute which served as a cloning factory, training facility, and homeland for quintessences. "Please step outside as we discuss your case."

Joseph turned without a word and walked out, certain what his fate would be. He had already admitted he was guilty of the charges.

A slight frown creased the elder C2 director's face. "Another hard case. His crimes call for the punishment of death." His short black hair was beginning to gray, and his face hinted of a few wrinkles. Though he had only been director for a month, he spoke with veteran authority.

"Yet he deserves mercy," said an AF2 model wearing a nametag with the wording *Mablevi*. His hair was styled into wavy cornrows, his intense eyes carrying the weight of centuries. The Synod secretly knew him as Mason, the Inquisitor. He was the most skilled at mind probing of any quintessence in the species's history.

"He kept to the Code, putting the welfare of his brethren before his own." The IN4 model's long hair was loose except for three thin braids, one for each of the children he and his wife had adopted. On his nametag was *Guyapi*, but the other Five knew him as Gabriel.

"This is the third time in eighteen months that quintessences have had to fight our own kind." The ME1 appeared as a human of Middle Eastern descent, perhaps in his late fifties, but he was really one hundred and seventy-nine. Well, Alec's body was that age. His memories were far older. "The ediethean are behind this. First they kept cutting our funding until we are at half production. Now they pit us against ourselves. How long until they order our extinction?"

"Alexander, you are seeing conspiracy theories again. This was a clerical error. The C2's were accidently assigned to Tamaris," said the director. This was the third time Caleb had served as the leader of Essence, each time only for a decade or two. Each of his other birthmates had been the director for at least a century, but he continued to fall into the rotation as a short filler.

"Three clerical errors in eighteen months? Surely you don't believe that, brother? This was done intentional to demoralize us. Destroy us from within."

"You speak without proof."

"You deny the evidence which is right in front of you."

"Brothers," cut in Gabriel. "Enough. You have forgotten the purpose of this meeting. We are deciding the punishment for Joseph."

Alexander and Caleb quieted, but the tension was still there between them, the argument to be picked up again later.

Mason spoke, "I will not give a death vote. I suggest we demote him to office worker, as we have done with several others lately."

"I agree," said Gabriel.

"Will this satisfy the Galactic Senate?" said Caleb. "If we continue to give lighter punishment for serious crimes, they may doubt our authority."

"They already do," said Alexander. "They have been testing us, and we are failing."

"Do you really believe Joseph should die so we can appease our political enemies?" challenged Mason.

"Time to vote," said Caleb. "Should Joseph die?" He looked each birthmate in the eyes but none spoke. "Do we agree that he will be demoted to a clerical position?"

"It is agreed," said the others in unison.

Joseph was called back in. He stood at attention in the middle of the egg-like room, his face blank, waiting to die.

Caleb sternly spoke. "Joseph of Company C5-20453, you have been found guilty of disobeying authority. As punishment, you will be demoted to desk clerk until your years of bondage are completed."

Puzzlement came to Joseph's face. "Sir?"

"This penance is not to be taken lightly. You will be living here in dishonor while your birthmates continue to fight, yet you will be helpless to aid them. To many quintessences, the separation from birthmates is worse than death. As you have been a dedicated lieutenant who cares deeply for his brothers, I predict that the last eighteen years of your bondage will be torturous. You will be assigned to a barracks to live with others who share your fate. Dismissed."

As Alexander watched Joseph leave, he felt pity for him. He remembered too well the frustration of being grounded while birthmates bleed for the empire. After the meeting ended, Alexander ate dinner alone in his penthouse on the top floor of Richton Tower. His apartment was the only place he could go without being tagged by a Shadow Guard. He had long grown used to having them around, a safety measure in case a Five ever went insane. No secrets were kept from the Shadow Guard or the Synod who were the other two governing powers at Essence.

Restless, he stepped out onto his balcony and studied the vista of barracks, plazas, hangers, and training grounds. A monorail whizzed by far below, taking workers to homes in the nearby city of New Hope, separated from Essence by a massive wall. Several fighter jets flew by in formation, and he felt the urge to fly himself. Perhaps tomorrow he would. Separating Essence from the ocean was another wall, this one smaller. Several quintessences strolled along the sandy beach with their families.

Loneliness prodded Alexander. He had not remarried since Lashana's death. While most of his brothers took a new wife after every blending, he had not. Even Mason has found someone this time, a powerful telepath who shared his talents for mind-reading. The other brothers kept secret from their wives that they had lived multiple lives, but Mason shared everything with his wife, just as he had with his previous wife Yaira.

Alexander could not move onward. His love for Layla, later reborn as Lashana, was too great. No one could measure up to his creator, his soulmate. His brothers warned him that he needed to truly let her go. Yet he could not. This was his punishment for immorality. To live century after century away from his beloved. Joseph may think his punishment of separation from birthmates for a few decades as harsh, but it was nothing compared to Alexander's agony.

Stepping back into the penthouse, Alexander looked around his luxurious home. The furniture had been changed several times over the centuries, each refurnishing being starker in design than before. Shelves held ancient heirlooms given to him and Lashana from visiting dignitaries. The second bedroom Lashana had used as a study still remained the same, even after three centuries. He walked into the study and sat at her computerized desk, the programing long ago obsolete.

For a while he relived memories of her. The smiles, laughter, tears. They had lived two lifetimes together, more than what most got. Through her daughter Yaira, several of her descents still worked at Essence. Alexander watched over them, secretly helping when they needed aid. They shared Yaira's brilliant genes, and usually held high positions at Essence. Alexander made sure of that, but they did not know an ancient relative guided their lives.

The argument with Caleb drifted through Alexander's mind. The Five were the first of all quintessences created. His greatest fear was they would become the last. The Ediethean High Council and the Coalition of Human Advancement had been at odds for centuries. The quintessences were pawns moved around the political field, sacrificed when one group or the other felt the need. Now with funding cut by half, Alexander feared that one day the Galactic Senate would vote to cease funding Essence Institute altogether. When that happened, within two centuries the last of the quintessence would die from old age. Then his species would become extinct.

The curse of being a clone race of only males.

Alexander touched the cold, dark surface of the desk, wishing again Layla was here. It was from her brilliant, gene spliced mind that quintessences came into existence. With her profectus gene, she had been the greatest geneticist the galaxy had known. He needed her so much now. Her advice, her warmth, her touch. Only she had the skills needed to make female quintessences.

An idea wormed its way into Alexander's mind. He tried to dismiss it, knowing it would require breaking galactic law, yet the idea persisted. He went to bed, trying to forget it, but it haunted his dreams. It clung to him the next several days, refusing to be ignored. Finally, he called a secret meeting with all of the Five.

Surrounded by five thousand empty incubators, Alexander stood in the middle of the second section of the Fetus Department. The vast chamber had once been a clean room protected by sonic rays to keep pathogens at bay. Now a thin layer of dust settled on the machines after a decade of nonuse. Only emergency lights lit occasional spots, casting most of the huge room into deep shadows.

"Strange place for a meeting," said Jacob, walking down the aisle, his Shadow Guard keeping back in the darkness.

"Enjoying your vacation?"

"Quite. In fact, it is so delightful, I'm thinking about extending it by a year or two." Jacob had selected a H1 as his host this generation. His model looked like a mid-twenty Hispanic human, young and strong. Desmond worked in the Security Department at Essence. Until Jacob was officially appointed as a Five, he would continue to live Desmond's life.

"Oh, no you don't," said Gabriel, approaching from the opposite direction. "Alexander and Caleb have been arguing again. We need you to smooth over the meetings."

"Ah, you miss my jokes."

"And your company," added Alexander.

"Your jokes are an atrocity," grumbled Mason, moving to stand beside his birthmates. "Still, we do miss you."

"How goes wife hunting?" said Caleb, the last to arrive. His Shadow Guard, along with the others, held back, almost invisible in the darkness, but was close enough to eavesdrop.

"Ah, I almost got Firestrike to agree to a marriage battle, called a *pugna* to you outsiders."

"I cannot believe you are courting a fjouwer. They are known for being very violent," said Gabriel.

"And we are not? You are just jealous cause of their four arms. Most are trained warriors from childhood. Tough to beat in a fair fight."

"Like your Firestrike? Why would she want an underling like you?" jested Caleb.

"She works in security too. And she can type on two keyboards at once when filling out reports. Very impressive."

"So she outperforms you even in the office," said Mason.

"I am her equal in battle. You should see our practice spars. She knows her blades well, but so do I. There is nothing more exciting than flirting while trying to kill each other."

"You have strange taste in women," said Caleb.

"And you do not? Your wife is a sundancer. They have hard spikes instead of hair. How is that romantic? You cannot run your hands through her hair."

"And a bride with sharp knives aiming to kill you is romantic?"

"Brothers," cut in Alexander. "I brought you here to discuss wives."

"Really?" said Jacob. "I thought we were here for another one of your conspiracy theories."

"I do believe the ediethean and their allies are trying to destroy us. Sooner or later our funding will be cut, and we will become extinct."

"How does this relate to wife hunting? You might not be so pessimistic if you actually tried finding a new lifemate."

Alexander tired of the jesting. "I'm talking about the future of our entire species. Until we can reproduce naturally, our species cannot control our own destiny. We need female quintessences. Technically there is no law that forbids their creation. Layla never made any because it was against BFG standards."

"And how do you propose we create them?" said Caleb. "It will be difficult, at best, to design one. And if the ediethean do find out what we are up to, they may use it as an excuse to cut the last of our budget."

"We do it in secret. Using only a few scientists at most."

"It will take decades, if not centuries," said Gabriel.

"Good thing we are a long-lived species. We will need a skilled geneticist to pull this off. I recommend we create her."

The brothers glanced at each other uneasily. Gingerly, Jacob said, "Layla is gone forever. She made sure her memories would not be passed to another. You know this."

"I am not proposing to bring Layla back, but a clone of her with the same talents she possessed."

"Cloning of sentient species is still illegal," said Mason. "You are asking us to break the Purity Law while we are supposed to be the enforcers of laws. This is against our Code."

"If we do nothing, we will eventual perish. This at least gives us a chance. Imagine that one day we may be able to stand in front of the Galactic Senate, an equal among all the other sentients. Our species's destiny finally in our own hands instead of our enemies."

"And if that day comes," said Caleb, "they will seek retribution against those who broke the law."

"Then hold me responsible." Alexander looked at each of his brothers. "I will pay whatever punishment the law calls for when the time comes. But first we must be successful. This project will take decades to complete."

Jacob suddenly burst into laughter. The others looked at him sharply. While quintessences did joke, rarely did they laugh out loud.

Seeing his birthmates startled looks, Jacob tried to appear a bit serious. "I have been an AS model for the last two centuries, which as Alexander knows, are very emotional. Your plan is ingenious, like…well…half your other ideas. Technically Alec will be dead within three decades along with the rest of you. Break laws as much as you wish. By the time all this comes to light, the ones responsible will be dead, at least to the universe."

"Accept you," pointed out Gabriel.

"Me? I'm just a computer technician in security. I have no direct contact with the Five. If they started an illegal operation before I was appointed a Five, I am not responsible."

"Your transfer of blame is intriguing," said Alexander, "but I do not take breaking the law lightly." He glanced into the darkness at the Shadow Guards listening to the conversation. If they decided the Five were abusing their power, they have the authority to act against the Five, even killing them. "I only ask this because I believe there is no other way to save our species. If you agree to this, it must still be brought before the Synod in a private session."

The birthmates looked at each other, seeking opinions. They may have skirted around laws at times but never outright broken one. To the galaxy, quintessences were the perfect enforcers of justice who could never be tempted by bribes, revenge, or pride. Now they were considering breaking a part of their own Code in order to preserve their whole species.

After sober reflection, Caleb said, "Do we agree to break the Purity Law and clone another profectus?"

"It is agreed," said the other four voices in unison.

Chapter Three

Students bent over their computerized desk, working on various assignments. Children sat by adolescents, grouped by families. The computers pulled up assignments appropriate for each. Their teacher, a slim sundancer with dozens of golden spikes on her head, walked down the aisle, giving advice as needed. She paused by a preteen human and smiled reassuring, knowing her student worked on a college exam.

Hennah returned the smile then finished the last questions of her biochemistry test. A bit challenging, but she knew she had passed with top marks. She always did. After completing the exam, she placed her thumb on the screen. It flashed green in acceptance and sent her test electronically to the university where she was taking online courses.

She sighed, wishing yet again she could physically attend college. Her parents were sternly against a child wandering around a campus alone, and they were too busy with their jobs in the Infant Department at Essence to escort her every day to classes. So she continued to go to school with regular students while taking college courses.

The exam had been her last assignment. Hennah sat quietly and looked around the room at students working. There were eighty-six others sitting at the computerized desks in a room designed to hold one hundred. Before the cutbacks, this had been a quintessence classroom located in Opal Barracks. Several decades ago, the building had been turned into apartments for workers at Essence, mostly for families with a quintessence father. Yet some were like her family, both parents holding prominent positions yet nether were quintessence.

To Hennah's left sat her siblings. Her sister Aashi was seventeen, beautiful and smart—yet annoying. When they were both younger they had been great playmates, but as Aashi became more aware that Hennah was far smarter than her, she spent less time with her sister. Now she was far more interested in boys than hanging with her little sister. Her brother Dhruvi, at nine, still thought it cool to play with Hennah. Having a genius sister meant little to him, at long as she found time to play videogames with him. He could still beat her in many games that relied on reflexes.

To the right of Hennah, a fjouwer was finishing a pre-algebra assignment. Two hands worked on the assignment, another tapped impatiently against the desk, with the fourth absently tugged at her coarse, thick hair. Her body was stout, her jaw line firm. Her strong fingernails were useful for fighting or digging—but not for academics. Darkfern hated math with almost the same equal passion she felt for her love of knife fighting. Her lips puckered in frustration as the timer counted down.

The sundancer said, "The day slips away. Finish your final assignments, and then you may leave."

Darkfern quickly sent in her quiz, though she still had time to finish several more problems. "What was on the twisted minds of those who invented math?"

Her younger brother Rockgem grinned. "The test was not that hard. I passed. How many times have you failed that same lesson?"

"By the moon, your daggers are dull."

"By the sun, your wit is daft."

Angrily, Darkfern pulled out a small knife and stabbed at her brother. He jumped back out of his seat and pulled his own weapon, laughing at the challenge. Fjouwers had thick hides so minor duels rarely led to serious wounds.

"Stop!" yelled their teacher. "I have told you both before, no fighting in class. Detention tomorrow. And Rockgem, if you say another sun oath, I will personally call your father." In sundancer culture, stars were considered sacred.

The smirk on Rockgem's face disappeared. "Yes, ma'am. Sorry about that. It just slipped out." He quickly tucked away his blade. Being discipline by a parent was one thing, but when your father was a Five, it was far worse.

Hennah's brother had already left with friends, but her sister stood in the doorway, shaking her head in disapproval at the fjouwers' behavior. Aashi did not understand why Hennah choose to be friends with Darkfern.

"At least your detention is not today. You can still come to my birthday party," said Hennah, gathering her belongings.

"As long as my brother is not invited."

"Hennah," called out their teacher. "A word please."

The preteen walked over to her teacher's large desk while the others left.

"I just checked your scores. Congratulation. You just finished your Bachelor of Geneticists. They will send you the diploma soon. Have you put in an application to Luncaster University yet?"

"Um, I have been trying to talk my parents into it, but they think I'm still too young to live on a college campus, even if it is Luncaster." The renowned university only accepted prodigies, but students had to attend in person. No online classes were offered.

The sundancer smiled sadly. "I really have no more material to teach you. Perhaps you can apply for a higher degree at a different university. I'll talk with your parents about it."

"Thanks." Hennah hurried out of the room to catch up with Darkfern. She tried to downplay how smart she was with friends, but the frown on the fjouwer's face told her that her friend had been eavesdropping.

"You didn't tell me you were finishing up with college." Darkfern led the way down the long hallway, passing apartments.

"I was more focused on my birthday."

"What are you going to do now?"

"I don't know. Try to get into Luncaster again. My parents wouldn't let me go two years ago, but surely they will now. I mean, it's only two cities away. By monorail I can get there in just a few minutes. I don't have to stay in the dorms, but that would be nice."

"And leave me, your best friend?" Darkfern made a comical sad face. "Who else is patient enough to tutor me in math?"

Hennah laughed. "Even if I make it in to Luncaster, we will still see each other a lot."

They passed the dark cafeteria which had been permanently closed. Many areas in the barracks were not in use, but the training room was visited often. Darkfern paused wistfully at its door, watching her ten-year-old brother face off against a taller neodite youth while a quintessence father supervised the match.

There were seventy-eight families living in Opal Barracks, sixty-nine of them had a quintessence in the role of husband—yet no quintessence was a biological father. Their offspring were ether step-children from a wife's previous relationship, adopted, or genetically engineered from donor sperm and the wife's egg. The wives came from many different mammal species, some facing persecution for marrying outside of their own kind.

"Come on," said Hennah. "Mamma said the party was immediately after school."

They turned down another hallway and entered an apartment which had once been a dorm room for a company of birthmates. Then it had held fifty bunkbeds but now thin walls divided the dorm into smaller rooms. The family prepared meals in a small kitchenette. Not fancy, but it was home to Hennah.

On the dining table was a bright blue cake shaped like a giant DNA strand. Several banners with blinking lights hung from the walls.

"Congratulation on your graduation," said her mom Pallavi, who had taken the afternoon off work at the Infant Department to prepare for the party. "Your teacher messaged us with the results."

"Proud of you," said her dad, pouring punch into cups. As a teenager working in the Infant Department, Kaushal had developed a crush on Pallavi. It had taken him four months to work up the courage to ask her out. "Another college graduate in the family."

"A birthday and a graduation at the same time," smiled her grandfather. Chandresh was head of the Research Department. At sixty, he was still energetic and outgoing, highly respected by his co-workers. "We have truly been blessed."

"Happy twelfth birthday," said Aashi from a couch, too busy texting her boyfriend to look up.

"Can we eat the cake now?" said Dhruvi, staring at the blue icing.

"Not yet," chided Pallavi. "First the blessing and prayers."

Hennah knelt solemnly on a small mat in the middle of the crowded living room. Her mother held a silver tray on which burned two candles. She dipped her finger into a red mixture and placed a dot on Hennah's forehead. She then feed a sweet to her daughter. Next, Chanresh stood in front of his granddaughter and said a prayer over her.

It was strange to have parents of different religions. Pallavi was Hindu but Hennah's dad and grandfather where Catholic. While her parents usually got along well, holidays sometimes led to conflict, like when her father had tried to put candles on a birthday cake when Hennah was five. Pallavi had snatched the candles away, fussing about sacred flames.

The rituals finished, the hazelnut cake was cut by Kaushal. Darkfern took two pieces, eating both at the same time with two forks while Dhruvi watched enviously. When he tried to mimic her by grabbing a second piece, his mother cut in, taking the plate for herself. Pallavi then served dinner of beef vinaloo, biryani, and rajma soup. As soon as the meal was over, Aashi left to hang with friends, though she paused long enough to give her sister a small wrapped present. The rest of the family gathered around as Hennah opened her presents. Darkfern had given her a book about weird species, Aashi a silver necklace, her grandfather a specialized e-band, her parents some clothes, and Dhruvi a video game—though the latter was really more for him than her.

As the family chatted, Hennah brought up the topic of attending Luncaster. The most she could get from her parents was they would think about it. As Pallavi tossed ripped giftwrap into the recycler, Chandresh beckoned his granddaughter away from her presents.

"Tomorrow, I would like for you to go to work with me."

"Sure, Dada," smiled Hennah, using the Hindu word for *grandfather*. During school holidays, she sometimes hung out with him at work, especially when she was a child. He would let her play with lab equipment, even perform basic experiments, never fussing if she messed something up. She felt important when walking beside him down hallways as workers greeted him respectfully. Sometimes she received compliments that someday she would make a great scientist. As a child, Hennah would giggle shyly, determined to grow up to be just like her grandfather.

The next day she was up at her normal time for school, excited. It was always more fun exploring the labs of the Research Department than going to class. She ate breakfast with her family, ignoring her sister's scowl because Hennah no longer would be attending classes, at least for now.

Chandresh met her in the hallway. "Ready for an adventure?"

"Always, Dada."

"That's my poti."

Hennah smiled at his use of the Hindu term for *granddaughter*. Using the ancient language of their ancestors created a special bond between them.

She rode across the huge complex of Essence in Chandresh's small hover car. As they neared the enormous Richton Tower, Hennah peered out the glass roof of the vehicle, trying to see its top. The huge building mushroomed near the top, with its final ten levels larger than those below. Several times she had visited Darkfern's home on the top floor. The fjouwer lived in a lavish penthouse near an indoor garden.

Hennah envied all that space Darkfern's family had compared to her cramped home. She had to share a bedroom with her sister while the entire barracks shared several bathrooms. Living in a college dorm room probably was very similar to growing up in a barracks, at least from what she had seen in movies. Still, she would love to be away from her sister, having her own space.

Chandresh parked then escorted his granddaughter to the Research Department. She proudly walked beside him as he visited various labs, encouraging workers and patiently listening to problems. They ate lunch at the food court in the Grand Forum. Hennah expected for them to return to the Research Department, but instead he took her to an elevator and punched in the number forty-five.

"Why are we going so high up, Dada?"

"There is someone important I want you to meet." His mysterious tone hinted that this was not a normal meeting.

Curious, Hennah followed her grandfather down the hallway and entered a huge office. One wall was made of curved glass offering a splendid view of Essence Institute far below. Near the door, couches surrounded a sleek, black coffee table. Two quintessences stood quietly beside bookshelves filled with antiques from many cultures. At the far end of the room an elderly quintessence sat behind a huge oval desk.

"Welcome, Chandresh." He stood up and walked over. He was over one hundred and ninety, reaching the age of decline in which quintessences rapidly age, hair graying, wrinkles deepening, reflexes slowing. "Hennah, I am pleased to finally meet you."

The preteen smiled shyly. "Good to meet you, Alec of the Five."

"Take a seat." The elder gestured towards the thickly padded couches. "Your grandfather tells me you have finished your Bachelor's. I would like to offer you a job here at Essence."

"Me?" Hennah glanced at her grandfather in surprise. "I was thinking about working on another degree."

"You can still do so while working on the project I have in mind. You would have your own lab and all the equipment you need. I will even pay you a small allowance. At sixteen you will get a raise. At eighteen you will receive the same salary as adult researchers."

"Wow. That's a lot." Hennah scooted to the end of her cushion, intrigued. "What is the project about?"

"That is classified. If you agree to work on this, you cannot talk about it to anyone who is not in this room without my permission. The nature of this project is quite serious. As you have the knowledge of an adult, I will treat you as one, Hennah. You need to be aware that if you leak classified information, the consequences are severe, including death." His dark, unnatural eyes bore into her.

The preteen shifted uncomfortably on the couch. "I can keep secrets."

"You cannot brag about your work to friends or enemies. The most you will be allowed to say is that you are working on a research project for your grandfather. Nothing more. Do you agree with these terms?"

Hennah glanced at Chandresh, uncertain. He smiled and patted her hand. "You were made for this, Poti."

She relaxed. "Yes, I agree."

"Good. The goal of the project you will be working on is to create female quintessences."

Hennah laughed, thinking he was joking. When he continued to watch her soberly, she looked in confusion at her grandfather. "Surely you have told him why that is impossible?"

"I have explained it to him."

The Five leaned forward. "Explain it to me again, Hennah, why you think it cannot be done."

The youth spoke as if talking to her teacher. "In a normal mammal species, there are genes in the Y chromosome that active male traits. Take away the Y chromosome, then the X chromosome activates the female traits. At least it typically works this way. But with the quintessences, Layla Rangan broke a lot of genetic rules. While trying to design the perfect genes, she avoided duplicate DNA

36

sequences which are actually a natural safely measure in case something goes wrong during mitosis. She compacted things so much that she only used twenty-one chromosomes. Humans have twenty-three, yet quintessence are more complex. She pulled that off by not designing female traits. None whatsoever. Two X chromosomes make, well, maybe a mutated male, but not a female."

"You have an excellent understanding of genetics. Now I want you to look beyond what you know, experiment with theories. Break the rules of nature as you see fit. Find a way to make this dream a reality."

Hennah worriedly looked at her grandfather. "But it can't be done."

Chandresh said, "He knows it cannot be done quickly, but over time, decades perhaps, I believe you can achieve this."

"Dada, you are a geneticist. You know genes don't work that way."

"You have a mind for this. You can see the coding in ways that no one else can, including me. It is your gift. And it is your responsibility to help."

"I…I will do my best." She looked back to Alec. She hated to disappoint him, but she knew what he asked for was impossible. It would be terrible for her to make false promises and years later he become mad at her when those plans failed. "But most likely I will fail."

"You need to prepare for success. If you believe you will fail, you will. If you believe you will succeed, then you will."

"Faith is not the same thing as reality."

Alec and Chandresh looked at each other. The grandfather said, "She needs to know everything."

The quintessence nodded and reached over to the low table in front of the sofas. When he touched its dark surface, it came to life. He navigated through a few menus then gestured upward. A vivid hologram created from a photo appeared in midair above the table. A middle-age woman of Indian descent smiled at the camera while holding an e-tablet.

"Who is this?" asked Alec.

"Either Layla Rangan or Yashana Kalkar who is my great, great, great something grandmother."

"It's Layla." He switched photos. This one was of a preteen with long, black hair standing indoors, but the background details were cropped. "Now who is this?"

"Me. But I don't remember taking that. Where was I at?"

Alec gestured and the rest of the photo revealed itself. The preteen was surrounded by two older sisters and parents—but they were not Hennah's family.

She frowned, confused. "Who is that?"

"Yashana's family. What have you realized?"

"I look like my ancestor, but I already knew I sort of resembled her."

37

"You do not resemble her. You look exactly like her. Your grandfather was careful to keep childhood images of Layla and Yashana away from you, but it is time for you to know that you are a clone of them."

Hennah opened her mouth, closed it, and then tried to speak again. "How is this possible?"

Chandresh gently took his granddaughter's hands. "I did it. As you know, your parents used a genetics company to customize the genes of their offspring. A common enough practice for those who can afford it. When it was time for you, I secretly stepped in and switched the egg that was to be implanted in your mother. You are the clone of Layla."

"That's…uh…illegal isn't it? There's some Purity rule about that." To Hennah, reality itself seemed to have suddenly, violently altered. Her mild mannered, reputable grandfather had purposely committed a crime to make her.

"Yes, Poti, I broke the law so you could exist. And I am glad I did so. You are a beautiful, talented girl who I am very proud of."

"Why would you do that? Why make me?"

"I asked him to," said Alec. "We need to be free of the yoke the Galactic Senate has us bound by. Layla was the only one talented enough to create female quintessences. Her unique talents are also yours. What she can do, you can too. We were careful raising you to give you the best possible advantages."

"You didn't raise me." Hennah felt a stab of anger. How much of her life had been controlled by Alec?

"You are right, your parents did so. And your grandfather has been very active in your life, advising you. You were created for this project, this purpose—to be the savior of the quintessences."

Hennah studied the elderly Five, appalled that he had secretly been controlling her life even before birth. "Did I ever have a choice? Was that stuff you said earlier about choosing even real?"

"You could have said no and walked away without ever knowing. We would have been disappointed, but I would never force you down this path. We tried to develop your interests so you would want to do this."

Hennah felt dizzy. "You have been manipulating me my entire life?"

Chandresh squeezed his granddaughter's hands. "Poti, I love you. Do not doubt my feelings. I have trained you for this moment out of love. I wanted you to have a big heart, to care for those needing help. And the quintessences need you."

The twelve year old tried to steady herself. "I will do my best."

"That is all I ask," said Alec.

Her parents were delighted when Chandresh told them she would be working in the Research Department. Hennah smiled, pretending she was happy with the decision, wishing she could talk with her parents about her DNA. The secret that she was not really their daughter burned within her.

She had the weekend to ponder the conversation with Alec. She tried to keep to herself, sitting on the top bunk of the bed she shared with her sister. Aashi kept playing music too loud while Hennah tried to ignore her. Dhruvi lured her out several times to play the new video game he had given her. She did chores of washing dishes and sweeping while her family went about their normal lives, not knowing hers had been altered forever.

She felt stabs of anger at Alec for controlling her. He said she had a choice, but did she really? He had specifically had her grandfather create her so she would one day create quintessences for him. If she had said no, would he had really just let her go after that much effort? She felt no resentment towards Chandresh. She had always cherished her grandfather, and even now could feel no bitterness that he had purposely made her. It was strange that though he was her grandfather, genetically she was his ancestor. Even weirder, she was sort of a great grandmother to her own father, though there were quite a few *greats* that needed to be added to that title.

Perhaps she ought to be upset she was a clone, but the feeling was fleeting. She had grown up surrounded by them. Her best friend's father was one. Most of her neighbors had one in their family. Really, being a clone was no big deal—except she happened to be illegal. She had the better end of the deal though. Unlike the quintessence, she did not have to serve fifty years as a slave warrior. Then again, perhaps this futile project of Alec's was her penance for existing.

If so, how long did she have to work on it? A decade? Or fifty years like the quintessences? She would be an old woman by the time she could pursue her own interests. Then again, genetics had been the only career she had ever considered, thanks to the careful guidance of her grandfather.

She felt a tightening of her chest. They really have been trying to turn her into a copy of Layla as much as possible. Alec lied when he said she had a choice. He had controlled her life so much that he knew exactly what to say to manipulate her into doing what he wanted. *I wish Aashi would turn down that loud music. Peace. I just want peace.* She buried her head under her pillow, wishing both her sister and Alec would disappear.

Monday she rode with Chandresh to work. He led her deep into the Research Department to the area that had been shut down thanks to budget cuts. As they walked down dark, barely lit hallways, Hennah imagined she was in a horror movie where a monster would rush out of an abandoned lab to attack.

Finally, they stopped in front of a security door. It was the fourth they had come through so far. Chandresh placed his thumb on a sensor then typed in a code. The door slid open to reveal a large, well-lit room, mostly empty except for metal tables along three walls. The creamy painted ceiling was high enough that there could have been a second floor. Instead, a twisted stairway led to an office with a glass wall which overlooked the lab.

Chandresh gestured with a grin. "Your first lab, Poti. We will get you a desk and other equipment. You will need to make a list of what you want and give it to Joseph."

"Who is he?"

"Me," came a voice from the doorway of the office seven feet above them. A C5 model stood on the small balcony, watching them. "We meet again, Hennah."

The preteen looked puzzled at her grandfather while the quintessence walked down the narrow, twisting stairs to join them.

Chandresh explained, "He was at the meeting when we met with Alec."

"Oh." Hennah had forgotten till now that there had been two other quintessences in the Five's office listening silently. "Hello, Joseph," she said politely.

"I will be your direct supervisor who will report your progress to Alec."

"I thought my grandfather was my supervisor."

Chandresh smiled. "I am, but Alec is both our superior. Joseph is here to help you. Whenever you need anything, he will get it for you. I will visit when I can, but I have quite a few other labs to oversee. Also, we need to keep things as discreet as possible, not letting the other researchers know this lab is active. Did you get her the e-tablet I asked for?"

"Yes." Joseph climbed back up to the office then returned with a thin, black computer. "It has been heavily encrypted and will only respond to your fingerprints. Due to security risks, you are not allowed to take any material out of this room, including notes."

"So I can't work on this at home at night?"

"No homework for you," laughed Chandresh. "Besides, you will spend enough hours working here that you will soon appreciate the breaks at night."

Chapter Four

Digital soldiers marched across a grassy plain on a giant hologram hovering above its circular display. Kylen showed no reaction when the brutes reached his iron mine and quickly defeated his few guards. They then began slaughtering the workers. His fingers quickly flew over the smooth surface of the display in front of him as he zoomed to another area on the map.

On the other side of the hologram, Marco grinned, pleased as his success. He was determined to beat Kylen this time. Last time he had lost when Kylen had focused on using the iron to build tanks which crushed his forces. He kept several of his solders at the mine to guard while others scattered to look for loot nearby.

Calmly Kylen zoomed his version of the map out, seeing that his scouts had located Marco's main base. He varied his strategies when in competitions. This time he had used the iron mines as a distraction for his real purpose. Near the back of the map he had workers mining gold then vehicles transported the ore to his city where it was smelted into coins. Then he raised the taxes super high. Soon it would led to riots in the streets, but he was unconcerned. He would win the game before unrest reached dangerous levels.

With the quick money he hired a company of quintessences and directed them towards Marco's base. By the time his opponent realized what was happening, it was too late. Most of Marco's forces were too far away to rush back to the base in time.

"You win," appeared on Kylen's version of the hologram while Marco grumbled at another lost.

"He cheated! There is no way this early in the game he could have hired energy leeches."

"It was a fair fight," said Doctor Kent, tapping notes into his e-tablet. The fortyish human was alethic, his eyes harsh, his judgement final.

"But how? The math does not add up."

"Your punishment for losing is to write an analysis explaining your logic for your conclusion. Then give me three theories how he succeeded. Six pages this time."

Marco scowled as he stormed out of the room. Kylen stood, allowing a small smile to be visible, but not a grin. He must avoid the appearance of gloating. The researchers were always watching them, judging. Kylen, in turn, was observing them, figuring out what they wanted then giving them those results.

"Good work again, Kylen. This win assures that you will be one of those selected to see a movie this evening."

"Thank you, Doctor Kent. I am sure I will enjoy it." He walked out the hologram chamber, keeping hidden the smugness he felt.

For thirteen years he and several dozen other children had grown up in an underground research lab. The results of the activities, lessons, and games they did was used to administer weekly punishments or awards. Competition was stiff between them. Awards included being allowed outside for short periods of time, special foods, and points for buying music or games for their e-tablets. Early on, Kylen realized there was a larger purpose to the contests.

They were being measured for what assignments they would be given once they became adults. Kylen made it a game to figure out what the researchers wanted. He noted that they frowned when kids became upset when losing, so he sometimes on purpose lost a game while showing politeness to the victor. He may not have always earned the weekly awards, but he had earned the admiration of the adults and that was far more important.

He still had not forgotten his most important lesson from a boy named Timon who had a bad temper which the researchers spent years trying to cure. When the boy was eight, he went into a rage when a lady reprimanded him for snatching a cookie from a plate of another child. He grabbed his glass and smashed it against the table. Then he picked up one of the large fragments and slashed her across the face. She withdrew from the cafeteria, holding her hand to her face, blood streaming down her arm.

A few hours later, Doctor Kent had entered the play room where the kids relaxed before bed. Two stout men with him escorted Timon out of the room. The boy never returned. When kids asked what happened to Timon, they were told he had been taken to another area where he was receiving treatment for his anger. But Kylen knew it was a lie. Eventually the other kids stopped asking about Timon. Due to his violent outbursts, he had been unpopular with the others.

Timon's disappearance initiated Kylen's understanding of power. Currently the adults were in control. They provided for the basic needs of the children, handing out awards and punishments. The young profectus went along willingly, playing by the adults' rules. But it would not be like this forever. Each of the children was a genius who would one day reshape the galaxy, changing human destiny. Well, that was what the kids were told in the lectures they had to attend. Kylen believed them, at least about this.

The young profectus were told that the Coalition of Human Advancement had sponsored their creation, but it had to be done in secret due to the malevolent race of ediethean who had fought for centuries against humans for control of the

Galactic Senate. Profectus had once been legal, their achievements far reaching. But the law changed. Eventually they had all died out, and new ones were rarely naturally born due to the genes being recessive.

Kylen liked being told he was special, that he was destined for greatness. All the kids believed it. The researchers promised that though they had to hide in secret now, someday they would walk freely among humans, becoming great leaders. That was, as long as they obeyed the orders of the Coalition who would direct them in which jobs to take and who to marry. They were warned repeatedly that they must either marry another profectus or a descent of one who carried the genes. It was vital that natural born profectus become a part of regular society.

Reaching the playroom, Kylen sat on a couch and watched the others. Several juveniles competed in games. Amy used building blocks to craft another elaborate castle, experimenting with how much weight the arches she had used in the base could take. Using an e-table, Marco creating math formulas to show how fast resources could be gathered within the game he had lost. In a far corner, Julian read digital magazines on one screen while typing out a forum post on another. Her thoughtful responses had become popular online, and she had a huge following, her fans presuming she was a highly educated adult.

After a few minutes, Kylen left the room and headed to the dorm he shared with seven other boys. He sat on a bottom bunk and pulled out his e-tablet. He navigated through menus and hacked into the Zaklanco's computer system. Most likely the researchers knew, but he was unconcerned. He was a clone of a famous hacker, so it would be expected for him to experiment.

What he had uncovered he kept from the other profectus. He knew instinctively that the adults would not want him to share their dark secrets. Repeatedly he had examined the blueprints of Zaklanco Bunker and knew there was no place Timon could have been kept. Zaklanco Bunker had several levels, but the other sections served as living quarters for the researchers, a lab where he and the other profectus were created, and storage areas for supplies. He had found a note in a daily log on the day that the boy disappeared which stated, "Subject 16 again showing signs of extreme aggression. The panel voted for termination."

Today Kylen wondered if for fun he should hack into another company's network and pull a prank. When bored he sometimes did that. Other times he wrote computer programs that suited his whims. He was tired of waiting for destiny to happen. All those lectures about how great he was, yet he slept in a drab cave and rarely saw sunlight. How much longer did he have to wait on the Coalition's Great Plan?

With a sigh, he pulled up pages of data he had long ago memorized about the two men who shared his same DNA. A picture of Richard Cambridge appeared on the screen along with his long list of awards and accomplishments. Among other things, he was famous for creating a software company which was still considered preeminent, designing the city of New Hope then becoming its beloved mayor, and giving large sums of money to charities.

Kylen flipped to a page about Ethan Covey. This clone's greatest achievement had been creating robotic animals which aided the handicap—at least that was what his public profile said. What intrigued Kylen was that Ethan was also a talented hacker who went by the name Prankster Brainster. Ethan had used the account on and off throughout his life. As an adult he had entered legal hacking contests, winning most. Prominent companies paid him to break into their systems then report ways to fix their issues. But Prankster Brainster's greatest conquest was when Ethan, only fourteen, had hacked into the renowned Essence Institute. While it earned Ethan a police record, it also made him infamous to techies. As far as Kylen knew, no one else had been successful in repeating the feat, though that had been four centuries ago.

Kylen was determined to break that record. Like all of Generation Three, as the young profectus were called, Kylen's chief goal was to achieve far more than what his clones had done. Still, Kylen could not do serious hacking from Zaklanco Bunker. As the base had to remain hidden, he could not risk being tracked by authorities. The planet they were located on was on the outer edge of the Core worlds, meaning it took a long time for information to be relayed through space from communication station to station, eventually reaching its destination. Annoying when you needed to be quickly in and out of a system. So Kylen limited his hacking experience to small companies on this planet, only doing minor pranks that workers would think were computer glitches.

Doctor Kent's voice boomed over the intercom, "Winners to the front elevator for movie night."

After turning off his e-tablet, Kylen joined the other nine fortunate profectus going on the outing. Several researchers dressed in casual clothes smiled at them, just as excited as the youths to be going outside. They too were usually just as trapped as the kids inside the bunker.

The group rode the elevator up to a garage built into a mountain. Then the kids were split into groups of two along with one adult. Each took a different hover car which zoomed along hidden paths through a thick forest which filled the mountain valley. Eventually they joined up with a main road that headed into a small city. They arrived at different times to the theater.

Ethan was paired with Amy who could not stop grinning. It had been six months since she had been outdoors. Their adult, a tall woman with a thin scar on her cheek, bought them snacks. The youths savored the spicy cornpuffs as they followed the researcher down the aisle to seats. Ethan sat beside Amy as the lights dimmed, drinking in the experience. It had been several months since the reward was a movie. Huge 3D actors appeared in the air above as the audience leaning back in their seats which vibrated and rocked at appropriate times in the story. Ethan laughed along with the crowd at the antics in the comedy. It felt good to be part of the human race, even if it was only for a few hours.

Chapter Five

Bored, Hennah spun her chair around, watching her lab fly by in a swirl of motion. She kicked her legs, making the chair go faster and faster. Feeling dizzy, she finally slowed to a stop. After the room stopped spinning, she checked progress on the Nanotech DNA Builder. Only half of one percent completed. She sighed and looked at her e-band. Nearly two hours until quitting time and she could go home. What to do till then?

Already today she had finished cleaning petri dishes from yesterday's failed experiment, edited an X chromosome for several hours, and then programmed it into the NDB where nanites now worked on making it into a reality. Once they finished the entire genome, it would be placed in an egg waiting to be fertilized. Tomorrow she would place it into an incubator where it might divide a few times into mush, well mush was too strong a word as the final results would be too small to be seen with the naked eye. Still, it would be a mess when she examined it under the Electrical Molecular Microscope. As she had explained to Joseph daily for the last week since she first began experimenting, two X genes did not make a female quintessence. He only answered by telling her to think creatively until she found a solution.

She sighed deeply and glanced around the lab. On metal shelves she had neatly stacked beakers, petri dishes, and other supplies. Drawers were organized with utensils, pipettes, and cleaning supplies. She even added labels to everything. She was not nearly this neat in her own bedroom, but she had delayed as much as she possibly could before facing the inevitable Project Absurd, her nickname for Alec's mission.

It had taken nearly a month to set the lab up properly. Joseph had gotten her everything on her list, often having to seek out supplies in the other research labs at night after the workers had left. She had joined her grandfather in helping Joseph sometimes, but as some higher level staff often worked late, she had to keep her appearance to a minimum to avoid drawing attention to herself. Occasionally visiting her grandfather in the main labs was normal, her taking off with a huge NDB's, cryogenic freezers, and incubators was another matter. Joseph enlisted the aid of several Shadow Guards to move over the heavy equipment in the middle of the night when there was no staff left in the labs.

Not in the mood to edit another chromosome, she wandered about the lab, wasting time. She glanced up at the glass wall of Joseph's office. Talking to him would be something to do. She climbed the steps to the small balcony and stood in his open doorway. The office was actually large with each glass wall offering observation of four labs at once, except the other rooms were unlit. Hennah felt like she stood at a mouth of a giant cavern, with most of the world plunged into darkness and only her lab leading to safety.

Joseph's office was completely bare except for his old fashion wooden desk and the chair he sat in. The few file cabinets and shelves were empty, and his desk unembellished except for an old computer.

"What do you need?" Joseph turned away from his monitor.

"I was wondering if you finally asked Alec if I can attend Luncaster University." She had been pestering him for weeks to ask, but he kept brushing her off.

"Yes, I talked with him yesterday. He said you could not go, but he would provide the funding for you to take online classes at any other college of your choice."

"But Luncaster is the best in the galaxy. And it is only a few miles away. It is where I belong. Both Layla and Yashana attended."

"Luncaster does not offer online classes."

"I could still work here in the evenings after classes are over."

"Hennah, Alec was very clear in that you are not allowed to even visit Luncaster. He said there are pictures in the hallways of famous graduates including profectus. You might be recognized as a clone."

"I can just tell people that I'm a descendent of Yashana. That is why I look like her."

"The answer is no."

The preteen looked away, her lower lip trembling as she fought back tears of disappointment. He could not know the depth of her longing to be around other prodigies. Since a young child, she had constantly downplayed her genius, but all the other students in her class had known she worked on material far advanced than them. It had become a barrier that separated her from her peers, and they avoided her outside of class. Even her sister Aashi had been affected by it.

If was difficult for her to make new friends. With her brother she lost games on purpose so he would keep wanting to play with her. At least with Darkfern, there was a balance in their abilities. She patiently tutored Darkfern, while evading bragging about how easy math was to her. Both she and Darkfern knew the pressures of having prominent family. Hennah's grandfather was head of the Research Department while her parents where supervisors in the Infant Department. Darkfern's father was a Five and her mother chief of security for all of

Essence Institute. Talented with blades, the young fjouwer knew the mockery of others who did not understand her fierce culture where status was attached to an individual's combat skills.

Still, Hennah yearned to be around others prodigies like herself. Where she did not have to constantly worry about being mocked or shunned because she knew more than everyone else.

Joseph spoke gently, "You can still earn your PhD or Doctorate. Alec has offered to pay with his personal funds to help you. He does ask that whenever you can discreetly merge your classwork with real work on this project, that you do so. While he wants you to continue your education, he also does not want you distracted from the project."

"How considerate of him." Hennah forced a smile.

Quintessence and girl stared at each other in silence for a long moment. Finally, Joseph said, "How goes your work today?"

"The same."

"Enjoying spinning in chairs?"

She shrugged. "Do you do anything besides stare at me all day?"

"Actually, I do a lot of paperwork."

"About me?"

"No, you are a second, secret job. We keep nothing on file about you or this project."

"Ah, Project Absurd must stay invisible. So what is your other job?" She walked over and peered at his computer screen which showed a partially filled out form. "What is this?"

"A quintessence applying for marriage."

"That's your job? Certifying marriages? I thought you would be doing something more…uh…dramatic. Like coordinating spies."

"This was the position I was assigned. My work is important to those seeking marriage."

"Sounds boring. Thought about a transfer?"

"You are the transfer, but as this project is secret, I must still finish a daily quota of applications to appear I am still serving my sentence."

"Sentence? Are you being punished for something?"

"I am bonded for five more years. This is what I was assigned to do until then."

"Why are you here at Essence and not in space, fighting?"

"You ask too many questions."

"I'm a researcher. That is what we do." Curious, Hennah scrolled down the screen. "There are over three thousands questions on this. That's insane."

"They do not answer all of the questions, only a short general section, and then the area which relates to the bride's background. Marriage laws vary widely across the empire, affected by both culture and local governments. The application tries to cover every known variation. My job is to make sure it has been completed correctly."

"So if you say no, then the couple can't be married?"

"If there is a mistake, then they just send me the corrected form."

"Have you ever denied a marriage?"

"Only when the law is being broken. As these are all quintessence marriages, that is rare. Usually caused by oversight."

"Oversight of what?" Hennah leaned closer to the screen, reading questions.

"I will show you an example then you will go back to work. Is that clear?"

"Yes, sir." The preteen gave a military salute.

Joseph exited the form and a long list of applicant names appeared. "There are two type of applications we deal with: pre and post marriages. That is, some of the marriages have already taken place and been approved by the planetary government where the nuptials took place. Mainly our purpose is just to validate what has already happened and add the info to the personal records of the quintessence. In pre marriages, the couple is waiting for us to give the final verdict. Marrying outside of one's species is a social taboo in many cultures, and marriages may be blocked by local officials. Licenses certified by Essence are classified galactic level and override all local authority, but I can only do so if certain criteria is met."

He opened an application and let Hennah read the beginning of it. Then he switched to another application. "What do you notice about both of them?"

"Uh, wait, let me see the other one again." As the preteen examined the first one, she frowned. "Is this one bride marrying two birthmates?"

"Yes."

"How is that possible? You are denying these, aren't you?"

"I approved both of them yesterday. But first I had to research to see if the bride's culture approves polygamy. It did. Next, I had to verify if polygamy is lawful on the planet she lives. It was. So I approved both her marriages."

"But I thought quintessences only have one wife. I have never seen a duel marriage before."

"Polygamy is rare for quintessences, but it does happen. I have seen applications of up to four birthmates marrying the same wife before."

"Four?" Hennah grimaced, not sure how such a marriage could work.

"The record is ten, set over five hundred years ago."

"Ten? I don't believe that."

"I did not either until my co-workers showed me the files and explained the story. The bride was a princess in line for a throne. She rebelled against her tyrannically father who had arranged her marriage with an enemy when she was only five. He threatened to assassinate anyone else she married, so she wed a squad of quintessences. Needlessly to say, her father's plan was thwarted and she became a powerful queen."

"Nice story, but ten is way overdoing it. So is two." Hennah pointed to the screen. "Surely one of the birthmates could have found someone else."

"Only a third of quintessences will ever marry for it is difficult for us to find wives who are willing to give up having biological children with their spouses. For some, the sacrifices are severe, with some women choosing banishment from their families in order to marry a quintessence."

Hennah frowned. "My friend, Darkfern, her mom had those issues. And she is married to a Five. Well, before her husband was a Five, her family mostly stopped talking to her. Once her husband became a Five, she was able to win some honor back. Then she became chief of security and her family is proud of her again. But it took many years before they accepted her back."

Joseph nodded. "That is why Project Absurd, as you call it, is so important. We need quintessence wives. It will allow more of us to marry who would never have found someone. And our spouses can give birth to biological children. The impact on our culture will be vast. Quintessences born into freedom instead of bondage. Slaves to no one."

The preteen shuffled her feet. "What if I can't pull it off?"

"What if you can?"

"I'm trying. But wishing for something to happen when nature says otherwise won't make it a reality."

"Neither will spinning in chairs. Hennah, I believe you can do this. But it is not my faith, but yours that matters. You need to believe in yourself."

"I'm trying. Really, I am. "

Chapter Six

"Milk, please," said a ten-year-old, holding out her cup.

A beautiful, blonde woman in a business suit poured milk into her daughter's bowl. "You are already late. Eat fast before the bus comes."

Her husband looked up from his e-tablet. "There is a traffic jam on the highway. We have best take the longer route to work today."

Their teenager son grinned, "Can I drive you to work then take the car to school? I promise to pick you up this afternoon on time?"

Quietly Kylen, now seventeen, watched the family interact as he ate breakfast with them. So this was a normal human household. So polite and helpful to each other. It was often different in the shows he had streamed growing up in the bunker. Then again, the family was most likely putting on a show for him. He did not mind for he liked the foster family the Coalition had assigned him to. They were volunteers who supported the Great Plan and knew he was a profectus. For a month now, they had opened up their home to him, helping him to adjust to living on a heavy populated Core World which had been colonized many millenniums ago.

Generation Three had been told they would be separated and sent to foster families where they would learn to assimilate into human culture. The profectus had welcomed the news with excitement, as they had long ago began seeing the bunker as a prison and were more than ready to leave. They had all completed their educations, and some even held online jobs. In the last year or two, some had become restless, testing the authority of their watchers. Kylen, though, had never showed disrespect to the adults. To him, pleasing them was still a game where the reward would ultimately be substantial. He just had to be patient.

Soon the family headed off to work and school, leaving Kylen alone in their spacious suburban house. For a while he relaxed on a couch and watched their huge vid, still marveling at live television. The bunker had been too deep underground and everything the children had watched had been prerecorded or from the internet. Now, Kylen could access a wealth of communications channels with the touch of a remote.

After a comedy went off, Kylen went to the bedroom he shared with the teenager son and picked up his backpack. He passed by a new, sleek e-tablet the family had given him and picked up an old laptop he had built with scraps he had purchased from several junk stores. He tossed the computer into the backpack. In the kitchen, he grabbed some snacks and a drink, packing them beside the laptop. Then he put on his new, denim jacket.

Locking the front door behind him, he headed outside, pausing to admire the bright flowers blooming from manicured flowerbeds. *Someday, I will own a house even bigger than this one,* Kylen promised himself. He followed the sidewalk to a bus stop and sat down, waiting. His foster family had encouraged him to explore the city and tutored him on how to travel using city buses and monorails. Each weekend, they planned adventures for him. So far they had taken him to a six-floor mall, a renowned museum, and an amusement park.

Kylen relished the experiences but also enjoyed exploring alone. What he was doing today was too dangerous to evolve the family. He rode a city bus to a large park. Then he walked along a path, admiring the tall, fragrant trees and huge skyscrapers beyond. Nearing a lake, he sat on a bench, quietly watching the cool autumn wind blowing brightly colored leaves and creating ripples in the water. Kylen closed his eyes, listening to a dog barking excitedly, young children laughing on a playground, and distant traffic on the roads. The teenager breathed deeply, savoring the sensation of being alive, surrounded by nature instead of bare rock walls.

Eventually he took out snacks and munched on chips, tossing some to birds. He watched in amusement as the bluish green creatures fought over the food, snatching morsels from the beaks of others. *They fight just like we kids used to over awards. Humans are really not that much different than animals, just a bit smarter. They need great leaders to unite them, turning them into a cohesive force.*

Kylen pulled out the laptop and turned it on. Soon he was scanning the networks, looking for a particular one. Once he found it, he activated a hacking program he had written himself. Within a few minutes, he was within a bank's encryption channel. His program observed and learned, recording its findings. Kylen studied the logs, satisfied with the results. Then he went to the bank's main webpage and signed in as a new user, creating a dummy account. He then asked for a money transfer from a major company whose interactions his program had been observing. With his hacking program still active, he tricked the host company into transferring a million credits to his dummy account, thinking he was a legit client.

Then he split the money, transferring it in equal amounts to ten different accounts he had made at other banks. Still not satisfied, he had the money split again, this time sending the accounts through high security channels to off planet trading companies, buying stock. His hack would most likely be detected and some of the funds confiscated, perhaps all of it. He was unconcerned. Money meant little to him. To Kylen, this was a game. The higher the stacks, the greater his thrill. Perhaps he should develop a hacker name and leave it to be found by authorities.

He sighed, wishing to brag of his exploits to the universe. But his watchers wished for him and all of Generation Three to remain anonymous, quietly moving into positions of power through legit channels. The profectus had been told that after a year or two with foster families, they would be assigned their own homes and given special jobs tailored for their talents. Then they would begin climbing in power, positioning themselves to reshape their chosen fields, aiding the Coalition in secret.

Still, it was difficult to be patient. Kylen knew the Coalition would frown on his prank which served no greater purpose than to amuse himself. If he was caught and it became public knowledge that there were profectus clones, then he would be jeopardizing not only his life, but many others. The plan was for all the profectus to be in respectable positions for several decades before their identities were revealed.

Reluctantly, he reversed his actions, selling the stocks he had just bought and sending the money back into the original dummy account. Fortunately, he made a small profit which covered the fees he had to pay. Then he transferred the million credits back to the original company.

There, no one will know I stole a fortune. And no one would know how skilled a hacker I am. He would remained quiet, cordial Kylen living with a friendly foster family—for now.

On his computer, he typed in the command for a memory wipe to erase everything. There was a backup of his hacking program on another junk laptop at the house. He stood up and strolled passed a stylish woman walking two genetically altered poodles, one with pink fur, the other with purple. A flirting couple holding hands zoomed by on hover skates.

When Kylen reached a trash can, he tossed the computer in it then threw on top of it the wrappers of the snacks he had eaten earlier. He continued his stroll through the park, just another teenager enjoying the cool autumn day.

Chapter Seven

A large crowd gathered around the central raised platform in the huge gym, rooting for their favorite combatant. Today was the annual Blades Tournament held in the Hall of Challenge, a vast wing of Essence Institute consisting of many gyms each dedicated to a different sport.

The first match was only an exhibition, as both contenders were too high ranking for a fair match against challengers. Jacob, inside of Desmond's agility H1 body, whirled, dodging two curved karambit blades aiming for him. He sidestepped, and sliced his dagger across his wife's side. Firestrike barely felt it as she twirled, cutting across Desmond's shoulder, leaving a streak of blood.

"Go, Dad!" yelled Rockgem, leaning against the platform, his four hands moving as he reenacted out blows.

"Come on, Mom!" shouted Darkfern, her eyes intense.

Pale-face, Hennah watched the fierce match. She had seen such bouts before, but still she always worried about injuries. The blades used were dull but still could be lethal. Unlike sword fighting, combatants stayed close when using knives, their movements fast, using their entire bodies and unarmed limbs to block and deflect blades of their rivals.

Firestrike lived up to her name, her four arms a deadly whirlwind of blades, but Desmond was quick, leaping and twisting out of her reach, using his free arm to deflect blows, looking for brief moments he could slip pass her defenses to deliver a cut.

A bell sounded and the fight ended. The combats bowed to each other as some in the crowd chanted their names. The thick hide of Firestrike had absorbed most of her cuts without the flesh being pierced. Desmond bleed from multiple shallow wounds, yet he kept a stoic face, not flinching from the pain.

Three judges, all quintessences, compared notes of blade contacts they had counted. The oldest judge climbed onto the platform and announced, "Firestrike wins again."

Quintessences in the crowd clapped but did not cheer, as it was their way. Other sentients cheered or yelled out jests about fighting spouses. Firestrike grinned and waved her blades high in the air. Then she and Desmond climbed down from the platform. As soon as their feet touched the floor, Desmond wrapped an arm around his wife's waist. With his other hand, he brushed her thick hair away from her neck.

She remained still as he bit. He kept the contact brief as his wounds healed. Even after he finished the bite, he held her close. She twisted in his arms. Desmond kissed her passionately on the lips, while her four arms wrapping tightly around her husband.

"Mom does enjoy her fights. That's how she fell in love," whispered Darkfern to Hennah. "When Dad finally beat her in a tournament. Before then, she only saw him as a flirting co-worker."

As two new combatants hopped onto the platform for the first official tournament bout, Rockgem bounded over to his parents. "Awesome, Mom. When do I get to fight?"

Firestrike pulled away from Desmond. "As we have told you before, only adults may enter tournaments."

"Which means I can," grinned Darkfern who had recently turned sixteen, the traditional transition age recognized by her species.

Hennah stared at two quintessence striking each other with daggers, blood specks sprinkling the mat. "Are you sure you are ready?"

"Of course. I have trained hard. Besides, my first pailuk is a month. I better be ready."

Desmond gave his daughter a firm pat on the shoulders. "You will do well. Keep to your mother's strategies. Use your extra hands to your advantage. Make them bleed tenfold for every strike they place."

Darkfern nodded, determined to bring honor to her parents. "I won't forget."

Several rounds went by before Darkfern was called. The mat had been washed by a small cleaning bot between bouts to remove blood and sweat. The fjouwer youth took her place across from a freed ME2 model. Despite her opponent being much older than her, Darkfern radiated confidence, holding her two curved karambit blades in tight fists, her index fingers in the circles at the end of the handles, making it difficult to disarm her. With a flick of her wrist, she could rotate the blades into an extended grip. The quintessence used a straight edged dagger.

Soon the two combatant were whirling around the mat, Darkfern striking fast, keeping her blows coming with two hands while her other arms blocked her opponent's attacks. She was skillful, but so too was the ME2. He deflected some blows and dodged others, several times causing her to lose her footing while he delivered strikes which would have killed her if his full weight had been behind the stab. The judges gave higher points for each kill stroke.

Firestrike frowned. "Roger is better than this. He is going easy on her. I told everyone to do their best. I'll give him night duty for this."

Desmond smoothed his wife, "Let it go. She is young, and he is testing her."

"Fights are far more brutal at the Kilpailu. How can she prepare if they do not push her here?"

To Hennah, the fight was intense. She saw no indication that Roger was taking it easy on her friend. When the bout ended, there were cuts on both opponents. Only a few wounds on the fjouwer bled slightly, while streaks ran down the arms of Roger. The score was close but Darkfern was announced the winner. She had landed only one kill blow, yet she had many more strikes. After Darkfern rejoined her family, her father and brother congratulated her, but Firestrike frowned, giving advice on how to perform better in the next round. Darkfern's bleeding wounds were patched up with a skin glue from a medic on duty.

Hennah walked with her friend through the crowd to a water dispenser. "You looked spectacular up there with your fancy blades. Are you hurt much?"

Darkfern gulped down all her water at once. "Nah. Our god blessed us fjouwers with thick hides. Mom is right. I need to be better. If this was a real fight, I would have lost. He killed me multiple times."

"You will get better."

"With my first pailuk a month off, I don't have much time. Still, as a newbie, I won't be a serious target."

Hennah shuddered, visualizing hundreds of fjouwers fighting in pairs in a vast, dark cavern. Kilpailu was a huge deal in fjouwer culture. It was a holiday celebrated twice a year by all the tribes. The most anticipated event was pailuk where unmarried fjouwers, along with spouses who wanted to reenact out their marriages, gathered for pugna matches. On the fjouwer homeworld, pailuk traditionally took place in the huge mushroom forests deep underground. Females were given a few hours head start then males rushed into the forests, seeking females to fight. If a male won, he coupled with her then bit her on the shoulder deep enough to pierce the skin, marking her as his wife.

"Aren't you afraid you will accidently be married to someone detestable?"

Darkfern laughed. "I will let no man take me before I am ready. If he tries, he will only know the taste of my blades. Besides, this will be my first time. No male wants to marry a newbie. Females earn status by making it through pailuks unmated. Make it past twelve, and you become legendary. Those are the ones the males target."

"But don't the less skilled males settle for less adept brides?"

"Sure, but I am talented. And ready for my next round." Darkfern grinned and headed back through the crowd to watch a match.

Darkfern made it through three more bouts, eventually winning fourth place. Rockgem kept trying to steal her bronze trophy, bragging he would earn a platinum one someday. Hennah was invited to dinner with the family. She followed them through the Hall of Challenge, passing its many gyms, competition rings, and ball courts. In Richton Tower they took the elevator to the top floor where their penthouse was located. To celebrate, Firestrike fixed a traditional fjouwer meal of spicy mushrooms, steaks covered in a sizzling sauce, and sweet yellow pods which popped when chewed.

Afterwards, Darkfern and Hennah strolled through the nearby huge indoor garden filled with exotic plants from various planets. At the center of the garden grew a huge rosa vine tree, its strong branches stretching two thirds up towards the glass dome over the garden. From its thick limbs hung vines with small red leaves which gave the appearance of the tree always in bloom. The girls stepped through the veil of vines. Deep violet flowers grew in the grass under the red canopy.

"It always feels magical here." Hennah breathed deeply the perfume of the flowers.

"That is a marriage hot spot. Dad says most of the married members of the Synod choose to have their weddings here."

"It's romantic. Maybe I will someday."

"You plan to marry a quintessence?"

"I've not seriously thought about that. But I worry about you. You could be a bride in a month."

"Not going to happen. I plan to make it to legendary status. Mom had the talent to be one, but she only made it through eight pailuks before falling in love with dad. She gave up a lot marrying him. My grandparents felt she shortchanged herself."

"At least your parents' story has a happy ending." Sadness came to Henna's eyes.

"Has your grandfather heard from the doctor yet?" Darkfern immediately knew the source of her friend's unhappiness.

"Not yet. But he has lost weight and missed a lot of work recently."

"Well, he is not going to get fired. He is a department head."

"He is thinking about retiring. Work won't be the same without him." How can she continue with Project Absurd without Chandresh's daily encouragement? For four long years she had labored fruitlessly in her lab. Earning her PhD had been a nice distraction, allowing her to do some research unrelated to quintessences. But now that she had her degree, she was expected to put her full attention on the project.

"You need a vacation. How about you come to Shah Luna with me?"

"I thought you were going to Bayoom, your mom's home planet?"

"Nah. Shah Luna is much more exciting. There are only a few hundred fjouwers living on Bayoom. Their version of Kilpailu is meeting in one of my uncle's warehouses and fighting in a makeshift arena. No forests to run in. Though there is

57

a lot of food, dancing, and singing. Fun when I was little. But I want my first pailuk to be more traditional, and there is no place more glorious than Shah Luna. An entire moon filled with huge caverns mined out by fjouwers centuries ago. Forests that are endless."

Hennah shook her head. "Oh, no. I don't want a bunch of guys chasing me with knives in a dark forest."

Darkfern laughed. "Our forests are luminescence. Many of our plant and fungus species glow. You will not find a more beautiful landscape in all of the galaxy than our subterranean forests."

"To a fjouwer. I prefer green trees and open sky. And I'm not about to take part in a battle marriage."

"Kilpailu is about more than just pugnas. It's about rejoicing for being alive. Everyone celebrates, both children and married couples. We dance and feast. Wow, do we eat. Here, Mom tries to create versions of our food with what she can buy in supermarkets. But on Shah Luna, you can eat our real foods which taste so much better. And we will be in the capitol city. New Werjouk has a huge city park that you can walk in for days and not find all its boundaries, at least Mom could not and she went four times. Pugnas only take place in the park, so if you avoid it, you will be safe. You can stay with my family while I enjoy fighting the boys. Please come. I promise you will have fun."

"I don't know. Sounds dangerous."

"You will be with a Five and his warrior family. You can't get any safer than that. And this will be my first pailuk. My best friend should be supporting me."

Hennah sighed deeply. "Alright, I'll ask my parents if I can come."

"Awesome." Darkfern took out her karambits and flipped the blades in circles around her fists, switching rapidly from reverse to extended grip.

"The boys won't stand a chance against you."

Darkfern grinned. "I know."

The next day, Hennah worked in her lab, trying not to give in to boredom. She was attempting to write the genes for a female quintessence from scratch, but the work was tenuous. Over six hundred thousand DNA strands was used to create the quintessences. She needed to isolate male traits and then replace them with female traits. But first she had to create an organic blueprint for those traits which was compatible with the entire genome. As she was using DNA from over sixty species, there was countless issues with proteins, enzymes, and mitosis. Some sources were cold-blooded while others warm-blooded. The very cell structure they originated from was far different from each other. Chemical reactions conflicted between species.

Hennah tossed down her e-tablet onto a metal table in frustration. "This is impossible!"

Joseph appeared as the doorway of his office, used to her outbursts. "What has you upset now?" He walked down the stairs to her.

"Everything. How in the universe did Layla get it to work the first time?"

"With patience."

"I lack that trait."

"Perhaps you should take your lunch break early." Calming her when she was upset had become one of his routine chores.

"Yeah." Hennah stood up, stretching her arms after sitting for hours. "Oh, I'm going to be gone for two weeks. I'm going with Darkfern to Shah Luna. Her family is celebrating Kilpailu."

A slight frown appeared on Joseph's face. "You can't go."

"I already asked my parents, and they said I could."

"You will need Alec's approval. Two weeks is too long a delay on this project."

"Approval for a vacation? I have worked four years and rarely taken a day off. Maybe some time off will rejuvenate me, and I can finally make a breakthrough."

"Still, you must have Alec's approval. I will ask him today."

"Sure." Hennah shrugged, and headed over to the small refrigerator where she kept meals. Sometimes she ate with Chandresh in the Grand Forum, but he had missed work again today due to sickness.

The afternoon hours dragged by. Finally she headed home, taking a hover bus which ferried workers across the huge campus. *Too bad I can't afford to buy my own car.* Once she had turned sixteen, she had been given a small raise but it was still too low to be helpful. *Why do I have to wait until I'm eighteen to receive regular pay?* Just one of many things which seemed unfair to her, like having to ask permission to go on vacation.

When she reached home, she headed to her bedroom, grateful that Aashi was away at college. Still, Aashi's stuff was scattered around the room. At least her stereo was silent. On an e-tablet, Hennah watched silly videos for an hour, not wanting to think about anything that related to work. Hearing her mom call that dinner was ready, Hennah headed to the table, happy to see Chandresh was joining them tonight. He had his own apartment nearby.

"Dada, you are looking handsome today."

Her grandfather smiled, but weariness was in his eyes. "Poti, you are as beautiful as ever."

Hennah placed flatbread on her plate then spooned spicy baingan bharta into a bowl beside it. "Mm, delicious Mamma. You found fresh eggplant."

Pallavi smiled. "It's in season now. After dinner Chandresh wishes to talk with you both." She glanced at Dhruvi reaching for some baked samosas.

After the meal was finished, the family sat on couches. For a long moment Hennah's parents and Chandresh looked at each other, unable to speak. Finally, Chadresh said, "The doctors have found out what is wrong with me. I have lysinuric morbus."

The room seemed to darken to Hennah. "Lysinuric? But, Dada, you are too young for that. Only really, really old people get that."

"My poti, I am old."

Dhruvi looked at the tense faces of his family. "What is lysinuric morbus?"

Kaushal explained, "It is a human disease which is similar to another that came from the Stardancer's homeworld. Most likely it mutated, adapting to humans. It's rare and usually affects only elderly humans. So far there is no cure. The subject will grow weaker as the body loses the ability to breakdown proteins correctly." His voice broke, and he fell silent.

Chandresh finished for his son. "I will experience muscle weakness, impaired immune system, and brittle bones. My liver and spleen will enlarge. My kidneys and lungs will develop serious complications."

"Will you die, Dada?" Dhruvi asked wide-eyed.

"We all die sooner or later. I just happen to know my time is sooner."

Hennah began weeping as her world collapsed. She moved close to Chandresh, burying her wet face in his shirt.

"There, there, Poti. I'm not dying today." He stroked her long, black hair. "I have several years. And I'm going to enjoy my retirement in the time I am allotted. I need you happy to cheer up an old man like me. Can you smile for me?"

It took some coaxing before Hennah could control her tears. Dhruvi wiped several away from his own eyes, trying to keep his grief hidden. Their parents attempted to cheer them up, pulling out a favorite board game. Chandresh won twice.

That night, alone in her bedroom, Hennah cried as quietly as she could so her parents would not be disturbed. For once, she wished Aashi was here so they could comfort each other, that is if Aashi would carry on more than a one minute conversation with her.

At work the next day, she barely could focus. She found herself redoing the same calculations three times, forgetting each time what the answer was. At lunch, Joseph sat beside her at a metal table in the lab, both eating sandwiches.

"I heard your grandfather is retiring. Is that why you are sad today?"

Hennah stared at her half-eaten sandwich, feeling as if she would never know happiness again. "He's dying. He has lysinuric morbus."

"I'm sorry to hear that."

"The doctors say he has a few years." She nibbled on chips, not tasting them.

Joseph watched her silently for a few minutes, trying to find something positive to say. "A panel will choose his replacement. Alec will make sure the new head of the research department is trustworthy and will be supportive of your research."

Hennah did not respond. Instead, she stared at her cup, her fingers encircled it but she did not drink.

"I did talk with Alec about your request for a trip."

She looked at him. "What did he say?"

"That you cannot go."

"Why not? You did tell him I was travelling with a Five?"

"Actually he and Desmond discussed the trip together. Both came to the conclusion it would be too risky for you. Darkfern had not asked her father's permission before inviting you."

The teenager felt upset at being forced to disappoint her best friend. "Project Absurd must be completed, no matter what. Don't want their lone researcher accidently dying while on the only vacation she has asked for."

"I apology that you cannot go."

"Then I ask to go with Darkfern when she visits her grandparents next time. Kilpailu on Bayoom is more tone down."

"Hennah," Joseph's voice was gentle. "You are not allowed off planet at all. Ever."

The teenager looked at him, slowly realizing the implication. "Wait. Are you saying that my boss is keeping me prisoner?"

"You are not a prisoner."

"But I can go where I wish. Can't I?"

"Yes, with certain limitations. You must avoid any place where the knowledge you are a clone might be revealed such as Luncaster University. And you cannot travel far without Alec's permission."

Hennah pondered his words for a bit. Her frustration about Chadresh's illness along with a Five trying to control her slowly turned into anger. "He can't do that. You tell Alec I am a citizen of the Basanti Empire. I can do what I please."

Joseph looked at her without speaking.

"Go, tell him right now. If he tries to control my life, then I quit. What do I care if this project is ever completed?"

"Hennah," Joseph spoke cautiously, trying to be as tactful as he could. "Technically you don't exist."

"What?"

"Your existence had to be hidden very carefully. Your birth records contain fake fingerprints and DNA. Even your pictures submitted when you applied to colleges were altered. Alec and others have tried to protect you as much as possible. Travelling off planet carries too many risks. Security checkpoints do face scans, fingerprints, and voice recognition. Computer databases will recognize you as Yashana Kalkar, not Hennah Kalkar."

"So I can never leave Xi'an. Ever?"

"Correct. The Five can control information about you on this planet but not other places."

Hennah looked away, clenching her fists. Life was so unfair. Chandresh was about to lose his existence while she did not exist at all. "If I'm not a citizen of the empire then what am I? Am I like you, a bonded clone? Am I a slave to the Five?"

"My understanding is…" Joseph paused, trying to find the right words. "…you fall in the middle. You are not a slave. They try to give you as much freedom as possible, but with limits."

"Do I belong to the Five or to myself?" Hennah angrily emphasized each word.

"You are like quintessences in that you live for the whole, not for yourself."

"They made that decision, not I." Hennah stood up and tossed her half-eaten meal in the recycler. "I'm taking off the afternoon. Do you have a problem with that?"

Joseph studied her, noting her hostile stance. "No, spend time with your grandfather. He would like that."

Hennah stormed down the hallway, fuming at what he had told her. *I am a slave to them. Joseph should have just straight out said it. They choose my family, my home, my job, my education, even my body. I have no say so about my own life. What else am I but a slave created to make more slave masters?*

Not wanting to be around others, Hennah wandered about Essence, passing young quintessences practicing bōjutsu in plazas. For a while she watched freed adults target practice with laser guns, competing with birthmates to see who could earn the highest score. At an obstacle course, she studied C6 models who appeared about her age climbing ropes, jumping across gaps high in the air, and leaping to the ground without pausing as they dashed to the finish line. Soon they would be fighting in someone else's war. Dying because they were ordered to do so. *Life is not fair to them. Or to me. Why does slavery have to exist at all?*

Eventually she headed home, arriving at her normal time. As she walked through the door, she was shocked to see Alec sitting on the couch chatting with her parents as they showed off family photos. Anger flashed in her. *He has no right being in my home!*

Pallavi smiled as her daughter entered. "How was work today, hon?"

"The same," Hennah kept her voice flat but glared at Alec. He had aged a lot since she had last seen him four years ago. His hair was completely white, his arms thin, veins in his wrinkled hands visible under his skin.

To her parents, he said, "Again, you have my sympathy. The Synod and I are deeply sadden by Chadresh's illness. He has been a trusted and loyal member of our family. We will pay for his medical treatments. Do not worry about money."

Kaushal nodded. "My family and I appreciate your help."

"Now I must be leaving." Alec stood and pressed his palms together. With a slight bow, he said, "Namaste."

Hennah's parents returned the ancient gesture. "Namaste."

As Alec walked towards the door, he paused. "Hennah, may I have a private word with you?"

She frowned, glancing at her parents. Though he was making it sound like a choice, she knew it was an order. She followed him out into the hallway.

"Your parents are very special."

"You don't have to put on a show for me."

"I care about your parents and your grandfather far more than you can understand. I feel a kinship with them."

"I feel nothing for you."

"Walk with me."

Alec led her down the long hallway and outside into the bright sunshine. A Shadow Guard followed them, keeping twenty paces behind. They strolled in silence pass other barracks where young quintessences lived. Alec turned into a small courtyard surrounded by high bushes and took a seat on a marble bench. He indicated for Hennah to sit beside him. She almost refused, but after a long pause of him silently staring at her, she sat down.

Alec looked at his Shadow Guard who remained standing by the entrance to the courtyard. The guard gave a slight nod then the Five said, "We can talk here in safety."

"I have nothing to say to you."

"You had a lot to say to Joseph, but he could not answer your question. I can. Yes, Hennah, you are a slave. Unlike my brethren, you do not belong to the Basanti Empire but to Essence. It is the Synod that ordered you into existence, so it is the Synod who are your owners. As I am a Five over the Synod, I am your master. Is that a satisfactory answer?"

"No." Hennah's body trembled in both anger and fear. "Slavery is illegal."

"So is your existence. We have tried to give you a good life. You have a loving, supportive family. An excellent education. You have far more freedom than a bonded quintessence."

"But I can't go where I wish."

"Off planet. Xi'an is large with many places to explore. The limits we have set are more than fair. There are many sentients born into freedom who never experience space travel. Many who can't afford a college education. Some who are unable to go to school at all. You have never experienced the despair of poverty or the horrors of war. Your life is not perfect, but you have been blessed far beyond many. I am sorry you now carry the burden of knowledge that you are a slave. All quintessences, including me, have known this feeling of not owning one's self."

Hennah stared down at the brown bricks by her shoes. She hated how he had turned the conversation. "You want me to be grateful for being a slave?"

"No, I want you to understand. And offer you hope. Quintessences are freed after fifty years of satisfactory service."

"I will be an old woman."

"Your condition for freedom will not be based on age, but progress. Once the first healthy female quintessences are born, I will remove all limits I have set on you. You may do anything you wish then."

The teenager continued to stare at her shoes. "What if I never succeed?"

"Then you will never be free. But I believe that you will be successful."

"I may look like you by the time I do."

"Maybe this will motivate you to try harder. Joseph reports you feel apathy towards your work, often wasting time and becoming easily frustrated."

Hennah looked at him. "Because you ask the impossible."

"You were created to make the impossible possible. Do not give up. Buried within you is the same passion Layla had."

"You're wrong. I don't care if there are more quintessences. I don't care about anything but my grandfather. And he is dying."

"I wish I could prevent that." Alec looked across the courtyard, silent for a moment. "I too am dying. Like your grandfather, I also know how long I have. One of the benefits of being a clone. We die by the clock."

Hennah looked at her hands clasped tightly together. "I…uh…am sorry you're dying."

"Death comes to us all, sooner or later. The question is how do you live your life? You can rant about the unfairness of life or you can embrace your destiny. You did not get to choose your path, but you can choose how you travel it." The elderly quintessence reached over and took the teenager's hands. "I wish great happiness for you. Your life can be abundant. Do not allow yourself to become bitter."

Hennah looked at the veins standing out on his deeply wrinkled hands. His skin was similar to Chandresh's. And he was dying like her grandfather. She would do anything to help Chandresh. Could she get over her anger to help Alec? She did not sense cruelty in him. Still, she resented that he had created her into slavery, no matter how sugary he tried to make it appear.

She pulled her hands from him and looked him in the eyes. "I want a raise. The same pay other researchers get with PhD's."

"Alright."

For a moment she stared at him, uncertain what else to say. With a proper salary, she at least felt some validation for her existence. She could afford a car, claiming the limited amount of freedom that came with it.

Chapter Eight

The list of marriage applications on the computer screen remained untouched as Joseph looked at his e-band for the hundredth time this morning. He should be working but he had been waiting eighteen years for this day. Everything else paled when he was about to be reunited with this birthmates.

"Our ship is now in orbit around Xi'an," read Philip's last message.

Unable to work, Joseph stood up and walked to the glass window to watch Hennah. The seventeen year old was bent over her e-tablet editing DNA. There was a mix of intensity and frustration on her face. Ever since she had learned that the Synod considered her property of Essence, her efforts had increased dramatically. Now she stayed focus all day, sometimes even working overtime if in the middle of something when quitting time came. Yet despite her best efforts, her experiments always failed. She rarely complained now. She just recorded the results and tried a new approach.

Alec was pleased with her new maturity and improved progress, believing it was only a matter of time before she found the correct combination. Joseph, though, sometimes missed the younger, happier Hennah. She may have wasted time, but she had sometimes been entertaining, like when he caught her testing freezing speeds of various sodas using the cryogenic freezer. She had grinned at him and offered him a soda popsicle.

She rarely smiled now. And she was not happy. He knew part of it was watching her grandfather slowly die. Chandresh was often in the hospital for a few days at a time, then sent back home until the next reoccurrence. Week by week he grew weaker and thinner.

Seeing it was finally lunchtime, Joseph climbed down the stairs and headed to the refrigerator, taking out both their lunches. Today, Hennah had brought leftovers from her mom's delicious home-cooked dinner. Joseph ate a sandwich and chips yet again, which he had picked up in the cafeteria of his barracks this morning.

They ate mainly in silence. Hennah spoke briefly about her latest attempt, but as he did not understand most of her scientific jargon, she kept her comments short. Joseph glanced at his e-band again, reading the message, "Our shuttle is launching now."

Excitement filled him, but he kept his face stoic. "I am taking this afternoon off."

Hennah stared at him in surprise. "You never take off early."

"My brothers arrive today."

"Oh, that's right. Your Day of Commendation is soon. Congratulations."

"Thank you." Joseph studied her face, noticing various emotions she tried to hide, but he had become good at reading her. She felt enviousness he was about to be free while her sentence still had no end, anger at Alec, and guilt that she was jealous when she should be happy for Joseph.

The teenager forced a smile. "You deserve your freedom. I am sorry you lost so many birthmates."

"No more died after Philip became lieutenant." Guilt of lost lives stabbed at Joseph. Logically he knew their deaths were not his fault, but the knowledge did not ease his grief. At least after his company had dropped below the fifty percent death rate, the other assignments had not been on warfronts. "Will you come to our Day of Commendation?"

"I…uh…might. I have been to a few with my family." The event took place every four month and lasted for hours. With it being so commonplace, turnout was low, though most workers at Essence had attended the ceremony at least once.

"I will be taking the next two days off to be with my brothers."

"Have fun."

Joseph nodded as he tossed his trash in the recycler. Then he headed out of Richton Tower to the landing pads. He walked under a metal frame canopy supporting its glass roof as he passed busy shuttles bringing down the thousands of quintessences who were returning to Essence after being away for fifty years. After checking his e-band, he found the right landing pad and waited eagerly. Eighteen years of separation. Long months of loneness and guilt of having an easy life at Essence while his brothers risked their own. No matter how pleasant life was here, he would have given it all up to be with his brothers again.

A large shuttle slowly landed on the pad. After a few minutes, quintessences began walking down the ramp. Members of Company C5-20453 separated themselves from the others and walked towards Joseph. They gathered around him, faint smiles on their lips. If they were human they would have hugged him; instead, they stood close, saying friendly greetings.

"It has been a long time, brother," said Philip.

"We have missed you. Our current lieutenant made us eat only vegetables at our last post," jested Ryder, giving Philip a glance.

"The entire planet was inhabited by vegetarians. It would have been an insult if we ate meat," explained Philip.

Joseph smiled. "It has been too long, brothers." Warmth filled Joseph as he looked over the forty-six who have survived. His throat tightened as he thought about the ones missing. "You will be staying in Sebok Barracks, not too far from where we grew up."

Each of them carried a duffel bag containing all the items they owned, including clothes, a knife, a bedroll, and an e-tablet that had been issued to them. They took a bus to the barracks and found their new quarters. Joseph had already brought his few things over the day before. He had been staying in a different barracks with other dishonored bonded quintessences serving out sentences similar to his. The mismatch group called Gray Unit had formed a loose community but never shared the deep connections of birthmates.

Philip beheld the plain room with foot lockers beside fifty bunkbeds. "Looks like we never left."

The quintessences began to unpack. To claim the footlockers, a quintessence scanned his hand over the lock, letting it read the microchip embedded in the flesh when he was an infant.

Joseph waited until Philip had put away his clothes. He then walked over and turned his back to his birthmate, signaling an invitation to merge minds. Philip bit him. The brothers swapped stories, sharing favorite adventures they had missed out on, joking about several of their birthmates. Then Philip became serious, revealing his fears of being a lieutenant, watching two brothers almost die due to a bad judgment call he had made when pursuing criminals, wishing often that Joseph had been there to give advice. Joseph shared his own loneness over the years of separation, of monotonous work of certificating applications, the self-punishment of avoiding recreation activities he had once shared with his brothers. The only thing he hid was Project Absurd since it was classified.

Philip broke contact. "No basketball for eighteen years? We have to fix that oversight."

"I was waiting for the right team to play with."

Soon the whole company headed to the Hall of Challenge and sought out the basketball gym which held twelve courts. They split into several teams rotating between courts as they held an unofficial tournament. They played for hours, not only against birthmates but other quintessences as well.

For dinner they ate in the cafeteria at Sebok Barracks then headed to the huge Recreation Center which was shaped like a giant ball. Late into the night they competed for high scores in video games, hologram simulators, and table games. As Joseph lay on his bunkbed listening to his brothers sleep, he felt a deep contentment he had never known before. No longer did he have to fear their deaths at the hands of indifferent politicians. From now on, they choose their own fates. And when they did meet death, it would be on their own terms.

For the next two days the birthmates were inseparable. They explored Essence at their own pace, visiting many of the gyms. They hiked in the nearby forests and swam in the ocean. They swapped stories with other quintessences who were staying in the same barracks and challenged them to competitions. Life seemed perfect for the first time.

The third day they proudly marched in formation to the vast parade ground which could hold twenty thousand quintessences at once. On two sides of the field were tall bleachers which could seat thousands of guests, but the attendance was low for the Day of Commendation. Few of the bonded quintessences had friends who had traveled to Xi'an to attend the event. The remnants of the five thousands who had left Essence fifty years ago stood in formation by company, only two thirds of the originals who left so long ago. On the other side of the field twenty-five hundred young quintessences stood at attention, ready to begin their years of servitude. Until the budget cuts, five thousand new soldiers were always sent to the Basanti Military every four months.

On a raised platform stood the Five. Several camera drones zoomed about, their recordings showing up on several huge screens positioned so the whole audience could watch. The fifty members of the Synod stood in a straight line on the ground near the platform, tables near them stacked with plastic cards.

The director walked forward to a glass podium. "Today we honor our brethren who have completed fifty years of service. The price of freedom you paid was high. You faced many trials. Lost friends along the way who have not been forgotten. We welcome you back as equals to enjoy the freedom you sacrificed for."

Caden moved back, and Alec took his place. "We also honor our newest generation about to embark on their journey. You have completed eight years of intense training to prepare for combat in inhospitably environments. But the skills you have learned will not be enough. You will need to rely on each other, protecting your brothers in times of weakness."

Desmond stepped to the podium. "What is the Code?"

As one, thousands of voices recited in harmony, "All quintessences shall place the welfare of their brethren above themselves. Each must live an exemplary life, obeying superiors, avoiding vices, protecting the weak."

The Five nodded soberly. "This is your guide in the darkness. Both free and bonded quintessences must never forget. You were created for a purpose higher than freedom. That is the protection of others."

Guyapi spoke next. "While we shield each other, we also look out for those in need who are not our brethren. Remember our history, where we came from, who created us, who taught us. We have kinsmen among many sentients, many species who are part of our larger family. Never forget."

Mablevi was the last to speak. "Eights, look to your right. In fifty years this could be you if you fight well and live honorably by the Code. We wish to one day welcome you all back to celebrate your day of freedom. Company C1-20558, step forward."

On one of the huge screens, Joseph watched the company march to the line of Synods members who handed them citizenship ID badges. Then they marched slowly down the huge field to the back of a row as another company rotated forward. As Joseph waited for his company's turn, he scanned the bleachers, which were mostly empty. He did spot members of Gray Unit who had been demoted like him. After living with many of them for years, he viewed them as friends. It was not until he was nearing the platform that he finally spotted Hennah sitting high up near the top, alone. He felt warmth for those who had come to support him.

Company C5-20453 was called. Along with his birthmates, Joseph marched forward, face blank, heart full of joy.

An elderly H3 handed him the hard plastic badge. "Congratulations."

Joseph nodded, overcome with emotions he could no longer hide. Philip flashed him a big grin. The company marched to the back of the line. Only then did Joseph examine the badge. It had a picture of him, his thumbprint, and his ID number which matched the microchip embedded in his hand. Today he was a citizen for the government he had bled for. He could go where he wished, do as he pleased. He closed his fist around the badge, feeling its sharp edges against his skin, visualizing each of his birthmates who were not here, memorializing them in his own way as he silently said each of their names.

After the last company had been called, attention was turned to the young quintessences. Each of their companies were called forward to the line of Synod, but instead of badges, they were giving their first assignment. Their faces were void of emotions. Today began their lives of slavery, along with the heavy burden of knowing not all of them would be alive in fifty years to become citizens.

After the ceremony ended, Joseph and his brothers grinned at each other and joked about who looked more handsome on their badges. Then they debated how to celebrate. Spotting his old barrack friends walking down the bleacher steps, Joseph walked towards them. Ahead of them a female human in her twenties was trying to rush through the crowd, finally climbing over the railing and dropping five feet to the parade ground. She was immediately embraced by a C6 model who kissed her deeply on the lips. Joseph paused along with others nearby to watch, knowing this was the couple's first kiss. Until a few minutes ago, it would have been a death sentence for the C6 to display affection for her. Joseph glanced at the C6's name badge, guessing there would be a marriage application turned in before the end of the day.

Joseph caught up with his own friends who congratulated him. He brought them over to his birthmates and introduced them. Then he scanned the crowd for Hennah. He spotted her at the end of the line waiting to exit the bleacher stands.

When she reached the ground, he said to her, "Thank you for coming out."

"It was a nice ceremony." For a moment there was silence. "Can I see your badge?"

Joseph held out to her the ID. Thoughtfully she studied its shiny surface. "Looks proper. Has the correct picture with your name." She handed the badge back to him.

"Your time will come too."

She shrugged. "Perhaps. Will you still be working with me or will you be taking a sabbatical like your birthmates?"

Joseph studied the tired sadness in her eyes. He had been so focused for years on this ceremony that he had not considered how it would impact her. "Most likely I will keep working, at least for a while, if Alec still wants me to."

"I'm sure he will. He appreciates what a great spy you are for him."

He noticed several of his birthmates walking towards them. "This is Lieutenant Philip and Sergeant Ryder. Hennah is a co-worker."

"Good to meet you," said Philip. "Is he flirting with you already?"

Hennah's mouth opened in surprise at the comment while Joseph gave his brother a sharp, warning look.

Ryder peered closely at her, "You look remarkable like Layla Rangan."

"She's my ancestor. Well, not her but Yashana. Uh, I got to go. See you Monday, Joseph."

After she has disappeared in the crowd, Joseph reprimanded his brothers. "You were both very rude. Just because you are free does not mean you say whatever you are thinking."

"I apologize," said Philip. "I just saw a kissing couple and wondered if you would be next."

"Our relationship is nothing like that."

Ryder looked in the direction Hennah had disappeared, a slight frown on his puzzled face. "She looks too much like Layla to just be a relative."

A warning tone came into Joseph's voice. "Quintessences who live at Essence know there are certain questions which should never be asked. That is one of them."

They joined the rest of their company who had decided they would climb a famous cliff in the nearby national park. They ate lunch in the cafeteria, excitingly planning the adventure. Then they grabbed climbing gear from a storage warehouse

71

and joined five other companies. After a four mile hike through thick forests, they reached the base of the thousand foot cliff and set up camp. As night fell, they roasting food over firepits and slept under the open sky.

Half asleep, Ryder mumbled, "First time I ever liked camping."

"This is the first time we have hiked without being on a military campaign," responded Philip. "Nice not having to worry about being shot in your sleep."

Joseph lay on his bedroll, studying the bright stars above, his brief anger with his brothers had long vanished. He breathed in the scent of crushed leaves, wood smoke, and cooked meat. "The rewards of freedom."

"Swimming? That will be fun," muttered Ryder, his voice fading as he fell asleep.

The next morning the companies rotated turns climbing then propelling down the mountain face. Joseph had climbed before but this was the first time he had done so for sport. He liked the feel of testing handholds, of muscles stretching as he pulled himself upward, the heat of the sun on his back. As he pulled himself over the lip of the cliff, he looked downward at the forest far below, adrenaline pumping, feeling very much alive. He shared grins with birthmates, relishing the thrill.

Monday he felt like a new man as he sat in his office. The day moved as any other, with Hennah working quietly, not complaining as she recorded the results of yet another failed experiment. Joseph read over applications, noting that the couple he had noticed at the ceremony had married that very evening. He carefully read forms, researching government laws occasionally. Today's work felt pleasant, not ponderous like when it had been a punishment.

Mid-morning, he received a message to meet with Alec. He headed up to the forty-fifth floor and entered the Five's office. The elder invited Joseph to sit on a couch. A silent Shadow Guard with the nametag of Miles stood near a bookcase.

"Congratulation on completing your bondage. I presume you wish to keep working on this project, as you came in today when you could be spending time with your brothers." Alec looked thinner, his skin sagging.

"I will be seeing them this afternoon. Hennah is used to my encouragements when her work becomes too taxing."

"You have been a positive influence on her." Alec touched the computerized coffee table and pulled up Joseph's files. "I will put you officially on the payroll. I can either list your job description as classified or you can keep your cover as a desk clerk."

"I would prefer keeping my old post, as it gives me something to do while watching Hennah."

Alex entered in data. "I know it may be too early, but have your brothers started considering what they will do once their sabbatical is over?"

It was customary for freed quintessences to spend six months to a year at Essence, enjoying a long vacation. They lived in barracks where food and clothing was provided for them, along with three hundred credits per month. The funds allowed them to explore nearby cities and shop for the first time. After six months, they began job hunting. Essence had a limited number of job openings, including positions in its own space fleet. Offers were regularly sent to Essence from planetary governments, politicians, and private companies who wanted to hire quintessences.

ME and C models preferred keeping birthmates together so they usually only accepted posts for the whole group. While bonded, IN's usually served as peacemakers on long term posts. Once freed, many headed back to their last post where they had already assimilated into the culture and sometimes had brides waiting for them. As talented technicians and mechanics, HC's were used to working in smaller groups and often took positons in private companies. The AS and AF models were kept in low production and almost always chose to continue to work for Essence until their retirement.

"We have not discussed that yet."

"As your company is small, if your brothers wish to work for Essence, I am certain we can find positions for all of them."

"I will pass the information on to them."

"You may work here as long as you wish, but if you do choose to leave after the sabbatical is over, please give us enough warning so you can train a replacement. It will be difficult for Hennah to trust another as she does you."

Joseph nodded. "Yes, sir."

"One final thing, tell Hennah she is allowed to date. The condition is he must be trustworthy, someone I would approve, and he must be associated somehow with Essence. Due to security risks, she cannot date outsiders."

"She will resent the limitations."

The Five closed the file on the table. "I know. But at least she will not have to wait until her work is completed to marry."

After Joseph left the office, the Shadow Guard sat down on a couch across from the Five. "Are you certain he is the one?"

The elder quintessence nodded. "Yes, I must not rush him too soon. He deserves some time to enjoy his freedom."

"Is it because of her you choose him?"

Alexander pointed to his own nametag. "I picked this body because Alec's name was similar to my original name. What does it matter if Joseph happens to work with her?"

Miles leaned forward, eyes intense. "She will never be Layla."

"I know."

"Are you certain?"

The Five looked away, studying a photo of his long dead wife. "I have accepted her death a long time ago."

"Your brothers do not agree. They believe you still mourn her after all these centuries."

Alexander fixed his stark gaze on his Shadow Guard. "After you have loved deeply and watched you wife die of old age while you stand helplessly nearby, then you may advise me about moving on."

"I apologize. I cannot understand what you are going though. Still, you must not forget Hennah is not Layla."

"I know that better than anyone."

Chapter Nine

Hennah walked into the Grand Forum beside Joseph. Now that he was finally getting a salary, he had suggested they eat at the food court. As they passed a museum, Hennah glanced away, refusing to look at the huge portrait of Layla on the wall. They stood in line for Asian food then found a table near a potted tree and flowers, away from other people.

As Hennah used chopsticks to eat sushi, she finally glanced at the portrait still visible across the huge chamber. "How long before more start recognizing me like your brother?"

"He spoke out of line."

"Still, he knew I looked like her."

"Many quintessences recognize you as a clone but keep silent. You will have no problems from them. Most other sentients will not notice even when you stand by a picture of Layla. They are too busy with their own lives to notice a ghost walking among them."

"A ghost? Nice wording." She munched on a roll. "As I get older, someone is sure to notice."

"Your own parents have not, and they see you more than anyone else."

"My mom has commented that I look like Yashana more than once."

"She believes it is because you are related, not that you are a copy." They ate in silence for a few minutes before Joseph said, "Alec asked me to pass on a message that you may date but with restrictions. The person must be associated with Essence, someone trustworthy that Alec would approve."

Hennah kept her voice monotone. "It's another leash he is binding me with." She dapped wasabi on her sushi.

"You are not required to date."

"What does it matter? I will never be free anyway."

"I do not believe that."

"I do."

Again they ate in silence until a beep came over both their e-bands. They read the urgent message then looked at each other, puzzled.

Hennah frowned. "Why is Janet calling us for a staff meeting? She knows no one is supposed to be aware of me." Janet Cashman had taken Chandresh's place as head of the Research Department. Like her predecessor, she was related to several founders of Essence Institute.

"She would not do so unless she believes it is vital."

They finished their meal and walked down long hallways to the meeting room. Top staff glanced curiously at the couple as they walked in and took seats in the back of the room. They were used to seeing Hennah visit Chandresh but never attend a meeting.

Janet stood at the front of the room, barely containing her excitement. She was usually a stern, commanding leader, but today she looked like a giddy school girl. "Something has happened that is unprecedented. As its impact is far reaching, I invited you all. I would like to introduce you to Dyjuna and her husband Todd."

Through the door stepped the couple. Todd was a strong, strapping C2 model in his seventies, but it was Dyjuna who everyone's eyes were drawn to. Beautiful fell short as a description for her exotic, full-figure body. Her skin was pale green and her long wavy hair a bluish lavender. She had no need for make-up as her lips were naturally violet, her slanted eyes highlighted in teal. Her abdomen was slightly swollen, hinting of a coming child.

Todd did not speak, but Dyjuna smiled warmly. "Hello. I send greetings from Z 5907, as my homeworld is called to you. My people call it Yunikinniah." Her musical voice carried an accent, hinting that Standard was not her first language.

Janet grinned boldly. "Anyone here recognize which planet that is?"

The researchers glanced at each other, but none spoke. Finally Hennah said, "Is that the planet where the epulo infestus comes from?" She had only recognized the name because she had recently been editing some of its DNA and read its backstory. Three researchers had died on the primitive jungle planet when it had been first visited hundreds of years ago. It had been avoided since then, as far as she knew.

"Yes. Dyjuna is from the same planet. Ten years ago, a team of researchers visited the planet to collect samples. For safety, they brought a squad of quintessences. Turns out that there are several sentient races which live on Z 5907. And one in particular who is curious about us."

Dyjuna squeezed her husband's hand. "He was brave, attacking a knokpawn with just a knife. I could not keep hiding in the bushes watching. So I came out and sung a peace song. The knockpawn left, and we have been friends ever since."

"My wife is very friendly and curious." Todd kept a stoic face as he talked, but continued to hold Dyjuna's hand. "The researchers were shocked and excited to meet her, as it had been presumed no sentients lived on the planet. Dyjuna explored our camp, and quickly began learning our language by singing new words."

"My people sing a lot." Her voice rose and fell in musical tones as she spoke.

"The researchers nicknamed Dyjuna's race *sirens* after a mythical creature from their homeworld. The sentients on Yunikinniah never developed written languages or advance technology. Sirens live throughout the tropical areas of the planet and are amphibious. That is they can breathe both in water and air, preferring to give birth in water. Each clan has sacred pools hidden in the jungles where their elders live."

"No outsiders may visit our sacred pools."

"There are three other sentient races on the planet beside sirens."

"Four."

Todd glanced at her. "Three. The other one is a myth."

"You talked to too many tineeths. The unspeakable ones are real."

Todd turned back to the scientists. "There are three species you can visit. They are friendly as long as you have a siren they trust with you. Hostile if they do not know you. One is an insect species which lives in giant hives. The other two races, tineeth and bitrool, most likely shared a common ancestor thousands of years ago but split, the tineeth settling in villages in the jungles while the bitrools prefer building homes on the side of mountains. The sirens marry into their tribes but only give birth to new sirens. There are no hybrids."

Janet stepped forward. "This is where it gets interesting. Real interesting."

Todd glanced towards his wife's slightly swollen belly. "Dyjuna carries my child. My biological offspring."

Dyjuna rubbed her stomach. "She is a girl. All siren children are."

"Impossible!" said half the staff in unison. The room filled with many conversations going on at once.

Hennah leaned forward, heart pounding. After all the research and experiments she had been doing for years, a quintessence was about to be a father without need of her work. She looked towards Joseph. He met her eyes firmly, puzzlement on his face.

Janet quieted her staff. "Dyjuna is indeed pregnant with Todd's child."

"I don't mean to be rude," cut in a neodite, "but the child's father may be someone else's."

"The child is mine." Todd spoke with steel authority that do one else dared challenge.

Janet spoke into the sudden silence. "There are no male sirens, at least not any more. Dyjuna has been away from her homeworld for two years, since her last visit. Her species has the rare ability to breed with others but only produce its own." She looked directly at Hennah. "This will not make new quintessences nor hybrids, but we can learn much from understanding how this genetic process works."

Hennah swallowed. For a brief moment she had hoped she was no longer needed. That the universe had created a genetic equal for the quintessences. She wanted to be free from this burden so much, but she could feel the iron bars growing tighter around her. Joseph looked at her, questioning. She shook her head, silently telling him this would probably not help her research.

The staff questioned the couple, wanting to know more. Dyjuna spoke freely, enjoying the attention, singing the history of the lost males in her native tongue. Her voice was hypnotical, and the listeners felt the deep sadness of the song as it finished, even when they did not understand the words.

Dyjuna translated as best as she could, speaking in singsong. "Long, long ago there were both male and female sirens. We were happy together. But then some females turned their eyes towards the handsome hunters of the tineeths. We were forbidden to mate outside our kind, but some did so anyway. Always they gave birth to females. Overtime in some clans it became fashionable to take tineeth and bitrool mates. Less and less males were being born, but it went unnoticed for many generations. We sirens often live scattered, only visiting our sacred pools from time to time. Finally, some elders in one clan became concerned and talked with elders from other clans. They tried to prevent the mating with outsiders, but it was too late. There were no longer enough males for the females so they had to continue to find lifemates with the bitrools and tineeths. Eventually there were no more siren males. We grieve for our lost males but cannot bring them back. So we sing their story to remember from generation to generation."

There was silence for a long moment. A few researchers wiped tears away. As Dyjuna had spoken, her profound emotions were conveyed to her listeners. Todd and Joseph were the only ones not affected.

Janet broke the silence. "The researchers on Z 5907 discovered that one of the sirens' defenses is telepathy. Through singing, they can cause some subjects to feel the emotions of the singer."

"Quintessences are immune," said Todd.

"They still make good lifemates," smiled Dyjuna. "That is why when we went back to Yunikinniah, we took more of Todd's brothers. I found lifemates for all of them." The siren smiled proudly. "My clan sisters travel the stars now, like me."

The meeting ended with Janet promising to send DNA of both parents to the researchers to study. Todd and Dyjuna refused prenatal testing of the fetus, but promised once their offspring was born they would allow a sample of her DNA to be taken.

Back in the lab Henna began analysis the siren's DNA. Janet also gave her access to the notes of other researchers doing the same thing. A week later, Joseph asked her how it was going.

Hennah pointed to the screen of her electrical molecular microscope. "We still don't understand the process of how the egg only needs a small percentage of the sperm's DNA. Being able to compare the parents' DNA to the offspring will be helpful. Several researchers came up with theories based on how other *referent disjunctus* reproduce, but they are all lower life forms."

"So this has happened before?" Joseph looked at the screen of the EMM, not understanding what the tissue blobs and statistics meant.

"Yes, but we are talking about worms mating with polyps which produce more worms or flowers breeding with an unrelated vine which produces the original flower. It's rare but has been documented on some planets. Never in a sentient before or any high level animal."

"Can this help with finding a method to create female quintessences?"

Hennah sighed. "No. It's fascinating, but pointless. I'm sure there will be several geneticists who will make a career out of publishing papers about siren reproduction, but it will not help me. Quintessences reproduce, or should be able to, like normal humanoids."

"Perhaps you should be looking beyond the normal."

Anger flashed in Hennah's eyes. "Should quintessences reproduce by parthenogenesis, gemmules, budding, or sporulation?" Joseph looked at her blankly. "You don't even know what I am talking about. Of course, I have considered other methods. Every single one known to botanists and zoologists. You already reproduce asexual through cloning. Alec wants a sexual method where DNA of a male and female mix together to produce a unique offspring. Todd fathering a child proves quintessences can reproduce normally. You just need a female with compatible traits."

"Which you are designing." Joseph kept his voice calm, knowing Hennah needed to rant, letting off her frustrations.

"Do you know how complicated it is to design the DNA for ovaries, uterus, and fallopian tubes? Let alone feminine bodies which look curvier, has larger breasts, and different face shapes? And the hormones I have to deal with! Don't get me started on that. And the final results is supposed to look human but behave like a quintessence."

"You have made progress."

"No! Nothing I have created in five years is useful. Nothing."

"I have seen some of your creations on the computers which look promising."

"You and Alec still don't get it. When I try to design a female, I keep making something brand new that is not genetically equal to a quintessence. Which is pointless because if they became real, then they would demand a genetically equal male version of their kind, which would just recreate the same problems I already have. Pointless. Everything is pointless."

"You will find the right combination someday."

Henna put her forehead in her hands, letting her long, loose hair hide her face. "You will never understand. If I replaced the X chromosome in the quintessence genome with any version I create, it will always become a different species. Always. Because I can't take that same X chromosome, add a Y chromosome from a quintessence and get a normal male quintessence. The X chromosome of quintessences actually contain some of your male traits. When I replace those traits with my versions of female traits, I get flawed mutations. Female traits should have been designed within the genome before the first quintessence was created. Because Layla did not do so, she sabotaged all future attempts to create your dream woman. She should have at least written the female traits into one of the autosomes and allowed them to be turned on with a gene in the X chromosome. But no, she did not even bother doing that. "

Joseph stood beside her, wishing to comfort her, but knowing no words. Finally, he said, "I am sorry you are dealing with this dilemma."

"Well, I should get back to my Sisyphean task, my penance for existing."

Hennah worked the rest of the day in silence, her dark outlook worrying Joseph. He had hoped that the siren would be the key to unlocking the iron door she was trapped behind. Instead, Hennah had become even more despondent.

Towards the end of the day, Chandresh stopped by. He looked extremely thin, skin splotchy.

"Dada, you should be home resting."

"Ah, my poti, I had to come meet Dyjuna after Janet told me about her. Sirens are quite remarkable. Do you know some of them live to be over three hundred? Their elders are revered in their society."

"So are you."

"But I won't even reach one hundred."

"Don't say that."

"I have accepted the fact. Will you come with me after work today? I am visiting the Quintessence Retirement Home."

"Sure, Dada. Let me clean up."

Henna put away supplies and turned off machines. She then dove Chandresh across the campus in her small yellow hover car she had bought last year. It had a polycarbonate dome which could be retracted, allowing riders to enjoy the open air.

She parked near a huge oval building that was twelve stories tall. Its walls were made of glass which reflected the cultivated gardens surrounding it. Hennah had never been inside before but knew Chandresh had made weekly visits for years. She followed her grandfather in where he greeted nurses by name. They passed rooms, each containing ten beds. Some quintessences were sleeping but most wandered about visiting with each other. He led her to a large game room where elderly quintessences played board games or watched programs on huge vids. All of the patients were nearly two hundred or older, their bodies feeble, their minds slowed. Still many joked as they tried to outwit opponents in games, thriving on competition even when death was imminent.

Chandresh sat down at a table where three quintessences played cards. "Got room for me and my granddaughter?"

"Of course, Chandresh," said a ME1 as he passed out cards to the newcomers. As he handed Hennah her cards, he studied her face intently. Then he turned towards Chandresh. "Your granddaughter you say?"

"Yep. I got two of them and one grandson."

A HC3 staring at Hennah said, "Are you a geneticist?"

"Yes."

The three quintessences shared glances then dropped the subject. They played four games. Chandresh won once and the quintessences three times.

After the final hand, Chandresh asked, "Where is Ricky?"

The three glanced at each other, and then the C7 said, "Top floor."

"Ah. Well, Hennah, we should go say hi before we leave. Good playing with you boys."

"Boys? When you think you can beat real men, come back again."

Hennah followed Chandresh to an elevator which took them to the top floor. Chandresh walked over to a nurse and asked which room Ricky was in. As they slowly moved down a hallway, Hennah stared into the rooms, feeling nervous. On most beds lay debilitated quintessences, most asleep.

"Are they dying?" whispered Hennah, wishing her grandfather had not brought her here. She had grown up her whole life around robust quintessences who rarely became sick. To see them like this was disturbing.

"Yes, Poti."

"Do all quintessences eventually come here to die?" She spoke hesitantly, unsure how to word her question.

"No. Those with families on other worlds prefer to stay with them. Most of the ones here either have no families other than birthmates or they had chosen to work at Essence and their families live near here."

They entered a room with ten beds, only five occupied. Chandresh greeted the three quintessence who were awake then introduced Hennah to an IN4 whose long hair was solid white. Beeping equipment monitored Ricky as he weakly turned his head towards his visitors.

"Glad to see you one last time." Ricky spoke slowly, his words slightly slurred. "Looks like I will be winning this one."

"Coming in second is not so bad, in this case," said Chandresh. Seeing Hennah's questioning look, he explained. "Several of us have been competing to see who makes it to the afterlife first."

"I win," mumbled Ricky.

Hennah opened her mouth but could not speak, such a contest horrifying her.

Ricky stared at her for a long moment, eyes partly unfocused. "You look familiar."

"I get that sometimes."

"Layla. Are you here to take me now? You are the most beautiful death angel I have seen."

Not knowing what to say, Hennah glanced at her grandfather.

Chandresh leaned closer to Ricky. "You have not won yet. This is my granddaughter Hennah."

"She looks just like…"

"I know. Remember, Yashana is my ancestor."

"Ah, yes. The blood of the creator in you. Still does not give you special privileges to go first when we play cards."

"Can't blame an old man for trying."

Ricky's eyes half-closed. "Would have been nice seeing her."

"You will soon, my friend. Very soon."

Seeing that Ricky was asleep, Chandresh and Hennah began to leave. The beeping equipment at another bed flashed a red warning light. The quintessence on the bed lay completely still. A nurse entered and studied the monitor. She entered information into a data pad then she began turning the machines off.

"He's dead? Just like that?" Hennah trembled, staring at the nurse. "Shouldn't you be doing something to bring him back?"

The nurse, a sundancer with ritual tattoos on her face and arms, looked with kind eyes at the teenager. "Bring him back to what? His body has played out and his organs have shut down. It is his time. His death was painless. We make sure of that."

Hennah swallowed and followed Chandresh down the hallway. She held it together until they were in the elevator. Then she began weeping. She had not known the quintessence, but the reality of someone dying just a few feet away shook her to her core.

Chandresh wrapped his frail arms around her. "It is alright, Poti."

"No, it's not. It will be you soon."

Chandresh tenderly touched his granddaughter's wet cheeks. "I am ready. I am at peace with my maker. I will be going to paradise."

"But I don't want you to go."

"There are somethings no one can prevent. We must accept and be thankful for the time we do have." The elevator opened to the first floor. "Now I'm ready for a hearty, home-cooked dinner."

Hennah wiped her tears away, knowing her crying saddened her grandfather. She forced a smile. "Mamma is a great cook."

Chapter Ten

Unopened boxes cluttered the apartment, some containing new furniture which needed to be put together. Kylen looked over the mess. It was his first apartment. Now eighteen, he was finally on his own. He began prioritizing the boxes, moving the ones he would not immediately need against a wall. He opened one that contained kitchen utensils, a gift from his foster family. They had been reluctant for him to leave, showering him with advice and presents they believed would be helpful.

Now they were several sectors away. Kylen had been asked to list three planets which interest him to live on, but he only put one down—Xi'an. Like the other profectus from Generation Three, he was drawn to his own clones. Having no real family, he needed a history and roots. Long ago he had memorized every known fact about Richard and Ethan, but it was not enough. He wanted to walk where they had, see buildings with his own eyes that they had looked upon. The desire to connect with them was powerful.

Hearing a chime, Kylen opened the door and was surprised to see Amy, dressed in jeans and a tank top, standing there with a plate of brownies.

She smiled as she entered. "I saw you moving in. Thought you might like a snack. I live three doors down. Moved in two weeks ago."

"I didn't know you were assigned to Xi'an also."

Amy moved to a window and looked out at the distant massive wall surrounding Essence Institute. It rose high above the nearby homes and apartments. "You're not the only one with ties to it. Diane designed the entire campus."

"I'm sure there have been additions since then." Kylen sat the plate on a counter and took a bite of a brownie. "When did you learn to cook?"

"I picked up a lot of skills living with my foster family. Perhaps I will be a gourmet chef instead of a pop star or architect. You are lucky that your path is so easily laid out."

Kylen had not seen another profectus in a year and was grateful for a friend. Knowing that Amy harbored insecurities, he flattered her. "Perhaps you are the lucky one. I am expected to be a great programmer. But what is something new I can offer that has not already been done by others? Millions of programs have been written by others since my clones lived. You have a talent for being creative."

"You think that is easy? The Coalition does not place high value on singers like Ice Babe. They wish for me to be like Diana, building monuments to their greatness. Perhaps I will design a singing building."

"Amusing. Then I will create a program to control its lights, changing colors with your music."

Amy laughed. "That will get their attention, proclaiming us the greatest profectus that ever lived."

Kylen chewed on another brownie. "I am glad you are here. It is nice knowing a least one person."

Amy pulled out a scrunchie and pulled her brunette hair into a ponytail. "Let's get you unpacked."

She opened a box and began putting together a shelf while Kylen unpacked silverware. As they worked, they chatted.

"Did they get you a job yet?" Amy laid the last piece on the floor then began assembling them. "I'm working at a small architect firm which designs commercial buildings. The Coalition wanted me in a larger city working on a major project, but I talked them down, saying I needed a few years to develop my skills on small things. Got a hammer?"

Kylen searched through a box until he found one. "I start working Monday at an educational software company in Luncaster. I can do most of my work from here and take a monorail to the office when I need to."

"Why did you decide to live here in New Hope instead of Luncaster?"

"Why did you?"

"You know why. Because she designed it."

Both turned towards the window, looking again at the huge barrier which hid Essence Institute from the city.

Kylen put knives in a drawer. "One of mine designed the security and the other broke it."

Amy banged a shelf into its support grooves. "Your bookcase could had been designed better. It will not take a lot of weight."

"I bought cheaply. Trying to make the funds they gave us last as long as possible."

"Yeah, my money is almost gone too. Takes a lot to properly furnish an apartment. My bed alone took up a third of my money. Good thing I will be getting my first paycheck soon."

She hammered the last shelf into place then Kylen helped her stand up the bookcase. They pushed it against a wall.

Amy moved to another box and pulled out parts for a chair. "I plan to get into Essence."

"Why would you want to do that? We are supposed to be keeping a low profile." Kylen tossed an empty box beside the door.

"Maybe their database has been purged, and I won't be recognized. It's not like I'm trying to do anything illegal. Just walk around the campus for a few hours. See what she built with my own eyes. Looking at photos is not the same."

"Essence is the one place the Coalition does not want us. Their security is designed to handle clones. They will have all our profiles in their database." Kylen opened a new box and pulled out plates.

"It's been centuries. Most places don't keep data that long." She screwed the seat to its base.

"I would if I was running Essence. As my clone designed its security, I am sure that is exactly what they have done. There is no way you can walk through their front door without being noticed by a face scan."

"I thought about using prosthetic makeup to change my face shape. Fingerprints of clones are similar but never the same. Our retinas are unique to each individual. Unless they ran a DNA test, I should be fine. All I need is a legit way in for a few hours. That's all."

"You're reckless."

Amy paused in her work. "Actually I have spent years thinking about this."

"You know, there are other structures Diana designed that tourists are allowed to visit."

"I know. I visited several with my foster parents. But Essence is the one she won the Zelzer for." Amy sat the chair upright and gave it a whirl. "It's just that...well...I need to be there. See the buildings from different angles. How the sunlight reflects off them. Study the landscape. Touch the walls with my own hands. I know it sounds silly, but it's worth the risk to me."

Kylen finished stacking the few cups he had brought. "It's not silly. Why do you think I came here?"

Amy studied him. "You feel the pull of our clones too?"

"We were given nothing else to cling too while growing up. No religion, no traditions, no family. Nothing. Just a legacy. It is the only thing which defines us." Kylen allowed anger to seep into his voice. Normally he would never show his true emotions, but it was only Amy he talked to. No hidden cameras monitored his apartment—that was first thing he had checked when moving in. For once, he could be honest.

Living with a foster family for a year had been too pleasant, forcing him to acknowledge all that he and the other profectus had missed out on while growing up. Instead of parents, they had caregivers who never connected emotionally with them. The profectus had been constantly monitored, their every action recorded and analyzed. The Coalition told them which jobs to take and where to live. Eventually who they would marry. If they rebelled and their misbehavior became too extreme, they would disappear. As they had no family, who would miss them?

Amy studied the dark look on Kylen's face. "So, great hacker of the galaxy, will you help me get in?"

"When the Coalition asked where we wished to be appointed, I refused to give them any other option but here. I came for only one purpose—to break in."

Amy smiled. "Excellent."

Chapter Eleven

Bright afternoon sunshine lit the practice field where participants fired off various guns at targets, some moving on tracks.

"Remember to line up your sight," said Darkfern.

"I still don't know how you talked me into this?" mumbled Hennah with one eye closed as she attempted to focus on the raised metal of the sight on the handgun's barrel.

"Because you got bored watching me. And it is a disgrace that you have grown up on a military base and never even touched a weapon."

"This will probably be the one and only day I do so." Hennah fired several shots that completely missed the paper enemy a hundred feet away. "This is harder than it looks in the movies."

"Make sure to look at your target, not just the sight."

"The sunlight is too bright."

"We could go back inside and practice laser shooting."

"You beat me twice already in that." Hennah fired off the final rounds, wincing at each loud bang. "I don't think I hit it once."

"You nipped it a time or two. Ready for a bigger gun now?"

"No, thank you." Hennah flipped on the safety and handed the weapon to her friend. "It's a good thing I'm not taking the test to be a security officer tomorrow."

"I am ready."

Darkfern reloaded the handgun and took careful aim. She fired off ten shots, each hitting critical spots on three targets which represented popular sentient body shapes. Then the teenagers walked across the huge field, passing other shooters. They paused to watch a neodite shooting a long-range sniper rifle that hit his target every time.

"There are only so many spots open." Darkfern studied the shooter. "The competition will be tough."

"Don't worry. You're going to get the job. You began training from the day of your birth."

"I will not be hired because of who my parents are. I have to prove myself worthy."

"You are one of the best knifers I know."

"Takes a lot more than that to qualify, including the hundred yard pursuit run, the two mile dash, procedure quiz, and weaponry knowledge."

"At least math is not on the test."

Darkfern chuckled. "Would that not be something, chasing a bad guy, catching him, then quizzing him on the polyhedron formula?"

"So if he gets the question right, do you let him go?"

"How would I know if he said the right answer?"

They entered the large Shooting Center where Darkfern checked the handgun in to a quintessence standing in the doorway of a storage room. As they walked down the main hallway, signs gave directions to the sections for laser, virtual reality, archery, and live ammunition. Darkfern paused in front of the hallway leading to the virtual reality simulators, yearning for another go. She had spent half her morning in one before Hennah showed up for a visit.

Knowing Hennah was ready for lunch, Darkfern followed her friend out of the building. "We make an interesting pair. I have been an adult for two years but only recently finished my schooling. You will be an adult in a few weeks but have had a job for nearly six years."

"I think our laws are lacking in defining what qualifies someone as an adult."

"It will be my job to know those laws because they affect how we process criminals based on if they are a minor or adult."

As they ate lunch in the Grand Forum, Darkfern chatted excitedly about her next pailuk, though it was still several months away. "We are going back to Shah Luna. I enjoy being with my relatives on Bayoom for Kilpailu, but nothing beats pailuk at New Werjouk, the capital of Shah Luna."

"I still don't understand how you find it fun being chased by armed guys in an underground forest. This will be your fifth pailuk. You are becoming a greater target."

"On Bayoom I am a big target every pailuk as there are only a couple dozen unmarried adults. There the focus of Kilpailu is more on uniting our people by celebrating our culture. There are some pugna battles but also duels of friends showing off their skills and other athletic contests. Plus tons of food. At New Werjouk there are thousands of fjouwers along with some other brave outsiders who join the pailuk. I am just one among many. Three days of surviving by your skills and wit. It is magnificent."

Hennah shook her head. "You're crazy."

Darkfern grinned. "Then all my people are. Really, it's fun. I wish you could come."

"I have too much work. They can't spare me. Perhaps they think quintessence society would collapse if I took a vacation." Hennah kept her focus on her pizza, trying to pretend she did not mind, hiding that she felt jealous of Darkfern's adventures.

Several weeks later when her birthday came there was no celebration. Instead, the family took turns sitting by Chandresh's hospital bed as his breathing became shallower, his heartbeat fainter. For four days he fought for breath, for life. On the fifth, he lost.

The family was ushered into the hallway as doctors and nurses worked to bring him back but could not. Aashi sat beside her fiancé, tensely holding his hand. Dhruvi stared at the closed door, his eyes wide and face pale. Kaushal held his wife tightly, tears flowing freely. Hennah sat by her parents, trying not to cry. She had shed too many tears already in fear of this day.

A doctor came out and informed them that Chandresh had died. Aashi burst into tears, and her fiancé wrapped his strong arms around her. Pallavi began comforting her family while Kaushal dealt with paperwork. Both Hennah and Dhruvi fought hard to keep sober faces. A priest who had known Chandresh soon arrived. At Kaushal's request, he had administered Last Rites two days ago. He led the family away to a quiet room where they could grieve.

Later the family returned home. Friends came, bringing food and chatting about old times. Hennah hid in her room, avoiding people as much as possible. The next day Kaushal and other men attended a cremation ceremony for Chandresh's body. On the fourth day, friends and family gathered at the beach beside Essence as Kaushal sat in a small boat which was paddled by friends away from shore. Then he spread his father's ashes into the salt water.

Hennah cried then as she ached for her mentor. Her grandfather. Her creator. No one else in her family understood her struggles, shared her secrets. Loneliness filled her, despite Darkfern standing beside her. She could not even tell her best friend about the heavy burden of her job, of why she had been made.

Chandresh had been well-liked and several hundred gathered along the beach for the funeral, including all of the Five. After the ceremony was finished, Alec came up to Hennah, offering his condolences. For a moment she felt angry at him, as she often did when she thought about him, but then she looked into his wrinkled face and sad eyes. She thought of Ricky the quintessence who had died in the Retirement Home. Alec would not live many more years himself.

"Thank you for coming," she said as a peace offering.

"Take as much time as you need to grieve."

"It is traditional to mourn for thirteen days."

"Then take the time off, with pay."

Hennah moved through the crowd, wishing to be home. Joseph appeared and walked beside her. Darkfern, dressed in her new security uniform, followed on her

90

other side. Nether friend spoke. Just being present was enough. When Hennah reached her barracks, Joseph left, but Darkfern hesitated.

"Do you wish me to hang out with you?"

"You're on duty right now. I'm fine."

"Are you sure."

"Yes, I'm fine."

"If you need me, call."

There was a busy flow of friends and relatives visiting the apartment, many bringing food. Hennah supported her parents by cleaning up after meals and leading groups of kids in games. Aashi stayed a few days then headed back to college where she was finishing up her Master's. Dhruvi, now fifteen, preferred hanging out with his friends than staying home.

By the third day, Hennah headed back to work, needing the solitude of her lab. Joseph was surprised to see her.

"I thought you were taking two weeks off."

"Too many people at home right now. Besides, I need something to keep my mind off of…." Hennah could not finish.

"I have missed you while you were gone. No one has been banging on equipment," Joseph jested.

"It's been a while since I took my frustrations out on machines." There had only been a few incidents when she was younger when she had smacked the NDB or tossed her e-tablet.

Hennah threw herself into her work, trying to honor Chandresh's faith in her. But as weeks turned into months with no progress, Hennah's grief turned into depression which clung to her, draining her emotions. Knowing her own family still grieved for Chandresh, she buried her own troubles, pretending all was normal. Guilt that she was letting down Chandresh, the Five, and Joseph smothered her. No matter how hard she tried, she could find no solution.

She began spending less time hanging out with Darkfern on the weekends. The fjouwer had begun to befriend co-workers who enjoyed extreme sports. When Hennah did eat with Darkfern, the conversation often turned to sailing, parachuting, mountain climbing, and fencing. Hennah pretended to be interested, but felt herself drifting away from her best friend.

Darkfern did notice and tried to get Hennah to talk about her job, but Hennah could only give vague responses. She wished she could be open with someone who understood genetics, but as the project was classified, she was limited to only talking with Joseph and Janet who occasionally stopped by to see how things were going. The chief was supportive but could provide no insight into the project.

Hennah sat down across from Joseph in the food court. She nibbled on a salad, barely eating, as she had little appetite lately.

Darkfern settled into a seat beside her friend. "I came in early today just so I could eat lunch with you."

"Thanks. I appreciate that."

"I'm leaving in two days for Shah Luna. Sure you won't come?"

Hennah glanced at Joseph. "No, I can't."

"I'll bring you another moon rock as a souvenir. Or perhaps one of the glowing mushrooms."

"The last one you brought me died."

"It was getting too much sunlight. They grow best in near darkness."

A dozen of Joseph's birthmates spotted him and came over with their trays of food. Hennah preferred quiet meals and felt irritated at the sudden increase of people. Darkfern was soon planning a mountain climbing trip with the quintessences when she got back from Shah Luna.

Hennah ate in silence. Suddenly something she overheard caught her attention. She turned to Ryder. "Where did you say you were going?"

"Rowan. It's a good job offer. A mostly human Core planet where we aid the police force. Exciting, and best of all, it's a long ways from a warfront."

Hennah glanced at Joseph. "You did not mention you were leaving."

"I was waiting till the right time." His face was blank, his emotions hidden.

"Oh." She felt a tightness in her stomach. "Tired of sitting at a desk?"

"That is not why I am leaving. I will be with my birthmates."

"Family is important." She tossed down her fork onto her half eaten salad. "Time to get back to work." She averted her eyes from Joseph and Darkfern who looked at her in concern.

She hurried to the lab and tried burying herself in her work. He was leaving her. *Why am I upset?* It was expected for quintessences to take jobs after their sabbatical was over. Still, she had presumed he would keep working here. But if his brothers wanted to leave, why would he stay doing a boring desk job when he could have an adventurous career?

When Joseph entered the lab, Hennah ignored him as she peered into a microscope. He walked over and stood beside her, waiting for her to finish her work and acknowledge him.

After several minutes of her silence, he finally said, "You are upset."

"I'm just busy."

"I was trying to find the right time to tell you."

"There is no right time."

"I will begin training a new co-worker in a few weeks."

92

Hennah typed data into her e-tablet. "I'm sure the training will be very intense. First lesson: How to stare at Hennah while she destroys another embryo. It's a very impressive job."

"Hennah, I…"

"I have work to do," the teenager glared at him.

"I will get out of your way then." Joseph climbed the steps to the office, pausing on the balcony to watch her work, a concerned frown on his lips. He had been her co-worker for six years, the one who heard all her complaints. Would she trust his replacement? Despite telling himself she would be fine, he felt he was abandoning her.

Hennah rarely spoke with Joseph the rest of the week. She began eating lunch again in the lab, avoiding others. By Friday, she was irritated and restless, frustrated that yet another prototype had failed, despite she had predicted it would. She stood in front of a microscope, looking at dead, mutilated cells.

My life's work. The legacy I pass on. I will live and die, with almost no one knowing I existed. No fancy awards for this profectus. She can't even complete one successful experiment in six years. What's the point? Why do I keep torturing myself with this?

Darkfern was off on another adventure. Joseph soon to sail away with his brothers. Aashi had her own life and upcoming marriage. She rarely saw Dhruvi except at meals. Her parents were getting older. *Everyone leaves me, sooner or later. I am alone.*

Alec her slave master. When he died another of the Five would replace him as her supervisor. Would it be Desmond? How ironic if her best friend's father was her master. A former slave owning a slave. *I can't even tell Darkfern what her saintly father has been doing all these years as a Five. I'm tired. So tired of this. I want a way out. But there is none.*

Rage kindled in Hennah at her helplessness, at the uselessness of her experiments, of her life. She picked up a beaker and threw it against a wall, coldly watching it smash into fragments like her life. Angrily, she grabbed a stack of petri dishes and began throwing them around the room, hearing equipment break. She wanted to destroy everything, including herself.

Joseph stepped onto the balcony. "Hennah, stop."

The teenager glared up at him. Without a word she reached over to the broken bleaker and picked up the largest shard of glass. She thought of Darkfern's curved karambit, how quickly it could slice through skin. With a quick jab, she cut into her wrist, wincing at the excruciating pain of the jagged cut. Blood flowed down her arm. Trying to ignore the pain, she made another cut, this one deeper, hitting an artery.

"Hennah!" Joseph leaped off the balcony, not bothering with the stairs. He ran to her and snatched the glass out of her hand. She continued to stare at the gushing blood as she wobbled. He caught her and held her wrist tightly.

"What were you thinking?"

"I want out," she mumbled, feeling lightheaded.

"I'm not about to lose someone else under my watch. You hear me, Hennah? You are going to live."

Joseph grabbed a cleaning cloth and tied it the best he could around her arm. Then he wrapped more cloth around her arm. Still keeping a tight grip on her wrist, he spoke a command into his e-band. "Call medical. I need an emergency team to meet me in front of the Research Department immediately."

He picked her up and hurried out of the room and down the hallway. At several security doors he had to pause, using his thumb print to unlock them. Somehow he managed to keep his tight grip on her wrist. Hennah was only vaguely conscious. She felt guilty for the trouble she was putting him through. When Joseph reached the final door, several medical staff stood with equipment in hand. He laid Hennah on the floor.

"Her wrist is cut. She is bleeding out."

The bloody clothes were removed from Hennah's arm by an aid as another grabbed a skin clue gun. Hennah stared at the hot, red liquid flowing down her arm as unconsciousness claimed her.

Chapter Twelve

Hennah woke up in the hospital ward. Her left arm was bandaged. On each side of her bed sat her parents, their worried faces showing relief when she opened her eyes. Joseph stood against a far wall, watching her face carefully.

Pallavi held her daughter's uninjured hand, tears streaming down her face. "Hennah, my dear beti."

Guilt tore at Hennah. "I'm sorry, Mamma. So sorry."

Kaushal leaned forward, his voice tense. "Why would you do this?"

"I…uh…don't know." She looked at Joseph. "I promise I won't do it again."

Pallavi brushed hair away from her daughter's face. "I know you took your grandfather's death hard, but this is not the way to deal with it. He would want you to be happy, not depressed like you have been."

"I'm really, really sorry. I wasn't thinking. I was being stupid."

Hennah's parents did not leave her side all night. The grief on their faces felt like salt on an open wound to her. She had acted on sudden rage, forgetting how her death would affect her family who had just lost Chandresh. Joseph left around midnight but was back the next morning.

As he watched her eat breakfast, he said to her parents, "You both need some sleep. I will stay with her."

Reluctantly they left, heading to their apartment for food and sleep. Hennah nibbled at eggs and toast, not liking his constant staring.

"I'm okay, really." She held up her bandaged arm. "I'm all patched up, ready to work again, boss."

"You cannot leave. You have been placed on suicide watch until further notice."

"How long do I have to lay here?"

"Until it is decided you are mentally stable."

"I'm not crazy. Not now. I just went a bit bonkers for only a moment. I'm fine now."

Joseph continued to watch her silently.

Mid-afternoon her parents came back with her brother. Joseph left for some rest. Dhruvi had brought several board games and her e-tablet with him. A table was pulled over to Hennah's bed and the family played games to pass the time. Dhruvi was soon joking, causing others to relax and sometimes laugh. Hennah tried to appear normal, like she was in the ward due to a natural injury. No one mentioned the incident.

For three days Hennah's family and Joseph took turns watching her, never leaving her alone for a moment. By the third day, Hennah was restless, ready to leave. Late that afternoon, Alec stopped by for a visit. Hennah's family had already left.

"How are you feeling?"

"Fine. I'm ready to go back to work. Can you get them to let me out?"

Alec looked at Joseph. "If your guardian believes you are ready."

Joseph firmly meet his supervisor's eyes. "She is not ready."

"Yes, I am. I'm tired of being in here. The project is everything. I need to be working on it again instead of wasting time here."

"You are not ready."

"Yes, I am."

Alec cut in. "As you seem eager to continue, it may be time to let you out."

"Sir," said Joseph, "May I talk with you in private."

"Alright." Alec left his Shadow Guard to watch Hennah as he and Joseph walked down the hallway, looking for an empty room. Finding one, they locked the door behind them.

Joseph stood several feet from the Five, his eyes challenging. "She needs a long break from the project."

"Why did she try to commit suicide?" asked Alec.

"Because of you. She has been pushed too far for too long and tried to push back in the only way she knew how. She will try this again, maybe not now but perhaps in a few months or years. This time she reacted in rage, but next time she will be thoughtful, careful. And she will succeed."

"I will assign her a psychologist."

"She already talks with me about her problems. She feels trapped and wants a way out. If you want to save her, take her off this project."

"I can't do that."

"Sir, she cannot handle the pressure."

Feeling weary, Alec sat down in a chair. "I know you care about her. But I must look beyond just her. As a Five, my duty is to the whole. While you daily watch her in a quiet lab, I watch our society slowly unravel. There have been many more accounts of quintessences being put into situations where they must fight their brethren. As you know, doing so takes a heavy toll on us. Some quintessences refuse to fight and their commanders send them back to us for discipline, putting us in a difficult situation. No longer do the edietheans hide that they are behind this. They use each failure as a rally call to decrease our funding. A bill to cut our budget by twenty-five percent is soon to be voted on. "

"Will it pass?"

"We have allies fighting against it. They have stopped a few before, but our failures are growing greater. While the empire fights among itself for power, entire quadrants on the Rim have seceded. Our brothers are being sent to deal with that while senators war with each other over feuds that date back millenniums. Our numbers have already dropped because of budget cuts, and these new wars are intense, making our average death count spike much higher than normal. Every day we become weaker as a society. One drastically wrong move on the part of our soldiers could become political fodder to be used by our enemies to have our funding completely cut. Every day we are one battle away from extinction. That is the realty I deal with. We all must do our part to prevent that, including Hennah."

"She is just one girl."

"Who holds our fate in her hands. She can unlock our freedom."

"Yet you have locked her in a cage."

"I provide well for her. She has been given far more advantages than many. Layla and Yashana both loved working on genetic projects."

"They believed in their work. Hennah sees the task you have given her as impossible."

"She just needs to work harder. The solution will come."

"I have watched her labor for six years, sir." Joseph raised his voice. "Pushing her more is not the answer. You will only break her permanently."

The two men glared at each other for a long moment, one feeble and worn from a long life of service, the other strong and fierce.

Finally, Alec said, "Find a way to fix her but keep her working."

"Working? That is what is destroying her. Let me give her a break. A real vacation."

After a long pause, Alec nodded. "Alright. I place her into your capable hands."

"Thank you, sir."

The two men walked back to Hennah's room. She looked at Alec, hopeful that she could leave, but he shook his head.

"You will be here longer. Joseph has been given the authority to say when you will leave. I do wish for your full recovery, Hennah." He and his Shadow Guard left.

The teenager glared silently at Joseph as he took a seat by her bed. For a while they just sat, doing nothing. Hennah pulled out her e-tablet and played on it for a while.

Bored, she finally said, "When do I get out of jail, warden?"

"When I think you are ready."

"What test do I need to take for that? I already said I'm ready to work. I'm embracing the purpose for my existence. What more do you want?"

"Your words are empty. You care little about Project Absurd. You only say what you think I want to hear."

"What do you want from me then?"

Joseph moved closer and studied her face. "What do adolescent humans do for fun?"

"Fun? For a teenager? Go to the mall. Watch a movie."

"Then we shall do that."

"Go out to a movie?"

"Yes. I have never been to a theater before."

"Your fifty-eight and never seen a movie?"

"Movies I have seen on vids, but I never experienced them in a theater. Or do you prefer to sit here and do nothing?"

"I'm ready to get out of here."

Hennah quickly packed the few belongings her parents had left for her into a backpack and followed Joseph outside to her hover car. Joseph sent a message to her parents that he was taking her out.

"I'm driving," said Joseph, moving to the driver's door.

"It's my car."

"You are still on suicide watch."

Hennah rolled her eyes at him but opened the door with her thumb print then walked around to the passenger side. Once seated, she placed her hand on a sensor and the car's engine turned on. Joseph drove while Hennah gave directions, complaining more than once that she should be driving.

They finally pulled up to a huge theater located beside the boardwalk which ran parallel to the beach. They bought tickets to an action movie and settled into seats which leaned far back. Above them on the huge ceiling the movie played out in 3D. During intense scenes, their chairs vibrated and explosions could be heard from speakers built into the chairs near their ears.

As they left the theater, Hennah felt relaxed, the tension she had endured for weeks had melted away. "So did you like your first movie?"

"Yes, it was worth the high price. Now where should we eat dinner?"

"Depends on if you prefer cheap or fine dining?"

"Expensive works for me. I need to spend some of this money I am earning."

They settled on a jungle themed restaurant that had artificial trees, vines, and animatronic animals. Hennah munched on fruit in a tropical salad while Joseph explored the rich flavors of a fish taco. The lights dimmed and fake lightening flashed across the room. Rain fell onto the plants and a gorilla popped out from behind a rock. A young boy at a nearby table ducked behind his mother then peeked out, staring at the animatronic. He became braver and walked closer to the gorilla. Slowly he reached out a finger to touch it. Suddenly the gorilla stood on its hind feet and beat its chest. The boy dashed back to his mom and hid against her leg while his parents chuckled. Watching the boy, Hennah smiled.

"That is your first real smile I have seen in many weeks," said Joseph.

Hennah looked down at a strawberry on her fork. "I have not had a lot to smile about."

"Then I need to change that. I told Alec that I am giving you a long vacation."

"To do what? I'm not allowed to do much in case my face triggers some security alarm somewhere."

"That is only an issue at spaceports or if you are breaking into a building, which I hope you are not planning to do. My brothers and I have been exploring a lot lately. There are some fascinating museums you may like."

"Um, there is an aquarium I like in Luncaster. Also a zoo I have not been to since I was a kid."

"Then that is where we will start."

"Oh, but you are supposed to be spending time with your brothers. I don't want to interfere with that."

"I can spend time with them in the mornings then pick you up in the afternoons."

"So I don't have to go back to the sick ward?"

He leaned close and looked her directly in the eyes. "If you promise me you will meet me every day, healthy and ready for adventure."

Hennah met his eyes, determined to prove she could be trusted. "Yes, I promise. I'm more than ready for adventure."

They left the restaurant and wandered about the boardwalk, visiting random stores. Joseph had never shopped for clothes so Hennah began teasing him, picking up gaudy outfits, claiming they would look great on him. He countered by suggesting outrageous hats for her. When she refused to try on a spiked hat shaped like a giant purple starfish, he placed it on his own head. Hennah burst into laughter which caused him to smile faintly.

As they headed back to the car, Hennah said, "Thanks for…well…everything."

Joseph stopped and looked at her soberly. "I wish you had talked to me instead of taking drastic measures."

"I have been talking to you for years. I feel like I have been shouting and no one was listening."

"I was always listening, Hennah. I warned Alec more than once he was pushing you too much. Often I have pondered how to help you, but I know little about genetics. I cannot ease your burden."

"You doing a nice job now."

"Good, because I am going to keep doing it. I'm not leaving with my brothers."

Guilt stabbed at Hennah. "No, you can't do that. They are your family. You were separated for eighteen years. I'm not worth that."

Joseph reached out and took her hand. "Yes, you are."

"No, my incident was just a brief act of mad selfishness. I was not trying to bind you to me. Or hurt my parents. I broke the Code, thinking of only myself. I'm sorry. I won't do it again. Don't stay because of me."

"Hennah, I have made my choice. Even before your incident, I wavered several times and almost stayed. I know now, for certain, that my place is supporting you."

"But…"

"No more trying to convince me otherwise. I can still have you locked in the medical ward, young lady, if you argue with me."

"Not fair abusing your powers." She gave a smile as a peace offering.

He drove her home and they parted ways, heading to different barracks. Kaushal and Pallavi greeted their daughter when she entered the apartment. Conversation was polite but strained. Hennah could see concern and fear in their eyes.

"I had a great time. Joseph and I went to a movie then ate dinner. Tomorrow we are going to Luncaster Aquarium."

Kaushal looked relieved. "It is good for you to have fun."

Pallavi said, "Yes, be a real teenager for a while. You grew up too quickly and missed out on so much." Her eyes became misty with tears.

"I'm fine now. Really. I'm sorry I worried you, but you don't have to be upset anymore. I'm never going to do anything crazy like that again."

Pallavi embraced her daughter in a tight hug. "Tomorrow I will cook your favorite foods."

As Hennah lay on the top bunk of her bed, she found sleep elusive. She could still see the upset faces of her parents and Dhruvi. The pain she had caused them cut into her sharper than the glass had. And Joseph giving up being with his brothers because of her. Guilt plagued her. She was a terrible daughter and friend, hurting those who cared about her. *You stupid girl, only thinking about yourself. So what if I never finish Project Absurd. I can't let my family down again. Ever. I must stick to the Code, putting others before myself.*

Several times during the night, Hennah heard her bedroom door open and one of her parents standing there, listening to her breathing. She pretended to be asleep, feeling regretful that she was the cause of their sleeplessness.

For the next two weeks, Joseph spent every day with Hennah, exploring the nearby cities. Concerned she was taking away his family time, she insisted that some days they did activities with his birthmates. One day they hiked to a waterfall. Another time they rented boats and went deep sea fishing. The birthmates sometimes joked about her stealing their brother from them until they saw her wounded look.

Darkfern finally arrived back home. As soon as she heard the news about what happened to Hennah, she came for a visit. Mid-morning she marched into Hennah's bedroom and stood, with both pairs of arms crossed, glaring up at her friend.

"Hi, Darkfern." Hennah lay on the top bunk, reading a novel. "I'm glad to see you are back."

"What were you thinking? Suicide! Don't both your religions condemn it? Why would you do such a dishonorable thing?"

Hennah turned off her e-tablet. "I, uh, was not thinking clearly at the time."

"Not thinking clearly? You are a genius. You think more clearly than most. If you ever try that again, I will personally beat some sense into you. Do you understand me?"

"Yes. Now is it safe for me to come down, or should I stay up here to avoid a thrashing?"

"You can come down." Darkfern settled into a chair by the desk, her eyes still angry.

Hennah climbed down the ladder and set on her sister's bed. "I am glad to see you again. How was Kilpailu? Are you still single?"

"Of course I am. No guy will take me until I am ready." Darkfern rolled up one of her sleeves, showing the new hieroglyph tattooed next to four others. On the fjouwers' homeworld fiber plants did not exist and paper had never been invented. Since ancient times they recorded important events on skin.

"Nice tattoo." Hennah could not read the hieroglyphs but Darkfern had explained their meaning to her several years ago. She knew on one of Darkfern's other arms was a spiral family tree with symbols for her parents, grandparents and other important relatives. When Darkfern married and had children, their names would be added.

"I can't believe what you did. No fjouwer would dare do such a depraved act, no matter how terrible life was. And how is your life bad? We have been friends our whole lives. What would cause you to want to end yours? Did someone hurt you?"

"No one hurt me. Look, can we talk about something else."

"I want to understand."

Hennah looked away, guilt causing her muscles to tense. She wanted to tell Darkfern everything, but she remembered Alec's gag order. The true source of her unhappiness she could not speak about. "Just the pressures of work and losing my grandfather. I became depressed, and, well, just lost it for a bit. But I'm fine now."

Darkfern was unsatisfied with the answer. "Work gets hard for me too, but I don't kill myself over it. Maybe you should get a transfer."

"Actually I have been taking a vacation. That is, Joseph and I have been just hanging out, doing things together. Today we are going to see a play. You can come if you like. It's a musical with good reviews."

"Are you and Joseph dating?"

"Dating? He is my co-worker."

"So? My mom married a co-worker. In human culture, is not dating when a couple do things together? Like going to plays and movies?"

"I…uh…" Hennah was unsure how to answer. In her mind, dating involved kissing and eventually marriage. She and Joseph were going on adventures, not romantic trysts. Courting meant a whole new level of pressure she was not ready for. "We are just friends. He knows I'm going through a hard time and is trying to cheer me up."

"Is it working?"

"Yes, I'm happier now."

"Good, because I would hate to have to beat you up if you did something foolish again."

Darkfern opted out of joining them that evening. Hennah sat by Joseph in the dark theater, trying to enjoy the play, but Darkfern's words kept whispering in her mind. What was Joseph's intentions? Other than a rare brush of hands, they did not touch. That is what she preferred, no flirting. No pressure. Just friends. That was what she needed now.

But would Joseph want more? He was giving up his brothers for her. Surely he wanted more from her than being a friendly co-worker. Of course, he wanted her to be sane, to keep working on Project Absurd. That was what Alec wanted also. Could Alec have ordered Joseph to befriend her? Henna looked at Joseph in the darkness, studying his face. A thin smile on his lips told her he was enjoying the musical. His friendship seemed genuine, but was he acting on orders?

After the play ended, they dined at a fancy restaurant serving sundancer cuisine. The spicy meal was nearly over when they received messages on their e-bands that Dyjuna had given birth to a healthy girl. Deciding to see the firstborn offspring of a quintessence, they headed to the hospital.

The hallway of the Maternity Department was filled with visitors gathered by the glass wall which looked into a room filled with cribs. Nineteen quiet quintessences stood by their elated siren wives, some singing lullaby to the various sentient babies through the glass. All the sirens were gorgeous, like Dyjuna. Their skin varied from shades of green to beige. Their hair was a wild mix of greens, yellows, blues, reds, and purples.

Janet and several other researchers from Essence talked excitedly. There were other visitors that Hennah did not recognize. It seemed that Dyjuna and her clan sisters had a knack for making new friends.

Hennah managed to find a spot near the glass and looked at the dozen or so babies. Over half were human. Dyjuna's child was easy to spot because she had sea green skin and a fuzz of blue hair.

A new song was begun by the sirens. This time all of them joined their voices into a joyful tune, some humming the melody while others sung the words in their native tongue. Hennah felt their powerful emotions fill her, washing away fear and doubt. Hope for a bright future shimmered like a dream. Though she knew what she felt was caused by the sirens, she let the music flow through her, controlling her feelings. Even when the tune ended, she was still mesmerized by the deep emotions it stirred.

Slowly she became aware of her surroundings again, noticing that Joseph stood beside her, holding her hand. She smiled at him, feeling blissful. He leaned over and kissed her on the lips. The contact was brief but still caught Hennah by surprise. If she had not still been under the siren's spell, she may have panicked. Instead, she leaned against Joseph, content. He wrapped a muscular arm around her shoulder.

Janet squeezed in between Hennah and a sundancer. "She's beautiful, is she not? Todd already allowed me to get a DNA sample. I will send it to you tomorrow—that is if you will be at work."

Hennah glanced at Joseph. "I guess it is time."

He squeezed her arm. "Yes, you are ready again."

Chapter Thirteen

Joseph stood beside Hennah as she pointed to notes in her e-tablet, explaining her latest failure. He quietly moved behind her and brushed long hair away from her neck. Before she could react, he bit her with the epulo. He had done so many times over the years, always erasing her memory of it.

Knowing Hennah's emotions was only partly helpful. Despite his constant monitoring of her, he could never had predicted her suicide attempt. She had reacted on a whim with no preempt warnings, at least none he had noticed. He had known about her depression, but he had attributed it to the normal grieving of losing her grandfather. He now understood differently. She was battling clinical depression.

Before her incident he had only read her mind weekly, now he did so daily. He knew the vacation and outings with him had helped, but once back in the lab, her brief contentment had drained away again. To spend a large part of each day tackling problems that always eventually failed took its toll. She continued to view her job as hopeless, hating the drudgery. The only reason she came each day was because of him.

Joseph had asked Alec to remove her completely from the project for a few months perhaps even a year, but the Five had refused, saying her work was too vital. So Joseph came to the lab each day because of his concern for Hennah while she came because she felt she owed him for losing his brothers.

Joseph broke contact and moved to her side. Hennah blinked a few times, and then continued her one-sided dialog, not knowing she had been interrupted.

When she finished, Joseph said, "I am taking off the rest of the afternoon. My brothers leave today. I want you to take off too."

"Do you want me come with you?" She pretended to care, but she really wanted to avoid the final goodbye, fearing the birthmates would look at her with accusing eyes for stealing their brother.

"No. Go relax. Finish that novel you are reading."

He wanted to give her a goodbye kiss, but he restrained himself. Not since that night with the sirens had he kissed her. When he had looked into her memories the next day, he realized she had been caught in their enchantment, happy at that moment, but the feeling had been fleeting. She felt no romantic feelings for him, only desiring friendship. Following Alec's advice, he had talked to a psychologist who worked at Essence about how to deal with someone with deep depression. He had learned that the lack of physical desire was one of the symptoms.

After seeing Hennah drive off to her apartment, he headed to the launch pads and met his brothers. They formed a loose circle around him, saying their goodbyes. While the parting was bittersweet, it was not painful like last time. His brothers were no longer slaves forced to fight for uncaring masters but could now choose their own fates. They felt excitement for their coming job where they would be police officers helping a peaceful society. Their profession would still be dangerous, but quintessences thrived on challenge. They would have salaries and share several apartments that were designed specifically for quintessences.

"We will take vacations together," said Philip. "Rowan is not too far away."

"I look forward to that," said Joseph.

"When will you marry her?" asked Ryder.

"When she is ready."

"You better hurry if you wish to be the first. I intend to find a bride soon myself."

"You just have forty-four brothers to compete with."

"I'm more handsome than them." Ryder gave a faint, playful smile.

The brothers picked up their duffle bags and boarded the shuttle, leaving Joseph watching silently as their ship lifted off the pad. Sadness lingered, but he knew they would do well. He wanted to be with them, sharing their adventures, being a part of their lives. As he wandered about the huge campus, he felt emptiness. For the last seven months, when he had not been with Hennah, he had been with his brothers. There were thousands of quintessences at Essence, but competing in sports did not feel right without his birthmates.

A message showed up on his e-band from Alec. After reading it, Joseph headed back to Richmon Tower and took the elevator up to the Five's office. Alec sat on a couch with his Shadow Guard on another. Joseph sat on the third couch across from the Five.

"You have my gratitude for choosing to stay and work on this project." Alec's hair was almost pure white, his body thin and frail.

"I did it for Hennah."

"I know. You care about her very much. I am concerned about her too."

"But not enough to pull her off the project."

"I cannot do that. She was created solely for this purpose. Hennah is not why I asked you to come here today." Alec looked exhausted. "You have already sacrificed much for the betterment of your brethren. I ask yet more from you. A mission that will alter your life forever, if you choose to take it. If you decide not to, all information about it will be erased from your mind."

"What is this mission?" Joseph asked cautiously.

"Many centuries ago, Alexander, the firstborn of all quintessences, accidently found a way to cheat death. A method using the epulo to create a mega ziphema which contained all the memories of an individual. This ziphema can be transferred to another who can absorb the memories, in essence becoming the previous person yet still keeping his own personality. Alexander passed this information on to his brothers and the Synod who have closely guarded this secret. Together they decided that the Five would preserve themselves using this method in order to continue to be guardians for our species."

Joseph leaned forward. "What are you implying, sir?"

"That I am not just Alec but also Alexander. Also Ariyo and Ace. I have lived in four bodies and am ready for a fifth. I would like that to be you."

Astonished, Joseph looked towards Miles who watched the conversation silently. There was no surprise in the Shadow Guard's eyes. Obviously Miles knew about this. Joseph took a moment, taking things in. "You want to take over my body?"

"No. I want us to become one. You will not lose yourself, only gain new memories which will aid you when you become a Five. That will be the new position you will be promoted to after a few months. You dislike my decisions about Hennah. Now you can become the one giving the commands. I am offering to make you one of the most powerful quintessences at Essence."

"I have never sought power."

"I know. If you had, I would not have chosen you."

"Why did you pick me?"

"Because you believe strongly in the Code, putting it before your own life. I began watching you after your trial, eventually moving you into a position to watch Hennah. You have grown to care about her, placing her even above your own brothers. You have the courage to stand up against me when you believe I am in the wrong. Not many will talk back to a Five."

"You are wrong about Hennah."

"Say yes to my proposal and you can change all of that, if that is what you wish after you have my memories."

"Will I still really be me?"

"Yes and no. Once a blend happens, you will be different, not me or you, but something more. Your personality will still be there and everything you cared about. But you will also have access to all my memories, of everyone I have known, of every mistake I have made. Hopefully this will keep you from making the same errors, but I am sure you will make new ones. We are not perfect beings. I will not lie. Carrying the legacy of Alexander will not be easy. He...I...loved Layla very

106

deeply. Those emotions will become your own. But your feelings for Hennah will be just as real. You will become a respected leader with heavy responsibilities. If you want an easy life, this is not the path to take."

"You ask a lot."

"Yes, I do. Shadow Guards will watch you the rest of your life." Alec glanced towards Miles. "They have the authority to kill any of the Five if we ever go insane or abuse our position. In the beginning we decided to give them these powers as a safety measure. So far, extreme measures have not been needed."

Miles replied, "You do like to test me some days."

"I would not wish for you to become complacent." Alec turned back to Joseph. "You have several days to think about this. If you choose no, I will ask another, but I prefer it to be you."

After Joseph left the office, he again wandering randomly about Essence, passing companies of freed birthmates marching together towards a new venture. Acutely Joseph missed his brothers, but even if they had been here, he would not have been allowed to talk with them about Alec's proposal. This was a decision he had to make on his own.

If it had only been Alec asking, Joseph would had refused immediately. To have someone else's entire essence become part of him was far different than sharing a few memories among friends. It would alter him forever, making him someone new. He would no longer be Joseph the marriage license clerk. Or Joseph the lieutenant of his company. He would become Joseph of the Five, with authority over his entire species. It was not a responsibility he wanted.

But it had been Alexander who asked him to share his life. Like all quintessences, when Joseph was four years old and learning how to use the epulo, he had been given the Canon, a ziphema which contained the core memories of Layla and Alexander which explained why the quintessences had first been created and the need for the Code. All quintessences revered the original Five, never guessing that they still existed over four hundred years after their deaths. The Canon showed both the flaws and heroic acts of the Five as they learned what it meant to be quintessence. It was a guide for each new generation in understanding themselves and their place in society.

Joseph had respected Alec's position as a Five, even when he disagreed with him. Alexander was a legendary hero to him. It was difficult to perceive them as the same individual. Now they were asking him to become a part of them. It was a high honor he wished had been passed to another. Yet he had been asked. Joseph, the desk clerk.

Eventually he found himself standing outside Hennah's barracks. For a while he just stood there. When he sent her a message asking if she wished to go out to dinner, she soon came to him, dressed in casual jeans and a tan blouse.

Hesitantly she asked. "Are you okay? With your brothers gone?"

"I will miss them, but we will see each other again. Often as Rowan is close. Where would you like to eat?"

They headed to a nearby café in New Hope. The conversation stayed light with both avoiding mentioning his brothers, but he knew she thought about them. He did not wish for her to feel guilty for his separation from them.

As they stood to leave, he reached out and took her hand. "Hennah, I am content. Do not blame yourself because I choose to stay here."

"How can I not?"

"If you understood my feelings for you, you would not be upset but happy, perhaps even joyful."

Uncomfortable with his words, Hennah pulled her hand from him and walked down the aisle between tables. He followed, knowing he had said too much. She was not ready to love, but he was. He wished he could share his life memories with her like he did with his brothers. His emotions, his dreams, and fears. He desired a soulmate. She just wished for each workday to end and dreaded the next one to come. Still, he would not give up on her. The depression had to end sooner or later. Alec offered to give him complete power over Hennah's life. He could then have her transferred into the regular Research Department and take a break from Project Absurd.

After he had dropped her off at her barracks, he messaged Alec with one word, "Yes."

Several days later as Hennah cleaned up the lab before heading home for the weekend, Joseph joined her wiping down the tables. They worked in silence, as they often did when he helped her.

As they put away the cleaning supplies, Joseph said, "Alec has a special assignment for me for a few days. I will miss work Monday and perhaps a few more days after that. But I will be back soon."

"Okay." She turned and picked up her backpack.

"Take Monday off. And perhaps a few more days. I will message you when I return. I want you to stay out of this lab until I come back."

Hennah frowned. "I can work just fine without you. I don't need a babysitter."

Joseph stepped closer. "I know you can, but I prefer it this way."

"The work is too important for me to stop just because you're gone on some assignment."

"Do this for me."

Her fists clenched. "You still don't trust me."

Joseph reached out and touched her cheek, forcing her to look him in the eyes. "Hennah, I trust you. Now trust me. Do not enter this lab without me. Please."

She flinched and stepped back. "Sure. Do I still get paid for this forced vacation?"

"Of course."

After she was gone, Joseph wandered through gyms watching various competitions. He avoided the basketball courts as they reminded him of his brothers. After he ate dinner at the food court, he checked his e-band, watching the pink dot which represented Hennah on a map. He always knew her whereabouts. All workers at Essence were required to have a tracking microchip to allow them through security checkpoints. Some employees wore the microchip either on their ID badges or in jewelry. Others preferred to have the implants in their hands. At birth all quintessences received the implants. Hennah had one in her hand, placed there by Chandresh shortly after she had come home from the hospital as a newborn. As a toddler she had been told she had the chip, and she accepted its existence as a normal facet of life at Essence.

Hennah was at home eating dinner with her family. He could see the dots for each of them in the dining room. Over the weekend Darkfern would be with Hennah as they attended several tournaments. After putting away his trash, Joseph took the elevator up to the top floor. He paused outside of Alec's penthouse. This was his last moment to only be Joseph. Part of him wanted to turn around, to keep being just himself. He pictured Hennah's weary face, sapped from a week of fruitless work. For her he would do this.

He entered the penthouse, finding it crowded. All of the Five were present, along with several of the Synod and Shadow Guards. They had come to say goodbye to Alec. They knew he was to be reborn, yet the process was still a form of death. Tobias, the AF3 who had replaced Mablevi nine years ago, stood beside his wife Amaka, a powerful telepath. While the other Five kept their previous lives hidden from their wives, Mason shared everything with Amaka. When Mablevi had died, Amaka waited two months then married Tobias, only a few knowing she was remarrying the same man.

Gabriel, now an IN1 for the last four years, went by the name of Skyler. Both he and Jacob did not bring their wives. Celeb was the only elder Five in the room besides Alec. He would remain director for a few more years, then pass that position to Gabriel upon his death. The brothers rotated the title, each shouldering its heavy responsibility for a while.

Joseph tried to keep a calm attitude as the others joked or said heart-felt farewells, but he felt apprehensive. This was like an execution where the victim knew he was going to die while Joseph waited to take over that person's life. It felt wrong, unnatural.

"Relax," said Tobias, walking up to Joseph. "I promise you, it will be better than you believe."

"I hope so." He felt a chill down his arms as the reality hit that he spoke not to just Tobias but Mason the Inquisitor. Even centuries later, whenever anyone spoke of Mason's deeds, it was with dreaded respect. Among other achievements, he was the founder of the Death Force, the elite unit who always got their target. Their main objective was to hunt down the rare corrupt quintessences.

Amaka smiled and laid a comforting hand on Joseph's arm. "Your love for her is strong. Hold on to that. It will see you through." She was a slender kuawazo with dark gray skin, jet black hair, and eyes of gold.

Joseph looked into her large eyes, feeling the eeriness of knowing she read his mind. He had never met her before but he knew the stories. Quintessences were immune to almost all telepaths and empaths, but Amaka was the exception. She was one of the most powerful telepaths ever born among her race, so talented that she had to flee her homeworld while still an adolescent because of an assassination attempt by those jealous of what she might become.

One by one the others began to leave until only Joseph, Alec, Miles, and Desmond remained. When Joseph glanced at Desmond, he again felt eeriness, knowing he looked into the ancient eyes of Jacob. What was it like to be both young and old at the same time?

"Ready?" asked Alec. He sat on a couch for he tired quickly when standing long.

"Yes, sir." Joseph felt tense.

Everyone moved to the bedroom and Alec laid on the bed. Joseph had already been instructed on what to do, yet still he hesitated. He was about to kill a Five. The ramifications scared him despite Alec had given him permission to take his life.

"All will be well," said Desmond. "We have been through this many times."

Joseph lay on the bed and bit Alec. As their minds meet, he saw a young, robust ME1 standing before him in a garden. Without a word, he knew he looked upon the living legend of Alexander.

"Relax," smiled Alexander. "This will be painless for both of us."

"I'm trying to relax, sir."

"No longer will you call me *sir*. We are equals, now and forever, Joseph. Take all that is me. Make it part of you. Serve our brethren well."

Following instructions, Joseph begin ripping all the memories in the mind of Alec, compacting them into a mega ziphema. The process could be done rapidly, but Joseph took his time, being careful as possible. Eventually there was nothing left, leaving Alec's mind completely blank. At this point, Joseph could withdraw and leave Alec braindead, but he had been requested to do more. Joseph began draining Alec's life energy, drinking the electrical impulses of the nerves until death resulted.

Finished, he broke contact and sat up. Alec lay still beside him. "It is done."

"Good," said Desmond. "Miles will take you to the apartment where you will be staying for the next few days. I will see to notifying the medical ward of my brother's death."

Joseph stood up and followed Miles. He felt tired, heavy, thoughts slow. They took the elevator down several floors and entered one of the apartments set aside for top aides who worked at Essence. Joseph headed to the bed and fell asleep immediately. A few hours later he woke up long enough to break the mega ziphema, sending millions of thoughts splintering through his mind. Then he slept for days.

Occasionally he woke enough to eat, but he barely noticed his surroundings. He was vaguely aware that visitors came and went. Shadow Guards rotated every twelve hours. On the fourth day, he finally became conscious. He lay in bed, eyes closed, hearing the sounds of a vid in the living room.

Images swirled through his mind, many far older than himself. Four other lifetimes. Six centuries. So many experiences, friendships, and responsibilities. Five generations of birthmates he deeply cared for. Three generations all dead now. Along with their wives and children. His extended family was vast. Then there was the Five: Joseph, Caleb, Gabriel, and Mason. While time continued to flow and the universe constantly changed, it was these brothers who were his rocks. Together they had weathered many storms. Lived on while spouses and offspring eventually died. He reflected on various individuals who had once meant much to him.

Then he looked into the core of who he was and saw Layla, his beloved creator. He relived vivid memories of their double lives together. Then endured watching helplessly as she died her final time. Grief filled him, fresh and raw as he felt his heart wrenched from him. Without her, how could he continue to go on? He was so tired of this endless cycle of rebirth when what he wanted most he could never have again.

Joseph shuddered and fought against the melancholy. Layla had been Alexander's wife, not his. But it did not feel that way. The memories were not like watching a movie or peeking into a ziphema. He was not observing someone else's life. He had been the one who kissed Lashana. Watched her kids grow up to become grandparents themselves. Her descendants he cherished as family, secretly watching over them through the generations. *Eventually everyone dies while I am cursed to live on. Perhaps one day I will be the last quintessence to exist.*

Again Joseph fought darkness, grief, and depression. Alexander, Ariyo, Ace, and Alec were a part of him, along with their fears, dreams, achievements, and mistakes. So much history of pain, suffering, and loneliness. But there were many moments of happiness. Of contentment in helping others. Sharing in the joy of birthmates who had found soulmates. Watching the quintessence society grow. Wars prevented. Millions protected. So many accomplishments. But while he had saved lives, as a soldier he had taken many too. When bonded, he had been a pawn in too many schemes of politicians. Once freed, he learned to manipulate the lives of others—for their betterment, so he believed.

Five overlapping lives led to eight-hundred years of collective experiences. The memories washed through him like a tsunami. He struggled to keep his identity while accepting the others as part of himself. *I am Joseph. And I will not give up on hope. I will not be the last of my species.* Hennah's face came to his mind. *Nor will I give up on you.* He focused on her, remembering her as a smiling youth spinning in a chair. Then the depressed adult demoralized by the heavy weight pressed on her by Alec. *By me*, he corrected. Alec was part of him now, and he was determined to undo the other's mistakes. The galaxy was in turmoil, but Hennah was the one individual he wished to save above all others.

He slowly sat up in bed. Miles had been watching a movie in the living room but quickly came to him.

"How do you feel?"

"Tired of being in bed."

"Do you know me?"

"Miles." As he looked at the C3, he remembered heated conversations. "The thorn who insist that I am not always right."

"Someone has to keep you balanced."

"You take your position too seriously."

"No problems with your memory, I see. Or humor."

"What humor?"

"Exactly."

Miles prepared a meal while Joseph took a shower. Then they ate together, chatting a bit. Joseph checked Hennah's location several times on his e-band. She was with Darkfern at another tournament.

"Your funeral is in three days, in case you wish to attend." Miles began to stack dirty dishes.

"That late? Usually they are much quicker."

"Your brothers decided to wait until the competitions were finished."

Joseph faintly smiled. "Glad to know where my brothers' priories lay."

"Jacob did not want to cancel the tournaments his children were to be in. This will be his son's first time."

"Ah. Family first. The living ones, that is. We will head to the tournaments ourselves."

Miles gave him a stern look. "Do not even consider entering one yourself. You will need to take it easy for a while after the merge."

"No need to be concerned about me. I am only going to watch." *And see Hennah*, but he kept that thought to himself. The urge to see her was overwhelming after wading through the memories of too many dead comrades.

After the dishes were washed, Joseph and Miles headed to the Hall of Challenge. They moved through the crowd in the popular bōjutsu gym, passing the large, circular platforms where matches were held. Today only one was in use. Two skilled opponents bowed to each other then began battling with metal bōs that had dull blades on each end. They twirled and leaped, their staffs moving so fast they appeared to blur. Around the room on several large screens the fight was shown live as it was recorded by a hovering camera drone.

Joseph found Hennah among the thick thong near the fighters. The moment he saw her, his heart quickened. In the chaotic swirl of five lifetimes of memories, it was she who drew him, who held him grounded. The purpose of his current existence. She needed help, and he wanted to be her savior, her protector, her friend.

Darkfern and Rockgem stood near her, both cheering loudly. Joseph reached out and touched Hennah's hand. She immediately pulled back and looked sharply at him. Seeing his nametag, she relaxed and gave a brief smile.

"You're back."

"Yes, finally. I missed you."

As they watched the fight, Joseph felt disoriented. While he had some training in bōjutsu, his talents lay in other areas. Yet as he watched the experts battle, he knew the name of each move, predicted how the contestants would respond to each other. His hand itched for a bō as he remembered his first experiments with sticks and brooms. Then becoming an instructor to the second and third generations of quintessences. Later as Ariyo he had broken several records including being the youngest master champion at Essence. Now part of him wanted to grab a bō and join the fight.

To restrain himself, he reached out and took Hennah's hand. This time she did not pull away. She remained quiet beside him while her friends yelled along with others in the crowd. The battle ended and judges announced the winner. Several bouts later the champion was declared and the crowd began to disperse. Joseph caught Mile's eye and tilted his head towards the door, hoping the Shadow Guard remembered the rules allowed for the Five when courting.

Darkfern noticed Joseph for the first time. "You missed my fight. I won first this time in knifing. Sixth in short sword."

"Congratulations."

"I got fourth with knives," said Rockgem. "Next year I'm beating my sister."

"As if you could."

"I have beaten you during practices."

"Only some. But practices don't count."

Joseph cut in. "Hennah and I are about to head to dinner. I will watch the recordings of your fights later."

He led Hennah away through the crowd towards the exit. Miles followed but at a distance.

Hennah was quiet until they were near the parking lot. "You should have invited them to come with us."

"You have spent days with your friends. I would like some time alone with you." He hoped Miles heard the last word and got the hint. Reaching Hennah's car, he took the driver's seat.

"Must you always drive?"

"Yes." He noticed that Miles walked casually pass. Later when he returned, Miles would probe his mind, checking that he behaved himself. That was the agreement when a Five asked for private time when courting. Irritating, but Alexander had agreed with those terms long ago.

He drove to the boardwalk and parked near the theater.

"I thought we were eating."

"It is a bit early. I thought perhaps a movie first." As they looked over the list of what was showing, he pointed to a romance.

"We always watch action or comedies."

"Today I feel like something different."

Hennah frowned but bought a ticket. They settled in chairs which leaned far back. In the darkness, he reached out and took her hand. The movie was lighthearted, and he sensed Hennah relaxing until there was a kissing scene. She pulled her hand from him and kept it away until the movie was over.

Joseph chose a fancy restaurant built out over the ocean, its lower floors below the waterline. They were seated by a window offering a submerged view of the ocean. As they ate, fish swam by, attracted by food which occasionally appeared from feeders.

"You are different today." Hennah buttered a roll.

"Different? How?"

"I don't know. Just different. Did something happen on your mission?"

"I had time to think about how short life is."

Hennah stirred her bouillabaisse soup then spooned up a shellfish. "I guess it is strange to go on a mission for someone and he dies while you are gone."

"Are you glad Alec is dead?" He studied her face carefully, looking for a reaction.

"No. Why would I be glad anyone is dead?"

"You did not like him."

"So? It's not like his death bought my freedom. Another will take his place. Nothing has changed for me."

Joseph flinched, feeling conflicted. He had wanted to immediately have her transferred, but now he was haunted by his predecessor's fears of extinction for his species. The continuation of the quintessences was one of Alec's top priorities, and he saw Hennah as the key which could save them. There had to be a way to make her happy yet keep her working at the same time.

"Hennah, is there anything you want besides a new job? Anything at all?"

The teenager shrugged. "Not really. I guess more time for sleep. I really just wanted to stay home over the weekend but Darkfern kept insisting I attend all those tournaments. I'm tired of people and crowds. I guess I'm ready to get back to my lab tomorrow. Quietness."

Joseph hid his disappointment. He needed to find a way to break the depression which held her captive. After the meal, they walked along the beach, watching the sunset. Hennah was ready to head home, but Joseph led her further away from the buildings and tourists. A cliff rose to their left. At the top, homes overlooked the ocean. They finally stopped by large boulders which formed part of a cape that led into the water. Hennah leaned against a boulder, watching the waves gently lap against the white sand in the moonlight.

Joseph stood beside her, studying her instead of the water. Memories stirred of two others who had the same slim body as her. He remembered kissing both of them, touching their smooth skin. Minds linked, souls bare.

"I wish you would not look at me that way," said Hennah.

"Which way is that?"

"Like…well…how you are now. I think it's time to go."

Joseph moved closer to her. "I want to remove your unhappiness. I would like to try something."

"What is that?" she asked warily.

"This." He kissed her gently on the lips. She tried to pull back, but she was against a boulder. "How was that?"

"Um, nice."

"Nice? A kiss should be more than nice."

He stroked her cheek, feeling her tension. "Trust me, Hennah. I want to help you."

He kissed her again, gently at first, but then he applied more pressure, moving one hand into her hair and the other along her back, pulling her against him. When he finally stepped back, she stood still, uncertain what to do.

115

He looked into her eyes. "Did you feel anything?"

"You kissing me."

"Anything else?"

"I don't know what you mean."

He signed in frustration. "I love you, Hennah."

"I guessed that."

"But you do not feel anything for me?"

"Sorry, I can't really feel much of anything. But I want to, if that helps. You have been a good friend."

He held her hands and touched his forehead against hers. They remained standing this way for a few minutes, each lost in thought. Then Joseph knelt in the sand while continuing to hold her hands.

"Marry me, Hennah."

The teenager opened and closed her mouth several times, unable to answer. Finally, she said, "I already told you I don't really feel anything."

"You may not feel love right now, but you still recognize it. Love of parents, love of friends, love of husbands. That is what I want to be to you. A helpmate. A friend. Your lover when you are ready. Marry me."

"I...uh."

In the moonlight he could see uncertainty in her eyes. He guessed the thoughts she pondered. She did care about him, that he was certain, but her feelings were muted by depression.

"I'm broken." She looked down at his hands holding hers, seeing the thin white scar on her wrist.

"I want you as you are, flaws and all. I am not perfect either."

"But I don't know if I can ever feel love, not like what you are seeking."

"That is okay. My love is deep enough for both of us." He stood up and held her hands to his chest. "I vow to be there for you, through darkness and light. We will come out of this together."

She leaned against him, and he wrapped his arms around her, holding her close. In a voice barely louder than the wind, she whispered, "Yes."

Chapter Fourteen

Tall trees swayed in the summer breeze, casting shadows on shoppers strolling along sidewalks and wandering into stores at an outdoor mall designed to resemble a modern village. Aashi paused in front of a jewelry store. A hologram image of a diamond ring appeared beside her then transformed into a gold bracelet.

She ignored the advertisement. "Are you having an engagement party?"

"We have not talked about it." Hennah shrugged, holding several bags which displayed logos from nearby stores.

She was weary of shopping with her sister. Aashi had graduated college two days ago and was home, planning her own wedding which was to take place in a month. Like their parents, Aashi was thrilled that Hennah was getting married. They presumed it was a sign she was getting over her depression. Wanting to please them, Hennah pretended to be happy, but the sham was taking its toll. She was often fatigued, wishing for solitude instead of being with family and friends.

"Engagement parties are huge in Hundi culture. Surely you will have one. Last year mine was quite exciting."

"I was there, remember? Your wedding is almost here, so me having a party would be a distraction. It's your big day."

"Have you set your wedding date, at least?" They strolled passed a bakery that displayed hologram dancing buns in front of its window.

"No, we have not even been engaged a week and there was your graduation to attend and the Five's funeral." The week had seemed endless to Hennah with its many social obligations, including a formal dinner with the family of Aashi's fiancé.

Aashi studied her younger sister for a long moment, deep in thought. "Quintessences are notorious for short engagements. He will want to marry soon."

Hennah glanced away, feigning interest in a pink kitten playing in a pet store. "We are not in a hurry."

"You may not be, but I know stories about quintessences who have gotten engaged and married on the same day. I don't want my coming marriage to interfere with yours. How about we combine and have a double wedding?"

"Like I said, it's your special day, not mine."

Aashi stopped walking and glanced at the faint scar on Hennah's wrist. "Look, I know I was not the best sister growing up. Let me make that up to you now. I don't mind sharing the spotlight with you, not anymore. And a double wedding will save money. I already have most of it planned out, but I can still change details, if you wish."

"Um, sure. Joseph will probably be fine with it." Hennah felt relief. With Aashi handling the planning, maybe a wedding would not be so excruciating. She just wanted it over with so she could fall back into her normal, bland life.

They bought coffee drinks and cheese cakes then sat at a table in a plaza. Hennah ate slowly while Aashi talked almost nonstop about the weddings, coming up with dozens of new ideas. Hennah nodded when she should, wishing to be home, but Aashi would be there too, still dreaming up wedding plans. Right now it was exhausting being Aashi's sister.

A beep on Aashi's telecom caught her attention. "Oh, there is a sale going on at Lucy's. Twenty percent off for one hour. We have to go." She glanced towards the building down the street where several shoppers had already changed their course and began to head to the department store.

"I'm not done eating. How about you go without me."

Aashi frowned as she counted a dozen customers entering the store. "Are you sure? I won't be long."

"Go, have fun. I need to rest for a bit." Hennah sighed, grateful for a break from her sister. For years they had barely talked to each other. Now she could not get Aashi to stop talking. Hennah took another bite of the turtle cheesecake, grateful for the brief silence. Once she had loved the nuts and caramel swirls, but now food held little interest to her.

"Is this seat taken?" A young man with brown hair slightly out of place sat down across from her and placed his coffee cup and e-tablet on the table. He was dressed casually in jeans and a buttoned shirt.

Hennah frowned at his rudeness. "My sister was sitting there."

"She is gone for the moment. Is she really your sister? I didn't recognize her." He glanced in the direction Aashi had disappeared.

"If I say she is my sister, then she is."

The stranger studied her closely. "Are you a backup? Was there a second bunker? Your clone died in ours during a plague outbreak when we were eighteen months, I believe. Thirteen died. Most likely a caregiver picked up the virus when visiting the city for supplies."

"Backup? No. What are you talking about? Thirteen died?" Hennah's heart quickened at the word *clone*. Who was this stranger?

"Our numbers are down to thirty-four, the last I heard. They began with fifty of us. How many was in your group?"

"I don't know what you are talking about. I'm not from a group. There is just me."

"You said you have a sister." The stranger frowned. "I have all the profectus memorized. She is not one of us. Did they actually place you in a family? They chose to do that with a second group and never told us?" His last words came out angrily.

Hennah glanced around at other shoppers relaxing at nearby tables. Perhaps she ought to feel fear, but instead she felt curiosity at his words, *Not one of us*. Could he be another profectus? A thin thread of excitement and hope broke into the emptiness she had known for too long. She leaned forward and whispered, "Who do you think I am?"

"A clone of Layla Rangan, of course."

"You are mistaken."

"No, I'm not."

"Why do you say that?"

He leaned forward also, looking intently into her eyes. "Profectus know their own. Tell me, who am I?"

Hennah tilted her head slighted as she studied his face. There had been five hundred profectus originally engineered. While she had studied the more famous ones, she had never tried to learn them all. She cycled through the ones she knew. Suddenly her eyes widened. "You are Richard Cambridge. I mean a clone of his."

"Call me Kylen. What is your name?"

"I, uh, should probably not tell you that."

"Good to be cautious, as we just meet." Kylen continued to study her, trying to figure her out. "They did not tell us they made a second group. Is there another copy of me?"

"No. Like I said, I am alone. Really alone. I didn't know there were any other profectus." Real excitement filled Hennah. *I'm not alone anymore. This changes everything.*

Kylen was deep in thought. "I am curious about why they did not tell you about us. Why keep you apart from the rest of us?"

"Who is *they* that you keep referring to?"

"The Coalition, of course."

"You mean the Coalition of Human Advancement?" Hennah had studied about the group years ago. She knew it had sponsored the creation of the first wave of profectus over six hundred years ago. And created the illegal second group. Outside of that, she knew little.

Kylen frowned. "If the Coalition did not make you, who did?"

Hennah sat back in her seat, warily. "I have said too much."

"I told you who made us. It is only fair you tell me your story."

"I'm…um…not allowed to do that. My existence is classified."

"Intriguing." Kylen took a sip of his coffee. "I accept your challenge. So the Coalition is not your creator. You are unique, one of a kind. Grew up hidden with a real family. Who would have the motivation to clone Layla and the facilities to do so?" His eyes wandered in the direction of Essence Institute, its massive wall peeking up beyond the nearby shops. "I'm guessing it's not a coincidence that you live on Xi'an."

Hennah tried keeping her face as blank as a quintessence, but she failed.

Kylen smiled. "Classified, hm. Now why would the leeches want you?"

"Why did the Coalition make you?"

"If you do not share your story, I cannot share mine."

Hennah leaned forward again, keeping her voice low. "It's not that I'm being unhospitable. I'm under a gag order punishable by death."

"Sounds like what the leeches would do. Are they cruel to you?"

"No, not really. My family really cares about me. How about you? How do your masters treat you?"

"We are not slaves." Kylen's face darkened, anger flashing briefly in his eyes.

"Really? I am. One of them didn't want to use that term, but another was straightforward with me. I prefer honesty than pretending. It's best knowing where I stand. Can you go where you wish? Do want you want?"

"We have…limits. They treat us well—as long as we follow their agenda. We have no families, just each other, but that counts for little. We were trained to compete against each other, always trying to be the greatest. That is our purpose, to outshine our clones which came before us."

"Technically the first profectus were not clones, as they were the originals."

"We prefer calling them clones," explained Kylen. "Easier to say in conversations than I have an original and another clone."

Hennah noticed Aashi walking towards them, a new bag in her hand. "My sister is coming. She knows nothing." She drank coffee, pretending she had not been engaged in the most interesting conversation of her life.

"Hello," said Aashi, pulling another chair to the table. "A new friend?"

"We are acquaintances," said Kylen. "It is good to meet you…" He paused, hoping she would fill in her name.

"Aashi. Soon to be Aashi Gupta. I marry next month."

"How was shopping?" asked Hennah, noticing Kylen's trick to get names.

"I got a great deal on shoes which will match my saree. We need to find you a pair. And a new saree for your wedding."

"You getting married too?" Kylen studied Hennah who averted her eyes. "Was it an arranged marriage?"

Aashi laughed. "We don't do arrange marriages anymore, at least not most Hindus. We do keep our weddings very traditional. Our ceremonies are quite festive. My sister and I are doing a double wedding."

"Both your grooms are very lucky. What careers are they in?"

"Mine just graduated like me. He will be a lawyer, and I am a statistician. And before you have a chance to say my job sounds boing, I will let you know it is very fascinating."

Hennah cut in, "You don't have a job yet." Trying to find a way to keep her sister from revealing more personal information, Hennah quickly finished the rest of her dessert.

Kylen turned to Hennah. "So what does your fiancé do?"

"Stuff." She gulped down the last of her coffee.

Aashi said. "He has an office job at Essence. Pays well enough, but not nearly as much as a lawyer. At least it's not dangerous. You know those quintessences. Many prefer jobs which require them leaping out of planes every day."

"A quintessence in the family. Does your parents approve of this?"

"We are not backwoods yokels. In fact, we are related to several famous quintessences who are held in high regard."

Hennah picked up her shopping bags. "I think we should investigate that sale before time runs out."

As the ladies stood, Kylen said, "I am delighted to have met you both." He looked Hennah in the eyes. "Enjoy your marriage."

She looked down at the table and picked up her cup and plate to toss away. "Perhaps we can talk again sometime."

"I would like that. I can often be found here, enjoying the open air."

Aashi and Hennah walked across the plaza and entered Lucy's. Hennah pretended to be interested in shoes, but only thought about the conversation with Kylen. She was no longer the final vestige of her subspecies. There were other profectus like her.

She wanted to ask Kylen many more questions, but her sister had shown up, revealing too much information. She had not planned to tell Kylen that she was engaged. He might want nothing more to do with her, yet at the end of the conversation he had hinted he could often be found in the shopping plaza. She needed to find a way to come back and see him alone.

Chapter Fifteen

Joseph greeted Hennah and Aashi in the lobby of their barracks. From the many packages they carried, he could tell their shopping had been successful. Aashi happily chatted about her favorite purchases, while Hennah silently stood, looking weary. Joseph reached out and took the bags Hennah held then he followed the sisters to their apartment.

As Aashi began retelling her shopping adventure to her mother, Joseph cut in, "Hennah and I are going out for dinner tonight."

"Oh, before you leave, Hennah and I discussed combining our weddings, if you don't mind."

Joseph looked into Hennah's eyes before saying, "Yes, that will be fine. You might already have a place planned, but I do suggest you check out Bellus Garden at the top of Richton Tower. Many weddings have been held there. The rosa vine tree can act as a natural mandap. It is the spot where both your ancestries Yashana and her daughter Yaira were married."

Aashi's interest was immediately peaked. "I would love to take a look, but I don't have clearance for the top levels of Richton."

"I will have that changed tomorrow. If you decide to hold the weddings there, I can get temporary passes for all your guests."

Joseph led Hennah to the parking lot. As Hennah fashioned her safety belt in the passenger seat, she said, "How do you know so much about Hindu customs? I have not talked much about them with you."

"I did research." He drove to Richton Tower and parked. "Before we eat, I would like to show you our new apartment."

"I thought we would be living in the barracks."

"No, I got us something a bit better." He gave a faint, mischievous smile.

They took an elevator up to the thirtieth floor and walked down several corridors. Joseph stopped in front of a door and waved his hand over a sensor to unlock it. They entered a small, cozy apartment furnished modestly. The living room and kitchen were combined. The one bedroom had a bed, large closet, and cabinet. As it was an inner apartment, there were no windows.

"It is not big, but it is already furnished." Joseph pointed towards the bathroom. "And you will not have to walk across half a building to take a shower."

Hennah toured the small living room, noticing the gray couch and the video screen on the wall. "You choose well. We can be at work in just a few minutes. Just an elevator away."

"I was not thinking about its closeness to work when I applied for it. I wanted you to have a real home."

"Living in a barracks is home to me." She walked over to Joseph and gave him a brief kiss on the cheek. "Thank you. It is nice."

He hid his disappointment at her lackluster response. They ate at the food court in the Grand Forum, mostly in silence. Joseph tried to draw her into a conversation, but her responses were short. Hennah did not want to return to her talkative sister, so they took a stroll on the beach.

The massive, protective walls of Essence ran into the ocean, cutting the beach off from the city of New Hope. On the institute's campus, a second, smaller wall ran parallel to the beach for nearly two miles, built several hundred yards from the water. The results was a private beach that employees and residents of Essence could enjoy.

Joseph held Hennah's hand as they passed heated volleyball competitions, swimmers frolicking in the water, and children playing in the sand. They walked north away from the popular areas, passing other couples, some with kids in tow. From piers squads of birthmates tried to outfish each other.

Several rocky capes stretched out into the ocean. They walked along a path that weaved between boulders on a cape. Eventually they settled on wet sand by a large boulder. Joseph sat behind Hennah and wrapped his arms around her, resting his chin on her shoulder as they watched the sun slowly set. Once darkness descended, he bit her, probing her mind.

Almost immediately he found that her private thoughts focused on a stranger she had met earlier today while shopping with her sister. Her emotions were of curiosity and excitement, something she had not felt in a long time. Concerned, Joseph played out the entire conversation in her memory. The more he saw, the more troubled he became. The Coalition had created profectus and one of them was now aware Hennah existed. Briefly he was upset with Hennah for revealing so much about herself to Kylen, but just as quickly he forgave her. She was not a trained spy. At least she had gleamed a lot of information herself.

What did bother Joseph was that she had told him nothing about Kylen. She was fascinated by the profectus and was scheming to meet him again, alone this time. That, Joseph could not allow.

He broke contact with her mind but still held her close to him. "Did you enjoy shopping with your sister?"

"She had fun."

"Meet any new friends?" Joseph felt her body tense.

"No. Just shopping."

"Your sister mentioned while you were putting away your things that you made a new acquaintance." Joseph lied, something he usually avoided doing.

Hennah shrugged. "Just a guy who chatted with me a bit while I was eating."

"What did you talk about?"

"Nothing much."

Joseph's arms tightened around her. "It can be dangerous talking with strangers."

"It's New Hope. You know, the city with the lowest crime rate in all the empire. Nothing happens to me here, ever."

"Still, you need to be cautious of what you say. I do not want you shopping again without me."

Henna pulled away and looked at him. "You're not jealous, now are you? You never acted like this before, and I have talked with other guys."

"You were not my fiancé then. And the other guys were not hitting on you. Also, you rarely say a word to others you do not know. You carried out a long conversation with this one."

"Kylen was not asking me out. In fact, we talked about you and my coming marriage." Hennah stood up and brushed sand off her pants.

Without another word, she marched down the path. Joseph walked beside her as they headed to the security gate to enter Essence, concerned that she was trying to hide from him that Kylen was a profectus. There should be trust between them, but instead there was deceit on both sides. He could tell her about his ability to read her mind, but he had planned to wait till their wedding night to share the experience.

After seeing her home, he sent messages to the Five, asking for a secret meeting immediately. Half an hour later they met in the abandoned section of the Fetus Department. Joseph waited for his brothers in the middle of the huge, poorly lit chamber, studying the rows of empty incubators which once grew his brethren. One of the glass canister may have been the one that protected him as a helpless fetus. Miles and other Shadow Guards held back in the darkness.

"This better be important," grumbled Jacob. "I was enjoying game night with my family. I had just reached the level Fearless Privateer and my craft was about to destroy a loaded merchant ship."

"This is more important than winning a board game," said Joseph.

Gabriel displayed a slight frown. "My new wife does not like me spending so much time working late. Could this not have waited till tomorrow?" He had been married less than a year to a human who worked in the Toddler Department.

"I did not want a record of this meeting, as I am not an official Five yet," said Joseph.

"As director, I would have appreciated an advance warning of a meeting." Caleb was the only one in the group with an older body. At one hundred eighty-seven, he would soon hit the Age of Decline when his body would rapidly age in just a few years.

Mason was the last to arrive with his wife Amaka. Shortly after his first marriage to her as Mablevi, Mason had begun bringing Amaka to many meetings held in the Chamber of Five, something even Layla had avoided. When his brothers had given him questioning looks, he had stated that it saved him time by not having to retell everything to her later.

"Alexander, why have you summoned us?" asked Caleb.

"Hennah met someone while shopping today. It would be best for me to give you the memory of her conversation and then we discuss it." One by one, he bit each brother and passed a small ziphema to them. He skipped Amaka, knowing she would read her husband's mind as he played out the memory.

Joseph waited patiently, giving them time to process the ziphema. "As you can see, the Coalition has decided to create another batch of profectus. This is quite serious."

"Are you wanting us to arrest scientists and teachers, like last time?" Caleb frowned slightly.

"That would make us hypocrites," said Mason, "as we have also broken the Purity Law."

"The profectus themselves are not the problem," said Joseph. "Do you remember what Senator Moyers said when we were investigating him? The Coalition's Great Plan implied a good deal more than creating profectus."

"Genocide," came Amaka's grim voice in the dimness. "They wish to wipe out the upper classes of the Ediethean. My own people feared that the Coalition would also turn against us, slaughtering our telepath class. The Coalition hates for any sentient species to have an advantage over them."

Joseph nodded. "If the Coalition has grown bold enough to have dozens of cloned profectus living in society, what else may they be doing? How far reaching are their plans?"

"We need to start an investigation immediately," said Gabriel. "We can start by probing Kylen's mind. He told us where to find him."

Jacob added, "I can arrange for security cameras in New Hope to start searching for profectus and track them."

"Most likely Kylen will know little about the bigger picture," said Joseph. "The profectus are pawns. We will need contacts higher up within the Coalition."

Mason said, "Amaka and I will head the investigation. I can pass among the humans better than any of you."

Caleb took a step forward. "Do not forget that a bill to cut our budget is soon to be voted on in the Galactic Senate. The Coalition and their allies are currently standing with us against the bill. If the Coalition becomes aware we are investigating them, they will turn against us. Losing their support can mean our extinction will not be far off."

Amaka's golden eyes reflected the dim emergency light coming from the ceiling. "What about the annihilation of my race or the edietheans? Will you allow the fear of your own deaths to blind you to the suffering of others? You may have to make a public stand against the Coalition or become the tool they will use to eradicate my people."

"We obey the government, whoever is in charge."

"What if it is evil?"

Caleb looked away from her probing eyes. "Hopefully it will not come to that."

"Do you have the courage to take a stand against evil if the cost is your own species?" Amaka continued to challenge the director, knowing his inner fears.

He looked back at her. "We will take one step at a time. Now we vote. Do we open an investigation into the Coalition?"

"It is agreed," spoke the other Fives in unison.

"On a lighter note," said Joseph, "I invite you all to my wedding in a month."

"How goes Hennah's work?" asked Gabriel.

"The same."

"We need a breakthrough," said Caleb. "Soon."

"I know. She is trying her best. If I push her too much she will break. After the wedding, she will become more focused again." Joseph hoped by finally revealing the secret of the epulo to Hennah, they could fight the depression together. With their minds connected, their souls joined, he could help her feel real emotions again.

"My daughter worries about her," said Jacob, "though she does see you as a good influence. Yet secretly you can be blamed as a bad influence."

"I am seeking ways to lighten the pressure Hennah feels."

Mason said, "You have not done enough. Hennah is one of my descendants, and I take it very personal that you pushed her to attempt suicide."

"And I have tried to make amends for that."

Amaka said, "Have you considered adding more researchers to the project?"

"None would have her talents for coding DNA. Layla and Yashana did much of their work alone."

"The burden you have placed on Hennah is too big for her to bear alone. Having someone with whom you can discuss problems with can be helpful."

126

"She can talk with me."

Mason said, "That has not solved anything so far."

"I will consider your advice." Joseph turned and walked down the aisle, Miles following a few feet behind.

Chapter Sixteen

Hennah kept her eyes closed as she listened to Aashi grabbing clothing from their closet then leave to take a shower. She hoped there would be a long line and it would take a while before Aashi returned. For a few minutes Hennah listened to the gentle hum of cool air blowing through a vent in the ceiling. *Peace, that is all I want.*

She peeked over the railing of her bed, looking down at the room she had shared with Aashi her whole life. Small, semi-messy, cluttered with childhood toys and mementos from adolescence. Posters on walls, shelves holding figures from popular movies, board games stacked in a bin. Everything changed today. Both of them were marrying and leaving behind the home of their youth forever.

"Hennah. Dhruvi. Time to get ready. My sisters will be here soon," called Pallavi's cheerful voice beyond the bedroom door.

"I'm getting up," said Hennah, but she continued to lay in bed.

She studied the henna patterns of flowers and abstract swirls tattooed on her hands. Two days ago she had to endured hours sitting still while the temporary tattoos were applied. Her cousins and aunts jested as they got their own tattoos. Hennah choose modest patterns, but Aashi had went all out. It took six hours to finish the tattoos which covered her entire hands and lower arms.

"Are you up, Hennah?" came Pallavi's voice again.

"Yes, Mom." The teenager flipped over her hand and examined her wrist. The henna covered up the thin scar. *You can do this. Just this final day to endure. Keep being the happy bride everyone expects.* When she had first told her parents about the engagement, they had been excited, seeing it as marking the end of her illness. They believed Jacob would make a fine husband for her as he was attentive and caring.

The door opened, and Pallavi peeked in. "You are still in bed. There is much which needs to be done. You have not even gotten a shower yet."

Hennah sat up. "I'm up this time." She climbed down the ladder and began pulling out clothes she would wear for a few hours before changing into her wedding dress. Then she walked down several hallways to the showers. There was a line of women waiting, but when they saw Hennah, they insisted she go first as it was her wedding day.

By the time Hennah made it back to the apartment, it was full of excited relatives. They lavished attention on her and Aashi, giving marital advice and making jokes at their expense. Hennah smiled and even sometimes laughed, but it was fake.

She wanted to be happy, to feel the joy that lit up Aashi's face. Instead, she felt nothing but apathy and weariness. It was like she was in a cave looking through a veil at happy people going about their normal lives while she was cut off from love, joy, and bliss. She could see the bright world around her but she was trapped in darkness that held her bound, devoid of strong emotions. Guilt she knew—and despair. *Why can I not feel one positive emotion on my own wedding day? Joseph is a good man. I should love him. Why can I not?*

Kylen's image popped in her mind. She had tried for weeks to find a way back to the shopping plaza but always her plans were blocked, usually by Joseph. Sometimes she was angry at him, but the emotion was too strong for her to hold on to for long. Instead, it was replaced with despair. All her life, even before she knew she was a profectus, she had desired to be around others like herself, geniuses who could talk freely without having to hide their intellect to fit in. Her greatest desire and deepest disappointment was not being allowed to attend Luncaster University. And now she had met another profectus. She wanted to ask him so much, to connect with others he had mentioned. She fantasized being in a room full of her kind. What wonderful conversations they would have. Jokes too lofty for others to understand. Truly she would feel happiness then.

How could Joseph understand the need to be around your own kind? He had always been surrounded by quintessences while I have had no equals. Chandresh was the closest I knew and now he is dead.

"Hennah, your henna looks cool," said Dhruvi with a grin while munching on a pastry.

"That is for the wedding reception," fussed his mother.

"It's time to go," called out Kaushal. "Everyone grab a bag."

Loaded with packages, food, and clothing, the large family took three vehicles to Richton Tower. Then they rode a private elevator up to the top floor. Firestrike had volunteered her penthouse for the family to prepare for the wedding. The brides were surrounded by women pampering them, applying makeup, and adjusting clothing. Hennah felt smothered by all the attention and just wanted it to end. Aashi radiated with happiness and excitement.

Darkfern whispered to Hennah, "Are you sure you would not prefer our way? Knife in hand, just you and your want-to-be-mate?"

"Too violent for me."

"You're missing out."

Finally the brides were escorted by family down the hallway to Bellus Garden. Both sisters wore red saree dresses which wrapped around their waist and draped over a shoulder. From their arms and ankles clinked bangles. Veils covered their hair.

In the central area of the huge garden was a plaza large enough to seat the two hundred guests dressed in bright, festive outfits. The brides walked down the aisle to the rosa tree. Its dangling red vines had been gently pulled back and tied to form a mandap canopy. A temporary raised platform had been set up under the tree. On it sat the two grooms dressed in embroidered sherwanis, long red scarfs, and safa turbans on their heads. A firepot was in the middle of the platform.

The brides sat beside their fiancés as a priest presided over the ceremony. Hennah felt Joseph's warm hand squeeze hers. Hennah gave him a brief smile then turned her attention to the service.

Aashi was the first to walk around the fire with her husband as the priest read the seven sacred vows. Then came Hennah's turn. Seeing two hundred guests looking at her as she rose sent a wave of anxiety through her. Everyone expected her to be a jubilant bride, but she was a pretender.

Joseph sensed her fear and squeezed her hand. In a low voice, he said, "We will come through this together, beloved."

She held his hand tightly as Pallavi tied the corner of Hennah's dress to Joseph's scarf. Then the couple slowly walked around the firepot as the priest read. Hennah bowed to Joseph as he applied red power to the parting of her hair, marking her as his wife. Then he placed a beaded necklace around her neck from which dangled three touching circles.

The guests moved to a dining room adjacent to the garden which was used for social engagements. The dancing and music lasted for hours. Aashi twirled around the dance floor with her groom, looking like she belonged in a musical. Hennah danced twice when she was prompted, but most of the time, she just sat quietly by Joseph, briefly chatting to well-wishers who came to congratulate her.

Eventually Joseph and Hennah left, though the party continued. They took an elevator down twenty floors and walked to their apartment where they changed into normal clothes. Joseph carried their luggage as they took another elevator down to the bottom floor of Richton Tower. Soon Joseph was zipping through traffic as Hennah silently watched the landscape zoom pass. Their destination was a fancy resort hotel several hours away. Aashi and her groom had selected a different resort further south.

Once they were on the open highway, Joseph increased his speed. "You make a beautiful bride."

"Thanks."

"How about me?"

"You don't make a beautiful bride."

"I'm glad to hear you joke." Joseph glanced at her, seeing the tiredness in her eyes. "Sleep if you like. It will be a long drive."

It seemed to Hennah that she had barely closed her eyes when they pulled into a parking lot at the resort. A bellhop carried their luggage to their honeymoon suite which had rose petals on the bed and a hot tub in the bathroom. The digital walls in the living room and bedroom rotated ocean scenes. A balcony with exotic flowering plants looked out over the nearby beach.

"This is fancier than even Darkfern's penthouse."

"I'm glad you like it." He wrapped his arms around her, holding her close. After a few minutes, he said, "You are exhausted. How about we sleep now?"

If Hennah had normal emotions, she would have felt nervous, but she only felt fatigue. She opened her suitcase and pulled out a nightgown, ignoring lingerie that an aunt or cousin had snuck into her luggage. She changed in the bathroom. Then she lay beside Joseph, falling asleep almost immediately.

She awoke near noon but continue to lie in bed, reluctant to get up. In the living room she could hear Joseph watching a movie. Remorse stabbed at her that she was not behaving as a proper bride. *At least I was honest with him. He knows I am depressed.* Still, guilt clung to her as she lectured herself for not being a good enough daughter, scientist, and wife. *You must do better.*

"Ready for lunch?" Joseph stood in the doorway, watching her.

She yawned, pretending to have just woken. After changing into brown slacks and a black blouse, she followed him downstairs to a fancy restaurant.

"They have a well stock fitness center where I worked out this morning," said Joseph, eating a lamb kebab. "There are five pools of different shapes, a spa, salon, ball courts, and numerous shops. What would you like to do?"

"Um, whatever you want to do." Hennah focused on her pasta salad.

"Our honeymoon is not about just me. I want you to have a good time. You decide what we do this afternoon."

"I guess just walk around and explore. See what's here."

They wandered around the resort, visiting stores and snacking on treats from vendors. Joseph took an interest in watching a volleyball match and performers doing waterskiing tricks. *He would have more fun if he was here with his brothers instead of me.* Trying to find something Joseph would like, Hennah suggested they take a boat tour around the bay. As night fell, they ate at another five-star restaurant.

They finally headed back to their room. Hennah was ready to sleep again, but as she exited the bathroom dressed in her nightgown, Joseph stepped behind her and wrapped his arms around her waist.

"There is something I have long wanted to share with you," he said as he brushed her hair away from her neck.

"Alright." Hennah braced herself, certain it was time for her to perform the expected duty of a wife.

She felt a brief prick of pain then found herself standing on a beach with a high wall in the distance. She recognized the volleyball nets and piers. She looked around in confusion. Joseph stood several feet away instead of behind her.

"How did we get back to Essence? Why are there no people here?"

"We are not at Essence. This is a memory. We are still in the hotel room. The epulo allows us quintessences to see into the minds of others. This is a secret we guard very closely, only sharing with our lovers."

"A memory?" Hennah looked around. She could smell the salty sea breeze, feel the cool air blowing her hair. "This feels real."

"We are in my memory of a real beach that we have both visited. I can show you many other places but I thought it best to start with a location you like. I have more to share with you."

Suddenly Hennah felt an emotion surge through her. It was of warmth, companionship, and protectiveness. She gasped, shocked at its intensity.

Joseph smiled broadly. "These are my emotions. Your depression has robbed you of real feelings for too long. My gift to you is to feel again, at least while we are connected."

Emotions wrapped around her like a cozy blanket, then rushed through her soul. She felt happiness, joy, peace, laughter. As the emotions changed, so did images around her. Joseph shared potent times in his life, delight in meeting his brothers again after the long separation, the thrill of getting his citizenship badge, the euphoria of being in love with her.

After showering her with a whirlwind of his emotions, he switched to her memories, reminding her of happy times with family and friends. He pulled from her own memories she had forgotten of laughter with Dhruvi as she played games, singing silly songs with her father, playing hide and seek with Aashi, learning to cook with her mother, listening to Chandresh share stories of family history, joking with Darkfern.

"You have lived a good life, Hennah. This depression has stolen the joy of life from you. You are loved by many, including me." He sent tender, caring emotions to her.

She drank in the emotions, wishing they would never end. "I want to love back, but I don't know how."

"Guilt controls your thoughts too much. We all make mistakes. You need to learn to forgive yourself when you mess up. Love yourself, Hennah. Know my love for you."

Strong, warm emotions filled her, washing away all else. She basked in it, relishing the sensations of being cared for. Guilt, low self-worth, and despair were all scrubbed away.

Joseph broke contact with her mind and held her. She trembled in his arms, overwhelmed by what she felt. Tears flowed down her cheeks. He gently brushed them away.

"The emotions I have shown you are temporary. They will fade, but I believe over time, you will begin to experience your own emotions again. One method of fighting depression is when guilt comes, try to replace it with positive thoughts."

"That's easier said than done." Hennah turned in his arms and looked into his eyes. He had given up his brothers for her, turned down an exciting job to be a desk clerk. "You are a good man, Joseph. I don't deserve you."

"It is I who does not deserve you. I want to honor the trust you have given me. To make you happy." Gently he traced henna patterns on her hand.

"Do you see my name?" she asked, wondering if he knew the custom that a marriage could not be consummated until the groom found both their names hidden in the tattoos.

"Yours is here." His finger traced over her name hidden in the swirls of petals. He searched her other hand, finding his name worked into an abstract pattern. "I am here."

She held his hands for a moment, remembering the feeling of love he had shared with her. "There was one emotion you did not show me. Passion."

"I can wait patiently until it is real for you."

"I'm willing to try now, if you wish."

Determined to be the wife he deserved, she kissed him on the lips. He pressed back, wrapping his arms around her body. As their kissing became more intense, Joseph paused long enough to tell the auto lights to turn off.

Chapter Seventeen

Bubbles rose in a beaker as its liquid began to boil. A sea laven moved his head closer to the flames, turning up the temperature of the burner with his webbed hand.

"You're going to burn it again," complained his wife. Lark'ukva was a lighter shade of purple than her husband. She wore a Tiara of Joining over the ridgelines of her head.

"Not this time. Are you recording the temperature?" The ridgelines on Fran'ukva head were twice the height of his wife's.

"Of course. It's too hot, just like I predicted. If you mess this one up, you're washing up the mess this time."

Hennah glanced from her monitor she had synced with her e-tablet. Following Joseph's suggestion, she had selected two researchers to aid her on Project Absurd. After reading through the list of qualified employees, she had decided on a married couple who would not suffer the feeling of isolation she dealt with. They could freely talk with each other without having to hide the purpose of their work.

When asked to join the classified project, Lark'ukva and Fran'ukva had been excited, honored to be selected. They came eager to explore new ideas. At first, Hennah had shot down many of their concepts because she had already attempted them. They pointed out that maybe she had missed something the first time. After she gave them access to all her files, she decided to allow them to do things their way, even though they were retracing her older research.

It was pleasant having the sea lavens in the lab. The couple was cheerful, having not become jaded by six years of failures like Hennah. Barely married a year, they often flirted as they worked. At least Hennah now had others she could talk with who understood her lingo and she could discuss new ideas with them.

Hennah glanced up at Joseph's office where he worked on marriage licenses. She wondered if he had certified his own. Would that be legal? Probably not.

"That's it! Another experiment ruined," said Lark'ukva. "You are not only washing all the dishes, but you will mop the floors at home."

"We have a bot that takes care of the floors. We could buy an android to handle the dishes too. That will leave time for other things." Fran'ukva bushed his hand against his wife's arm.

"We can't afford another one of your bots right now." Lark'ukva pretended to be irritated, but she moved closer to her husband as he poured the vile liquid down a sink.

Hennah felt a pang of guilt that she did not flirt with Joseph like the sea lavens did with each other. She went about her job, only occasionally speaking to him when he came out of his office, just like the days before their marriage. Recognizing the feeling of guilt, she forced herself to think of something positive instead. *At least I'm not distracted this way.*

Joseph had been coaching her to change her thought patterns. It was still bizarre having a husband that could peek into her mind whenever he wished. When she had learned he had been doing so for years then erasing her memory of it, she had become upset, refusing to speak to him for two days. Still, she liked being able to feel his emotions. They had both hoped that doing so would pull her out of the deep depression which plagued her.

During their honeymoon she had begun to almost feel like a normal person, but once back at Essence, Joseph soon realized Hennah was relying on him for feelings and still could mustered few on her own. Not wanting her to become reliant on him, he limited the sharing to only a few times a week. She had been content for a while, but as weeks went by, she began to fight bleakness from the daily grind of failures in the lab. Hennah was drained from the frustration of knowing the Five were counting of her but her best efforts were always fruitless.

As the workday drew near its end, Joseph climbed down the steps and helped clean up the lab. After the sea lavens left, Hennah flipped off the lights, and they headed down the hallway.

"We are to attend a meeting in the Synod Chamber now."

"Why?" Hennah looked at Joseph in puzzlement. "When did you find out?"

"Earlier today, but I did not want to bother you while working."

"So I would not be distracted from my vital research," she said in annoyance. "I'm not properly dressed. We need to stop by our apartment."

"We are to come immediately." He glanced at her slacks and pink blouse. "You look fine."

"Not for a formal meeting. I have no make-up on."

"You rarely wear make-up. You are beautiful, Hennah, as you are."

She gave him a scowl but followed him. They took an elevator up to the fortieth floor then headed towards the large ornamental double doors where Shadow Guards served as sentinels.

As they enter the huge, oval chamber, Hennah glanced around in curiosity. Arena style seating was along all the walls, leaving a large open area in the middle. A section was marked off for visitors, another for department heads. The rest was reserved for the fifty members of the Synod, their aides, and the Five. It was Hennah's first time visiting. *Why did they ask for me? To reprimand me for not completing Project Absurd? But they would not do so publicly.* Every seat was filled, including the visitors section, except for a spot by Desmond. Camera drones zoomed about the room, controlled by several workers from the Publicity Department. Whatever was going on was important.

Joseph stood near the door and waited. Hennah glanced towards the visitors' section for a seat, but none were available. *We should have left work early so I could change and we could have gotten a seat,* she thought, annoyed again with her husband for not telling her earlier.

The Five were seated high up, directly across from the main door. The director stood and the room fell silent as every eye turned to him.

"It is time for us to select a replacement for the open position of Five." He glanced towards the empty seat beside Desmond. "The responsibilities are arduous. A Five must place the wellbeing of all quintessences above himself, sacrificing much."

He sat down and Skyler stood. "After looking over the many candidates, we have selected one which has repeatedly put others before himself, even when doing so endangered his life."

Tobias rose up. "We, the Five, nominate former Lieutenant Joseph to the position of Five."

Shocked, Hennah glanced at her husband. He kept a blank face, not looking towards her, only staring at the speaker. *He knew this was coming yet did not tell me.*

"He refused to allow young quintessences from another squad to be slaughter after they had surrendered in battle, knowing such an action could possibly result in his own death. For eighteen years he served out his sentence as a desk clerk, while at the same time, learning much about the operations of Essence Institute."

Desmond replaced Tobias. "Does anyone have cause to deny Joseph this position? Once voted into this office, a Five cannot be removed accept by death." He slowly looked around the room at the many gathered.

Hennah glanced at the somber faces of the quintessences. Some looked at her husband while others watched Desmond. In the department head section, Janet flashed a smile at Hennah. No one spoke.

"For the record, none have spoken against Joseph." Desmond sat down.

The director stood again. "The members of the Synod shall now vote. Shall Joseph become a Five?"

Fifty-three voices said in unison, "It is agreed."

"Joseph, step forward."

Hennah watched her husband move to the center of the room. Despite her depression, she felt jittery. Joseph now held the second most powerful position at Essence.

"As a Five, do you accept the heavy responsibilities of this office?"

"I do. I will endeavor to always place the welfare of my brethren above myself. I will live an exemplary life, avoiding vices, protecting the weak. I will uphold our entire Code as I perform my duties."

"We accept your oath. Be received by us."

The audience begin to rise and walk down the steps to the floor to greet Joseph. He beckoned Hennah to his side. Feeling surreal, she gave formal greetings to the top leaders of Essence. Having no greeting gestures in their culture, the quintessences stood stiffly, saying quick congratulation before moving on. Other species' greetings were widely varied. Humans shook Hennah's hand, though one kissed both her cheeks. Sundancers formed a large circle with their fingers which Hennah touched with her forehead. When unfamiliar with a culture, she watched Joseph for clues. He never once missed giving a proper salutation.

Firestrike, wearing a red security uniform, held her four fists up forming a V shape. "Proud to have you, Hennah, as one of us. If you need help with anything, let me know. The duties as a wife of a Five can be taxing at times."

Hennah copied the gesture the best she could with two fists. "Thanks. I will." The strangeness of everything overwhelmed her. Firestrike was her best friend's mom who she had always looked up to. Now she was suddenly her social equal.

Amaka and Tobias greeted Hennah. Though of different species, both looked similar. They dressed in neutral, matching colors. Amaka's thick hair was braided with gold ringlets worked into the design. After his marriage, Tobias had grown his hair out into dreadlocks.

"You are part of our family." Tobias' eyes were intense. "If Joseph gives you any trouble, let me know."

"Uh, okay." Hennah glanced at her husband who was shaking hands with Skyler's wife.

Amaka held her palms out flat. Not sure what to do, Hennah placed her hands on top. Amaka smiled and gave the teenager's hands a friendly squeeze. "You have never really been alone. Always there have been others looking out for you. Now you are moving into a position where you can look out for others. Trust your husband, forgiving his faults. He has suffered far greater than you know."

Hennah felt uncomfortable being so close to a telepath. "I will remember."

She was relieved when the last person went by. As Joseph and Hennah left the Synod Chamber, a Shadow Guard fell in step behind them, following them to the elevator. At they stepped inside, the guard came too. Hennah glanced uneasily at Miles, vaguely recalling he had served Alec.

"Is he following us?" she whispered to Joseph.

"Yes, the Five always have Shadow Guards." He touched the button for the top floor.

"But we're inside Essence. No one is going to try to assassinate you here."

"It is a requirement for Fives to be accompanied by Shadow Guards their whole lives."

Uncomfortable, Hennah glanced back at Miles whose face revealed no emotions. She had seen guards around Desmond and Alec, but she took them for granted. It was eerie for one to be following her.

The doors slid open, revealing a large, airy hallway. Only then did Hennah realize that Joseph had led her to a private elevator that reached the top floor of Richton Tower.

"Why are we here?"

"To see our new home."

One end of the hallway led to the magnificent Bellus Garden enclosed with a glass dome. Joseph turned the other direction, soon stopping in front of embellished doors of a penthouse. He waved his hand over a sensor to unlock the door, and they stepped in. Miles took up post outside the apartment.

The lofty living room's ceiling had embellished borders. A wall of windows looked out onto a balcony where vines twisted around the railing. The furniture had dark gray upholstery. Black shelves held relics from various cultures. Green houseplants grew in decorative pots. The floor was thickly carpeted. Doors led off to three bedrooms, an elegant dining room, and a large modernized kitchen.

Hennah stood by a couch, looking around without speaking, her mind reeling from the suddenness of it all.

"Would you like a tour?" asked Joseph.

"Why? It's just like Darkfern's." She had visited her friend's home many times over the years, envious of the two bathrooms the family did not have to share with an entire barracks.

"The furniture is different, which we can change to suit your taste."

"You have been in here before." Accusation was in Hennah's voice.

"Yes," Joseph's face hid all emotion. "Why are you upset?"

"Because you knew you were going to be promoted to a Five and hid it from me. How long did you know?"

"For a while."

"How long is a while?"

"Alec told me in person that he had selected me as his successor."

138

"We have been married over two months, and you never once spoke a word about this."

"It was classified. Until I was officially appointed, I could not speak of it to anyone, including you."

Hennah turned away from him, walking into the hallway to the nearest door. It led to the master bedroom with a king-size bed. Not wanting to explore that room, she moved to the next one. It was a study. Shelves were cluttered with antique books, figurines, and awards. A large computerized desk sat against a wall. Attached to it was a huge, flat screen. A tall jewelry box and full length mirror took up one corner of the room. Beside them was a table with makeup and a brush.

"This room was used by a woman," said Hennah. "I don't understand. I thought Alec lived here. He never married. Why would he have a hairbrush?"

"These are the belongings of Yashana. This room has been preserved as a memorial to her and Layla who lived here before her."

Intrigued, Hennah picked up the hairbrush which still contained a few strands of gray hair. *This belong to my ancestor. Well, my clone also. I am standing where Yashana once dressed for work.*

"This is your study now," said Joseph, carefully watching her.

Still annoyed at him, she pretended not to care. "This stuff is old. Most of it will have to be thrown away." She put the brush down and walked over to a shelf containing trophies and plaques. Inscribed on some was Yashana Kalkar, on others Layla Rangan. "My dad would appreciate them, as Yashana is our ancestor." She picked up the heavy gold Zelzer Award, studying its polished surface. "Oh, this is Layla's. The awards can be donated to the museum downstairs. They are being wasted here. The rest can be thrown away."

"Wasted? These artifacts were considered valuable by the previous occupants." There was an intensity in Joseph's voice which puzzled Hennah.

"I'm surprised nothing is dusty, despite this stuff is hundreds of years old."

"A housekeeper comes regularly to dust and water plants. Also, there are cleaning bots for the floor."

Hennah moved over to the old desk. As she swept her hand across its smooth surface, it came to life. Words and icons appeared on the screen as an outline of a flat keyboard materialized on the desk. "This still works?" She tried navigating through a few programs. The computer responded sluggishly, taking a long time to load. "Well, barely works. We can throw this away too."

"Perhaps not yet." Joseph's voice was tense. "This computer has not worked for centuries. I thought it was broken, but it woke for you."

"Voice or face recognize. Why would the other Fives leave a broken computer in here anyways? Surely at least one of them had a wife who would not want all this junk lying around."

"Neither Alec nor Ace married. Before them was Ariyo who was married to your great grandmother. This computer has the personal files of both Layla and Yashana."

"There are a lot of *greats* before grandmother." Hennah slowly scrolled down a list of files. "I don't even recognize most of these file formats." She randomly opened a few which displayed family pictures. "These are so old that I don't know if my e-tablet can open them."

Joseph moved to her side and touched a file which opened to show a DNA pattern from a quintessence. "Her research is on this computer."

"I already have access to her work which is on the server."

"There may be material here that she did not download to the mainframe. I will have a technician make a copy of everything, then have the computer trashed. We will get you a newer model."

"I would appreciate that." Hennah studied the DNA of a C7 model. "Perhaps I can do my planning here, like her. Then copy my work to the computers in the lab."

"As long as we keep your computer off the network. None of your work can appear on the server."

Hennah imaged what it was like being Yashana, sitting at this same computer working. Did her husband stand beside her as Joseph did this very moment? Did he keep secrets from her or would he have told his wife he was becoming a Five. Again Hennah felt annoyed at Joseph, him probing into her mind, seeing her secrets yet keeping things from her. She thought of Kylen, how Joseph had kept blocking her from visiting the outdoor mall. With a jolt, she realized he had known all the time that Kylen was a profectus.

She stood up and walked to the doorway. Joseph's eyes followed her. "I want to see Kylen again."

"What? No. Why would you wish to see him?"

"You knew this whole time he was a profectus. Surely with all your memory thieving, you know how much I have desired to be among my kind. Kylen knows where other profectus are."

"Kylen is part of the Coalition. He is dangerous."

"So are you but I married you anyway. I could be a spy, getting information about the Coalition for you."

"We already know everything he knows. His mind was probed weeks ago without his knowledge."

"And you knew this? Why would the Five tell you that?" Hennah studied her husband. "Have you really been working on marriage certificates in your office?"

Giving himself time to think, Joseph walked into the living room and sat on a sofa. "Most of the time. But I was also in training for this job."

"What did you learn about Kylen? Where are the others at?"

"Scattered. Living hidden in main society while working normal jobs."

"I want to see him again. Meet the others. Find out what their lives are like." Hennah walked into the living room, standing near a second couch.

"I said no. The Coalition is too dangerous."

"But…"

"That is an order." The sternness in Joseph's voice meant the topic was closed for discussion.

"Order?" Anger flashed in Hennah's eyes. "I am your wife. You don't order me around."

"I am also a Five with more authority than you."

"You have barely been a Five for an hour. Marriage is supposed to be about cooperation. That is how it worked for my parents and their parents. You don't order your wife around."

"Depends on the culture."

"Argh!" Hennah grabbed a cushion from the couch and tossed it at his head. He did not try to dodge as it hit. "I am tired of you keeping secrets from me."

"You kept secrets from me."

"I *tried* to keep them from you but obviously failed. You know everything about me but tell me little about yourself. Modifying memories, distorting emotions, spying on me for years. Running off to tell Alec everything I was doing. Did he order you to date me? Did I even choose to marry you or is that something you implanted in my mind?"

Joseph reminded sitting on the couch, face stoic, saying nothing.

"Well? Are you going to answer me?"

"Are you finished with your rant?"

"No. Yes. I don't know. I'm sure you love being married to someone depressed. I can't stay angry at you long even when I want to." She slowly settled on the second couch far away from him.

"Alec never ordered me to date you. I did so because I love you. The only memories I have erased from your mind was of me biting you before our marriage. I have never manipulated your personal thoughts or memories in any other fashion. As for your emotions, you have always been aware of when I was sharing mine with you while briefly turning off your own gloomy ones. You freely choose to marry me. I would never, ever alter your memories to force you along a path you did not

141

choose by free will. If I had done so, it would had been quickly spotted by the Shadow Guards who have been keeping close watch on me since Alec's death. They take candidacy for the Five very seriously. If I was found guilty of such a crime, I would have been executed. As for keeping secrets from you, that comes with my job. I have access to classified information which I cannot share with you nor do you need to know. That is my burden to bear, not yours. Your weight is heavy enough without more problems being added. Does this answer your questions?" He stared at her, eyes piercing.

"Yes, I guess." Doubt was in her voice. "Still, you can't order me around, not the way Alec did. I know you're my supervisor, but I'm also your wife."

Joseph sighed and briefly closed his eyes. He then walked over and sat beside her. "Hennah, I am sorry that I come off harshly at times. I have always been a soldier. I am used to giving orders but also obeying orders, even when I disagree with them. I was expected to obey instantly without an explanation being given to me." He reached out and took her hand. "I promise to be more open with your when I can. You need to understand that there are members of the Coalition who are murderers and are using the profectus as pawns. Kylen is aware of this and hides your identity from them, just as you tried to hide him from me. He believes his activities are monitored by the Coalition. You meeting with him or any other profectus could endanger your life."

"Why could you not have told me this instead of giving me an order?"

"Because I think too much like a soldier sometimes." He gave her a brief smile. "Do you forgive me?"

"I'm thinking about it."

"I got you a penthouse to live in. Your best friend lives right next door, and you will be seeing each other more often. I was given a substantial budget for you to buy new furnishings. Anything you don't want we will get rid of. Your idea of donating awards to the museum is a good one. It is time to let them go."

Hennah glanced around the room, looking at the shelves laden with relics from numerous cultures. "Those can go to the museum too."

"Some can. A few I would like to put in my office."

"You will finally decorate your office?"

"I have a new office—Alec's old one."

"You won't be watching me in the lab anymore?"

"I will come visit, but you have the sea leavens for company. Besides, it's not like I was helping you with your research. You don't need me there."

"You trust me? That I won't go crazy again? No more guarding?"

"I trust you, Patni." He used the Hindu word for wife. "It's me who will have guards, whether I like it or not."

Chapter Eighteen

Shoppers wandered about the outdoor mall, many with packages in hand. A few wealthy ones had androids following them, holding items. Kylen sat at a table at the edge of the central plaza. His seat offered a view of all the tables where shoppers rested or ate. He came several times a week when the weather was good, enjoying working on his e-tablet in the bright sunshine. The tasks for his job were easy enough to complete, leaving him a lot of time to experiment with his own programs.

Today he observed the patterns of shoppers, wondering about the coding needed for a program which could predict where a shopper would go then advertise specifically for that individual. Most likely such software already existed, but he was certain he could write a better algorithm.

After living too long in a bunker, Kylen was fascinated by the behaviors of others, especially nonhumans. The patrons ranged widely in species, and many stores customized their stock to attract certain clientele. A helmeted squamiger oozed out of a shop which sold fish in large aquariums. A human might think the building was a pet shop, but Kylen knew the live fish swimming in a container the squamiger carried in its tentacles was its dinner.

A human with dark hair walking by caught Kylen's attention. He briefly thought it might be Hennah, but when she turned a corner, her face was different. It had been over two months since he had meet her, but he still searched for her, intrigued that she was a profectus who had grown up outside of the Coalition's influence.

The clues she left him were tantalizing. She said the quintessences were her masters, herself a slave, yet she claimed to be well-treated, growing up with a human family who did not know she was a clone. The sister had revealed enough information that Kylen was able to find Aashi on several popular social media sites, allowing him to see family pictures and learn names of relatives. Hennah had avoided the camera most of the time, but her sister had posted wedding photos of them together.

The mystery began to obsess Kylen almost as much as his desire to hack into Essence Institute. He had increased studying its security systems, but it was well protected by many levels of safeguards, some most likely designed by Ethan long ago. Sometimes Kylen wanted to force himself in. He might actually succeed for a few minutes, but he would be quickly detected and the leeches sent to hunt him down. He avoided them whenever possible, yet he saw them often walking around

New Hope. They usually traveled in groups with birthmates or with spouses, sometimes with children in tow. Rarely was one alone.

Kylen pondered why the quintessences had cloned Layla. From clues in that one conversation, he suspected that Hennah's marriage was arranged without the sister's knowledge. Hennah had avoided looking at him whenever the wedding was mentioned. Still, the leeches would not go through the trouble of cloning her just for marriage. There would be a far more vital purpose. Most likely it related to creating a new prototype that the leeches wished to keep secret.

A man carrying a plate of food sat down at Kylen's table. He was in his early fifties, a bit heavyset. "Been a while." The man began eating a burger.

"Hello, Doctor Kent." Kylen was instantly alert but acted calm as if it was a planned meeting. He had not seen the researcher since leaving the bunker nearly two years ago and had no desire to see him now. "Enjoying your visit to Xi'an?"

"It's been enlightening, this close to the death drinkers. You picked a strange place to live."

"I was following orders."

"Yet you only gave us one choice when we were giving out assignments. I have wondered why this place was so special to you."

Kylen shrugged. "One of my clones did design this city."

"True. Out of all of Generation Three, you have offered the most promise. I personally asked to be the one to bring you the news of your coming wedding."

"So it has been decided?" Kylen had presumed it would be Amy as they spent a lot of time together, yet he had hoped it would be another. Having grown up with Amy, she was more like a sister to him. To marry her would be awkward, at least at first. Still, he would do as the Coalition asked.

"Yes. Her name is Abarrane."

Kylen was puzzled. "Never heard of her. She is not from Generation Three."

The doctor smirked. "Abarrane Basanti."

"She is royalty?" Kylen's heartbeat quickened. Vaguely he remembered seeing a blonde girl in a few newsfeeds, but he never had paid much attention.

"Her father is Emperor Duyagni. Surely you have heard of him. Years ago he personally asked us to make a suitable husband for his only child who carries the profectus gene. His wife had been part of a closely guarded genetic linage that has occasionally spawned natural profectus, but never could we get two alive at the same time to produce more purebreds."

"So I'm to be your stud to sire a royal profectus."

"Exactly. You will be given a month to put your affairs in order here then you will fly to the capitol city for training in etiquettes and given a suitable job which will earn you an award to create some buzz about you in the local media. Then you will

144

meet your fiancé at a party. After a number of suitable social outings, the Emperor will announce your engagement."

"You have my entire life planned out." Kylen's mouth went dry.

"We have placed high hopes in you from the day you were born. You are even-tempered, sociable, and well-liked by both your caregivers and your foster family. When under pressure, you don't panic, quickly adapt, and find solutions overlooked by others. You will make a fine leader."

"I am a computer programmer, not a politician."

"You are the clone of Richard Cambridge, who I will remind you, was the beloved mayor of this city for thirty years, besides being its designer. He was also well-known for being a philanthropist who helped many charities. We will groom you in developing your political skills."

"You have left me no challenge by following this golden path."

"Oh, it will be challenging. Believe me, politics can be brutal." Kent finished the last bite of his burger. "Kylen, we are going to make you the most powerful man in the galaxy. As Abarrane is Emperor Duyagni's only child, guess who will be in line for the throne next? As you know, females cannot hold that position."

Kylen tried to look pleased. "I will endeavor to live up to this honor you have bestowed on me."

The doctor stood. "I know you will, son. You will be contacted with final arrangements in a month. Give your job proper notice that you are leaving for a new employer. You may share this news with Amy if you wish." Kent walked away, soon disappearing in a crowd of shoppers.

Kylen remained seated, pondering the implications. *A month of freedom is all that remains to me. One month to hack into Essence. Hennah was right in saying we are slaves to the Coalition. If I refuse to go along with them, they might kill me.* He did not know that for certain. Perhaps they would select another and leave him alone, but he doubted that. They had gone through a lot of effort to create and train him. He was their prize they wished to flaunt in front of the whole galaxy.

Packing up his e-tablet, Kylen headed home. On the bus ride, he wondered if he should be pleased or upset with the high position the Coalition had planned for him. Part of him had always wanted to brag to the universe of his greatness, but he wanted that on his own terms, doing something so big it dwarfed the achievements of his clones. Becoming emperor would definitely outshine the others, but it was being handed to him on a golden platter. All he had to do was follow along. The victory felt hollow, like cheating. And there would be a cost. The Coalition would expect him to support their agenda, passing their laws. He would be their lapdog.

He had barely entered his apartment before Amy walked in unannounced and went to his refrigerator. She pulled out ice cream and began scooping it into a bowl. "Want some?"

"Sure." He watched her put cream and nuts on his sundae, skipping the cherries that had she put on hers. It would have been a pleasant life married to her. They knew each other well.

As they ate, Amy chatted about the latest news she had heard. Unlike Kylen, she kept in regular contact with other profectus. "Julian said that Dave has been acting up again. Arrested for driving while intoxicated. He hit another vehicle and killed a child. Why would he do something so stupid?"

"The pressure can get to you sometimes."

"He is facing prison. There is no way the Coalition can cover up his crimes this time."

"Maybe they will make him disappear like a few others that turned out to be disappointments."

"They are supposed to be retraining them, getting them some psych help."

"Sure. That is why they fell off the radar for so long."

Amy become silent, her lips pressed into a firm line as she pondered his words. He wondered if she suspected they were dead like him. The Coalition did not put up with profectus who caused embarrassments for their Great Plan.

"Doctor Kent visited me today."

Amy's spoon paused halfway to her mouth. "Oh? What about?"

"My marriage has been arranged."

"To who?" She tried to look detached, but he guessed she had expected to marry him.

"To Princess Abarrane. The Coalition wants a profectus on the throne."

The spoon fell into the bowl, its contents forgotten. "You're marrying a princess? A real one? But she's not a profectus."

"She carries the gene, part of a line that has been doing arranged marriages for generations."

"But I thought that we…" Amy turned her back to him, hiding her face, brushing silent tears away.

An awkward silence fell between them. Kylen failed to find words to comfort. Amy was the only real friend he had ever had, the one he dared share his true emotions and dreams. "I still have a month. I'm going to get us into Essence. I keep my promises."

"You have not broken a promise yet." Her voice wavered.

"And I won't. You will always be my confidant."

"Who else would keep you in the loop?" She turned around and gave him a sad smile.

Sleep was allusive that night as Kylen pondered how he could hack into Essence. An inside contact was what he needed. Someone who could get him into the system, bypassing security protocols. He was up before dawn. By the time the sun had peeked over the horizon, he already had three junk computers he had patched together hacked into several systems of New Hope. A face recognizing program constantly monitored video feed from traffic lights, the outdoor mall, and other popular sites in the city. He knew he was taking a big risk leaving his computers jacked into the servers, but he could not go off blindly following the Coalition's plan without first achieving his only life goal.

Two days later, his program spotted Hennah at the boardwalk with her husband. Then next day she was grocery shopping with him. Hennah only occasionally left Essence and always with her guardian. For three weeks Kylen watched her, growing more desperate as his time ran out. Finally, on a Saturday, she went shopping with her mom.

Taking an e-tablet with him to monitor her, Kylen hopped on a bus and headed across town to the shopping center. He tracked her to a furniture store. He hid behind appliances, watching Hennah and her mother discuss with a clerk about upholstery colors. The worker touched a display, and a hologram caused the couch to change colors.

Peeking around a corner, Kylen caught Hennah's eye. She looked surprised, glancing in his direction several times. Then she came up with an excuse and left her mother still talking with the clerk.

Slowly she wandered behind a row of refrigerators, out of view of her mother. She pretended to be interested in a self-cleaning model with a video screen built into its door. "I have wanted to see you for a long time, but my husband forbids it."

Kylen stood across the aisle, checking out a different unit. "You told your husband about me?"

"No, my sister let it slip. My husband is very protective and doesn't like me talking with strangers."

"You know who I am, so I'm not a stranger. There is a bond between us profectus. That is why I sought you out to ask for a favor."

She glanced at him then back to the price tag for the appliance. "What is that?"

"I'm friends with Diane's clone. It has been her lifelong dream to visit Essence, to see the place Diane won the Zelzer for. We need you to get us on campus for just a few hours."

"I would love to meet her, but it would be too dangerous. Our security monitors for clones including profectus."

"We have ways around some of that. All we need is a legit invitation. Perhaps a work order of some kind."

"I, uh…" She hesitated, uncertain. "There is an old computer which needs some work in my apartment."

"I can fix it. Send two invitations to Bluered Technology."

"I never heard of that company."

Kylen grinned. "I just made it up. Give me a couple hours, and I will have a website up for it."

"You don't even know what is wrong with the computer."

"I'm the clone of two famous computer programmers. I can fix anything. What model is it?"

"Uh, I'm not sure. It's ancient, maybe four hundred years or more. It's a computerized desk with a monitor, if that helps. I think the brand name began with a D, maybe. We need the files taken off it, but our technicians were unfamiliar with it because it's too old."

"For it to work this long means it is a high end computer, very expensive. I can track down its model. Can you get us in Monday?"

"Uh, sure. I think. It's my first time doing something like this. I should get back to my mom."

As she stepped away, Kylen smiled at her. "Thanks. My friend will really appreciate this."

Chapter Nineteen

A quintessence guard stood by the exit to the monorail station. Hennah stood nearby, trying to appear relaxed as passengers walked pass, most heading to work at Essence. She checked the time on her e-band again. They should be here soon. Nervousness filled her. She had given the names Kylen had sent her to security which should allow them through the juncture to change from the public monorail to Essence's more secure system.

Pulling up a map on her e-band, she saw that Joseph had just reached his office. She had told him she was taking off work this morning because technicians were coming to look at the computer. No lies needed. She had been careful to avoid allowing him to probe her mind yesterday. He would learn about this later, of course, after she finally got to meet a new profectus.

A new train pulled in and a crowd exited the building after they had passed through a security check point. A men and woman dressed in business attire stopped in front of Hennah.

"Hello," said the man holding a backpack that had just been searched. His voice was that of Kylen but his face was wider with higher cheeks. "Ready to work, Mrs. Kalkar."

"Kylen? You look different."

He glanced towards the nearby guard. "I'm the one and only. This is Amy."

"Good to meet you." Hennah nodded to the woman, and then led them away from the guard, stopping near a terrace bordered with flowers. "Glad you made it."

"You do not know how excited I am to be here. And to meet you." Amy grinned. Her hair was loose, and her face had high cheekbones like Kylen. "I can't believe that you live here, right in the middle of the leeches. How do you manage that?"

Hennah shrugged. "I'm used to it. This is my home."

"I wished it was mine. The landscape is gorgeous. Look how function is blended with beauty." Amy walked onto the terrace, admiring how it offered privacy beside a busy sidewalk. "Elegant. Nice view of Richton Tower from here. Hides the elevation drop well."

"You could have gotten off the monorail much closer to it, but I thought you would like the walk."

"Excellent." Amy beamed in pleasure. "Diane was in full form when she drew up the blueprints."

The three slowly strolled along the sidewalk, passing asymmetrical buildings which rarely contained straight lines in their design. Amy bounded away at times to explore a new plaza or garden. When they reached Richton Tower, Amy marched up to the glass wall, closed her eyes, and placed both hands on its sleek surface warmed by sunshine.

"I think she is in love," said Kylen. "You may never get her to leave."

Hennah laughed. "I'm glad to see her enthusiasm. It's catchy."

"How about we leave her while I work on your computer, if you think it is safe."

"Sure. As long as she doesn't go into any restricted areas, she should be fine."

"Got that, Amy? We meet back here in two hours."

"Hmm." Amy opened her eyes, looking blissful. "Two magnificent hours. Got it."

Hennah led Kylen across the busy Grand Forum to a private elevator which went directly to the top floor. Before the elevator could even move, Hennah had to punch in a password for it to accept Kylen as a guest.

"Your security is well designed."

"Thanks, though I had nothing to do with it."

The elevator doors opened to reveal Darkfern standing with her four arms folded, foot tapping impatiently. She was dressed in a red security uniform with a gun and knives strapped to her waist. Kylen stiffened when he saw her.

"Finally." The fjouwer moved into the elevator. "I'm going to be late for work again." She barely gave Kylen a glance.

"You should have left earlier," replied Hennah, stepping into the hallway, followed by Kylen.

"I did, but I forgot my name badge again. Why can't they be sewed on instead of velcroed? Getting up early is hard."

"You could transfer back to the afternoon shift."

"Nope, I pulled off twelve years of schooling getting up in the mornings. I can do it again. Oh, a couple of my cousins and several other clansman from my mother's home planet are coming next week. They are trying out for jobs in security."

"If they are as talented as you and your mom, I'm sure they will be hired."

Darkfern lowered her voice. "I think a couple of them are coming specifically to flirt with me, being a daughter of a Five."

The doors closed, leaving the profectus alone in the hallway. Kylen let out the breath he had been holding.

"We're close," said Hennah, leading him to her apartment.

150

As they walked in, Kylen whistled. "This is some home. I thought foeditas horribilis lived modestly."

"Most do. I guess you could blame Diane who designed this area. She wanted it to be extravagant. My husband is working, but you should probably not utter insults around here."

"Sorry. Is the room bugged?" Kylen sat his backpack down.

"No. Definitely no surveillance in here. Fives insist on privacy in their own homes. The computer is in here."

She led him to the study. Some of the antiques had been sent to the museum, but Joseph had kept random items, claiming Yashana had been specially attached to a few of them. Hennah had been puzzled by the exclusive knowledge he had. She was a descendent of Yashana, not him. There were anecdotes about Yashana passed on through family tradition, none of which referred to old books or trinkets.

Kylen began examining the computer desk after Hennah woke it up for him. "A Divinus model. Well-designed and very expensive. Sluggish response, I see."

"Is it normal for computers to work when this old?"

"There are some over a thousand years old that still function." Kylen lay on the floor and scooted under the desk, opening a panel. "Most of those are organic and can heal when damaged."

"Living computers? You're joking. I never heard of one before."

"Cause you can't buy them at your local electronic store. That technology is closely guarded by alien governments who came up with the designs." Kylen used his telecom to flash light into the wires and microchips. "Hm. Not too dusty. There have been some added modifications to it after it was purchased which may have extended its working life. To speed it up, I will need to replace quite a few parts, many no longer being manufactured. It would be cheaper to buy a new desk, in my opinion."

"That is what we plan to do, but my husband wanted a backup of the files first. A technician from here already looked at it, but he didn't have a compatible hookup to transfer the files. The wireless is broken."

"Broken?" Kylen stood up and navigated through menus. "H'm, all access to Essence networks have been manually turned off. I can move your files over to another computer for you, but they will need to be converted for use by newer programs. Fortunately, I have the software to do that for you."

Kylen plugged in an old cord into the desk and copied all its files to his own computer. Then he ran them through a converter program. "This will take a while."

"My husband will be out until lunch time. We usually eat together."

"I'll be finished by then." Kylen sat in the chair by the desk while keeping a watch on his own e-tablet's screen. "Tell me, how do you like being in an arranged marriage?"

Hennah stiffened. "I choose to marry Joseph."

"Are you sure you were really given a choice? From what I have seen, the foeditas horribilis have been controlling you. And yes, I will call them what I wish. Do you really love him?"

"My feelings…are complicated. I'm dealing with clinical depression."

"So you are unhappy."

"Not because of the marriage. Really, these questions are too personally." Hennah walked into the living room and looked about for something to do.

Kylen followed, standing under an arch doorway. "I don't mean to upset you. Recently I was told about my own arranged marriage to someone I have never met. I had wondered if you could be happy in yours, maybe I would in mine."

"Oh. I'm not a good example. Joseph does love me. I just have a hard time feeling anything back. He is a good man. He tries to make me happy."

"Why does your expression tell me differently? Your life is similar to mine. Our masters are benevolent as long as we obey them. If we rebel against them, we face their wrath."

Feeling drained, Hennah sat on a couch. "That is just the way it is. Always has been."

Kylen sat down beside her, eyes burning with anger. "Why do we allow this? We are profectus, one of the smartest beings in the galaxy. It is time for us to break our bonds."

"How is that possible?"

"By taking control of our own lives. Let's leave, together. Fly far away from here."

Hennah shook her head. "We will be hunted down. You cannot hide from a quintessence for long."

"We are profectus and can outsmart them. Sectors of the Rim have seceded from the Empire. The leeches have no authority there."

"But those areas are warzones. It's far too dangerous."

"Then we avoid the battles. I can keep us safe, getting all the money we will need. We will have splendid adventures chosen by us, instead of others telling us what to do."

"Your plan sounds exciting, but you are acting without carefully thinking things through." Hennah moved further back from him on the couch. "You are asking me to leave my husband. I do care about him and my family. What about Amy?"

"She is like a sister to me. I can ask her to come, but most likely she would prefer the civilized life too much."

"I can't go with you."

"Why not? For once, think about what you want instead of what the mortis elixirs tell you to do."

Hennah pictured Joseph, how much it would hurt him if she left. She sought logically reasons to stay. "Our faces will be recognized in spaceports."

Kylen laughed and pointed to his own face altered by prosthetics. "I got through Essence just fine today. Besides, the databases on Core planets have been purged. They don't hold data over two hundred years, a regulation the Coalition put into place long ago when they were planning for us."

"I need time to think about this."

"Three days. That is all the time I have left then I am supposed to fly away like a happy bootlicker to the destiny that the Coalition has created for me. I'm tired of doing things their way. Tell me, Hennah, what is the source of your depression?"

"Um..." Hennah looked down at her hands. "It's classified."

"You can't even speak about what they have done to you. You deserve to be treated like a legitimate citizen. We both do. Let us take our fates in our own hands." Kylen reached out and held her hands. Hennah almost pulled back, but she remained still. "Come away with me. I promise we can safely get away and live exciting, adventurous lives. I have never broken a promise. Amy will vouch for me on that."

Hennah rotated her hand and looked at the faint scar on her wrist. Only once before had she tried to break free and that had not ended well. Which future did she want? Being the dutiful wife laboring on a task she loathed until she died from old age or be an adventurer roaming through the galaxy, free of responsibilities. "Your plan does sound appealing."

"Give me two days. I will arrange everything."

"I never leave Essence without an escort."

"Don't go to work Wednesday. Say you're sick. Wait for my message then follow the directions. You will be able to walk out, and I will be waiting for you on the other side."

"You make it sound easy."

"I will be doing the hard part hacking into their system. All you have to do is come to me." Kylen squeezed her hands in reassurance. "I'll add me to your contacts on your e-band."

Kylen scooted closer to her and took her wrist, keying information into her device. When he finished, he remained seated beside her, their legs touching. Hennah knew she should pull away, but she remained, her mind a whirlpool of confusion. Kylen offered a way out of the prison she had grown up in, but for her to gain the freedom she had long desired meant hurting family and friends.

She felt the gentle brush of Kylen touching her cheek. The he leaned forward, kissing her gently on the lips. Her heartbeat quickened. If she ran away with him, he would expected her to become his lover. She felt no attraction for him, but neither did she for Joseph unless he first bit her, flipping on those emotions for a while. *If I am away from Essence, then maybe I can also leave this depression behind. Feel human for once instead of a robot.* She kissed back, aware of the warmth of Kylen's lips.

"Files done," announced Kylen's computer.

For a long moment, Kylen ignored the machine, but eventually he reluctantly pulled away from Hennah. "I…will copy those files to your e-tablet."

Hennah nodded, getting up from the couch. She watched as he worked, her mind reeling at what she had just done. *I kissed another who is not my husband. I am a terrible person. I shame my family.* She imaged Chandresh looking at her in disappointment.

Kylen packed away his things. Standing close to Hennah, he said, "Two days and I will come for you. Wait for my message." He kissed her again. Hennah remained stiff, not responding back this time.

"You should go before my husband comes." She walked him to the door. "One question. If we were in a car together and I wanted to drive, would you let me?"

"Of course." Kylen gave her a smile then was gone.

Hennah leaned against the door, trying to organize her thoughts. *Am I really going to run away?* The idea was romantic, exciting, beckoning like a shiny jewel. But the price to be free from her gilded cage would be high, hurting Joseph and her family. Guilt consumed her as she wrestled with her conscience.

When Joseph showed up, Hennah was sitting on a couch, perusing the thousands of new files on her e-tablet. "Hi. The tech guy was able to copy the files over. And he converted them, at least most of them. Some still won't open."

"Anything useful."

"If someone was making a documentary about Layla or Yashana's lives, they would have a lot of video and pictures to use. But I haven't found anything useful for me."

"Ready for lunch?"

They ate in the Great Forum then Hennah headed to work in her lab. She pretended all was normal as she edited yet another genome. The two sea lavens experimented with splicing human female genes into a quintessence chromosome. After work, she cooked dinner in her stylish kitchen which was triple the size of her childhood bedroom.

"You went all out tonight," said Joseph. "A full course Indian meal."

"I thought you deserved something special." Hennah gave a forced smile, hiding the guilt which pulled her deeper into depression's grip.

"Tomorrow I will cook you an authentic Asian feast."

"Sounds great."

Hennah avoided being too near Joseph during the evening, never turning her back to him. At bedtime, she claimed to be feeling a bit sick, sleeping on the far side of the bed. The next day she kept to her normal schedule, working all day in the lab and eating meals with Joseph. She was restless during the night, barely sleeping.

At times she wanted to confess everything to him, begging for forgiveness. *He is a good man. A good man,* she kept telling herself over and over. *My place is here.* Yet she dreaded her life in the lab, the endless cycle of editing the tens of thousands of genes to make yet another genome which would fail. *I hate my life, but I care about my husband. I'm sure I do. But I'm so tired of being dead inside, no pleasant emotions unless he feeds them to me. I want to feel like a real person. To be free.*

In the morning she told Joseph she was not feeling well and was staying home. After he kissed her goodbye, she roamed about the penthouse, her guilt worse than ever. She changed her mind countless times while going over the cons and pros. Still, she packed a bag. Sitting at the computer desk, she handwrote a goodbye letter, tore it up, and then wrote three new versions. On her e-band she finally got a simple message that said, "Three o'clock."

She hid the note and backpack. When Joseph arrived for lunch, she was lying in bed. He cooked her a quick meal, and brought her the soup to eat in bed.

As he ate beside her, he said, "Maybe you should visit the medial ward."

"I'm sure I will be fine soon. If I am still sick tomorrow, I will go. Thanks for cooking."

After their meal were finished, he said, "I can stay home with you."

"No, your work is important. You have an entire civilization to oversee."

"If you need anything call me."

"Alright." As she watched him walk away, she realized it may be the last time she would see him. "Joseph, I love you."

Her husband paused at the door. "That is the first time you have said that to me."

"I should have said it sooner."

He gave her a brief smile and left.

She began her roaming again, telling herself she would stay, yet she placed her note on the desk. Glancing around the study, she noticed the large, decorative jewelry box standing in the corner. Needing something to do, she pulled out several of the necklaces and looked at herself in the mirror. She held up a three circle necklace Joseph had given her at the wedding ceremony. She placed it back in the box and keep looking. Most of the pieces were pretty but inexpensive. Only a few were made from real gems and rare metals. *Maybe I could sell them to help with travel costs.*

As she begin to sort the pieces, she came across a simple chain from which hung a crucifix. Hennah dropped it as if her hand burned, thinking of Chandresh. Adultery was a taboo in both religions her family belong to. *I never even decided if I'm Christian or Hindu. I just follow along, like I do with everything else. Well, I'm making a decision this time. I choose my freedom, my happiness.*

She closed the jewelry box, leaving the rest of the contents untouched. Walking to a shelf, she glanced at the books. She picked up one that Joseph had been especially determined to keep. The edges of *Frankenstein* were worn from its many readings. She wondered yet again why her husband wanted to keep it and how he had special knowledge that it was Layla's favorite.

After more roaming, she settled on a gray couch. *I never did buy new furniture. Joseph needs something brighter, more cheerful.* Guilt again. She should be here to help him decorate. She randomly looked through files on her e-tablet. She flipped through family photo of Yashana with her daughter Yaira. They always looked happy together. Suddenly Hennah pulled the screen closer. *She's wearing my necklace.* Hennah examined other pictures, seeing a beaded necklace with the three circles over and over again. It was the same color and size as her own. Curious, she found photos of Layla. Again, the necklace was present in a number of the pictures.

Hennah glanced back towards the study. *Joseph gave me the same wedding necklace that belonged to my clones. How did he know it was their mangala sutra?*

Puzzled, she returned to clicking on random family videos. It was strange to see moving images of her clones. They were older, but still had her face, her voice. Overall they seemed happy, in love with their husbands. Their work was paramount to them. Designing new quintessence models brought them pleasure and satisfaction. *I wish I felt like that about my work.*

She watched another video. Yaira's young daughter had turned on the camera without the adults noticing. The child joked with her grandparents about what she wanted to be when she grew up.

After the child left the study, Yaira leaned close to her mother and said, "I finished looking over the files for that special project we have been discussing."

"What did you think about them?" Yashana replied while putting on earrings.

"Perhaps your best work yet. Too bad no one else will ever see them."

"No one can predict the future. The possibility may open."

"At what cost? I fear only a great catastrophe will open such a path."

"Hope for the best, plan for the worst. That is the all we can do."

Hennah's heartbeat quickened. Surely Yashana could not be referring to hidden genes for female quintessence. But if the project was a normal male, then why would the files need to be secret? *I'm just jumping the gun, wishful thinking that they are talking about what I want most.* Still, Hennah replayed the video a dozen times. Then she began searching through the recovered files, looking for anything out of the ordinary that might be the secret files.

Her e-watch beeped. The message it displayed said, "Now. Take elevator to twenty-fifth floor. Then take service elevator to first floor."

Hennah tensely stared at the words. She had gotten so wrapped up in the mystery of the cryptic conversation that she had forgotten about Kylen. She might finally be on the edge of the breakthrough she had been working on for nearly seven years. Leaving now would ruin it all.

"Hurry," scrolled more text. "I am in the system and can see you."

So he had hacked in and was most likely watching her dot on a map, just like she could look up where Joseph was. Hennah stared at her watch, unable to decide. *My freedom at the cost of the quintessence species.* She trembled, wishing Alec had never told her that he believed creating female quintessences was the only way to save his species. *It's unfair putting that pressure on me. I want to be happy too. Why must I give up my dreams for them? Why?*

Joseph's gentle face appeared in her mind. His concern about her health. Him giving up his brothers for her. She had never asked him for that, but he had done so anyway. Fear in his eyes when he had carried her, bleeding, down the hallway of the Research Department.

A tear ran down Hennah's cheek. *He loves me. I can't betray him like this. I can't.* She tapped out a message on her e-band. "Sorry, but I am staying. Go without me."

"Don't let fear guide you," came the message back. "I can protect you. I'm in control right now. See." The lights flickered on and off several times in the room. "Come to me."

With trembling fingers, she tapped out, "Truly I am sorry." She took off the e-band and tossed it onto a sofa. Then she dropped to the carpeted floor and wept. The lights flickered again as Kylen tried to get her attention. She kept her eyes closed, ignoring the blinking lights, wishing she was not hurting Kylen. At least he could be free. The blinking became more frantic then suddenly stopped. A few minutes later Joseph opened the door.

Seeing Hennah on the floor, Joseph rushed over. "Are you alright? Do you faint?"

"No. I mean, yes, I'm okay now. I found a video you should see." She picked up the e-tablet from the couch.

Joseph knelt on the carpet beside her, still concerned. "You have been crying."

157

"I'm fine. Watch this." Hennah played the entire video.

As he viewed it, an odd expression came to his face that she could not understand. When the video finished, he stared at the screen for a long moment before saying, "Do you think she was referring to female quintessences?"

"I don't know. Maybe. I keep trying to find the files she was referring too, but there are thousands here."

"If she meant for them to be found some day, she would have hid them in plain sight, waiting for a trigger to have them revealed." Joseph took the e-tablet and began scrolling through the vast list of files. He occasionally opened one, only to quickly close it and continue his search.

Hennah leaned against him, watching the screen. "Why could she not make it obvious?"

"She had to keep it hidden from her husband, knowing the timing was wrong. Ariyo was too ambitious. He would have wanted to make them immediately. But she knew doing so might had led to his arrest by the Senate if they figured out what he was doing. She was protecting him."

"How do you know what she was thinking? And how could she hide secrets from her husband? Would he not have found them when probing her mind?"

"Most likely her husband did not look at the memories giving details about her research. We quintessences are not scientists and would find skimming through countless hours of work boring. Also, wives may ask for husbands not to peek into certain thoughts, especially if they relate to surprises and presents."

"We can do that? Ask for privacy with our thoughts?"

"Yes, of course."

"Why did you not tell me that before?"

"You did not ask." Joseph changed the topic. "Does any file stand out to you, as a researcher?"

"No, I was looking before you came in."

Joseph clicked of one titled "Sleep at work." The file refused to open.

Hennah said, "There are several that didn't convert."

"We should check the originals."

As they went into the study, she noticed her goodbye letter sitting on the computer. She stepped in front of Joseph and tossed it away, as if it meant nothing. Hopefully, he was too focused on the mysterious video to have noticed. Hennah awoke the desk. When she found the file, she touched it. Instead of opening, an outline of a hand appeared on the desk's surface. She frowned but laid her hand on top of the outline. Words flashed up, "Percent compatible." A light flashed from the monitor as Hennah's face was scanned. "Face recognized," flashed on the screen.

A video of Yashana in her sixties appeared on the monitor. "Hello. I am presuming you are a relative or another clone of me. If you are, then perhaps you opened this file out of curiosity. Perhaps you are seeking something. I don't know who you are, only that you are not me. I hope I can trust you. There is one I know I can trust. If he is with you, tell him to look in the prize that I least deserved. He will know what I am talking about." The recording ended.

Hennah frowned. "Great, another cryptic puzzle. If you are going to send a message from the dead, don't refer to other people who are also dead."

"It is in the Zelzer trophy," Joseph said with certainty.

"How did you come to that conclusion?"

"It is a guess." Joseph stood up. "Do you feel like visiting the museum or should I go alone?"

"I'm feeling better now."

As they stepped into the hallway, Miles left his post to follow them. They took the private elevator down to the first floor and walked across the Grand Forum. Hennah glanced at Miles several times. She still was not used to having a guard whenever she took walks around the campus with her husband.

On the wall outside the museum hung portraits of the founders of Essence Institute, the largest being of Layla Rangan which could be seen from almost anywhere in the food court. Hennah had visited the museum several times as a child, but had avoided it after she learned she was a clone. It consisted of several large chambers divided into smaller areas which displayed memorabilia, interactive hologram displays, and a souvenir booth.

A sundancer showed her two children a canister which held a fake fetus. As the children reached out to touch it, their mother explained how the quintessences were grown and her role in helping them to be born.

Joseph headed towards the museum curator who stood in the souvenir section. The neodite's blueish skin began to turn purple in his excitement when he realized a Five was visiting. "Is there anything I can help you with, sir?"

"Yes, I would like to borrow the Zelzer Award my wife and I donated last week."

"We were thrilled, sir, having that added to our collection. The Publicity Department is planning a new ad campaign around it and some of the other donations you gave. It's been awhile since anything this substantial has been given. Can I ask, sir, why do you need it back?"

"We would like to take a few private family photos with it. I promise to have it returned tomorrow morning, early."

"Of course, sir. Right this way." The curator led them through a doorway into the staff area where a new display was being created just for the awards. "We are still working on the holograms that will go with them." He pointed to a device in front of the Zelzer Award. The trophy was protected by a clear polycarbonate panel. "We will show the award ceremony of when Layla Rangan received it."

Joseph nodded. "I am pleased with your plans."

"Thank you, sir." The curator placed his hand on a sensor which unlocked the protected panel. He pulled out the gold trophy and handed it to Joseph. "We hope to have everything finished in two weeks to begin the publicity campaign."

So the award would not gather attention, it was placed in a box which Joseph carried back to the elevator. Hennah stood near him, glancing at Miles. She knew nothing about the Shadow Guard other than he worked the afternoon shift. Was he married? Did his birthmates work at Essence? How long had he chaperoned Alec before the Five had died? When they reached the penthouse, Miles again took up a silent post outside the door.

Joseph sat the box on a table and pulled out the Zelzer. "Hold this while I get a picture, so our cover story will be truthful."

He took several pictures of Hennah posing on the balcony with the heavy trophy. Then he carried it to the dining table and used a knife to pry the bottom panel off. An old memory drive fell out along with cloth used for padding to keep the device from moving around.

Hennah felt a thrill of excitement as she picked up the device. Could it hold the answers she had been seeking for so long? Still, she was puzzled how Joseph knew it was in this trophy and not another.

In the study, she plugged the drive into the desk and copied its files onto the sluggish computer. She opened the video titled "Watch first." Again an outline of a hand appeared on the desk and a light flashed from the monitor. After Hennah had passed those tests, a box appeared with the question, "What is my true name?"

Hennah stared at the screen. "How are we supposed to know that? Does she mean her birth name or a nickname? Or maybe it's a reference to her daughter or a movie I have never seen."

Joseph moved beside Hennah and typed in "Lashana." Hennah looked in puzzlement at her husband when the computer accepted the word.

"How did you know that?"

"Something Alec told me."

A video of Yashana appeared on the monitor. Again, she was in her sixties, wearing a blue blouse. "Hello, beloved. We meet again, though if this works out like I think it will, I will be dead when you see this. Strange talking about my own demise when I have decades yet to go, at least I hope so. Still, I could not share this with you during my lifetime. The political wind is not in favor of my little project. I don't know if there will ever be a correct time for it, but my intuition tells me that someday the galaxy will either be ready or the quintessences will face a great danger and will need this. As you may have guessed, I have a special gift for you. In the files I have provided, I have created ten genomes for possible females of your species along with variations for each. Since these were never tested, I am certain you will need to tweak them a bit before they can become reality. Because of both the secrecy of this project and the need for a gifted geneticist, the files will only open to a clone or relative of mine. Ethan actually came up with the programing for that, though he has no knowledge of what I am protecting."

Hennah leaned closer to the screen, heart pounding. Could Yashana had found the solution she could not? What method had she used? How had she gotten pass the flaws in Layla's design? She glanced at Joseph, seeing a strange look on his face. She frowned, trying to understand it.

Yashana continued, "Because I will most likely be dead when, if ever, you see this, I feel I should say something profound. It's a strange concept because I will see you in two days when you get back from that camping trip with your brothers. You know, the one where you plan to spend an entire week with only basic supplies, hunting for all the food you eat. I will find it quite amusing if all of you return home starving and ten pounds lighter. But most likely, you will have gained ten. If you bring any game home, you are dressing it, not me. But I'm procrastinating. What real message do I have for you from beyond the dead?"

A sadness came into the woman's eyes. "That I love you. I know you will have a hard time moving on without me. But it is your duty to, at least for a while. Your brothers will be there to support you. I hope you can find happiness and love again, but it better not be me. I'm sorry, beloved, but we humans, even profectus, can't handle it well. When you finally get tired and wish for an end, come to me. We have talked about my belief in the afterlife. I will be waiting, if you decide to take the journey I will be on." Yashana sighed. "It is weird talking so morbidly when I will see you in a few days. As far as I know, I still have half my life to spend with you, and I don't know if this message will ever be found by you. But if so, remember I love you. Have faith that good will come instead of being so pessimistic."

The video ended. Joseph stared at the screen, raw emotions on his face. Hennah watched him in concern. Quintessences usually only showed a hint of emotions through facial expressions, but Joseph looked like a human in deep grief. Without a word, he turned and walked out of the room. Hennah was uncertain if she should go to him. Why was he upset about her ancestor that had been dead over three centuries ago? It was like Yashana had been talking directly to Joseph, but that was impossible.

Hennah turned back to the computer and opened a file of a genome. For a while she became lost in the research, reading personal notes written by both

Yashana and Yaira. What they had created had a high chance of success. Excitement for Project Absurd pounded through her. For the first time she felt eager to return to her lab to test their theory.

Wanting to share the news, she sought out Joseph. She found him kneeling on the balcony. Realizing he was praying, she stopped in the doorway, surprised. He avoided talking about religion, though he was always respectful of priests and other clerics.

Sensing Hennah, he stood. His face had returned to its normal expressionless state. "You have questions."

"Yes. And news." She was unsure where to start. "Yashana is brilliant. Somehow she found out that Layla had a gene in the X chromosome which looked for a Y chromosome. That is normal. But Layla had also coded it so that when the Y was missing, look for a Z chromosome. It was there from the very beginning and not a single researcher noticed that tiny little extra message except Yashana."

"I have not heard of a Z chromosome. She created one with female traits?"

"Actually Z and W chromosomes are normal in some birds, fish, and insects. Layla liked to break natural laws, so she coded a future door where a Z chromosome could be used to make a female. I can do it now, Joseph. Even if Yashana had not went ahead and designed several versions of the Z chromosome, I could have done it. But this will save me a lot of time. Years of it." Hennah smiled. "I can give your species daughters now."

Joseph slowly sat down in a patio chair, relief passing across his face. "You have removed a heavy burden from me today. I have feared I would live to see the end of my species. Now I believe otherwise."

For a long moment neither spoke. Hennah sat in a chair beside him, struggling with what to say. Was now a good time to confess she had almost left him? She would not be able to hide her memories of Kylen much longer. Yet she was puzzled by her husband's behavior.

"Speak your mind, Patni. I can see you have questions."

"The necklace you gave me on our wedding day was the same mangala sutra that both Layla and Yashana wore. Why did you choose the same necklace? And how did you know the files were in the Zelzer trophy or the right password? When Yashana spoke, it was like she was talking to you. But that is impossible."

"Why is it impossible?" His eyes were perceptive, scrutinizing her expression.

"You are not even sixty, and she has been dead over three centuries. You could never have met her."

"But I did. Yashana was my wife."

Hennah opened her mouth but could not speak. She just stared at Joseph, unable to accept his words.

162

"Let me explain. Long ago, by accident, I discovered a way death could be cheated by passing all my memories to another through a mega ziphema. This became a closely guarded secret only known to the Five, the Synod, and our Shadow Guards. I am Ariyo, the husband of Yashana. Also, I am Alexander, husband to Layla. Plus I am Ace and Alec."

Again Hennah struggled to speak. Finally she said, "Did you run out of names which begin with A? How can you be five people? And I thought I was struggling with sanity."

"I am not five individuals but one with the memoires of five. I do not have split personality disorder."

"If what you say is true," Hennah felt bewildered, "that makes you my own grandfather. You were married to my grandmother. That's incest."

"No. There are a good many greats in front of grandmother. Twelve generations to be precise. I have no genetic link to you as I have never fathered children."

"Pallavi and Kaushal may not biologically be my parents, but they are still my parents. If you were really Ariyo, then it still makes you a grandfather to me."

"Step. Yaira was twelve when I married her mom. Her father was Seth Lanneret. Mason can actually claim closer kin to you as he was married to Yaira and raised her child Akari as his daughter."

Hennah shook her head, trying to understand this strange conversation. "Yaira was married to Marcus, not Mason."

Joseph leaned closer to his wife. "The Five are *the* Five, the first quintessences ever created. You now know Mason as Tobias. Gabriel is Skyler. Our director Caden is really Caleb. And Jacob is Desmond, the father of your close friend."

"This is too much. Darkfern's father is…is…ancient? Tobias and his wife kept saying I was part of the family, but I didn't understand what they really meant. And you," She stabbed a finger at him. "Alexander? Do you know how many stories I grew up hearing about the renowned Director Alexander, firstborn of all quintessences? I married Joseph, the desk clerk, not a legend. I no longer know who you are."

"I am still Joseph who loves you very much."

"But you love her. When you watched that vid, I saw your expression. You are in love with her."

"Yes, I do love Lashana. I also love you. It is possible to love more than one at the same time."

"Why do you call her Lashana?"

"Because Layla and Yashana are the same person. Layla's memories were passed to Yashana, again by accident. Your great grandmother was also the creator of the quintessences. That is why she knew about the Z chromosome."

163

Hennah stared at her hands, struggling to understand. "This is difficult for me to accept. You are altering the reality I grew up with. How many more people are not who I thought they were?"

"Only the Five and Yashana have experienced memory transfers. It was decided long ago not to involve more. The price for immorality is too heavy. If I was not needed to be a guardian of my species, I would have allowed myself to die from old age after Lashana's death. But I have carried on, alone, for centuries until you came along."

"You called me forth into existence. Did you marry me because I looked like her? It was really Layla...Lashana you wanted but you got me instead. A big disappointment I turned out to be."

Joseph moved over and sat beside her on the patio chair. "I, Joseph, married you because I love you. I cared about you before I was selected to be Alec's heir. There are many memories I would like to share with you." He reached out a hand and brushed hair away from her neck.

Panicking, Hennah pulled back from him. She was not ready for him to see her sins. "You are also Alec who I don't like. The slave master I despise."

"I am sorry how I pushed you."

"Sorry? I tried to kill myself to escape you, but instead I was deceived into marrying you."

She stood up and stormed off. For a few minutes she circled around the living room, ignoring her husband standing by the balcony door watching her. Finally, she sat on a couch not facing him.

In a voice barely above a whisper, she said, "I could hate you but it is myself that I despise. I had planned to leave you today. Even packed a bag. Wrote you a goodbye letter."

"You were going to leave?" Joseph's voice became deathly calm. "Why?"

"Cause I was tired of having my whole life controlled by you." She gave a bitter life. "You, Alec, decided my birth, my parents, my education, and my job. Most likely you arranged for Darkfern to become my best friend and Joseph to fall in love with me. You have been manipulating me my whole life."

"I tried to provide well for you to make you happy."

Angrily she spat out, "You gave me the illusion of freedom, without allowing me to know the real thing. For years I have not felt like I was a real person, just a dutiful puppet whose strings were controlled by others. I can't live like this anymore."

Joseph sat on the other couch and gently said, "I have made mistakes. As Alec, I did push you too hard. As Joseph, I opposed Alec's treatment of you. I only accepted becoming his successor because I thought it would allow me to help you

164

better. I have warred with myself over you. My two great desires are to please you and to protect my species. What do you want, Hennah? If it is within my power to give it to you, I will."

For a long time Hennah did not speak. Finally, she looked at him. "Forgiveness. I kissed Kylen."

"When was this?" A coldness came into his voice.

"Here on this couch when he came to work on the computer. I invited him here knowing you would not like it. He asked me to run away with him, and I said yes. And I almost went, but I didn't. The only reason I stayed was because of her." Hennah pointed towards the study. "I happened to see that vid, and it gave me a tiny speck of hope that maybe the project could be completed. I could not abandon you when there was a chance I might could actually help you."

"Do you love Kylen?"

"No. Love is an emotion beyond what I can feel."

Again silence reigned in the room. Joseph's fist clenched in anger. He breathed deeply, forcing himself to relax. Unable to look at him, Hennah studied the scar on her wrist.

When Joseph finally spoke, his voice was calm. "I appreciated that you stayed. I do forgive you and take part of the blame on myself. You are right that I have been manipulating you your whole life. Because I have been married to two versions of you, it gave me insight in how you think and react. I believed I was doing it for your betterment, giving you a good life. Instead, I smothered you. If you want a divorce I will give that to you."

Hennah looked at him in surprise. Divorce was unheard of among the quintessences. They married for life. The consequences of a Five breaking off a marriage would cause waves of doubt about his leadership.

"I won't seek a divorce. I care about the part of you that is Joseph. You have been a good friend to me. Today, I actually felt real excitement for Project Absurd and want to complete it, now that I know how. Hope. I feel it for the first time. And if I can feel hope, over time, maybe I can feel real love, not the emotions you feed me. That is, if we can start over."

"I would like that." Joseph held her eyes. "How can I help you know freedom without our marriage ending?"

"Ask but never order me to do anything. Vacations occasionally off planet. And allow me to drive my own car."

Joseph gave her a ghost of a grin. "I can teach you how to pilot a plane. I fly when I need to relieve stress."

"Fly? You are a pilot?"

"I am many things. Since we were married I have wanted to share all my lives with you. My brothers keep this knowledge from their wives except for Mason. They believe it is better on their wives to not know. I want to hide nothing more from you. Would you allow me to share with you?"

Hennah looked into his eyes, seeing not anger or revenge, but tenderness. "Alright." She moved to his couch and offered her neck to him.

Joseph bit and began shifting through his five lifetime of memories, sharing what was essential to him. He exposed who he really was, hiding no faults or offering excuses for mistakes. When she asked questions, he answered as truthfully as possible. He shared the anguish of watching two wives die while he had to continue on. Over the centuries he and Mason had secretly watched over the descendants of Yaira, unable to openingly acknowledge their kinship. His anger of sending young quintessences to die at the hands of manipulating politicians. Remorse he felt while presiding over trials where he ordered quintessences to their deaths over the crime of acting on love while still bonded. Concern about quintessences recently abandoning their posts in wars to avoid obeying corrupt leaders. Having to send the Death Force to hunt them down, though he agreed with their decisions. Torment of watching his species slowly falling apart while the funding was cut yet again. Fear of one day being one of the last quintessences in existence when all others had died.

After he broke contact, Hennah leaned against his chest and held him tightly. "Amaka was right, you have suffered more than I knew."

Joseph stroked her hair. "Today you have given me hope when I thought I was watching a ship slowly being pulled into a black hole. No matter how powerful we have become, the vortex will crush us. We are too close to the event horizon."

She kissed him on the lips. "I will give your species children, husband. Beautiful daughters."

Chapter Twenty

Kylen stared at his screen, trying to will Hennah to come. He sit in a rented hover car which would take them to the spaceport. Rain had begun to fall, distorting the view through the windows.

His plan had been perfect. While coping files from the old computer, he had also copied its protocols and security codes which had allowed it access to the network long ago. The codes had been outdated, but with a bit of tinkering, he had been able to fool the system into accepting his own e-tablet as a substitute. He had spent yesterday hacking into a bank for money and arranging for travel. When he told Amy he was leaving, she thought he was heading off for his arranged marriage.

He had parked in front of a store near Essence's massive wall. Then he had went on the institute's server, tricking the system into thinking his e-tablet was one of their own computers. He had entry level access to basic information without the need of further hacking which might draw attention to himself. While using Hennah's e-band yesterday, he had given himself permission to view her and her husband on the campus map. Once he had gotten use to Essence's systems, he had sent Hennah a message. All she had to do was walk out the building and drive her car to his parking lot. No one would have stopped her at the gate. They would hurry to the spaceport, taking a flight that was about to lift off. Together they would be off planet before her husband even knew she was gone.

But she had chickened out. Part of him was angry with her for being a coward. He knew she had been doubtful, but he had been certain after the kiss that she would come. She admitted that she did not love her husband. Why did she stay? He could have protected her from those monsters.

Kylen gripped the steering wheel tightly, telling himself to drive away. Yet he again watched Hennah and Joseph on the e-tablet's screen. Two dots sitting by each other on the map where a couch would be. He had watched them walk to the museum then back to the apartment, leaving him guessing about the purpose of the short trip.

Hennah was supposed to be his prize, the ultimate proof that he was a better hacker than Ethan. Who else could claim to hack into the military base and come out with a Five's wife as a trophy? Originally he had only planned to get into the system, maybe leave a tiny hidden code he could publicly brag about once he became Emperor many years from now. The leeches would have no authority to arrest him then. But once he had talked with Hennah, seeing her sadness, he had wanted to take her away, give her a new life. Just like with Amy, he wanted to help.

He had never planned to rebel against the Coalition until he had actually spoken the words. Verbalizing the wish he had long hidden in his heart had given him the courage to make it a reality. Roaming the galaxy with a beautiful profectus lover would have been a splendid adventure. The Coalition had long fingers in the tame Core worlds, but little control in the wild Rim where fewer humans lived.

The two dots were moving again, this time to the bedroom. Angrily, Kylen pulled the e-tablet out of Essence's system and turned it off. He sat there, staring out the foggy window as rain pounded the vehicle. Without Hennah, being on the run from the Coalition was not appealing. It would be a lonely life of wandering from planet to planet, associating with strange aliens while avoiding civilized worlds. He could have asked Amy to come, but he knew her well enough that she would prefer her current life. She was destined to create illustrious monuments to human greatness.

What was his destiny? Did he choose a lonely life of empty ventures or become the most powerful man in the galaxy by marrying a stranger?

Part II

"Be steady to your purposes and firm as a rock. This ice is not made of such stuff as your hearts may be; it is mutable and cannot withstand you if you say that it shall not. Do not return to your families with the stigma of disgrace marked on your brows. Return as heroes who have fought and conquered and who know not what it is to turn their backs on the foe."

—From *Frankenstein* by Mary Shelley

Chapter Twenty-one

Around a large purplish-green planet, an intense space battle raged. The government of Penmort had seceded from the Basanti Empire over a year ago. The Empire had retaliated by sending four battlecruisers and eight destroyers stocked with hundreds of Claw fighters.

A fast Vivere fighter zoomed passed Quinn, targeting one of his birthmate's vessels. Taking aim, Quinn fired, hitting its engine. The fighter swerved away. In the distance a transport belonging to Penmort blew up, sending out a brief fiery explosion.

"Target the space station," came the command through Quinn's helmet.

As major, Quinn gave directions to his birthmates, sending three squads towards the station while others focused on defending a battlecruiser under heavy attack from Viveres. Another fiery explosion announced his birthmates' success as the large station split in the middle, its massive sections beginning to drift out of orbit towards the planet.

"Clear a path in front of *Bismarck*, now!" barked a voice through the com.

Quinn and his fellow fighters swerved away, several barely missing the blast of dense energy which surged from the Galactic-class battlecruiser towards one of the largest cities on the planet. Upon impact, a huge cloud of debris swept outward from the detonation, killing millions.

The fighters continued to take out the remaining Viveres who could no longer return to their space station for repairs. Several headed towards the planet to land, but they were not designed to handle atmospheric conditions well. Another battlecruiser fired at the planet, destroying a second city. Just before the blast hit, a surge of merchant ships and private yachts burst from the atmosphere, fleeing in random directions.

A surrender message came over all channels from Penmort's government. The Empire had won. Expecting to be called back, Quinn turned towards *Bismarck*, his squad following his direction.

"Permission to board," said Quinn.

"Negative. Continue taking out all enemy ships," came the order over the com.

"They surrendered," said Quinn.

"Orders are to target civilian craft. Let none escape."

"But they surrendered." Quinn's kept his voice calm, but he felt frustration at the illogic. The battle was over.

A different voice barked into the headset, "Major Quinn, your orders are to target all enemy ships, rather they are military or civilian. Is that clear?"

"Yes, sir."

Quinn flew back towards the planet, chasing a merchant craft. His fighter was faster and soon caught up. His wingman fired across its bow, as he damaged its engine. Unable to move, the merchant vessel drifted helplessly. Quinn could turn around and finish off the lightly shielded craft, but he kept flying, seeking another. He may only be eighteen, but he knew killing civilians after a surrender was unethical.

The two Galactic-class battleships continued to fire at the planet, destroying several seaports. From other cities, waves of spaceships carrying panicked passengers lifted off, desperate to escape. While squads of Claw fighters chased after the fleeing civilian crafts, the battleships continued to obliterate cites, ignoring the surrender plea.

Fuel beginning to run low, Quinn returned to *Bismarck*. He could have stayed out a while longer, but his conscience bothered him. This was not war but butchery. Once in the hanger, Quinn climbed down from his fighter and met the eyes of his birthmates. He saw his own frustration mirrored in their eyes.

"I will speak with the general," he said. "This is wrong."

"You missed on purpose several times," said a birthmate, "letting some escape."

"You copied me." Quinn looked into the eyes of his squad members. None challenged his actions. "Go get some rest. Dismissed."

Quinn walked to the bridge of the battlecruiser. Soldiers sitting or standing at posts barely glanced at him. Over half of the fleet's population was human. The others came from a wide variety of species. General McLowary barked orders from his computerized chair built on a platform several feet higher than the deck. A gloating smile crossed his stern face as another city was annihilated. Quinn glanced at the huge screen on the wall displaying Penmort. The planet's atmosphere was filled with swirling clouds of debris and dust. Only the polar areas had remained untouched from the bombardment. Survivors would be facing years of intense climate changes of short summers and lengthy winters.

"Looks like we got all of the mongrels," said the general. "Call in the Claws. Good work, soldiers. That will teach those dogs to rebel against us." The fortyish human was athletic with a scar across one cheek. Half a finger was missing on his left hand, lost long ago in a fight.

Quinn stood near the platform for several minutes, waiting until the general had time to speak with him. Occasionally he glanced at his e-band, receiving reports from his lieutenants. Several officers glanced at him, including Colonel Gundry who looked back at the planet, frowning at the destruction.

Finally noticing Quinn, General McLowary said, "Report, Major."

"Sir, my companies lost eight fighters. Total Claws lost is thirty-six for the fleet. Thirteen of the pilots' escape pods have been recovered so far."

"Causalities are lower than predicted. Good work. The Penmorts didn't put up much of a fight after bragging that their organic technology was more advanced than ours. All bark and little carry through."

"Sir, may I speak with you in private."

The general frowned but walked with Quinn to his nearby office. McLowary sat at his desk while Quinn stood at attention.

"Speak your mind, Major."

"Sir, why did we continue to fight after Penmort surrendered? Why were we asked to target civilian ships?"

"Are you questioning my orders, Major?"

"No, sir. I am seeking to understand them. My birthmates were confused by the orders as we have been trained to stand-down after opponents are defeated."

The general folded his hands together and glared at Quinn. "The civilian ships may have contained spies and disguised soldiers. Could not have them fleeing to other safe holds to spread rebellion. As Penmort is seen as the leader in this sector, demolishing the planet sends a strong warning to the others. Fear can destroy an enemy before we fire the first shot."

"If you wanted to send a warning, why not spare the civilian ships to spread the word of what was done here?"

"A few did escape, thanks to your pilots' incompetence. More time needs to be spent practicing in the simulations."

"Yes, sir. I will see to that."

"Dismissed."

Quinn left the office and walked across the bridge. Colonel Gundry left his post and followed Quinn to an elevator. Once the doors closed, the colonel hit the pause button. When Quinn had first arrived as a fresh graduate from Essence Institute, Gundry had taken him under his wing, giving advice about leadership. Over the years, they often tested each other by playing strategy board game in the officer's staff room. Quinn had soon come to respect the human's intelligence and wisdom.

"Our orders from Command were to subdue the planet, not destroy it," said Gundry. Angry tinged the voice of the tall, alethic man. Despite he was only in his forties, his hair had already begun to turn gray. "McLowary has overstepped yet again."

"Why does he keep doing this?"

173

"My opinion, he loves mayhem."

"He deliberately ignored a surrender. That is a war crime."

"Who will hold him accountable? Back home he will be commended for his brilliant victories. Who cares what happens to rebels on the Rim, especially when they're not human?"

"Would that had made a difference?"

"Yes." Gundry looked uncomfortable. "When I'm with certain human officers, I hear their speciesist chatter. Some view slaughtering non-human sentients as equal to killing bugs. Even at Command, some would praise McLowary if they knew the details of what he has done."

"Why do you not feel this way?" Quinn knew Gundry well enough to ask personal questions.

"I do not judge an individual based on their species. Our Empire is made up of many sentients. As part of the Basanti Military, it is our duty to protect all of them. Over the years I have proudly served on several ships under the command of non-humans who did an excellent job."

"I have noticed that McLowary only promotes humans to top positions within his fleet."

"I noticed that too. There is resentment among some of the lower non-human officers who have been bypassed for promotions for years." The colonel hit the button for the elevator to continue.

Quinn headed to the quarters he shared with birthmates. The cramped room held thirty-three bunkbeds stacked three high. Their belongings were kept in lockers on the wall between the beds. Two of the missing brothers had been rescued after their ships were destroyed. That left one missing birthmate, the second they had lost in their eight years of service. The grief had only begun to be felt by the birthmates who were already upset about their orders. Next door were two more crew berths for the other ME units. They had also lost members today. As major, Quinn was responsible for overseeing all three companies.

As Quinn entered his dorm, his brothers gathered, asking about his meeting with the general. He shared the conversation and what Gundry had said in the elevator. Then he listened to their replies, many agitated that they had been ordered to murder the innocent. They saw a huge difference in shooting an enemy who could shoot back and taking down a lightly armored ship trying to flee a doomed planet.

Quinn had difficulty sleeping. As a soldier, it was his duty to follow orders, if he liked them or not. When he killed an innocent, was the blood on his hands or his superior? Disobeying meant his own death. Forty-two years he had left following orders from officers like General McLowary, that is if he did not die in battle first.

To quieten his doubt, he viewed memories in the Cannon illustrating why the Code was important. While *obeying superiors* was listed in the Code, it was closely followed by *protecting the weak*. Quinn's conscience continued to keep him awake. How did one decide which part of the Code was more important when they conflicted?

Colonel Gundry split his fleet into two groups, each exploring a nearby solar system which had been colonized by Penmort centuries ago. Reaching their destination, one battlecruiser and destroyer focused on a moon base near an outer planet while the *Bismarck* and its escort headed towards a rocky planet nearer the sun.

Dressed in flight suits, the quintessences waited in the hanger for orders. Quinn kept close watch on communication channels. From the planet came the surrender call. Quinn glanced at their birthmates, concerned as the battlecruiser begin lining up for position to use its fission weapon.

"All fighters launch," came a command over the hanger's intercom. "Target all enemy ships."

Clenching fists, Quinn remained still, feeling angry and helpless. Again, they were to be instruments in murder. How could he keep killing others and lie to himself that he was innocent? Better to die with honor than gain freedom by killing the guiltless.

"Belay that order," said Quinn, causing other M1 models to glance at him uneasily. "Stand down, everyone. That is an order."

Some of the quintessences were already climbing into their Claws. Hearing Quinn, they froze, uncertain if they should obey their major or general. Maintenance workers, some of them H3 models, stared in surprise.

"It's about damn time," muttered a fjouwer, pausing in his welding of a damaged ship. "Someone needs to make a stand."

"Out of the fighters, now," barked Quinn. "My squad leaders, to me." Nine birthmates hurried forward. "Follow me."

Quinn jogged down the hallway, closely followed by his brothers. When they reached the bridge, officers glanced their way as the quintessences marched to the general's chair.

McLowary glared at them. "Why are you not launching?"

"The enemy has surrendered. It is unethical to attack." Quinn stood at attention, voice firm, eyes intense.

"You are disobeying a director order, Major." McLowary leaned forward, a dangerous look in his eyes.

"I am obeying rules of engagement agreed to by our Galactic Senate."

"You are demoted and placed under arrest."

Several security officers stepped forward. Quinn's brothers stood near him, their hands touching their holsters but not pulling their weapons.

The general barked, "Commander, fire at the planet as soon as we are in position."

"Belay that order," said Quinn, his own hand touching his gun still in its holster. "The enemy has surrendered. If you fire, you are guilty of murder."

The security officers pulled their guns, pointing their muzzles at Quinn. His nine brothers pulled their own weapons and aimed at the two guards. The room became deathly quiet.

"Put away your weapons, leeches." McLowary said. "You are looking at a court-martial, Quinn. Do not make things worse."

"Sir, you are guilty of war crimes and should be the one court-martialed." Quinn looked towards the security guards. "Arrest General McLowary."

"You do not have the authority," said McLowary.

"I am taking that authority."

The two men glared at each other. The security guards, one a human and the other a neodite, glanced at each other then at the ten armed quintessences. Other officers on duty watched tensely. No one moved.

Colonel Gundry broke the silence. "Security, arrest General McLowary for murder of civilians after a surrender."

Uneasy the guards stepped forward to the general's platform. McLowary stood above all, silently calculating in his head various scenarios if there was a gunfight.

He turned to Gundry, "You disappointment me, Colonel."

"You disappointed me too, sir."

McLowary looked at Quinn. "I will have your head. When we get back to Basanti, my allies will see to your death."

Firmly Quinn meet the general's eyes, neither man showing fear. "The Five will decide my fate, not you."

As security escorted McLowary out of the room, the quintessences holstered their guns. The colonel stepped onto the platform and sat in the command chair.

He gave Quinn a nod then said to the whole room, "Tell the colony we accept their surrender. Then send a reminder to our other ships to not fire on civilian ships unless first fired upon." He turned back to Quinn. "Dismissed, Major."

Chapter Twenty-two

The large oval Synod Chamber was filled to capacity. The Fifty with their aids took up the higher rows in the amphitheater style seating. The Five sat across from the main door. In the visitor section, high-ranking dignitaries from several governments stared at the accused quintessence standing quietly in the middle of the huge room. Camera drones flew about, recording the trial, all controlled by the Publicity Department at Essence. A few outside reporters managed to be among the crowd as guests of politicians. Hennah sat with other wives of the Five. Near them were department heads and other high ranking non-quintessences at the institution.

Hennah tried to look poised, but being surrounded by so many important people with fancy titles made Hennah feel like a child masquerading as an adult. At nineteen, she was the youngest in the room except Quinn, a lieutenant with eight years of experience. A few days ago, the wives of the Five had met and collectively agreed to attend the trial. Hennah has remained mostly silent during their discussion, going along with what the others decided.

She preferred to be in her quiet, isolated lab. Cell growth tests were coming along well, too well. Yashana and her daughter Yaira had been masters of their craft and their designs needed little, if any tweaking. Still, Hennah and her two lab assistants were running every test they knew, checking all results twice. Before committing to actually growing a batch of cells to birth age, they needed to assure the DNA was perfect as possible.

Sitting to Hennah's right, Firestrike tapped orders on her e-band to one of her lieutenants. Today she wore a long red dress, a rarity for fjouwer preferred pants. Twisted across her shoulder and waist was a large, fashionable black slash, carefully arranged to hide the gun and two knives she carried. Though she looked the part of a dignitary's wife, she was on duty, constantly monitoring communication with her underlings.

Amaka sat on the other side of Hennah, constantly scanning the room, reading minds of any she wished. As Amaka was publicly known as one of the most powerful living telepaths, most of the visitors avoided looking at her. But it did not matter. She could still peer into their thoughts without the need of eye-contact. The silver dress she wore made her dark, gray skin seem a few shades lighter.

In the row directly below Hennah, the other two Five's spouses whispered to each other. Being married to the director of Essence, Aurora Curi, an elderly sundancer, was considered to be the most powerful woman at Essence. Aurora had retired as head of the Publicity Department a few years ago. Still, she was a master at manipulating information. Before the newscast of today's events was broadcast by her former department, she would review the final editing, making sure every detail was factual while accurately explaining to watching quintessences the impact of Quinn's trial.

Jennifer McMillian, the human wife of Skyler, leaned towards Aurora and whispered while pointing to an ediethean from the High Council sitting on the other side of the room. At twenty-four, Jennifer had been the youngest of the wives until Hennah joined the group. Jennifer had risen quickly in position within the Toddler Department. When she and Skyler first married, she had been a basic worker who tended youngsters. After Skyler began a Five, she was promoted several times. Now she was one of six supervisors who oversaw the entire department. Within a few more years, it was expected she would become its head. Such was the power of being the wife of a Five.

The floor of the Synod Chamber was white marble tile except at its center where a dark green circle formed the area for the accused to stand. Hidden microphones in the floor carried the speaker's voice clearly across the large room. Quinn showed no emotions as he recounted his story of why he challenged his superior. Occasionally one of the Five would interrupt him with a question. Each time Quinn answered in a calm voice then continued his story. Once he finished, various members of the Synod questioned him in earnest, seeking to know details.

Caden asked, "How much time passed between the surrender of the planet and General McLowary's command to continuing firing?"

Quinn replied, "Maybe one to two minutes from my perspective. After the first call for surrender came, I tried to return to the *Bismarck* but was ordered to destroy all foreign ships, including civilians."

"You lie!" shouted a trim human man from the visitors section. The officer stood and pointed at Quinn. "General McLowary has honor, unlike you, leech."

Caden turned cold eyes towards the human. "General McLowary is not on trial today, but Lieutenant Quinn. Only members of the Synod may question him. If you interrupt again, you will be removed."

The man gave the director a dirty look but sat down in silence. Firestrike typed orders into her e-band and two security officers moved across the oval room and took guard positions on the floor just below the man's seat in the first row. Mumbling from onlookers quieted as the trial continued.

General McLowary had been sent back to Command locked in the brig of a ship, but he had been quickly released by high-ranked supporters. The media was told he was now retiring as a victorious war hero. Several edietheans in the military sent word to the High Council on their homeworld that the general was guilty of war crimes and the Coalition was trying to cover it up. The High Council demanded for McLowary to be court-marshaled but Coalitions members pushed back, blocking all attempts.

With the retired general immune from prosecution, focus turned towards Quinn. The Coalition demanded Quinn's blood for treason. The High Council wanted the galaxy to see the speciesist views of the Coalition exposed, while at the same time desiring to force a wedge between the quintessences and their Coalition masters.

As Hennah continued to listen to the proceedings, she kept glancing at her husband sitting with the other Five. His face was stoic, but she knew he was deeply troubled. Late into the night they had discussed the impact of the coming trial. If the Synod found Quinn innocent, the Coalition might pull their support away, letting a pressing bill in the Galactic Senate pass which would slash funding by half yet again. If Quinn was found guilty, the High Council would still view the quintessences as puppets of the Coalition and push yet harder for the bill to pass. Either way, it was a no-win situation for the quintessences.

Hennah had tried to comfort her husband. He was concerned that the trial would ignite a spark which would eventually burst into a blaze incinerating the quintessences into extinction. That was his greatest fear. She knew no words to help him, only holding him tightly as he talked until sleep claimed him. Then she had lay quietly beside him, wondering what Lashana would had advised. Sometimes she felt jealousy for this ancestor who had bedded her husband in the same room. Lashana was long dead but her memories remained vivid to Joseph.

It had been three months since Hennah had learned the truth about her ancestors, but she still struggled with accepting that Joseph, Alec, and Alexander were the same person. It was challenging enough dealing with a husband she had thought was forty-one years her senior. With him having over six centuries of experiences, she was but a tender twig next to a massive tree.

Still, he worked hard at their marriage, giving her spontaneous gifts, usually cheap in price but powerful in meaning. Like a bangle which was identical to the one her dad had given her mom on their twenty year wedding anniversary. Or a marigold pin to wear in her hair. Wanting to share his passions with her, one afternoon he took her up in a fighter jet. He piloted while she sat behind him, feeling queasy at the high altitude and fast turns. Another time he had piloted a helicopter, flying low over the vast forests of the national reserve near Essence Institute. After getting over her uneasiness of flying, Hennah had enjoyed the splendor view of herds of animals dashing across plains and disappearing into the thick forest. Near noon he sat the craft down in a clearing then pulled out a picnic basket. They dined together, enjoying each other's company far away from civilization.

Hennah had begun feeling emotions again as the depression slowly faded. First had come hope when she saw the DNA designs created by her ancestors. As she began working on the patterns in her lab, she felt excitement for the first time for the project. She smiled more often, laughing at jokes again. From her apartment's balcony, she admired sunsets. When Joseph kissed her, she returned his passion. She could finally feel love for him.

Yet sometimes dark thoughts still pulled at her, threatening to draw her again into depression's apathy embrace. Such times came when she was alone or lying in bed beside her sleeping husband. Whenever she compared herself to Layla and Yashana, she came up far short. Did her husband only love her because she was a clone of his dead wives? He insisted that he had fallen in love with her as Joseph before the merge with Alec. Still, doubts ate at her. With regularly mind probing, he tried to help her identify bleak thought patterns and break their vicious cycle. It was not easy, but most days now she lived free of depression.

Hennah's attention was pulled back to the present as Quinn was replaced in the green circle by Colonel Gundry. The witness's account closely matched Quinn's testimony. Some Coalition members mumbled disgruntledly, but none dared speak openingly. A few other officers were called forth to testify. Two supported the general, claiming McLowary only gave orders to fire at civilian ships which shot first. The birthmates which served as Quinn's lieutenants supported his version.

After the last witness had been called, Caden called for a half hour break. The Five left to talk in private. Sentients milled about, stretching their legs. Animated discussions came from small groups. The Fifty sent some of their aids off on tasks.

Amaka lowered her voice, speaking so only the four wives near her could hear. "It is as we feared. If Quinn does not receive a death sentence, the Coalition will retaliate by allowing the funding bill to pass. They wish to remind Essence of the power they hold over us."

Aurora whispered, "Will the High Council support us if Quinn is set free?" The large spikes on her head were pale from stress.

"No. They still view quintessences as an abomination against nature. They will be delighted if there is a public rift between the Coalition and Essence."

A human reporter walked up to the wives, disrupting their discussion. He gave a friendly smile. "I'm from *Galactic Times*. I was wondering if I can get quotes from you ladies."

Amaka gave him a long stare with her large golden eyes. She must have liked what she saw in his thoughts for she relaxed and smiled back. "We can spare a moment."

"Excellent." The lanky reporter activated the audio recorder on his e-tablet. Essence security did not allow outsiders to have camera drones on campus. "What is your opinion of the coming verdict?"

Aurora answered, "The Synod will do as they always do—give a fair verdict based on the evidence."

"How will this verdict affect Essence's standing with the Galactic Senate?"

Firestrike spoke first, "The Galactic Senate long ago gave the Synod power to decide the fate of wayward quintessences. Normally such matters stay internal."

"Are you suggesting that because of General McLowary's high profile, this case is being treated differently?"

"Yes. Galactic senators don't usually attend our meetings here."

"If the accused is found innocent then Essence will seem to be supporting the claim that renowned General McLowary is guilty of war crimes. Do you believe he should be court-martialed?"

Jennifer could no longer hold back her anger. "Yes. The general is a monster. He ignored a surrender, killing innocent children, destroying whole cities. He should be held accountable for what he has done."

The reporter looked expectantly towards Hennah. "If other quintessences are given similar orders as Quinn, how will they response?"

"Um," Hennah was uncertain what to say. "I don't know."

The man asked a few more questions which the others answered. Finishing the interview, he said, "For the record, can each of you state your name?"

The others wives said their names and positions. When it was Hennah's turn, Amaka cut in, taking the reporter's arm. "I'm sure you will do a fine job with your article. Tell me, what is your personal position about the Coalition?"

The man turned off his recorder. "Off the record, I think their speciesist views are ripping apart our empire."

Amaka led the reporter away from the others as she continued the discussion with him. Hennah let out the breath she did not know she had been holding. She knew Aurora would make sure no images of her appeared in Essence's news vids. Having not said anything intelligent in the interview, she hoped to be quickly forgotten by the reporter. She should not have come today. The outside world could not find out that the Five had broken galactic laws for her to exist. The fallout would be far worse than this trial.

The Five reentered the room, and sentients began moving back to their seats. Amaka gave Hennah's arm a motherly pat as she sat down. Quinn moved back into the green circle, and the room became quiet.

Caden stood and slowly moved his stern gaze around the chamber. "We have heard the evidence and have had time to discuss the information. There will be one last opportunity to question the accused then we vote."

Various synod members asked Quinn questions about details, times, and specific comments by other. Everything had already been covered in the earlier testimony.

Impatient, Hennah whispered, "Why don't they just go ahead and vote?"

Firestrike answered, "Liars can sometimes be tripped up with tiny details."

"He is not lying. We know that." Quinn's mind had already been probed days ago, and the Synod knew the true events. Today's long proceedings was just a show for the visitors.

"Patience." Firestike caught Amaka's eyes. "How will they vote?"

Keeping her voice barely audible, the kuawazo said, "They waver back and forth. The impact of this decision is too great. I cannot tell which way it will go."

"He is innocent," said Hennah. "They should vote on the truth."

"Truth? He disobeyed a direct command from a supervisor. The Code states the punishment is death."

"But he did so because the order was immoral."

"That does not give him immunity from breaking the Code."

Hennah slumped in her seat, frustrated. Why was the Code written to be so inflexible? She would ask Joseph—or Alexander—later about that. Surely he had been one of the original writers. She felt a few harsh words coming to mind.

The large chamber fell into silence. The last question had been asked. Faces turned expectantly towards the director.

Caden stood. "Brothers, it is time to vote. Enter your choice."

Synod members touched screens built into the arms of their chairs. After they entered in passwords, their faces were scanned along with the microchip in their hands. Then they entered in their vote.

After all fifty-five votes were registered, Caden stood. "Lieutenant Quinn, this Synod finds you guilty of breaking the Code specifically for disobeying a supervisor."

The young quintessence in the green circle did not react. Quinn kept a stoic face as he looked up to his director.

"We have taken into account that you did so in order to obey other sections of the Code. Therefore, we will waver the death penalty. You are stripped of your command and will spend the rest of your bond years exiled from your birthmates preforming menial tasks."

Hennah mumbled, "That is the same punishment they gave Joseph."

Amaka frowned, "They still try to walk the middle ground, but it won't be enough this time to appease any side."

Angry shouts broke out from several human groups. A dark-haired man in a colonel's uniform yelled above the others, "Leeches! Foeditas horribilis! How dare you sit in judgement of General McLowary! You have no jurisdiction."

Caden turned cold eyes towards the man. "We have passed judgement on what we do have jurisdiction over. It is the Basanti Military's job to investigate General McLowary."

The trial over, sentients began moving about the room, groups forming to discuss the events. Several reporters sought out quotes.

Aurora shook her head. "My husband should not have made that last statement. Now he has publicly declared Essence stance against the general and the Coalition."

"He didn't mention the Coalition," said Hennah.

"Does not matter. They will take it that way. Our newsfeed will not contain that line, but others will publish it." Aurora glanced at the roaming reporters.

Feeling sick of the whole matter, Hennah broke away from the other wives and left the room. She very much wanted the comfort of her quiet lab where she controlled all outcomes.

Heading towards the elevator, she was halfway across the airy lobby before Darkfern, dressed in a security uniform, emerged from the crowd. "So what was the verdict?"

"Guilty. They gave him the same punishment as my husband."

The fjouwer frowned, "Wish I have been stationed inside where all the action was, but Mom thinks I'm too hot-headed."

"You are." Hennah relaxed a bit. Teasing her best friend relieved some of the stress which boiled inside. Jibes were part of fjouwer culture, and Darkfern would take nothing she said personally.

"Perhaps. I think we should just throw the evil general into a juttin pit and be done with the matter."

"How would putting him into a pit end things? His buddies would just get him out again."

"You don't know juttins. They are large, semi-intelligent beasts from the fjouwer homeworld. Some of the more barbaric tribes keep males in deep pits. I will spare you the details of how they are used as a punishment, only that it can last for years."

"I think your mom was right in keeping you away from the trial."

Darkfern grinned. "Don't worry. Modern fjouwers don't keep juttins. The only ones we see are in zoos on Shah Luna. You should come with me to the next Kilpailu held there."

"Maybe soon. There is much needing to be done at work."

"You always say that."

"My job is important."

Hennah hurried away to the elevators. She bypassed the closest ones which only stopped on floors that permitted visitor access. The one she chose was empty and took her directly to the Research Department. When she reached her lab, Lark'ukva and Fran'ukva greeted her by waving the results of another passed test.

"Really," said Lark'ukva, "there is no reason why we should not proceed to the next phrase—live birth."

"Too soon," complained her mate. "Alpha testing goes on for years."

"But these were designed by Yashana and her daughter, two of the most brilliant geneticists who ever lived, beside Layla. No offense, Hennah."

The profectus shrugged. "I know I'm not as good as them."

Lark'ukva turned her large, deep blue eyes towards Hennah. "Your name will be as famous as theirs someday, once this research goes public."

"It's still their work."

"But after we run though all these models, then you will be designing new ones. From scratch. You have the talent. You just needed the key."

Hennah gave a smile to appease the sea laven. Lark'ukva was too perceptive, knowing that her boss had carried the weight of failure for far too long.

Fran'ukva said, "We must proceed carefully. Not give false hopes. Keep to regulations as much as possible."

Thinking about the trial, Hennah said, "Regulations are important, but so is time. I will speak with my husband about moving to the beta stage."

Reaching the end of the workday, Hennah headed back to the penthouse. She found Joseph on the balcony, leaning against the railing, his broad shoulders drooping. Hennah walked over and wrapped her arms around him, snuggling against his firm body. He turned and hugged her close.

For a long time they stood, holding onto each other, as they surveilled the vast campus of Essence. Spaceships lifted off carrying passengers back to their home planets. Monorails zoomed along their high tracks, taking workers home. Squads of young quintessences marched towards their barracks after a long day of training. Families headed to the beach to spend time playing together in the waves and sand. Recently freed quintessences returned from fishing trips on sailboats. All was peaceful, calm.

Joseph finally broke the silence. "Amaka has informed us Five that the Coalition will let the bill pass. Soon we will be laying off half of our workers, over three thousand employees." His fist clenched. "There are generations of families, like yours, who have worked here for centuries. To layoff even some of them splits the entire clan. They have supported us, allowing my brethren to join their families by marriage. Many of the workers of Essence are part of my giant family. We are all connected."

"I'm sorry," said Hennah, giving her husband a tight hug.

"Today my brothers and I almost voted the other way. We almost sentenced Quinn to death."

"You were in his shoes once. You know he did the right thing."

"Yes, but if the death of one innocent quintessence will spare all the pain of what is to come, then the price would have been worth it."

Hennah pulled back. "How can you say that?"

"The Code states that all quintessences shall place the welfare of their brethren above themselves. Each of us must be willing to sacrifice our own lives for the good of all. Quinn's death would have kept the Coalition on our side. Instead, tens of thousands of my brethren will never be born. Generations of families will be split apart as they go to other planets seeking jobs, some never seeing each other again. That is the cost we pay for keeping Quinn alive."

"Then why did you let him live?"

"Because the Coalition will continue to put our brethren in the same situation over and over again, using them to destroy non-humans. We had to make a stand. Already quintessences have been used as tools in genocides. Entire species of sentients wiped out, the environments of their homeworlds made unlivable. All under the orders of the Coalition."

"It's not in the news."

"The Coalition can manipulate the news just like us, hiding genocides under the veil of rebellion. Quinn was not the first quintessence to stand up against such practices, but he is the first to survive a successful coup. Too often our brethren are killed immediately when they take a stand against superiors, but sometimes a few are sent back here for trials, like myself."

Hennah leaned against her husband, overcome by all the cruelties in the universe. "Essence should ally with the Ediethean High Counsel."

"Easier said than done. The elite of the edietheans despise us, and their hands are not clean of innocent blood either. They are almost as dangerous as the Coalition."

Trying to find something positive, Hennah said, "Lark'ukva thinks we should proceed with beta testing."

185

Joseph reached out and took his wife's hand. "Beta testing takes decades. By the time we know if the females are mental stable and can live by the Code, we may no longer have labs to grow new generations in."

"There is still hope for your species."

Neither spoke for a while. Hennah suddenly turned and faced her husband. "You need a vacation."

"My society is collapsing. Now is not the time for vacations."

"You promised months ago to give me a vacation off world. I have never been away from Xi'an, yet you have been to hundreds of planets having countless adventures."

"Adventure is not the word I would use. I was a soldier serving my empire."

"Not all the time. Anyway, you promised me. Let us visit your birthmates. They don't live that far away. You have not seen them in over a year. If we don't go now, there really will not be time once the betas are born."

When Joseph remained quiet, Hennah wrapped her arms around his neck, pulling him down to kiss him on the lips. She then gave him a comical, pleading look.

A faint smile crossed his face. "Layla would use that same expression when she wanted to talk me into something."

Hennah pulled back, frowning at being compared to his first wife. "I'm not like her at all."

Joseph wrapped his arms around her slender waist. "You are like her a lot more than you realize, and I am not referring to your lovely body."

"If you feel like flirting, then you must be agreeing."

"Yes, we will visit my birthmates."

She beamed as she gave him a passionate kiss which he returned, letting the frustration of the day fade away.

They left the planet two days later, telling only a few. Miles was the only Shadow Guard which accompanied them. Joseph kept their identities secret when they landed in the spaceport of Rowan. They arrived in a small space yacht owned by Essence. Visits by Fives to peaceful Core planets often led to political leaders throwing parades and parties to honor their prestige guests. Joseph wanted to avoid politics for the next few weeks.

When he and Hennah showed up unannounced at the apartment building that most of his brothers lived in, he enjoyed his birthmates' astonishment. Soon he was surrounded by his brothers, all trying to greet him at once.

"Do not let being a Five go to your head," said Philip. "I can still out gun you any time."

"You should see me at bōjutsu. I have improved."

Ryder said, "You may have been the first to marry, but I was not far behind. You must meet my wife. She holds several platinum metals from the Planetary Sports Tournament. You can stay with us while you are here."

The birthmates wanted to share everything with Joseph that he had missed out on. Having lost so many brothers in war, the birthmates were determined to embrace life. They talked and jested for hours the first night. Over the next three weeks they took Joseph to their favorite hangouts, teaching him new sports, and showing him off to comrades at work. Hennah came along at times, but when they tried talking her into skydiving from an airplane, she drew the limit. While they were enjoying extreme sports, she hung out with her eight sisters-in-law, well, the ones that preferred not to paraglide or mountain climb. Several of them were as athletic as their husbands. One was, in fact, a parkour star who had won over a dozen awards. Another held two platinum medals in xpogo ball.

While Joseph was with his birthmates, he was cheerful, joking right along with the rest, the responsibilities of a Five far away. On their last night before leaving, the couple went for a walk together in a popular park, pausing to admire a water show. Hidden pipes shot liquid up over a hundred feet in patterns while laser lights morph the water into different colors.

Hennah held her husband's hand. "I am happy to see you happy."

"You were wise in convincing me to come. I needed this." He kissed her hand. "Thanks for agreeing to me my wife—twice."

She grinned and gave him a playful pinch on his arm. He pulled her to him, kissing her in sight of all, something he had never done before.

"One question," she said when they broke apart. "Why does this planet look so much like Xi'an?"

"Because sentients tend to terraform their colonies to look like their homeworlds. Over millenniums, many of the Core planets are very similar, depending on which sentient race settled first. If you want exotic locations, then you must go to the Rim."

"Like Shah Luna? Darkfern keeps asking me to go with her there. Will you take me?"

"Yes, someday. But your research must be our priority for now."

"You promise?"

"Yes, Patni. I promise."

At the spaceport all forty-six birthmates, their wives, and a few girlfriends came to see Joseph and Hennah off.

Philip said to Hennah, "You have done well by him. He is happy. For years we have worried about him."

"You are part of his happiness. You remind him of why he must continue his fight. The duties of a Five are heavy."

Ryder's parting words to Joseph were, "If you need us for anything, we will come."

Joseph studied his birthmates. "My greatest desire is for you to live, to be free to enjoy the life that you paid so dearly for."

The trip home took several days. Once they were in orbit around Xi'an, they buckled into seats for the descent. Hennah sat by Joseph as they watched the planet loom closer through a window. She noticed her husband's shoulders drooping, the sternness of his face. The worries of the Five were back.

Seeking to console him, she wrapped her slender arm around his muscular arm and whispered, "I will give you a miracle, husband. No matter what, your species will survive. That is my promise to you."

He squeezed her hand as he watched the craft approach Essence.

Chapter Twenty-three

Melodious music filled the air as an orchestra played on a stage. Dancing couples in expensive garments whirled around the center of the ballroom while onlookers mingled or grabbed drinks from passing servers. Far overhead the enormous roof, made from specialized glass, gave the appearance of a sparkling diamond slowly rotating colors. The palace's roof was so famous that the entire capitol city of the Basanti Empire was named after it.

Kylen studied elaborate columns surrounding the edge of the marble dance floor. *Amy should be here to see this. She would know the name of every architectural component used to create this cave of wonders.* The tuxedo Kylen wore felt too heavy, like a shell hiding who he really was from the galaxy. His usually ruffled hair was sleeked back, and Kylen resisted the urge to run a hand through it to loosen it up.

"Smile," said Reynold Nash, Kylen's boss. "Look like you're having fun. You just won the prestige Humanitarian Award for saving hundreds of future lives."

The heavyset man owned a renowned software company that maintained programs for the Transportation Department for the city. The family-own company was over three hundred years old. Reynold knew little about coding himself, but he knew how to hire talented employees. Kylen had only worked there four months, and had little to do with writing the algorithm for the program which gave service and emergency vehicles faster routes through the city by delaying oncoming traffic. The program had been written over three years ago but kept secret until now. Kylen had tweaked the program a bit, so at least he could honestly say he had worked on it. Members of the Coalition on the award committee promoted Kylen above other contenders for the Humanitarian Award.

Kylen forced a smile. "Not every day I meet a princess, let alone my future wife." He wished again Amy had been invited. Her enthusiasm for seeing the palace would be catchy, helping Kylen to relax.

Reynold led Kylen through the crowd, introducing his employee to people he knew. Kylen had already secretly met a number of them over the last few months. He had been tutored in politics, etiquettes, and laws by various Coalition members determined to turn him into a proper prince. Kylen had been a quick learner, memorizing over a hundred greeting for prominent sentients, the proper silverware for fancy meals, even steps for traditional dances. Still, he felt inaccurate picturing himself talking to a real princess. He was a computer programmer, not a politician.

A herald announced, "I give you Emperor Duyagni and his daughter Princess Abarrane."

The orchestra played the national anthem as the royal pair entered. The tailored suit the athletic ruler wore was embroidered with symbols representing Basanti. The princess wore a blue flowing dress which simmered in the light. The crowd parted, giving them ample room to walk to the center of the dance floor. Guards stood at attention around the room, scanning for assassins. The music changed to a waltz. The Emperor bowed formally to his daughter, and she gave a curtsey. Then he took her arms, swirling her around the floor, her long blue dress twirled around her legs. Several dozen dignities joined the dance, forming a large circle. Couples rotated partners, moving in precise patterns.

From among the onlookers, Kylen watched, his eyes never leaving the princess. She was poised and confident, never missing a step as she switched partners. Her blond hair was bound in a tight bun by a sapphire pin. She was gorgeous, appearing far more radiant than the insipid princess he saw in vids.

When the song ended, the princess moved to the side of the room to greet acquaintances. The orchestra picked up the tempo with its next song, and more couples moved onto the dance floor.

Reynold smiled boldly. "Time to meet your bride-to-be."

Kylen attempted to hide his nervousness as they meandered through the crowd, slowly making their way towards the princess. They passed tentacled squamiger drinking fishy ales, humans sipping wine, and stardancers sampling spicy hors d'oeuvres. Dozens of different sentient species enjoyed the party. Kylen waved away a servant offering him a cocktail. He needed a clear head tonight.

Now he was twenty feet, then ten from her. Moments away from speaking with her, Kylen reflected on a secret meeting with her father which took place several weeks ago. Without warning a brawny man had shown up at Kylen's apartment, telling him to come. Thinking it was yet another tutoring session from a Coalition member, Kylen had climbed into the nondescript brown hover car. Even when it pulled into the wealthy estate located at the edge of the city of Diamond, he had felt no alarm, only curiosity. Then he entered a large room filled with a dozen guards, prominent Coalition members, and the Emperor himself. He had become wary, realizing immediately this was no normal social gathering.

For the next three hours, he was grilled with questions about himself, his training, and how he would behave in different scenarios. Kylen spoke calmly, even when some attacked him with insults, testing to see how well he dealt with pressure. The Emperor was especially bold, tearing him down in one sentence while flattering him in another. Kylen used wit against the insults, turning phrases back towards the speakers. Eventually the questioners were satisfied and sent Kylen away. Two days later he had received the invitation to the annual ball.

Reynold's voice pulled Kylen back to the present. "Princess Abarrane, I would like you to meet my protégé Kylen, winner of the Humanitarian Award. I taught him everything he knows."

Kylen's mind went blank, forgetting the words he had practiced. She stood in front of him, the stranger he was supposed to wed, her sharp eyes boring into him.

Abarrane frowned slightly. "Everything? Surely he picked up a few things on his own. I heard he was a genius. A silent one, I see."

Pulling his thoughts together, Kylen said, "I can speak quite a bit on subjects I enjoy."

"And what are those subjects? Computers and coding? I yawn thinking about them."

Kylen forced a smile. "While I am a talented hacker, you will find me very knowledgeable about many subjects." He noticed a new song was starting. "Like dancing." He held out an arm, inviting her.

With a tiny grimace, she studied his hand. A stern elderly woman beside the princess gave her a gentle poke in the side. Aberrance sighed and put on a fake smile. "I will be delighted to accept this dance, prince of the hackers."

As Kylen led, he occasionally misstepped, but Abarrane was talented enough to cover it up. When the music ended, Kylen followed her to the side of the room. The stern attendant stood within hearing distance, watching the couple.

Kylen gave a polite bow. "Thank you for the dance, Princess."

"The pleasure was not mine. When did you learn to dance? Last week?"

"Last month. Before that I was memorizing the faces of all your household staff. For example, your watchdog to the left is Suson Taklen. She was your mom's nurse then yours. She is also a trained bodyguard. You respect her yet secretly resent that during an assassination attempt five years ago, she saved your life and not your mom's."

Abarrane had remained aloof until he mentioned her mother. Anger blazed in her blue eyes. "Who told you that? I never made such a statement."

"No one had to. I see it in the way you interact with her. I am very, very good at reading people."

"If that is so, then what am I thinking right now."

"You distaste being told who to marry. You have already decided I am an unrelatable computer nerd. My objective is to change your mind in that regard." He held out a hand. "Will you walk with me?"

"Will you talk about technology?"

"No."

"In that case, we can speak in a more private location. There will be few in the Royal Garden right now."

As the princess led Kylen through the palace, Suson followed several paces behind. They passed large, elaborate rooms. Many held huge art pieces on walls and statures on pedestals. The vast garden was indoors, divided into biomes sectioned off to control temperature and artificial rainfall. Rare, exotic plants from across the galaxy grew in carefully maintained habitats.

For a while they walked in silence as Kylen admired the magnificent conservatory. As a child growing up in an underground bunker, he saw few plants except on reward trips to town. He breathed in the rich aromas of blooming night flowers in a hot, jungle environment. What had life been like for Abarrane growing up in this paradise?

They walked through a short passage and entered a wintery biome. Abarrane waved for her guardian to stay behind. The temperature was just below freezing. Gentle snow fell from overhead vents. Hearty plants grew among snowbanks and icicles. Kylen paused in front of a dark green bush with spiky leaves and red berries. How did such plants thrive in inhospitable environments? During winter on the planet he had grown up on, trees lost their leaves and other vegetation disappeared under the snow. Yet here was beauty when there should have been death.

"You are fortunate to grow up here, in a palace."

"Fortunate? You do not know what you are getting yourself into. Always I am watched. Never am I out of sight of a guard even in my own private suite. At social gatherings, my words are securitized. Have I offended this person or that one? This one wants a favor; that one wants me put in a good word with my father. Everyone tries to use me as a pawn—just like you. A bride so the nerd can pretend to be a prince."

"The marriage was not my idea. I prefer writing codes for the rest of my life. I am simply following the orders I was given, as you are." Kylen's breath fogged the air.

"Why did the Coalition choose you as their lapdog? Would not a politician be better than a nerd?"

"Surely you know who I am a clone of. Richard Cambridge was a well-liked politician and computer programmer who won the Zelzer Award."

"He was only a mayor, not such a big deal. And the Zelzer Award was rigged. My ancestor Emperor Kalyuga made sure Richard was given the award to produce positive publicity for his leech project."

"Something else my clone and I have in common. The Humanitarian Award I was given was also rigged."

Abarrane's frown deepened. "And you are just going along with it?"

192

"It is what they expect of me."

"Do you always do what you are told?"

"Do you?"

The princess glanced towards her elderly nurse standing near the entrance of the snowy biome. "My choices are limited."

"So are mine. Profectus who don't fit the Coalition's agenda have a habit of disappearing permanently."

"My father wields real power. He was born into his position and he understands nuances of dealing with the many groups all angling for control. As you are a creation of the Coalition, you will never be more than their puppet, expected to fulfill their whims."

"The Coalition does not act on whims. The plan to have a profectus as Emperor began many centuries ago. We both stand at the zenith of countless dreams of others—a natural born profectus ruling the galaxy."

"Nightmares are what I see. Do you really know everything the Coalition plans?"

"They tell me what they want me to know."

Abarrane leaned closer and whispered, "What about the genocides they have committed? And the ones planned?"

Kylen noticed her cheeks and nose had turned red from the cold. The foggy cloud from her breath blurred his view of her. Was she testing him or really concerned about other sentients? This whole conversation might be a trap, seeing if a beautiful girl could sway him from the Coalition's agenda. There could be hidden recorders catching his every word at this moment.

"You are referring to putting the Edietheans in their place. That will happen someday when the Coalition believes the timing is right."

The princess pulled back, disappointment on her face. "I guess they did pick the perfect dog for the job."

Chapter Twenty-four

The plate clanked as Hennah sat it on the dining table in front of her husband. Then she sat across from him, adding more spice to the chicken kozhi curry on her own plate. As she ate, she silently studied her husband. Quintessence expressions were difficult to read for outsiders, but Hennah had spent her whole life around them. She noted his slightly drooping shoulders, tired eyes, and straight lips.

"Did the Synod meeting go better today?"

"No, the budget debate still continues." He took a deep sip of water.

"Sorry about the spice. I may have added a tad too much."

His lips slightly curled into a smile. "With three wives who like spicy Indian cuisine, I am use to the heat."

"Others keep asking me when the layoffs will begin. I don't know what to tell them. People are worried."

Joseph's smile faded. It had only been a week since the Galactic Senate had voted to half Essence's budget. The Synod had met every day since then, debating how to manage funds to reduce layoffs.

"Today, we agreed to a ten percent budget cut for all lower staff. Twenty percent for upper staff. Synod members fifty percent. Except for the Five who will only get a five thousand credit supplement per year. Along with other measure, we are hoping to keep two-thirds of our staff."

"Five thousand credits? I know you are frugal with your money, but that is not enough to live on."

"You will still be getting a decent salary. Besides, my brothers and I have invested our money well over the centuries. If we wished, we could live extravagant lifestyles on the interest alone."

Hennah paused in her eating. "Exactly how rich are we…you?"

Joseph reached across the table and took her hand. "We are rich in love. That is enough for me. As for money, the values changes daily based on many stock markets across many planets. Every decade, my brothers and I siphoned off the excess and buy new ships for Essence. That is how we have built up a sizeable fleet. We then can provide jobs for freed birthmates who live on those ships, fulfilling missions approved by the Synod. As you know, we regularly get requests for help from across the Empire."

"Paid mercenaries, you mean. You charge a sizable fee for providing a helping hand."

"Ships need fuel; armies need food. And my brethren deserve a paycheck for their work, after giving free labor to the empire for half a century. What profit that is made it put back into Essence's budget. Occasionally we do mercy missions for free if the cause is dire enough."

"I'm not criticizing. I know that the quintessences have helped a lot of sentients. But yesterday in the Synod meeting, you discussed increasing your mercenary services and double the asking price. Less people will be able to afford your help."

"We are struggling to survive, Hennah. We do what we must." Joseph's e-band beeped, and he glanced at the incoming message. "Caleb sends a reminder of our private meeting tonight."

"You are tired, along with the others. Cannot it be postponed for another time?" Hennah chewed slowly on her last bite of chicken.

"You have twice already had it postponed. I am beginning to suspect that I married a shy bride who dreads public speaking—even if it is a secret gathering."

Hennah rolled her eyes. "Give me Desmond's humor over yours, anytime."

"I thought Firestrike was the only one who could put up with Jacob's wit. You surprise me, beloved."

"Flattery does not make me feel better."

"You will be fine. You are a wife of a Five. Just answer the questions matter-of-factly. They are just as eager as I am for Project Absurd to succeed."

After the dishes were cleaned, the couple headed down to the fortieth floor. Hennah paused in front of the ornament double doors leading into the Synod Chamber. She looked behind her at the large, airy lobby and the glass wall looking out over Essence. So many were counting on her. The reality was a heavy weight pressing upon her, causing her breathing to quicken, her chest to hurt.

"I cannot do this," she whispered.

Miles and other Shadow Guards watched silently as Joseph wrapped his strong arms around his wife, holding her close. Gently he kissed her, feeling her slowly relax. "I am with you, Patni. You have nothing to fear."

They entered the oval chamber partly filled with Synod members, several accompanied by wives. This was a closed, private session. Other than the Shadow Guards, no one else was allowed, not even aids. Recording devices were prohibited. There would be no record of what was spoken tonight.

High up, Joseph took a seat beside Jacob and Firestrike. Near him were the other Five and their wives. Hennah moved to the center of the room, standing in the green circle on the marble floor. Nervously she looked at the many faces surrounding her. They expected a miracle from her. Living female quintessences she

195

could give them, but how mentally stable the offspring would be was beyond her skills. What if she created monsters that would need to be culled? It had happened several times before. Even the exalted Layla Rangan had to put to death a young quintessence in Generation One after he had murdered his own brother.

Caden's voice resounded through the chamber. "Hennah Kalkar, we are eager to hear your report."

Hennah swallowed, steading herself. "Currently we are growing ten healthy fetuses in my lab. Their growth rates are following expected patterns. Five of them are CF1 models, predicted to look like Caucasian females with red hair. The other five are ASF1 models who will appear to have Asian descent, particular Indian, like me. Yashana patterned them after her family."

She went into more details, keeping her eyes on Joseph. As long as she pretended she was only talking with him, the nerviness faded. When she finished her prepared speech, she was forced to look around the room, waiting for questions.

"How long till their birth?" asked Jacob, excitement in his eyes.

"A month."

"Where will they be kept then?" Gabriel's blank face was unreadable to Hennah.

"In a connected lab. We will set up cribs. As they grow, we will add beds and toys. We will try to match the experience of the Toddler Department as much as possible. I suggest transferring over several workers to be their caregivers."

"That would be a mistake." All eyes in the room turned to Gabriel's young wife. Jennifer leaned forward, her body tense, ready for an argument. "We desire for these females to grow up to marry and have natural offspring. Without experiencing proper family life themselves, that process may be very difficult. Far too many psychologists at Essences have written papers detailing the difficulties of quintessences transiting from the role of soldiers to domestic husbands. They lack parenting skills. Only one-third will marry, and less than that take on the duties of parenting. Our traditional methods of rearing quintessences does not prepare them for domestic life."

Faces turned back to Hennah, waiting for her response. The palms of her hands began to sweat. "I...uh...am only a geneticist, not a psychologist. I deal with their DNA, not their behavior."

Caleb looked at Jennifer. "What do you propose we do?"

"Raise them like our daughters in families with a quintessence father and human mother. The children will blend into society, passing as humans. They should not grow up in a secret lab hidden from the world, rarely seeing the light of day. As much as possible, we need to give them a normal life."

Hennah felt a tightening in her stomach. "That may be dangerous. We do not yet know how mentally stable these models will be. They must be observed carefully, objectively."

"How will raising them in a sunless lab strengthen their mentally?" challenged Jennifer.

Unable to think of an answer, Hennah looked towards Joseph. He remained silent, thoughtful.

Gabriel said, "My wife's concerns hold merit. As a supervisor in the Toddler Department, she has had years of experience raising quintessences. I agree with her that we should explore alternative methods for raising the females."

Ideas began to be spoken around the room. Some, like Tobias, focused on complications which might arise. Others countered with solutions. Hennah stood in the green circle, dismayed by the turn of events. For seven years she had worked on this project in isolation. Now it was being snatched from her, others deciding the fate of her subjects. Joseph beckoned her. She left the circle and climbed the steps to him.

As she sat down, he squeezed her hand. "You spoke well."

"They do not like my plan. I was following protocol."

"Do not take the rejection personally."

She gave her husband a weak smile but still felt upset.

The debate continued for an hour, finally coming to the conclusion that the females would be raised in pairs, one from each model growing up in family units. When out in public, the pairs must stay away from each other to avoid arousing suspicious questions. In private they would study and train together.

After Caleb summed up their conclusion, he said, "That leads to one final question. Who will serve as parents?" He slowly looked around the room.

"We volunteer," said Jennifer. Her husband nodded in agreement.

"My wife and I also," said an IN3 named Stuart. His spouse Lissa was a supervisor at the Shooting Center.

"Add us," said a thirtyish woman named Reanne sitting beside a HC5.

"And us," said Joseph, ignoring Hennah's shocked look.

"I also and my wife," said Rodrick, a ME2. His wife Camila grinned in excitement.

As the meeting ended, Hennah remained seated, afraid if she so much as looked at Joseph she would start yelling at him in the middle of the crowd. *How dare he volunteer me to become a parent without asking!* She was supposed to be the objective scientist, observing from a distance, keeping careful records.

When the throng thinned, she stood and walked down the stairs, avoiding Joseph's eyes. From her body language, he had to know she was upset. The couple remained silent as they walked to the elevator and rode up to the fifth floor. Once they were back in the penthouse, away from Shadow Guards, Hennah let her rage fly.

"How dare you! You promised me you would never make any more important decisions about me without talking to me first. You lied to me!"

"There was no time. If I had not spoken, others would have taken our place."

"Then let them. Joseph, I am only nineteen. I am not ready to become a mom."

"Many younger than you have become parents."

"Do you understand my role in this project? I have to remain objective. If the infants turn out to be unstable or cannot live by the Code, I am the one who has to recommend their culling. How can I do that when I will also be a parent to two of them? Moms support their kids when they make mistakes. Scientists terminate their mistakes. I cannot do both roles!"

"Hear me out, Hennah. Afterwards, if you still do not want to be one of the parents, I will take our names off the list." Joseph's eyes were gentle, his voice calm.

Hennah stopped pacing and sat down, her hands still clenched in fists. "I will listen, but I will not change my mind."

"I have lived for many centuries, but I have never experienced being a real father, guiding a child from infancy to adulthood. I have trained many generations of quintessences, but that is not the same thing as being a father. I prepared them for war and death, but not for living a peaceful, domestic life. Jennifer is right in that we do a poor job in preparing quintessences for life once they are free. Many cannot stop being soldiers. It is the only lifestyle they know."

"You were married to Yashana, who had three kids."

"Two were already grown and attending college on another planet when I married her. Her youngest Yaira was a student at Luncaster University, living here on the weekends. Seth was their father, I only their step-father. I had little to do with their upbringing. I long for the experience of being a real father."

Hennah turned her head away from him, angry that he had put her into this position. He believed so strongly in this. How could she say no to him? Yet she was not ready for the responsibilities that came with being a parent.

"You ask too much of me. I'm not ready. Maybe after another generation or two, when we know if they are stable, then we can become parents."

Joseph sat down on the couch beside his wife. "Patni, I know you are afraid. But you will not be alone. If for any reason a judgement must be made for termination, you will not make that call, at most a recommendation. It is the Synod who will make the vote. I will carry the burden of it, not you."

"It's not as easy as you make it sound."

"I know." Joseph took his wife's hands. "Instead of thinking of worse case scenarios, reflect on the positive. Being the first real mom to a quintessence. Guiding two beautiful daughters as they grow up. Experiencing the joys of being a mother. New discoveries every day, you a pioneer. It will not be easy, but together we can reshape the destiny of my species. Create a new pattern, a new lifestyle that my brethren can follow. There is nothing in our Canon about being a parent, no guidelines. We can change that."

Hennah looked into her husband's eyes, seeing his excitement. The worries about budget cuts were banished for a while. This was not just Joseph she looked at but Alexander, the firstborn of all quintessences. A living legend she was married to. Sometimes, like in this moment, the reality both terrified and awed her. If he wanted to be a father, who was she to say no? Like the many times before, she agreed with his plan, despite her reservations.

She gave his hand a squeeze. "Alright. I'll become a mom, but I will still have to be the scientist too. I hope your faith in Lashana's work is rewarded."

A real smile lit his face. "Thank you for taking this journey with me."

Chapter Twenty-five

Hennah's lab had never been so crowded. With the entire Synod present, along with many wives and Shadow Guards, there was little space to move among the tables, shelves, and machines. Hennah stood beside the Automatic Fetus Developer, trying to appear calm. Her lab assistants grinned boldly, enjoying showing off their work, answering questions about how the project was conducted.

Births were commonplace in the Fetus Department, never drawing a large audience. Hennah had seen births a few times from the window of the observation room which allow visitors to watch without disturbing the workers. Now it was her turn to birth a quintessence and she felt fear. What if she accidently killed the fetus? Horror filled her as she glanced at the sharp knife laying at the edge of a nearby table.

Seeing that everyone had arrived, Caleb gave a brief speech of welcome then everyone look towards Joseph and Hennah. As Alexander had been first-born of all quintessences, the others felt it fitting that he would be the first to birth a female. Confidently, Joseph hit a button, causing the machine to drain away the amniotic fluids in a canister. Once it was empty, he unhooked the glass tube and laid it on a table which had raised edges to prevent liquids from running onto the floor. Gingerly he slid the wet, squirming infant out of the tube and carefully tore the placenta away from her face. He lifted her out of the slimy synthetic placenta. Next he clamped the umbilical cord then used the knife to cut it. He wrapped her in a thick towel while cleaning her mouth and nose. She began crying, taking her first breaths. He held his new daughter close, a look of bliss on his face.

The quintessences watched in silence while the others oohed and ahhed. Glad she had not been the first to go, Hennah copied the steps her husband had followed. Soon she had a squirming, wet infant on the table. She broke through the placenta and saw clearly her daughter's face for the first time. Large eyes stared at her from a bronze face. Weak hands flailed about. *She looks so human.* Carefully she pulled away the placenta and applied the clamp to the umbilical cord. Holding the knife, she found herself afraid to cut. *Why are we using a knife and not scissors? Leave it to soldiers to birth with weapons.* Taking a deep breath, she sliced across the cord. As she lifted up the baby, the infant cried out.

The lab and its audience faded from her awareness. There was only her and the nameless child. Wrapping the baby in a towel, she held her close, studying the face.

Large brown eyes and damp black hair. She had stared at the DNA on monitors for months. Now she beheld the results. Wonder filled her. *You are my daughter. My child. You are more beautiful than I could have predicted.*

She became aware that someone was standing beside her. Looking up, she saw Joseph studying her face. Tenderness was in his eyes as he gave her a smile, knowing the infant had infiltrated pass her researcher's detachment. For a moment she held his eyes, feeling a new connection to him, understanding why he wanted to be a father.

Lark'ukva and her lifemate cleaned up the table. Jennifer and Gabriel stepped forward for the next birthing. As Hennah watched the other births, she only partly paid attention. It was the child in her arms that fascinated her. After the tenth infant had been cleaned up, visitors crowded around the new parents, congratulating them. Fran'ukva injected each newborn with a microchip and entered their ID numbers into a computer. Lark'ukva weighed them on a scale, carefully documenting the notes in her e-tablet.

Eventually Hennah and Joseph headed up to their penthouse with their young family. In the elevator, Miles stood beside them, his eyes observing the infants, a faint, whimsical smile on his lips. *Even he is affected by them*, thought Hennah.

Joseph had already refurnished the second bedroom, taking away the bed and adding two cribs along with a changing station.

"I'll heat up the bottles," said Joseph, laying his daughter in a crib. "It's time to begin considering names."

Hennah laid her charge in the second crib. Worried that something would go wrong during the birthing, she had refused to discuss names whenever her husband had brought it up over the last month. Now she felt uncertainty. It was a heavy responsibility. A name stayed with someone forever. Normally quintessence infants were assigned random names from a database. Her daughters deserved better.

Joseph returned, passing a warm bottle to Hennah. His infant was soon feeding hungrily while Hennah struggled to get hers to take more than a few sips at a time.

"You are holding the bottle at the wrong angle. Lift it up."

"How do you know all this, as it's your first time being a father?"

"When Generation Three was birthed, my brothers and I were often put on feeding and diaper duty. Rosetta made quite a drill sergeant making sure we preformed our duties correctly."

"Rosetta Thomson? The one whose picture is beside the museum?"

"Yes, she was very important to all of us. Without her, Layla's little project would not have lasted long." He tossed a towel across his shoulder and placed his charge against it, patting her back.

"I forget sometimes that what is history to me was reality for you. That the strangers on walls were your friends." She felt again the eeriness of seeing the man she knew as her husband transforming into an ancient relict from another era.

Hearing a knock on the door, Joseph walked into the living room. Hennah followed, finally getting her daughter to suckle properly.

After having glanced at a small monitor showing who was in the hallway, Joseph said, "Door unlock." Louder, he called out, "Come in, Darkfern."

The fjouwer walked in, dressed in leather pants and tunic, knives attached to her belt. "Mom said you had a surprise to...." Darkfern's eyes grew large as she stared at the infant Joseph was burping then the one in Hennah's arms.

Hennah grinned. "First time I have ever seen you speechless."

"Are...are they yours?"

"Yes, I'm a mom now. I have two daughters."

After several false starts, Darkfern finally sputtered, "How? When? Why didn't you tell me you were planning to adopt?"

"I wanted to wait until it was official. And I like surprising you."

"Surprise me? That you did."

"Would you like to hold one?"

"Hold a baby?" Darkfern's mouth wrinkled into a grimace, and she stared at the infant in Hennah's arms like it was a dangerous bomb about to explode.

Joseph gave a rare laugh. "The mighty warrior defeated by a baby."

"I am not afraid of a baby. Give me one of those."

Carefully Joseph passed his over to her. As her four arms formed a cradle around the infant, she glared at it, expecting something terrible to happen any moment.

"Relax," said Joseph. "Babies cannot injury you."

"They use foul weapons. They poop and cry and throw up."

Hennah burst into laughter. "How are you ever going to make a mom yourself if you see them this way?" Hennah placed a cloth on her shoulder then laid her infant against it, coping her husband's example for burping.

"Fjouwer children are not nearly as fragile as yours. Besides, it will be years before I become a mom. I have four pailuks left before I will even consider marriage."

"We asked you here for another reason," said Joseph. "I am considering you for a job promotion."

Darkfern's eyes lit up as she handed over the infant. "Have you noticed I have been training hard during my off time? I'm ready for a new challenge."

"This job requires upmost secrecy and dedication. It will involve supervising underlings."

"I am the monarch of secrets."

Hennah giggled. The fjouwer shot her an annoying look. "Sorry, Darkfern, but you are not known for being discreet."

"My people boast. That is our way. But I also know when to shut up. I grew up with a Five for a father and a mom as security chief. At home, I have overheard many things I never spoke aloud. I can keep secrets very well."

Joseph leaned forward. "Such as?"

"I know where the....wait, you are not about to trick me. You're testing me."

The Five looked at his wife. "Will she do?"

"Yes, I vouch for her character."

Joseph looked somberly at the fjouwer. "You will oversee a unit which will provide security for our children."

Darkfern's face fell. "A babysitter? I know many parents think the world revolves around their kids, but a whole security detail for two children? My time is better spent elsewhere."

"Our children are very special."

"Hire a nanny."

"A normal nanny will not be able to keep up with our children when they get older. Who will teach them knifing? Keep them from hurting others if they become reckless?"

Darkfern frowned. "What type of children do you have? I presumed your goal was to make scientists of them? Why would they be dangerous, besides the pooping?"

"Down the hallway Skylar and Jennifer are welcoming two newborns, a light-skin and a darker one." Joseph smiled slightly.

"They adopted too?"

"Two floors below, three more families today have added two girls, each with the same faces as ours."

Darkfern crossed her four arms. "There is some mystery you are hinting at. You mock me because I am missing something important."

"You are a trained security officer. Use logic." Joseph said with a twinkle in his eyes.

The fjouwer looked at grinning Hennah and the Five. "Each set is identical to the others?"

"Yes."

"It's highly unlikely two different mothers gave birth to quintuplets then gave them up for adoption to elite quintessences. The babies would have to been artificially created somehow. Are they clones?"

"Yes," hinted Hennah. "But clones of what?"

Darkfern looked at the one now sleeping in Joseph's arms. "You said they could be dangerous. Surely they are not..." The fjouwers mouth dropped open in astonishment.

"Speechless twice in one day. The universe will freeze and planets stop rotating."

"How is this possible? Female quintessences are supposed to be impossible."

"My secret project I have been working on all these years."

"This is your doing? You created them?"

"Yes. Do you wish to be their guardian or should we pass our babysitting job on to another?"

"Of course, I want the job. This changes everything. And I don't mean about me and the job. Quintessence society will never be the same again. Its impact...well is beyond anything I could come up with. This is huge."

Hennah looked at her sleeping infant. "I know."

"What are their names?"

"We are still working on that."

"What about...hmm...Darkstone? Maybe Sunfate. Or Starvortex. Rockstorm."

Joseph said, "As we want them to blend in as humans, we will most likely go with more traditional names."

"Too bad. They need powerful, mysterious names. Galaxyeater. Deathbringer. Hurricanejustice."

"They need sleep now. You can begin creating a list of who you would like in your unit and bring it by tomorrow."

"Sure. I would like to include my clansmen. They may still be rookies here, but they are good fighters."

"Did not your mom hire them so you will have someone to flirt with?"

Darkfern pretended to be shocked. "My mom trying to set me up? No, she wouldn't do that. Besides, they have got to up their game, as none of them are even a close match in combat with me."

As the fjouwer headed out the door, she continued to come up with new names. After the infants were laid back in their cribs, Joseph cooked dinner while Hennah continued to watch her sleeping daughters, wondering what their lives were going to be like. She pulled out her e-tablet and began surfing through word lists. During dinner, the couple debated names.

"How about Alexandra?" suggested Joseph, eating masala pasta.

"I don't know." Hennah munched on a sheermal roll, wishing for more spice.

"Alessandra."

"You are determined to name one after yourself."

"Why not? Is it not fitting that the first born girl share a name with the first born boy?"

"Perhaps her father is getting a bit conceited."

"We could shorten it to Alexa for short."

Hennah sighed. "Alright. But I get to name the other one. How about Zara. In Hindu it means *little*. In Russian, *princess*. In Arabic *star* or *flower*. In Hebrew, it relates to a famous woman who could not bear children, yet she had one in old age."

"Then it is agreed? The ASF1 will be Zara and the CF1 will be Alexandra."

"Alexa. Officially she can have the longer name, but I will call her by the shorter version."

As the weeks went by, Hennah and her assistants closely monitored the infants. Twice a day their weight was recorded along with behavior notes. So far, their growth rate was similar to their male counterparts. They usually remained quiet accept when hungry or had soiled diapers. Many of the new parents took a week or two off work to focus on their children. Jennifer took things further, taking a long term leave of absence. She volunteered to watch the other children when needed. Soon she had a daycare going in her penthouse, using Darkfern and other security officers as aids.

Several times Hennah overhead Darkfern muttering about the villainous evils of dirty diapers. Still, the fjouwer took her job seriously, organizing two rotating groups of security officers during day hours. Half of them were her fellow clansmen, two were cousins. She forbid all flirting doing work hours, but off duty, several of the males kept attempting to impress her in combat practice. She returned their flirting with blades crossing their skin.

When a month had gone by and the infants still looked healthy, gaining weight, Hennah felt it was time to introduce her daughters to their grandparents. She worked for several hours cooking a complex traditional meal, trying to equal her own mother's talent—but she fell short. The curry was nearing done when Zara began crying due to a wet diaper. Joseph was busy feeding Alexa, so Hennah dashed to the bedroom to change Zara. By the time she got back to the kitchen, the curry was scorched.

"There is no time to start over!"

"Relax, Patni. Your parents will be so enthralled with their grandchildren, they will not care about the food."

Hennah added more water to the curry, wondering if she should throw it away or try to use more spices to cover up the scorch flavor. "I hope they like them. It going to be a shock."

A knock announced that time had run out. Hennah greeted her parents as they entered.

Joseph walked into the room. With a slight bow, he pressed his hands together and said, "Namaste."

His in-laws returned the ancient gesture. "Namaste."

Kaushal then gave a small reprimand. "It has been nearly two months since you last invited us for dinner."

"Sorry, Papa. We have been very busy," said Hennah. "I did go shopping with Mamma last month."

"You work too hard." Pallavi studied her daughter. "You look happy, even radiate. You have been eating better, filling out more." Pallavi judged Hennah's mental health by how skinny her daughter was. When Hennah had been depressed, she had eaten little.

"We have a surprise to show you," smiled Hennah mysteriously. "It's in the back bedroom."

They were still in the hallway when Alexa began crying. Pallavi and Kaushal glanced at each other, their eyes filling with excitement. They rushed into the bedroom, each quickly scooping up a baby. Having both spent their entire adult lives working in the Infant Department, they instantly took to cooing and fondling their grandkids.

"When did you decide to adopt?" asked Kaushal, making silly faces at Alexa who reached out her small hands, trying to touch his lips.

"Two months ago. We decided to keep it secret until…well…now." Hennah felt relief that her parents had been so quick to accept her adopted children. Perhaps in a normal human family, her parents might have been upset about her choosing a husband she could never have biological kids with. But many generations of her family had lived at Essence where marriages to quintessences were commonplace.

"They are beautiful." Pallavi kissed Zara on the forehead. "Yes, you are. Very beautiful. My naatin. My daughter's daughter."

"Aashi will be envious. You beat your sister who has been hoping for a child for a while now."

"Oh," Hennah averted her eyes, anxious about what she had to tell them after dinner. "I'm sure it won't be long before she will. Ready to eat? The food will get cold soon."

"Let it," said Pallavi, tickling Zara on the stomach.

Nearly half an hour passed before Hennah was able to distract her parents into eating. If her parents noticed the scorched curry, they did not mention it. They only wanted to talk about their grandchildren. Afterwards Hennah cleaned up while her parents played with the infants in the living room.

Finally, Hennah settled on a coach by her husband. On the other sofa, Kaushal and Pallavi each held a sleepy infant.

"You should have invited your sister and brother today," said Kaushal.

"Well...uh..." Hennah glanced at Joseph, not sure how to begin the conversation which she dreaded the most. "We thought it best to introduce our daughters to a small group first."

"Ah."

Joseph decided to be direct. "They will not be meeting our daughters, and you will not be allowed to share with others that you have grandchildren."

"What? Why would we not brag about our own grandkids? We are not ashamed that you adopted."

"You misunderstand. Alexa and Zara are part of a classified project which we are attempting to keep hidden as long as possible."

Puzzled, the grandparents looked at the sleeping infants in their arms. Pallavi asked, "Is there something wrong with them?"

"No," said Hennah quickly. "They are normal...for their species...as far as we can tell."

"Species? They look human."

"They are not." Joseph's expression was blank.

Hennah's mouth went dry in fear. This was the danger point where her parents might reject her children. "They are the project I have been working on all these years, the one Grandfather had me start."

Baffled, Kaushal peered closely at Zara, holding her small hand. Suddenly his eyes lit up with wonderment. Gingerly he opened her mouth and peered under her tongue. "She is a quintessence! You created female quintessences."

"Yes, I did." Hennah barely breathed, tensely waiting their reaction.

Pallavi beamed. "We knew you were gifted but never did we think this was possible. How did you do it?"

Joseph said, "That part is still highly classified. You only need to know your daughter is a brilliant, highly dedicated geneticist."

"We already knew that," said Kaushal, marveling at the sleeping infant in his lap. "You have created a miracle. We are proud of you, Beti."

Hennah's breathing became normal again as she relaxed. *They are okay with my children. Family means more than species. It means love and acceptance, no matter who you are.* She had hidden so much from her parents over the years. Suddenly she wanted to tell them everything. She and Joseph had debated for several weeks about the consequences of including her parents in the children's lives. He most likely would not approval of what she was about to do, but she did not care at the moment.

"There is something else I need to tell you. Something you may not like, but I have wanted to tell you for years. Since I was twelve."

"Hennah," Joseph's quiet voice carried a hint of warning.

She ignored him. "I'm not your biological daughter."

Her parents stared at her in silence, unable to accept her words. Finally, Pallavi said, "Of course you are. I gave birth to you."

"I know you did, but the genetically enhanced egg you had modified at Bontinc Genetics Foundation never came back to you. Grandfather swapped out the eggs before your implantation."

Kaushal angrily said, "My father would never had done such a thing. Who told you these lies?"

Joseph said, "Chandresh would have if a Five asked him to. Alec knew it would take an extremely talented geneticist to create female quintessences. So he made sure one was born into a good family who would raise her well. And you have done so."

Kaushal glanced at his wife, his anger fading. "I still do not understand. Are you saying that Alec orchestrating my daughter's birth just so she could create these babies?"

Hennah gave her husband a sharp glance. "Alec did a lot of orchestrating. Quite a bit, being a Five. Perhaps he got his kicks from manipulating others."

Joseph returned his wife's stare. "What he did was out of necessary. Being a Five, it was his duty to protect and preserve his species."

"Who are your biological parents," came Pallavi's strain voice.

"I...uh...really don't know. History never recorded that." Hennah swallowed. "Do you remember who you kept saying I looked like as a child?"

Pallavi's mouth opened in astonishment. "You are...no...can you be?"

"Yes, I'm a clone of Layla Rangan and Yashana Kalkar."

"But cloning of sentients is illegal. Why would a Five break the law? They are its enforcers."

"Good question." Hennah gave Joseph another dark stare.

The look he returned told her she was walking into dangerous territory. "The choice was between annihilation of his species or transgression against laws he had upheld all his life. He choose to protect his species."

"At what cost?" anger boiled in Hennah that she had been suppressing for a long time. Only once before had she openly talked about this topic with him, and that was the day she had learned her husband was also Alec. Since then, she had tried to pretend that part of him did not exist. She glanced down at the faint scar on her arm, and her lips trembled. "What cost did I have to pay for his dreams?"

Joseph glanced at her parents, unable to say what he wanted to in front of them. Seeing her daughter's distress, Pallavi gingerly laid Alexa on the couch by her husband and came to her daughter. She wrapped her arms around Hennah who burst into tears, all the torment, loneness, and despair of her adolescence overwhelming her.

"I wanted to tell you for so long. But I was not allowed to speak about any of it. Not about who I was, or the project. Nothing. Except with Grandfather. After he died, I just could not handle things any more. I had no one to talk to."

"You had me," came Joseph's gentle voice.

Through clinging strains of hair, Hennah looked at her husband. "Yes, you helped." *And left me a hollow shell. I hate Alec but love Joseph. Throw in the legendary Alexander. What am I supposed to feel for a husband who is so many? He is both my best friend and a stranger.*

After several more minutes, Hennah regained control of her emotions. Pallavi held her hands, tears running down her own cheeks.

"My dear beti, we love you, no matter if you are physically our offspring or not. I wish Alec had asked us about creating you instead of going behind our backs. I would, of course, had said yes. I would have chosen you."

Joseph said, "Alec was protecting you. If it became public knowledge that Hennah was an illegal clone, the first ones arrested would be her parents. By not knowing, you cannot be held accountable. Also, you would have raised her differently, putting her on a pedestal. Alex wanted her to have a normal life as long as possible. He did care about her, but he made mistakes. He died wishing for her forgiveness."

Hennah reached out and took his hand. Breaking the silence that had bound her for so long had allowed the tears to wash away her anger, healing years of emotional scarring.

After Kaushal and Pallavi left, Hennah stood for a long time by herself in the bedroom, watching her daughters sleep. She had sacrificed so much of herself so they would exist.

Watching Zara's chest rise and fall as the infant breathed, Hennah whispered, "You are worth it, little one. I would do it all again for you."

Turning off the light, she walked down the darken hallway, ignoring a small cleaning bot vacuuming the thick carpet. Joseph stood by the open door of the balcony, watching her, the gleaming lights of Essence beckoned from far below.

"We need to talk."

Hennah nodded, "I know."

"Today you broke a gag order from a Five. The consequences…"

"…is death. But we both know you will not enforce that. If you believed my parents were really a security risk, you would never have allowed them to meet their grandkids."

"Still, you should have talked with me first."

"There was no time. I felt the need to tell them, so I did so."

"That was not your decision to make on your own. The risk…"

Hennah reached out and placed a finger on her husband's lips. "Shush. Stop your lecture right now. You may be a Five and a living fossil, but I carry the genes of another legend within me. I may not be her, but you will treat me with respect. I put up with your gag order for years, despite how miserable I was. Now you will trust my judgment. If I wish to tell my parents who I really am, I will. And if I decide to tell Darkfern tomorrow, I will do that too. In fact, I am certain I will do so. I am tired of holding secrets from those I care about. Now are you going to accept what I did, or will you be sleeping on the couch tonight?"

Joseph studied her for a long moment in the dim light. A faint smile curled his lips. "No, ma'am. I trust you judgement completely. And I prefer a warm bed."

Chapter Twenty-six

The man's voice droned on as he pointed to statistics on a hologram chart slowly rotating above the large conference table. Kylen sat at the head of the table, barely listening. Within one minute of the speech beginning, he had already examined the evidence and concluded not to support the man's project. Still, he pretended to listen as his mind wandered through the long list of things which needed doing. Being the Technology Advisor for the Emperor's cabinet carried many responsibilities.

His top concern during the three years he had been the Emperor's son-in-law was the need to constantly prove himself. The cabinet position had been a prestige but hollow appointment giving the public the illusion of him being important. He needed to do nothing more than sire a profectus with the princess to satisfy the Coalition. Kylen, though, had his own agenda.

The day Kylen had received his appointment, he had showed up unannounced in the Security Department located deep under the palace. He behaved as if he outranked its chief, demanding to know how their systems functioned. Being the Emperor's son-in-law carried immense weight, and the others hastened to obey, even the chief.

Within a week, Kylen had formed his own committee, choosing advisors in key positions from the palace's security, city infrastructure, and local police. His contacts gave him the ability to know vital information about the coming and goings of politicians, of enemies and allies. Kylen soon had positioned himself into the core of power—the control of information. He was given passwords for many government computer systems. For the others, he could hack into them without concerned about being caught. If the hack was ever traced back to him, all he simply needed to do was claim he was testing their system.

The man's presentation finally ended. Kylen politely pointed out the flaws and asked him to keep working on the idea. Then he dismissed the meeting. Several of the men hung back, waiting for others to leave. They waited patiently as Kylen addressed each one's concerns or requests. He listened carefully, always benevolent and friendly. Even when Kylen rejected an idea, each went away feeling important and valued. Long ago Kylen had mastered manipulating people as easily as coding data on a computer. Everything boiled down to formulas. Find out the motives of a person, then use that knowledge to direct the individual along the path you desired for them. It worked for most people—but not for Kylen's wife. She saw through the illusions he wove.

Kylen walked down elegant hallways decorated with expensive paintings and statues. The marble floors gleamed in the bright lighting. Servants and aids gave polite, brief bows as he passed. Security officers stood stiffy at posts, their eyes following his movements. Several politicians stopped Kylen for short conversations.

Sometimes Kylen missed being able to walk unnoticed in pubic, to meander around shopping centers. Now if he went outside the palace, body guards surrounded him, making him even more conspicuous.

A tattooed man Kylen used to work with in street maintenance approached. Kylen waved away a concerned bodyguard. Making sure no one else was within hearing distance, Kylen asked, "How is my old boss?"

"Reynold sends you his greetings. He is proud of how much you have achieved in so little time. And that matter you asked him about a few weeks ago has been dealt with—permanently."

"Tell Reynold he has my gratitude. His help will not be forgotten."

The man gave a polite bow and left. A part of Kylen felt a chill at speaking of murder so casually in the gilded palace, though the walls had most likely been witnesses to far worst crimes over the centuries. Kylen had not set out wishing for Devin's death. Really, it was the man's own fault.

Devin had been the main developer of the software program that had earned Kylen the Humanitarian Award. Devin had been in the Coalition most of his life and knew how the rules worked, yet he was jealous that he had not received any credit for his work. A few weeks ago, he had spoken with Kylen in private, demanding a position on his committee or he would tell the press what he knew. Kylen had calmly said he would see about it but secretly planned not to give in to blackmail. Coalition members knew from the beginning that they worked together for the good of the human race, sometimes sacrificing to help the cause. Devin had broken a fundamental rule of placing himself over their ultimate goals.

Kylen had passed word to Reynold about what his employee was plotting, knowing the Coalition would silence Devin. Kylen cared nothing about the details. His hands remained clean, his reputation untarnished.

Entering the lavish suite he shared with his wife, Kylen barely gave the sundancer maid a glance. She bowed and left. The parlor was immaculate, fresh flowers in vases, polished shelves holding expensive books and heirlooms. Kylen walked down the hallway to his bedroom. Abarrane had her own bedroom at the end of the hall. Once a week they spent the night together, working on that long awaited child the Coalition desired—though Kylen felt little desire for his bride. She was beautiful but cold. Being with her felt like making love to ice.

Alone in his own room, Kylen finally relaxed. Here he could stop wearing the charismatic persona he was expected to be. He changed out of the formal, tailored outfit he had worn all day into casual pants and shirt, looking more like the computer nerd Abarrane accused him of being. Ignoring the expensive digital desk sitting near the huge vid screen and plush sofa, he knelt on the thick carpet beside a hunk of junk. Well, it looked that way to Abarrane, but he saw a treasure.

He had found it deep in the archives under the palace where it had been forgotten for decades. At least, someone had occasionally tended it or the living flesh would have died long ago. From the outside it looked like an ancient metal crate attached to an old monitor. The casing hid an organic matrix which computed at speeds for superior to digital computers. The alien technology fascinated Kylen. He nicknamed it Sundara, a Hindu word for *beautiful*.

After pulling out some tools, Kylen opened the metal casing and studied the living blobs of tissue surrounding components. Many decades ago, a military invasion on a faraway planet had netted this prize, but the invaders had little time to learn how to use it. They had scrapped up some of the living matrix of the aliens' huge living network and stuck it inside this contraption. Technicians had played around with it without success. Eventually it had been discarded in the archive.

Kylen reached out and touched the flesh with a finger. It changed from red to yellow as it reacted to electrical impulses in his skin. He suspected the original creators had communicated with it through touch, but other sentients could not achieve that same connection. The technicians had attached a keyboard and monitor to it, hoping to access it. In that they were successful, but the matrix did not respond to binary coding but processed data in a far more complex method. Trying to get it to run normal programs had not worked so far. Kylen was determined to find a way to make Sundara understand binary.

As he experimented, his body relaxed, the problems of the day forgotten. There was only him and Sundara. He thought of the living matrix as a woman, one he could touch and she in turn could respond back to him. They may not speak the same language, but she recognized he was living. Sundara also reminded him of the alternative life he still secretly dreamed of. The one he almost had with Hennah. He followed the Coalition's plan, allowing himself to be their perfect pawn while he positioned himself into the center of power. But it was all a game, a persona he played. What he desired most was to create an original legacy without the Coalition's help, one that would shadow his clone brothers. If he could make a huge leap in technology advancement, then he would be remembered for something he actually deserved.

The bedroom door opened and Abarrane walked in, wearing a stylish pantsuit. She closed the heavy door behind her, a scowl on her face. "Still playing with that gruesome gob? Why have you not thrown it away yet?"

Kylen frowned. This was the one place she rarely came, his sanctuary. When they slept together, it was always in her bed. "It can revolution our concept of computers as we know it."

"If that was true, it would have been done decades ago by others."

"They could not communicate with her, but I am making progress."

"You care more about talking with an alien computer than me. I have texted you three times today yet you have not responded once."

"I have been busy." He stood up, giving her his complete attention. "What do you wish to tell me?"

She stood by the door, arms crossed. "I'm pregnant."

"Congratulations." At least he would not need to sleep with her for a long time.

"You look as excited as if I told you I was changing my hair style."

"What else do you want me to say?"

"You are about to become a father. Some excitement is expected."

"I performed as expected. That is excitement enough for me."

Abarrane's frown deepened, a brief look of fear flashed in her eyes, but it was quickly replaced with determination. "I already had a genetic test done. The child is not a profectus. I do not care what anyone says. I am having this child."

Kylen was silent for a long moment. "I would not advice that. You know the Coalition wants a natural born profectus on the throne. The firstborn must be a profectus. With the odds being fifty percent, there is a high chance the next one will be one."

"This is my child, not theirs." Abarrane raised her voice. "I married you because of my grandfather's promise to them, but this is my body, my child. If you want no part in raising your own flesh, then leave me. You have already played your part."

"Actually, no. The goal was for a profectus child. We just keep trying until we are successful."

"And so casually toss away this one?"

"Abarrane, think logically for a moment. What happens if you keep this one and the next is a profectus? The Coalition expects a pureblood to sit on the throne. That means the firstborn must die at some point."

"You are a cold bastard."

"As I had no father or mother, I think you are using the term wrongly. Push aside your emotions for a moment. Think like the Coalition. The child must die sooner or later. Better now when it is only a mass of cells without personality than a child you have grown attached to."

The princess glanced at the open frame of the computer beside her husband. "If I destroyed that mass of cells in your precious Sundara, would you actually feel some emotion then?"

"This computer could change the galaxy."

"So could my child! You want to kill him before he even has a chance in life!"

"I do not care if the fetus lives or dies. It is the Coalition you have to deal with, not me."

"Screw the Coalition and screw you! Actually, I am never screwing you again." Abarrane stormed out of the room, slamming the door behind her.

For a while Kylen stared at the door, wondering why she had to be so difficult. Did she not see that she was making things harder for herself? Just get an abortion and try for another child. Problem solved. Actually the easiest thing was to have a baby designed at a genetic company using his sperm and her egg. It would break a long tradition of royal offspring being natural born and raise questions about breaking the Purity Law when it was realized the fetus was not completely human. Still, buying the silence of several geneticists and medical staff was better than dealing with this.

Needing to think, Kylen passed his bed and walked out onto a balcony. A beautiful vista of the city of Diamond stretched out before him. Gentle wind tossed his hair. Too bad this was an illusion just like his life. His suite was deep underground, part of a bunker that would be protected in case of bombardment. Sometime in the past, a previous occupant had the balcony built along with a curved wall which displayed videos of the city above him. It was realistic, giving a broad view of vehicles moving below and stars slowly rotating across the sky. Kylen leaned over the balcony, watching the recorded vehicles move along the streets.

In his head, he replayed the conversation with Abarrane. She had wanted support but he had only given her logic. Perhaps he should have just played along, pretending to be excited about the child, but deep inside knowing the child would never reach adulthood—as long as a profectus child was later born. Abarrane's current plan was a dangerous one—having no more children and force the Coalition to accept her only child. Most likely it would eventually cost the life of the child she loved.

Better to feel no love than face the pain of loss she would know one day. She had called him a cold bastard. *Perhaps I am, but it is how I have survived all these years. How can I love anyone? I have never felt the love of a parent. How can I be expected to love my own offspring? Love is just an emotion that can be used to control you, to destroy you.*

As self-pity and loneness filled him, he embraced the emotions for a few minutes. All his life he had been surrounded by people who either wanted to control him or seek favors. Senators had asked him to spy on their cheating spouses, corporations paid him to hack into their enemies' mainframes. Other cabinet members relied on him to keep tabs on their enemies. He wielded enormous power, but it left him empty. What he lacked was a true friend.

Amy. Her smiling face filled his memory, and he ached for her presence. She was the closest he would experience to a sibling. Yet she also bent to the will of the Coalition. She was off on various planets designing monuments displaying the superiority of humankind. Obeying the Coalition, she had married Marco. At least the two of them would have no trouble producing a natural profectus.

Hennah. The only other person he felt warmth for. Trapped in a loveless marriage like him, both trying to please their masters no matter the cost to themselves. He had wanted to free her along with himself. Time had allowed him to forgive her for letting fear control her, for remaining with the leeches. Still, a part of him fantasized showing up at Essence, demanding that the mortis elixirs release her. He could bring her here to this palace, giving her a better life, healing her depression. She could become his concubine. All their children would be profectus. Maybe over time he would even feel tenderness for them, as he had chosen their mother. Surely it would feel different to hold in his hands a child that was conceived in love instead of duty.

Kylen sighed, pushing away the dream. He needed to deal with reality, with facts. Emotions left one weak. He walked back into his bedroom and knelt beside Sundara. Codes he could control, could manipulate to obey his desire. Here he was the master.

Chapter Twenty-seven

Hennah, still dressed in a lab coat, stormed into Jennifer's penthouse. Two fjouwer security guards hurriedly moved out of her way. From the carpeted floor, Zara looked up from the board game she played with Jennifer's two daughters.

"Hello, Mamma," said Zara. The three years old could easily pass for a six year old human. Long, black hair hung loose around her face. Her bronze skin was almost the same shade as Hennah's. When out in public, they seemed the perfect mother and daughter.

"Where is your sister?"

"In the kitchen." Zara turned back to her game, moving a meeple onto a newly placed tile. Her birthmates frowned slightly, seeing that the move would earn Zara a large number of points.

Hennah hurried to the kitchen, her face alarmed as she spotted Alexa standing at a counter as Jennifer wrapped more gauze overtop a bloody bandage. Red stains covered the child's arm and darkened her blouse. Alexa kept her face blank as possible, pretending she felt no pain. Darkfern stood nearby, pulling out a glue skin canister from the first aid kit.

"How bad is it this time?" asked Hennah, noting this was the most blood she had seen from one of her daughter's accidents. She had been working in her lab when she received the message about the injury.

"It should stop bleeding soon," said Jennifer. "Then we can patch her up."

"How did it happen?"

Jennifer glanced at Darkfern. The fjouwer looked uncomfortable. "She…was looking at my karambit."

Hennah's pulse raced. The tension that had built up as she rushed from her lab to the apartment needed a release. "You gave a three year old a knife!"

"She was only supposed to look at it, not begin spinning it."

"Still, she is three!"

"We begin blade training with our offspring when only two. Besides, she is equal to a six or seven year old human."

"You don't give any child a knife!"

"Perhaps you fragile humans can't handle them, but we fjouwer can."

"You may have thick skins, but you have thick heads as well."

"Enough," cut in Jennifer. "The bleeding has stopped. Pass me that skin glue."

Alexa said, "Please, Mamma, do not be mad at Darkfern. It is my fault. I asked for days to hold a karambit."

Hennah sighed. "Your father and I have told you no weapons training until after you have master using the epulo when you are four. Then you can quickly heal if injured."

"I know. I apology." Alexa cast her eyes downward, looking genuinely repentant.

After the wound had been properly tended, Hennah watched Zara finishing her board game. Zara and the other ASF1 named Khloe kept stoic faces as they studied each new tile placed down. Natalia, a CF1, showed deep contemplation as she focused on the best moves to gain the most points. Like all quintessences, the girls loved competition. When Khloe won, a frown was visible on Natalia's face, but she politely congratulated her sister. Zara showed no visible reaction to losing.

Since their births, Hennah had paid close attention to the behavior of the two models, comparing them to each other and to males their age. So far, the ASF1's were fairly stereotypical for quintessence children. Quiet, deep thinkers. Well-behaved, quick to please adults. They did show emotions a bit more often than their male counterparts, but compared to a typical human child they seemed apathetic. Hennah knew that was only an illusion as ASF1's felt the same emotions humans did, just quintessence faces showed little of what they actually felt inside.

Well, most models were like that. The CF1's were too much like the AS1's and AS2's, which were kept in low production. Few outsiders even knew about the existence of those models who made excellent spies due to their ability to show emotions almost as well as a normal human. Glancing at Alexa's bandaged arm, Hennah worried yet again about her daughter. Alexa, like the other four CF1's, not only was more emotionally but pushed against bounties, not directly rebelling but looking for loopholes in rules. When challenged by an adult about their behavior, they would offer polite apologizes while explaining their logic.

Alexa sat on the floor to join a new game about to start, but Hennah intervened. "You need a clean shirt. Time to go."

Zara asked, "May I stay longer, Mamma?"

"Yes, when you finished the next game, come home. Dinner should be nearly finished then."

The front door opened and Reanna walked in, leading her two children. To try to hide that two groups of quintuples living in Richton Towers, each set of sisters had a different hair style from the others. Hennah's daughters either wore their long hair loose or pulled back in ponytails. Jennifer's two had layered, shoulder length hair with streaks of blue or purple. Reanna's children had long, curly hair styled with bright ribbons. No stranger glancing at them would guess that her cute, doll-like daughters had predator instincts. Lissa enjoyed creating complicated braids for her two. Camila's children currently had a simple pixie cut.

Jennifer greeted the newcomers. "When will you pick them up?"

"In about three hours. Kitoka and I are going to a party for my parents' fifth wedding anniversary. Wish I could bring them, but you know how it is. Can't explain to all my relatives why my children are aging twice as fast as theirs."

Jade, Reanna's CF1 daughter, paused in front of Alexa, noticing the dried blood on her birthmate's blouse. "Were you in fight?"

Alexa frowned slightly. "No, the karambit slipped when I was trying to do the extended grip."

Jade's eyes widened. "You were practicing knifing? I thought we had to be four?"

"I made a mistake." Alexa glanced at her mother.

"Oh." The disappointment on her Jade's face mirrored Alexa.

Her sister Pearl said, "Today we watched a company of C4's run an obstacle course. They were our age. We wanted to join them, but Mother would not allow us."

"I could have kicked their asses," said Jade, eagerness in her eyes.

"Jade!" reprimanded her mother. "We do not use that type of language."

"I apology. I mean, I could have completed the course much faster than them— I am certain. They slowed down too much on the bars."

Hennah looked away to hide a laugh. *No matter how you dress a quintessence, their combatant nature cannot be suppressed.* Jade wore a lacy, doll-like dress with matching green ribbons in her curly hair. She looked like she should be heading to a pageant not boot camp.

Once Hennah got Alexa home away from the others, she asked, "Why did you disobey your father and me? You knew we had said no combat practice until you were older."

"I only wanted to touch it, see what if felt like. Once in was in my hands, I was curious to see if I could flick it the way Darkfern does to switch the blade's position. It slipped."

"Curiosity can kill you, Beti. Never let it guide you. Use logic. Be patient. When you are older, then you may learn."

"Yes, Mamma. I will not make that mistake again."

No, but you will make others, thought Hennah. "You will have to explain what happened to your father."

Alexa looked worried. "Do we have to tell him?"

"Of course. Do you think you can hid a secret from a Five? Now go change your shirt while I start dinner."

When Joseph arrived home after a long meeting, he called Alexa to the kitchen. As Hennah spooned baingan bharta over rice, Joseph looked sternly down at his young daughter.

"You disobeyed us today, Beti."

"I apologize, Papa."

"You apologize often but still break rules."

"I did not mean to disobey. I only meant to touch it."

"Alexa, when we say no weapon practice until older, that also means no touching a weapon without proper training. Logically, you knew that but chose to reinterpret what we had said to you. That is still disobedience. Recite the Code to me."

Alexa looked miserable. "All quintessences shall place the welfare of their brethren above themselves. Each must live an exemplary life, obeying superiors, avoiding vices, protecting the weak."

"You broke the Code. For an adult, what is the punishment for disobedience?"

"Appearing in front of all the Five. And...death." Alexa studied her hands, unable to meet her father's eyes.

Joseph knelt so he was eyelevel with his daughter. "I never want that to happen to you, Alexa. When you try to skit the edge of a rule, in your heart, you are still disobeying. You need to learn now, while you are young, that it is wrong."

Alexa clenched her fists, her lips trembling slightly. Quintessences rarely cried after infancy, but Alexa was very close to it now. She had disappointed her father yet again.

"I am very, very sorry, Papa."

"Your punishment is no dinner. You will go to your room and write an essay explaining why what you did was wrong."

"Yes, Papa."

As Alexa walked across the living room, her sister glanced at her tense face. Silently Zara followed her sister to the bedroom they shared.

Hennah paused in her plating. Keeping her voice low, she said, "Did you have to be so harsh with her? Talking about death? And no food?"

"You know as well as I that they will be soldiers someday. Our laws must be strict to protect both ourselves and others from evils we are capable of."

"Yes, but she is still only a child. Telling her she could be killed?"

Joseph leaned closer, his voice barely audible. He knew the acute hearing of quintessences could pick up conversations in adjoining rooms. "I have put to death quintessence children who had murder in their hearts. Once they reach four...you know the dangers as well as I with the epulo. She must learn complete obedience now, before it is too late for her. Curiosity kills quintessences. Mason's curiosity almost destroyed all us long ago. "

Hennah pulled back and finished plating the meal. Joseph had touched on a subject that all the parents feared. But now was not the place to discuss it.

She called Zara in for dinner. The young girl sat silently at the table eating slowly. Occasionally she glanced at the empty chair where her sister normally sat.

When she finished eating, she said, "May I go work on homework now, Papa?"

"After you have thrown away the food you hid in your pockets for your sister."

A slight frown betrayed Zara's guilt. "I did not want my sister to be hungry."

"I commend your loyalty to your sister, but by helping her cheat a punishment, you are hurting her in the future. She must learn that it is important to always obey. In the battlefield, if you disobey your officer, it could lead to many deaths. Your officer will have more information than you, but he will not always have time to explain details to you. You must trust him and obey immediately. Hesitating or challenging your superior could mean the loss of birthmates. I have seen this with my own eyes."

"Yes, Papa." Zara placed two small plastic bags of food which had been in her pockets on the table and left.

Just before bedtime, Alexa approached her parents. She held out an e-tablet. "I finished writing the essay."

As her parents read it, Alexa stood at attention with hands behind back, face blank, determined to look the part of a sober soldier. The wording and spelling was simple, as the girls were currently on a second grade reading level.

Joseph nodded in approval. "A few grammar errors but your logic is sound. You may get ready for bed now."

A brief smile gave away that Alexa was relieved her parents had approved of her work. As she headed to her bedroom, her footsteps were lighter.

Hennah waited until the lights were out and she had snuggled up against Joseph in their bed before whispering her fears. "Can the CF1's handle the epulo?"

"Yes," Joseph wrapped his strong arms around her waist.

"How can you be certain? You said it destroys some quintessences."

"Those who let curiosity draw them into darkness. That is why I drill both our daughters about obedience. They will be fine."

"You are just saying that so I won't worry."

Joseph kissed her neck. "I say it because I believe it."

"I fear us being parents may blind us to their faults. I told you in the beginning that was a danger for us."

"That is why we have a specially selected team of psychologists who study the behavior reports all us parents write. And they question our daughters twice a month." He moved to nibbling her ear.

"You are trying to distract me." She closed her eyes, relishing his touch on her bare skin.

"Is it working?"

"Yes. Somewhat. Still I am concerned about the CF1's. They are too emotional, too rash at times."

Joseph sighed and looked Hennah directly in her eyes. "You forget that I once was Ariyo, a very emotional AS1 who was so rash that almost all the psychologists in the department wanted to discontinue my model. Yet, it was finally discovered that my model's so called weaknesses could be a great talent. The AS1's and 2's still make the best spies we have. Yes, the CF1's are prone to act on emotions more than their sisters. Is this a crime? No. As long as they keep to the Code, they will be successful. Stop worrying, beloved. You did not break out of depression to spend your nights haunted by fears."

"At times you worry a lot too."

"I'm learning to be more optimistic. Join me." He kissed her on the lips.

She pressed back, letting the concerns of the day slip away.

Chapter Twenty-eight

Ten young quintessences quietly tapped in answers for their math tests. Alexa studied the smooth surface of her computerized desk, frowning as she struggled with the answers. Why did Jennifer have to decide that her birthmates needed higher math than the males? And her own mom had increased the science rigor. *We are not scholars. We are soldiers.* Still, Alexa tried her best, certain she had missed a few questions.

"Time is up," said Jennifer, walked through the narrow aisle between the desks. An apartment on the forty-eight floor of Richton Tower had been turned into a classroom. The apartment was fairly good size, but having ten large computer desks took up a lot of space. Jennifer glanced at the e-tablet in her hand. "You scored seventy through eighty-five percent. Seeing you need more practice with fraction word problems, your homework will be to complete ten more. Pay close attention to the tutorial which explains the concepts to you."

Alexa hoped her grimace was hidden. There were so many better things to do, especially today. She could barely contain her excitement, wishing time would go by faster. She glanced at her e-band for the hundredth time. Not long now. Glancing at her birthmates, she saw her own eagerness mirrored back. Even the ASF1's were antsy. Today, they would become adolescents.

They had turned four just over a month ago. On that day, their fathers had bit them with the epulo, introducing them to its amazing abilities. The Canon was passed on to them, and they were taught how to open the ziphema, accessing its memories. It was far better than any historical textbook. Instead of reading static words or watching videos, they could experience history as it happened, feeling the actual emotions and thoughts of the participants. The Canon centered on Layla Rangan and the original Five, containing memories of why the quintessences were first created, their discoveries of their own abilities, and vital lessons learned as they grew up.

Lately, anytime Alexa and her birthmates were not busy, they browsed through the Canon, learning how to jump to particular memories they wanted to see. It was a bit strange at first to see her own mother's face in the Canon, but being a clone herself, Alexa quickly adjusted to the fact that Layla was not Hennah. Still Alexa had to restrain herself from bragging to birthmates that her mom was a clone of the legendary profectus.

Following their father's instructions, Alexa and Zara practiced biting each other and birthmates. For the first time, they could connect, sharing their own thoughts and emotions. There were many rules to learn, including separate standards between quintessences and other sentients. Never bite a superior officer or any adult without permission. Do not force oneself into the private thoughts of other quintessences. Most importantly, never let an outsider know of the epulo's ability to read minds. Either the outsider had to become a trusty insider or be killed.

There were lists to memorize. Sentient species from across the galaxy were categorized by how well they responded to the epulo. Many, like humans, could easily be manipulated without any awareness of what was happening. Others had a natural resistance or were instantly aware when intruders entered their minds, such as sirens. Only expert quintessences were allowed to probe them. Then there was the forbidden list of powerful sentients who could defend against probing. The list was short, containing nine species including kuawazo. Only AF masters were allowed contact with these, yet even they usually avoided those sentients. Alexa pondered why Tobias had married one. Of course, Tobias was an AF1 and a Five, but still she wondered why he had originally risked being around such a powerful telepath.

The classroom door opened to admit Amaka and Tobias. The ten girls looked expectedly towards them. Tobias dismissed the two guards on duty and slowly looked over his young charges, his dark eyes stern. Alexa kept her face blank but knew her thoughts could not be hidden from Amaka.

The Five said, "Today you leave your childhood behind. As you will now have the power to kill, you will be held to higher standards. If you abuse the epulo, you will be terminated. Is that clear?"

"Yes, sir," came ten young voices in unison.

Alexa knew the warning was due to a few young quintessences who went insane and tried to kill their hosts. It was extremely rare, yet the girls had been warned for weeks to be careful.

"Follow me." Tobias and his wife walked out of the room. The ten girls followed, each with stoic faces.

They took an elevator up to the top floor and walked through lush Bellus Garden to the open plaza at its center. Near its edge grew the huge rosa vine tree, its strong limbs reaching towards the glass ceiling high above. Alexa glanced around at the crowd watching them. All their parents were here along with many security officers, half of them fjouwers. Ten prisoners stood beside guards. Normally a company of young quintessences would visit the prison for this exercise, but the girls were not allowed to be seen together outside the top levels of Richton Tower.

The prisoners were relaxed, enjoying the scenery. Each had volunteered to be part of the training program in exchange for shorter sentences. They believed they were here so young quintessence could practice healing. Later their memories of today would be altered, leaving them thinking it had been an ordinary drill with boys.

Alexa stood at attention in line with her birthmates. She stared straight ahead, trying to keep her face blank. To her right, both her parents watched. *I will not shame you today. I can do this.*

A curious prisoner sat in a chair in front of the girls. He looked at the ten young faces in awe, realizing what they were. Tobias stood by the human prisoner with a sharp knife in his hand. He called Natalia forward. The CF1 walked to him and held out her hand. Her face stayed expressionless as he made a shallow cut across her palm. Ignoring the blood pooling in her hand, she turned towards the prisoner. She bit where neck joined the back of the head. For a few minutes the prisoner's eyes glazed over. Then Natalia pulled back. Tobias tossed her a rag and she wiped blood off her hand.

"Where you successful?"

"Partly." Natalia held up her hand, showing it had healed. Her phrase was a code indicating she had failed to find the memory she had been assigned to seek. The prisoner rose and another took his place.

One by one, each girl took a turn probing for memories. Alexa was to be the last one called. Three ASF1's and two CF1's were successful. The girls had been warned in advance that it was normal to fail the first few times. Still, none of them liked failure.

Zara gave a hint of a smile when she held her hand up. "Yes, I was."

"Good," said Tobias. He looked towards Alexa. "Next."

Alexa walked to him, noting both how tall he was and the knife in his hand. *I wonder how many he has killed.* She held out her hand, wincing as the blade sliced across her palm. *Wish I could hide pain better.* Trying to ignore the throbbing of her hand, she moved to the prisoner. Tynick was a neodite with blue skin, but his fingers and face were tinged purple, revealing he was enjoyed today's adventures away from his cell.

Alexa bit. The alienness of his mind caught her off guard. The minds of her birthmates had been similar to her own, easy to navigate. Tynick's consciousness encircled her, his inter thoughts rambling, tens of thousands of his memories forming a vortex surrounding her. Alexa tried accessing a few. They were random, seemingly disorganized. Yet there had to be some system that connected them. Remembering her lessons, she tried to project her own thoughts into his. It had to be subtle, his mind processing the information as if his subconscious had come up with the idea.

Driving. Vehicle. First time. Alexa projected the thoughts. Memories swirled around her. She reached out to the nearest.

Grinning, Tynick drove a roofless hover car. Wind whipped his short, blue hair. Scenery of strangely designed skyscrapers blurred pass. He drove through an endless tunnel made of hard, clear material that could support heavy weight. Far below lay the ground from which rose more buildings and parks. Nearby was another clear tunnel where traffic flowed in the opposite direction. A loud siren came from a police car following close behind. Tynick laughed in defiance.

Alexa was fascinated by how it felt to drive. There were two ways to perceive memories. You could watch as an outsider or slid into the host's conscience, feeling exactly what he felt. The girls had been warned that it was usually better to be an observer. *How can it hurt to feel what it is like to drive?*

Slipping into his conscience, Alexa felt his excitement. He controlled his destiny, not those idiot cops. Faster he zoomed, taking curves too fast, the vehicle tilting dangerously along the side of the tunnel. Far below the clear tunnel he saw the neighborhood he had grown up in. Spotting a school, he laughed. *Never will I allow myself to be trapped in one of those prisons again. I am free!*

Another police car entered the tunnel from a side passage. A neodite leaned out of the vehicle and pointed a weapon. Tynick tried to dodge, but the gun's glowing pulse hit the stolen hover car he drove. Immediately all electrical systems died. Tynick panicked as he fought to steer the car as it swirled out of control, eventually coming to a stop backwards in the middle of the tunnel. He looked about trying to find a way to escape as the cops ran towards him, guns pointed at his head.

Alexa pulled out of the memory. That was not his first time driving—perhaps his first time being arrested. Alexa touched another memory.

Tynick was a boy sitting on his father's lap in a hover car. The vehicle was in a parking garage.

"Ready to give it a shot?" smiled the father.

"Yeah!" beamed young Tynick, his skin very purple in excitement.

Alexa slipped into Tynick's conscience as the boy steered the vehicle around the garage very slowly. Happily he made zooming sounds, telling his father he wanted to go faster. After a few minutes, the father stopped the car and moved the boy to the passenger seat.

"Now to pick up your mother."

Tynick felt disappointment. "I want to drive the whole way."

"It will be a few years before you can do that."

"But I want to now!" The boy kicked his shoes against his seat. "Now, Dada!"

"Patience, son."

The memory shifted, catching Alexa off guard. She had not known the host could shift his own memoires while she was visiting.

Tynick stood in a crowded room by a glass coffin where his father lay. He was only a few months older than the last memory. Tears ran down his face.

"Dada, why are you leaving me?" the child whispered, tightly holding his mother's hand. "Come back to me. I promise to always be good. Please, Dada."

Alexa had never experienced grief before. As its pain filled her, she felt as if her own heart had been ripped out, happiness a forgotten dream. She pulled out of Tynick's mind, back in the peaceful garden again.

"Where you successful?" Tobias's voice seemed to come from far away.

Still overcome with grief, she was unable to answer. All she wanted to do was curl into a ball and cry for her dead father whom she would never see again.

"Alexa, are you alright?" came Joseph's concerned voice.

As the girl looked in his direction, relief flooded her. *Papa is right there. It was only another's memory. Not mine.* "Yes, I was successful."

She wiped blood form her healed hand and took her place in line. After the prisoners left with their guards, Tobias questioned each girl. Those that had been successful described the memories they had found. Those who had failed explained what they experienced then Tobias gave suggestions how they may do better next time.

Alexa dreaded speaking when it was her turn, knowing her expression had given away that she had experienced something terrible. "I found his memory of his father giving him driving lessons. Then the memory shifted to his father's funeral."

Tobias studied her face for a moment. "You were doing more than observing?"

"Yes, I felt his emotions, his grief."

"Now you know what it feels like to lose someone you love. Grief is a hard emotion to deal with. That is why we ask you to observe only. Being drawn into another's emotions can affect you, especially when so young."

"Yes, sir. I will be more careful next time."

Tobias looked at all the girls. "You are dismissed."

The birthmates headed towards their parents. As Alexa walked up to her father, she gave him a tight hug, needing the reassurance that he was alive. Quintessences were not natural huggers. If he was surprised by her sudden display of affection, he did not show it. After a moment he pulled back and studied her face.

"The sadness you feel will pass."

Alexa nodded and moved to stand beside her quiet sister. At least he had not reprimanded her. And she had not gone insane.

Hennah said, "Your father is cooking your favorite meal tonight to celebrate both of you doing well.

Zara allowed a hint of a smile to show. "We look forward to that."

Khloe and her sister Natalia walked up. "Will we have bōjutsu practice today?"

Joseph looked at the pair. "I was uncertain if you wished to practice today after your first healing drill."

Natalia eagerly said, "Yes, we want to."

"Then you may fetch the bō's."

Alexa watched her birthmates follow a path through the cultivated flowers and bushes. She felt pride that her father was the group's bōjutsu instructor. While Jennifer was their main teacher, all the parents were actively involved with their education. The mothers popped in as guest speakers, sharing about their interests. To help them understand genetics, Hennah had them grow plants from seeds then cross pollinate to see the results of the next generation. The fathers had begun to focus on basic defense skills. Once they mastered healing, Alexa looked forward to Darkfern's knifing lessons.

Khloe and Natalia soon returned with wooden sticks barely taller than themselves. Adult quintessences used bō's which were much longer and made from metal. Experts preferred spiked ends which could rip flesh besides break bones. The other girls noticed and quickly gathered in the plaza. Grins flashed between the CF1's. They loved this sport.

As Alexa practiced moves her father showed the group, she relaxed, the sad emotions from the neodite fading away. She paired with Zara, twilling and dodging, her blood pounding as she pressed the attack. Even when she felt a painful whack against her shoulder, she barely slowed down. This was what it meant to be quintessence. Strip all away to the basics of survival, the pounding of the heart, the movement of trained muscles, instinct taking over, pain only dimly felt. Alexa laughed, understanding how Tynick had felt when defying the cops.

After a while, Joseph said, "Good job today, girls. Who will put the bō's away?"

Jade and Pearl volunteered. Today they were dressed in oversize pink shirts with leggings, curly hair pinned back by large purple bows. Alexa's curled her lips at the comical view of them carrying the wooden weapons through the cultivated flowerbeds. She was uncertain how they put up with their mother's taste in fashion. Zara and herself dressed conservatively, plain blouses and slacks, usually in shades of brown, gray, or black. Better for combat.

Hearing Darkfern chatting with Hennah, Alexa walked over to her mother. Zara followed.

"Surely you will go this time to Kilpailu. This will be my sixteenth pailuk."

"You know I want to go, but I'm busy."

"Always your excuse. I understand why you are careful about visiting Core planets, but this is Shah Luna. It's on the Rim where the Coalition has no influence, no regulations. We live by the laws of my people."

"You have violent punishments for criminals." Hennah glanced at Joseph who had walked up beside her.

Alexa listened closely, wishing her mother would finally agree. Darkfern and her many stories had always fascinated her. While standing around on duty, the fjouwer often whirled her karambits to pass the time. During combat practice, she was a dangerous whirlwind of blades, her four arms expertly blocking and attacking.

"Our elders' decisions are fair. Because our punishments are brutal, our crime rate is low. You have said for eight years you wanted to come. I refuse to marry unless you come. Must I die a virgin warrior?"

"I thought those were the most regarded heroes of your legends."

"They are, but I never said I wanted to be one. Me make it through fifty pailuks? Some claim such stories are myths from our ancient past. No modern fjouwer has made it passed twenty-five. You will come this time?"

Alexa eagerly looked at her mom. "Please, Mamma, can we go? I want to see the giant mushroom forests."

Zara added, "It can be part of our social studies lessons. We will learn much from observing another culture firsthand."

Hennah looked at her husband. For a long moment he remained still then he gave a slight nod. Alexa flashed a grin at her sister. They were going on a vacation.

A few weeks later, Alexa sat by a shuttle window looking out at the vast moon of Shah Luna. The dull gray surface looked boring. No structures were visible. The orange gas planet it orbited was far more exciting. They had traveled by a large yacht to an orbiting space station. From there they had taken a shuttle which would carry them through one of the tunnel locks that protected the subterranean ports.

The shuttle was packed, mainly with fjouwers coming for Kilpailu. Darkfern's whole family was here along with all her clansmen that worked at Essence. Hennah leaned against Joseph as both looked out a window. Zara and Alexa had competed to see who sat beside Darkfern, who was the star of this trip. Zara won, so Alexa picked a window seat.

Darkfern smiled as she looked out at the moon. "For fjouwers there is no greater world except for Werjouk where our species originated. Pop quiz. Why did fjouwers first come to Shah Luna?"

Zara said, "They were miners working for a corporation that later went bankrupt."

"How did Shah Luna change from a small mining colony into the bustling metropolis it is today?"

Alexa glanced back at the dull moon. She saw nothing bustling about it, except other shuttles waiting their turn to land. Still, she quoted from her history lessons, "When it was realized the company was collapsing, some of the leading families of the clans formed an alliance and took out a huge loan, buying the entire moon. They continued to mine it out, turning it into the paradise it is today—except I do not see a paradise yet."

Darkfern flashed a big grin. "You will soon enough. What laws are in effect on Shah Luna?"

"Fire Justice," answered Zara. "Named after one of the founding leaders who believed fjouwers had to modernize in order to live peacefully with other sentients."

Darkfern nodded, pleased her pupils had been paying attention. "Before then fjouwers were considered barbarians to outsiders due to the habit of killing foreign males and taking their spouses as second level wives called *javes*."

"Do you still have multiple spouses?" asked Alexa.

"Yes, it is allowed," answered Darkfern, "but not by force. The wife must agree to the marriage, and no battle takes place. Javes cannot be from one's own clan. Hence why most javes are foreigners. No self-respecting modern female fjouwer will allow herself to become a *jave*. When we marry, we are *dijaves*, first wives."

"What is wrong with being a jave?"

"Nothing." Darkfern shifted her eyes away.

From across the aisle, Hennah said, "She is avoiding the darker history of her species. How on their homeworld clans often fought against other clans over territory. When raiding each other's villages, they kidnaped younger ones, forcing them into slavery, sometimes marrying them. *Jave* means slave wife."

"No longer. The word has a different meaning now to modern fjouwers. It just means *foreign wife* or *wife taken without pugna*."

Joseph looked towards his daughters. "On their homeworld of Werjouk, there are clans living deep underground who still live by the old laws. That is why it is dangerous for foreigners to travel there."

"Shah Luna is safe," insisted Darkfern. "There are generations of foreigners who are permanent residents. Here we live peacefully with others."

"*Peaceful* is not quite the right word." Joseph's lips slightly curled.

As the shuttle neared the moon's surface, Alexa finally spotted a vast tunnel dropping straight down deep into the moon's crust. After they entered, a massive metal gate covered the tunnel's entrance. As they slowly descended, lights illumined the rocky walls. Another large gate opened below them, and the ship entered a busy space port. Over a hundred ships of many styles rested on launch pads. Once their own ship had landed, Alexa was finally able to take off her safety belt.

Outside, she looked around, hoping for something interesting to see. The air was cool and damp. Groups of sentients walked towards a massive building. Many were fjouwers, some foreigners. Above their heads was a high rocky ceiling, lit up here and there by strange lights. Another ship exited a tunnel and prepared to land.

Firestrike led her large group to the building. From there, they waited in line to take an elevator downward to a large lobby. Then they had to wait in another long line to clear customs. Alexa quickly grew bored, but she tried not to show it. She quietly stood by her sister while observing others. Tourists chatted excitedly about their plans, many wearing sleek, stylish outfits. Locals preferred drab colored clothing, usually in earth tones. Many fjouwers wore leather or thick cloth made from natural fibers to protect their already tough skin from their active lifestyles.

The group began walking again. "This, you must see," grinned Darkfern mischievously to the girls.

They bypassed the closest elevator and walked down a broad hallway which opened into a huge chamber with a clear floor. For a brief moment, Alexa was taken off guard, thinking tourists walked on air over a huge chasm. Realizing the clear floor was safe, she walked carefully onto it then looked down, gasping in shock. The drop had to be over a mile straight down. Zara was equally impressed, though she was better at hiding her surprise.

Below were countless buildings. Many would have been called skyscrapers if on Alexa's home word, but there was no sky here. Only a vast rocky ceiling that stretched out until disappearing from view. Here and there were massive pillows at least a quarter a mile in diameter which rose from the city and widening at the top as they connected to the stone ceiling. Alexa realized that she stood in one of those pillows at the point where it connected to the sky roof—it helped her to imagine the endless ceiling as a stone sky.

Darkfern beamed. "Your first look at New Werjouk, capitol city of Shah Luna." She pointed towards the far horizon. "There's Thallus Park, but it is too far away for you to make out much, even with your sharp eyes. That is where the unmarried gather for pailuk—and the married who wish to relive the memories of their youth. There will be twenty thousand or more participating."

Joseph walked over the clear floor, admiring the view with the visiting fjouwers. Desmond pointed out key landmarks to his brother. Hennah stayed near the entrance, staring at the drop-off in horror.

"Mamma, it is safe. The floor is not glass. It will not break," said Alexa.

"I can see just fine from over here."

Darkfern challenged, "I thought you wanted to see New Werjouk? You live in a tower. How can you be afraid of heights?"

"Because I cannot see through the floors of my home."

The fjouwers shared amusing winks at each other at Hennah's expense. Then Firestrike led the group back to the elevator that carried them down closer to Primary Level. Alexa learned the term was used similar to sea level. Structures could exist both above and below the invisible line. The term had been invented long ago as a navigation reference in the underground.

They came out at the edge of a clear tunnel, similar to the one Alexa had seen in the memories of Tynick. Hover vehicles zoomed along the clear tunnels hundreds of feet above Primary Level. The group climbed into cabs which took them across the city to another massive pillar which rose up to the stone sky. During the ride, Alexa admired the strange buildings both below and beside the clear tunnel. The architecture contained few straight lines. While some rocky buildings stood away from others, many were connected by overhead walkways or built directly into the sides of each other. On the Primary Level were streets for pedestrians where vehicles were prohibited except small scooters and bikes.

 The cabs dropped them off at a hotel built into a massive giant pillar. The lobby was huge, brightly lit from electricity. Lichen and vines dangled from small overhangs in the stony walls. Water poured from a waterfall in the wall and followed a trench to a fountain. Chandeliers made from pale crystal dangled above Alexa's head. Waiting on the adults to check in, Alexa touched a rocky wall and frowned.

Seeing Darkfern's brother standing nearby, she asked, "Is this wall made from real stone? It looks like it but feels strange."

Rockgem glanced away from an ad for tailored leather armor he had been watching on a monitor. The youth had grown up to be brawny and stout. While he worked in security at Essence, he had refused to join his sister's unit. "Nah, it's an inner wall. We make our buildings appear to be carved out of living stone. It's our style, but we often use materials that are stronger than moonrock. Don't worry. Our buildings don't collapse, no matter how tall."

"Why would I fear collapse?"

"I've seen some tourists react this way. They worry about earthquakes, but what few we have, our structures can take."

Across the lobby, a fjouwer who worked at Essence brushed against Darkfern as he walked pass. She lashed out with a blade, striking his arm. He grinned as he jumped backwards.

Rockgem leaned towards Alexa. "There's bets on if my sister will wed Sparkrage or Nightstorm. Who are you for?"

Alexa gave a slight shrug. She liked both guys. Sparkrage loved showing off his blades when she asked. Nightstorm was quieter, spotting details others overlooked, using opponents' weaknesses against them. "She has not told me who she prefers."

"Our females never say verbally. You must look in the way they react. Cuts are shallow for those they like, deep enough to draw blood for those they wish to warn away."

Zara, who had been listening nearby, said, "Would it not be easier to just state intentions?"

Rockgem laughed. "What would be the fun in that? This will be my twelfth pailuk. My sister is not the only one who might wed this time."

"Who are you marrying?"

The fjouwer gave a mysterious smile. "The one I have my sight on shall remain nameless—until she says yes with her blades."

Hennah called her daughters over. They followed their parents to the elevator which took them up several floors. Their suite was fancy with two bedrooms opening into an airy living room with a glass wall that looked out towards Thallus Park. Excitedly Alexa studied the forest of huge mushrooms that stretched away until vanishing on the dark horizon. Some were shaped like common mushroom she had eaten in meals, just larger. Most were bizarre, twisted into strange shapes, lichen and moss hanging from them in large clumps. She had presumed they would glow, but the large ones did not. Instead, various lichen, small fungus, and vines gave off a faint light. A stony wall divided Thallus Park from the city, with the forest lower than the city by twenty feet or more. The park was not flat but hilly. Far away, Alexa could make out the faint glow of forest-clad hills raising higher than some of the skyscrapers in the city. Wisps of fog slowly swirled in the lowest valleys above streams of running water.

For dinner Alexa's family ate at a restaurant in the hotel with Darkfern's family. The other fjouwers from Essence headed off on their own adventures for the evening. The next morning—at least it was morning according to Alexa's e-band—the whole group meet for breakfast. The unmarried fjouwers were dressed for battle in hide armor, their favorite blades strapped to waists. Desmond and Firestrike jested with their offspring about the adventures which awaited them. Nightstorm and Sparkrage vied for Darkfern's attention which she returned with either a sharp tongue or blade.

After the meal was finished, they headed towards the park. Everywhere were sentients, most fjouwers but there was a fair mix of others species. Alexa kept close to her parents in the throng. Eventually they reached one of the ten gates of the park, each supervised by a different clan. Steps lead down to a plaza surrounded by the same wall which divided the park from the city. Only those registering for pailuk were allowed entrance. Alexa had to be content standing with her family on the walkway above the plaza, watching the lines of contenders giving their names to elders who typed info into e-tablets. Darkfern flashed a grin towards her parents and friends just before disappearing through the gate to enter the park. Rockgem silently nodded towards his parents as he joined other male participants.

Alexa's family along with Firestrike and Desmond followed the street built parallel to the wall, looking for a better view. The wall followed the natural curves of the land, never running straight for long. Finally they stopped at an overhang that gave them a view of thousands of excited participants below them. The females mingled at the edge of the subterranean forest while the males stayed near the wall, waiting for the signal to begin. Alexa leaned over the railing, trying to make out details in the dim light. Here the moist air smelt like rich, fertilized earth. Some participants wore cloaks with hoods covering their faces to hide their identity. Others kept their arms bare to show off tattoos depicting clan and family history. Not all participates were fjouwer.

Alexa squinted. "Is that a squad of quintessences over to the left?"

Desmond nodded. "Of course. You think I am the only one who wants a fjouwer bride?"

Firestrike twirled a blade in her hand. "I better be the only one you want."

"It was challenging enough winning you. I do not need another wife."

"Good, because if your hands every wander, I will cut them off." Firestrike's words were harsh, but a smile hinted she was flirting.

Hennah frowned as several males fought in a mock battle below. "Does anyone actually die during pugna?"

"It happens, but it is rare. Foreigners who register for pailuk are warned very clearly about the dangers. You enter at your own risk. Medics wearing red bands wander about the park to help any with serious injuries."

"How big is the park?" asked Zara.

"Endless." Firestrike's eyes took on a longing look. "The city wraps around its edge for five miles. The park itself merges with the wilderness beyond. You could walk the rest of your life and never come back to your starting point."

"Does anyone get lost?" said Alexa.

"From time to time. But we fjouwers have a good sense of direction in the underground. It is foreigners who are more likely to get lost."

"Why do many of the females wear colored bands?"

"White means it is their first time. Yellow indicates they have only completed two, three, or four pailuks. While males still battle the younger ones for fun, they will lose on purpose. No male wants an inexperienced wife. Honor comes from mating with the most skilled warriors—those wearing purple. They have completed pailuk twelve times or more and are considered legendary. You will also see wives wearing green. They are reenacting their pugna with their husbands. Joseph and I have done so a few times."

234

A loud siren blew from somewhere. With excited shouts, thousands of females dashed into the forests. The watching crowd around Alexa whooped, cheering the participants on their quest. The male participants continued to mill about near the city wall, eagerly awaiting the next signal. With her eyes, Alexa follow the females as they moved in groups or solo. They ran quickly away from the city, spreading out the further they went, soon disappearing into the thick foliage.

Hennah asked, "How long do the males wait?"

"Two hours. Then the chase will go on for three days. Eventually all will return to check-in with our elders at the gates."

With nothing happening for a while, the families wandered about, visiting nearby shops. Outdoor areas were lit by the soft glow of fungus spouting from lampposts, pots, or fissures in walls. Indoors, small traditional businesses preferred using the natural living lights, but larger modern companies preferred electricity.

Everywhere along the streets were vendor booths selling food, trinkets, and souvenirs. Performers put on mock combats, some enacting out ancient legends. Tourists and locals joined various competitions which seemed to be taking place on every street corner. Joseph and Desmond faced off, both climbing up a series of ropes to reach a bell at the top. Joseph barely beat the other Five.

When nearly two hours had passed, the families headed back to the wall. Another loud siren sounded. Yelling in anticipation, thousands of males rushed into the forest. Alexa hoped to see a pugna, but the females had not stayed near the city wall. After the males had vanished, Alexa competed with Zara to see who could climb a wall of ladders first. Zara won that prize. Alexa earned a bracelet made of colorful stones when she outshot a dozen children competing with laser crossbows. All the contests cost money, which Joseph paid without complaining. He even talked Hennah into entering a few competitions, but she only tried ones that tested intellect and not agility.

When they final reached their hotel room, Alexa watched the park from the window, occasionally spotting tiny figures moving between stalks of giant mushrooms. She rubbed her fingers along the smooth stones of her bracelet. "Papa, we need a holiday like Kilpailu at Essence."

"We have the Day of Remembrance and the Day of Commendation." Joseph sat on a sofa with Hennah. Using his e-band, he had projected a map of the city onto a wall. They studied it, seeing what attractions were nearby.

"I know both are important, but they are not fun. We need a fun holiday to celebrate being alive, like the fjouwer."

"We have annual contests in the Hall of Challenge."

"But not an official holiday. You should turn the contests into a holiday for all quintessences. You are a Five. You can do that."

Hennah leaned against Joseph. "I agree with our daughter. You should add an official holiday that is actually festive."

"You could call it the Days of Challenges. Should last three days like Kilpailu. Quintessences across the empire will come together not to fight but to play...well play fight."

Joseph's lips curled. "I will bring up your suggestion with the other Five."

Alexa smiled back. Perhaps the measure would not be approved, but just knowing she had a father who listened to her made Alexa feel special. It was nice having a father who was a Five.

The next day they attended a sports event. The stadium was oval with an obstacle course in the middle. Teams represented different clans. Parts of the course moved and changed as team members dashed through the maze trying to steal giant fake gems from each other's headquarters. Alexa found it quite comical as they raided each other, carrying the huge gems while navigating revolving walls, spinning floors, and spraying jets of water.

Afterwards the families wandered the streets, checking out stores. Alexa was fascinated by a blade shop. Everywhere on walls and racks hung weapons, many with designs she had never seen before. Joseph held up a short sword, testing its balance. Desmond tossed throwing blades at a target on a wall. Firestrike laughed, claiming she had better aim. She then picked up the blades and proved her words were not a vain boast. Alexa and Zara ran their fingers over the handles of polished knives, their eyes lit up with excitement. The girls silently looked at their mom, pleading with their eyes for one.

Hennah sighed. "You are four now." She glanced at her husband. "Do you think they are ready?"

Joseph stabbed the air with a flamberge sword, its wavy blade reflecting dim light of nearby luminosity fungus. He looked at his two daughters. "They have been patient long enough. You may select one knife each."

The sisters eagerly tested different blades, seeing how each felt in their hands. Eventually Alexa settled on a karambit similar to what Darkfern used. She loved how its blade could whirl around her fingers. Zara choose a double bladed knife. It could be used one bladed, but with a touch of a button on the handle, a second blade appeared facing the opposite direction.

While the girls shopped, Desmond picked up a curved sword and challenged Joseph to a duel. "Have at thee, villain."

"Thou art the villain."

The two danced around the room, sparring, dodging shelves and each other. Firestrike called out jests to her husband while Hennah just shook her head, muttering about men turning into boys when on vacation. The shop owner, a fjouwer, ignored the duel while giving directions to the girls about the best way to hold their new knives. Everyone bought a weapon but Hennah. Desmond walked out of the shop with three swords to add to his collection back home.

As they passed a booth near the city wall, Joseph purchased a bag of fruit. He held out one of the fruits to his daughters. Liquid swirled inside its translucent skin.

"Fireberries. Very spicy. They are hard to find on Core worlds."

Alexa reached out and took the fruit. When she bit into it, fiery juices exploded, causing her cheeks to puff out. The flavor hinted slightly of sulfur. Despite having grown up on Indian cuisine, her eyes watered from the heat. "It's like eating a star, Papa."

Joseph passed the bag around for others to try. Zara tried suppressing a giggle when the fruit exploded in her mouth. Firestrike grabbed a handful but Hennah hesitated.

"You should try one," said her husband. "Your ancestor Yashana helped make them popular on the Rim."

Hennah frowned for a moment then took a berry and plopped it in her mouth. Her cheeks puffed out and she coughed. "I can't imagine why she would win a Zelzer for this."

"Because they grow where many other crops cannot survive." He turned to Firestrike. "Are there underground volcanos here?"

"No. Just hotspots where we grow fields of fireberries."

Alexa was curious. "If it does not rain here, how do plants grow?"

"Actually we have both clouds and fog in our larger caverns like this one. Have you noticed how moist the air is? We keep it that way on purpose for our plants and fungus. There are some environments far away from cities that are dry and hot where our fireberries grow.

Zara leaned over the railing. "Look, there is a fight. Is it a pugna?"

Alexa eagerly looked down into the luminosity forest. Under a giant twisted mushroom, two fjouwers circled each other, both looking for an opening to attack. The male suddenly lunged forward, the female sidestepping. They went back to circling. Bystanders on the walkway above noticed the fight and an eager crowd grew, many calling out suggestions or jests to the combatants. The male moved in again, the female using two arms to block his movements while her two blades aimed for his vulnerable spots of neck and arms. Nether landed a killing blow as they swirled around each other, twisting, blocking, and dodging. Their bodies became closer, the male sliding a suggestive hand along his opponent's arm. The female stabbed his side, but the hide armor he wore took the blunt of it. As he twirled sideways to dodge her other blade, he suddenly dropped to the ground and rolled, knocking her feet from under her. She fell but was quickly up. He was faster, pressing a blade to her neck.

"Do you yield?" his voice was ragged.

She grinned. "About time, you fool."

The couple embraced, their many hands brushing the bare skin of the other's muscular arms. The male begin to unfasten his bride's armor.

"Girls, time to go," said Hennah.

"I wanted to see the bite," said Alexa, following her mother away from the wall. They passed a vendor selling grilled meat on sticks.

"You are too young to see that."

"They mate and the male bites the female, marking her his bride. Right?"

"I am glad to see you have been paying attention to your biology lessons—and to Darkfern's stories."

Alexa looked at her father, wondering if he would let them go back, but the sternness in his eyes told her it was no use asking. "Do they kiss like you and Mamma?"

Hennah cut in, "I am not sure this topic is appropriate for your age."

Joseph said, "You will have to have this conversation with them sooner or later."

"Not here."

Tempted by the odor of sizzling meat, Desmond stepped in line at a booth. Seeing that they would be waiting for a few minutes, Alex turned to Firestrike.

"Did Desmond bite you when you married?"

"Would not be a proper marriage without it." Firestrike pulled back her shirt on her right shoulder, revealing scars in an oval pattern.

"Did it hurt?" asked Zara.

"Yes, but it is only done once."

"And tasted terrible," complained Desmond. "Male fjouwers have it easy. Powerful jaws and sharp teeth to break tough hide. Glands in their mouth produce an enzyme that keeps the mark from healing like a normal cut. I had to chew on a foul tasting pill to produce the same effect. Took days for the flavor to go away." He glanced at the grilled meat the vendor was handing him. "I need two of these to make up for that awful memory."

Firestrike rolled her eyes. "He tries to make it sound like he suffered, but he had a good time during our pugna."

"Did you kiss?" asked Alexa.

"No, fjouwers don't have the instinct for that." She grinned. "But we have other ways to make up for that which are just as much fun."

Hennah cut in. "I have seen you two kiss before."

"You think I will give up kissing just because she lacks the instinct," said Desmond trying to eat from one stick while holding the other and balancing three dangling swords on his back.

Firestrike shrugged. "He likes to kiss so I let him when I'm in the mood, but he has to fight for it."

"Delighted to try it tonight. I have new weapons to break in."

Later, back in the hotel, Alexa again watched the forest, wishing to see more pugnas. The fighting was exciting. "Papa, I want to marry like the fjouwers."

Joseph looked up from polishing his new blade. "Your mother and I hoped you would marry a quintessence someday."

"I will, but I want it to be fjouwer style. A battle for my hand in marriage."

Zara stopped flipping the blades of her knife in and out. "Why would you want that? Mamma and Papa's marriage was romantic." The girls had seen vids of the wedding.

"It is nice, but not exciting."

Hennah frowned. "Normally quintessences follow the traditions of the bride's culture. That is what your father and I did."

"But what is quintessence customs? We have none of our own. Who is to say that fighting for marriage is not the right way? There have been no females before us. Is it wrong for me to want this?"

Joseph placed his sword on a table. "You have brought up a valid point we have not considered. We quintessences have few tradition or holidays of our own. What we do have is borrowed from other cultures. Zara, what do you think a quintessence wedding should be like?"

Zara looked between her parents and sister. "I like your wedding. I thought mine would be like that."

"Then that is what you shall have some day."

"What about me?" asked Alexa. "Can I have a battle marriage?"

"If you can get a male to agree to that, but that may be difficult. When there is no clear culture of the bride, I suspect most will lean towards what they saw in the Canon."

Alexa frowned but said no more. Most likely her father was right. Quintessences would follow the familiar when there was no clear path. She had seen Layla's marriage to Alexander in the Canon. It had actually been a Hindu wedding like her parents, though the Canon also contained Layla's memories of seeing several Christian weddings of friends. *Still, I will make it challenging for any male who wishes to marry me. There must be some type of conflict. Perhaps two guys fighting over my attention.*

The next day, they stayed near the park's gate as participants trickled out. Many walked through the gate alone or in groups with friends. Newly married couples held hands, grinning at their families waiting to greet them. It was near noon before Firestrike, watching from the walkway above the gate spotting her son.

"Rockgem is back. And he has someone!"

Desmond and Firestrike hurried down to the plaza by the gate where they waited until Rockgem and his bride reported in to the elders. Alexa watched from the walkway as Rockgem turned to greet his parents. He had several cuts covered by a paste made from lichen.

"This is Mistdawn. She is from Jadesmooth Clan. Her grandfather is chief."

Firestrike glanced at her husband, both stunned. "It is a great honor to welcome you into our family."

The bride grinned. "As it is my honor to be married into a family of a Five. My parents will wish to meet you. They wait at a different gate for me. You will come to our villa tonight for dinner?"

"Yes, of course."

Rockgem said, "Has my sister come out yet? I wish to brag about my bride."

"Not yet. Hopefully soon."

Mistdawn wrapped a pair of arms through her husband's arms as they walked to a nearby tattoo booth. They sat still, letting the artist add their spouse's name to the detailed spiral bands already on their arms.

"Related to a chief," said Joseph to Desmond. "You have moved up in the universe."

Firestrike grinned. "One of the ten ruling families. For fjouwers, we have just married into royalty. I had hoped my son would marry well but never have I dreamed this big."

Desmond took two of his wife's hands. "You faced banishment for marrying me. Now see how far you have come."

"Others only saw you as a low-level guard, but I knew you would make a respectable husband. You are worth the shame I had to endure for a while. My parents finally realized how special you are."

The quintessence leaned closer and whispered into her ear. She smiled back then allowed him to kiss her on the lips, though one of her hands stroked her knife.

The tattoos were finished by the time Darkfern showed up with Nightstorm beside her. "I finally decided."

"I see," said her mother. "Nightstorm, welcome to our family."

The fjouwer's brawny body had over a dozen fresh wounds. "It was an epic battle. Your daughter fought well."

"I expected no less."

Darkfern grinned. "It was a fight worthy of our bards. Is that my brother over there with an actual wife?"

Rockgem brought his bride over. "Mistdawn of Jadesmooth clan. Her grandfather is chief."

His sister's mouth widen in astonishment. She looked between her brother and Mistdawn. "You...married well."

"I outrank you now sister."

"I see that." For a moment Darkfern could think of nothing to say. Suddenly she turned to Mistdawn. "Of the thousands here, why would you choose my brother?"

The bride smiled. "He caught my attention a year ago. It was my eleventh pailuk and many sought me out. I defeated all of them, but your brother stood out. He is fast, adapts quickly when I changed things, like jumping off a ledge into an yluken den. Afterwards I asked around about him. Found out his father was a Five. When he found me this time, well, you know what happened."

"So you married my brother because he is a son of a Five?" Darkfern's eyes narrowed.

"Do you know how many have tried to marry me because of who my grandfather is? Rockgem is one of the few who can understand me. I purposely sought him because he is my equal, both in skill and position."

Rockgem grinned at Darkfern's flabbergasted expression. "Does she meet your standards, big sister?"

"I guess."

Alexa had to wait several hours before finding the opportunity to speak with Darkfern alone. They were in the lobby of the hotel, waiting on the last of Firestrike's clansmen to arrive before heading to Mistdawn's villa.

"Do you like being married?"

"I've barely been a bride for a day, but yes, I can say it's fun."

"I want to be a warrior like you. And to marry like you."

Darkfern looked at the karambit fastened to Alexa's waist. "Then it's time for you to begin your knifing lessons."

Chapter Twenty-nine

Cabinet members shuffled uneasy, studied their e-tablets, or listened with rapt attention to the speaker. Emperor Duyagni nodded every so often while studying the charts sent to him on his monitor. His chair at the head of the table was carved from ziricote wood, its grains a swirl of light and dark. Figures of the ten original species of the empire was curved into its unique surface. Several seats around the room were empty as the meeting had been called suddenly during late afternoon after some members had already left for the day.

Kylen pretended to listen to Shelby Hermes from the Basanti Food Administration, but her concern about genetic experiments being sold illegally bored him. His mind wondered back to Sundara. A few months ago he had finally made a breakthrough by getting the living matrix to understand binary coding. He could even run normal programs on it at speeds that beat the fastest computers on the market. Problem was he did not know how to replicate Sundara. Months ago he had several scientists clone the tissue, but their version retained no memory from its parent and could not function. It was nothing more than a mass of living cells that might as well be dead.

It would have been helpful if Kylen could speak with a technician from the species who had created Sundara. Too bad that six years ago their homeworld of Penmort had been almost completely destroyed by an overambitious general. Survivors were hesitate to trust the Empire. Kylen had even sent a task force specifically to find a technician for him. They caught one, but the woman had committed suicide after she realized why she had been captured. Better to die than give the Empire her people's technology.

The speaker sat down, and Bruce Higgins took her place. Gray hair accentuated his angular face. He supervised Internal Affair and was a top official in the Coalition. To aid several of his investigations, Kylen had hacked into computer systems for him on various planets.

"I thank everyone for coming today. This is a very special meeting, so I was careful about who was invited."

Kylen glanced around the room, noticing for the first time that only Coalition members were present. A late meeting and messages unsent had weeded out the others.

Bruce pulled up a file to display on the hologram while instantaneously sending digital copies to everyone in the room.

"This is the ultimatum of the Ediethean High Council listing one hundred and fifty grievances they have with our government."

"They are part of our Galactic Senate," said Shelby. "They vote on our laws, just like every other alien species."

"Let me rephrase my previous comment. These are grievances they have with our current administration. They demand an investigation take place."

The Emperor frowned as he read over the list. "Hmm, a fourth of these I approved myself, for good reasons. Some are cover ups like the Penmort incident. Others I do not recognize. Perhaps, Bruce, you can share some light on them."

"It does not matter if their claims are true or not. The Ediethean vermin have the audacity to demand we bend to their whims! Sire, we cannot continue to let them try to push us around. We need to make a firm stand."

Duyagni leaned back in his chair. "You mean declare war. That is where this is leading. As I have said so before, I will do nothing to split our empire. We have enough enemies at our borders. We do not need to make more among ourselves."

Bruce fought to keep his anger in check. "Sire, for centuries we have been pushing for the right moment to wipe out the Ediethean. This is it. Many of their ships are at the Rim. If we strike now, we can wipe out their entire council. Destroy their biggest cities. From there we can systemically eradicate the higher classes."

Kylen and the rest of the cabinet watched in silence as the Emperor stood, his eyes firm. "Then what? Their warships will turn on our imperial fleet."

"We ran the numbers. There will be some losses, but we will win."

"By leaving us vulnerable to rebels! If we show ourselves weak to outsiders, they will destroy us."

"Sire, your father agreed to this plan."

"Perhaps you have not noticed, but I am not my father. He dreamed of a pureblood profectus that would come from his linage. While chasing that fantasy, he showed your Coalition great favor, ignoring your zealot nature." Duyagni moved behind his wooden chair and pointed to its carvings of sentients. "I do not forget that I represent hundreds of species, not just humans. I will not declare war on our own citizens. Is that clear?"

The Emperor looked around the room, staring each individual in the eyes. Some firmly meet his eyes including Kylen. Others looked away, disturbed. Only Bruce dared to challenge the monarch.

"You are breaking your promise with us."

"No, there will be a profectus on the throne someday, but I intend to give my future grandson a kingdom that is intact. Kylen, chose twenty-five items from the list and open an investigation into them. Make sure the perpetrators are held accountable to the law. That should satisfy the edietheans."

Bruce refused to back down. "You are making a mistake, sire."

Duyagni gave his opponent a final glare. "Meeting adjourned." As members left, the Emperor said to Kylen, "I wish to speak with you in private."

After everyone including guards had left, Duyagni sat down with his son-in-law. "Do you know why I choose you to marry my daughter?"

Kylen studied the monarch, wondering what would be the right response the other wanted to hear. Uncertain, he took a literal approach. "I have good genes."

"Genes are not enough. You also think well under pressure, and I do not believe you accept all of the Coalition's rhetoric. They would prefer to destroy the empire than accept that another species is smarter than them. You are better than that."

"I rely on logic, sire. I have observed for years how you play one side against the other, always keeping each off-balance, never letting either have full control."

Duyagni nodded, pleased. "You play the political game nearly as well as I do. You have positioned yourself well, knowing the secrets of many. There is only one thing in which you have disappointed me. Why do I not yet have a grandchild?"

"Because your daughter will not let me touch her since the miscarriage." For months afterwards Abarrane had been distraught and withdrawn, barely speaking to Kylen. When she did, it usually carried an accusation that he had somehow been involved with the fetus's death. Most likely the miscarriage had been natural, not caused by the Coalition. Trying to convince her of that had not gone well.

"It has been over four years, more than enough time to grieve. I suspect there is more going on between you two."

"Sire, I have always been polite to her."

The monarch frowned. "Brains you have, but little in the way of women."

"I was given little life experience in preparation for marriage."

"You need to make my daughter feel she is the most important person in the universe to you. Apologize, even if you did nothing wrong. Give her gifts. Not expensive ones, but small things with meaning. Connect with her on an emotional level."

"I will try, sire." Kylen listened attentively. He had tried expensive gifts but she spurned them. In public she pretended to be a happy, supportive wife, but in private she avoided him, her short conversations insulting. She blamed the Coalition for the loss of her fetus and saw Kylen as the organization's symbol. She needed a face to hate and had settled on him.

"Take her to the performance tonight. She will like it. I have invited sirens to sing. Lovely species they are. Only a few of them have left their primitive home planet."

Heeding his father-in-law's advice, Kylen tried having a real conversation with Abarrane during dinner, but she cut him off, giving him the usual silent treatment. She at least agreed to attend the performance after reading a personal invitation from her father.

A few hours later Kylen escorted her to the palace theater. With security always an issue, the room had been built so the royalty family and their friends could enjoy live performances at home. Tonight nearly two hundred filled the crowded theater. Dressed in a tuxedo, Kylen sat between Duyagni and Abarrane, both in lavish outfits. Nearby sat ever-present Suson. Like the princess, she wore a long gown, but hid a weapon in her purse.

The lights dimmed. An ethereal figure stepped onto the stage. Every eye was drawn to her shapely body, pale green skin, and wavy lavender hair. She smiled, her lips a natural purple. Then she began to sing in her native tongue.

Kylen had seen many live performance since living in the palace, but nothing like this. The melody pulled at him. He did not understand her words, yet he felt an emotional connection, a yearning he could not understand. The song became happier, cheerful. A dozen more sirens walked onto the stage, adding their voices to the melody. Kylen was drawn in, forgetting that he existed. Their musical voices became life itself, controlling emotions inside him, feeding his soul with raw primal beauty. The sirens took him on a journey through heartbreak, hope, despair, and ultimately joy.

Two hours later when the last note faded, Kylen sat in the dim theater, only slowly becoming aware of where he was. Abarrane reached out and brushed a tear from Kylen's cheek.

She whispered, "You have a soul after all. Who knew?"

Kylen took her hand and held it. He felt a closeness to her that he had never experienced before. She smiled back, her own eyes moist from crying. The sirens' songs had affected her as well. Not wanting the emotions to fade, Kylen continued to hold his wife's hand the whole way back to their suite. Without a word, she drew him into her bed, for the first time in over four years letting him touch her.

The next morning, Kylen awoke with his arms around Abarrane. He did not know what magic the sirens wove, but he hoped it did not fade. For the first time since their wedding, he felt genuine warmth for his wife. He lay for a while, in no hurry to get up, watching her breathe. His princess. His wife.

Seeing her eyes open, he smiled. "You are beautiful."

"Every nerd's fantasy," she teased.

"Actually having an android which obeys your every command would be on the top of the list for many geeks."

Abarrane rolled her eyes then silently studied her husband's profile. "You are almost handsome."

"Thanks, I think."

"How about we stay in today. No meetings. No outings."

"Sure. I have a new hologram game we can try."

She grimaced. "And no electronics."

"There is another game we can play." He kissed her lips while pulling her perfect body to him.

Midafternoon someone knocked on the bedroom door. Abarrane pulled her mouth away from Kylen. "I said do not disturb me."

"Sorry, Princess, but it is your father." Distress was in Suson's voice.

Abarrane hurriedly put on a robe and opened the door. "What is wrong?"

The elderly nurse looked between the princess and Kylen still laying in the bed. "Emperor Duyagni...has been...has been assassinated."

"How?" Abarrane's body began to tremble. "I just saw him last night. He was fine. Happy."

"The details are still unclear. I came to tell you as soon as I heard. Your father was walking in the gardens alone. When he did not return when expected, his guards searched for him. They found him dead, stabbed in the heart."

Kylen sat up. "There were sentients on duty in the garden and cameras posted in every biome. There will be evidence of what happened."

Eager to investigate, Kylen reached for his pants, forgetting that Suson was still in the room. Suson turned her back as Kylen dressed. Abarrane stood silently, her face pale as she fought to control her emotions.

Kylen turned to his wife. "I will find out who did this. There will be evidence. I will see personally that he is held accountable."

He headed down the hallway to the living room. Suson followed behind him and caught his arm. "Do not leave her now."

"What?" Kylen turned, startled.

"If you abandon her now, she will never forgive you." Suson looked like an harmless elderly aide but her commanding eyes were a reminder she was still a trained bodyguard.

"I am not leaving her, just heading to my office for news."

"Others can investigate, including me. You need to be here. She has lost her mother and now her father. She has no close family left but you. If you walk out now, you might never be invited to her chamber again."

Puzzlement filled Kylen. He was a man of action. When he saw a problem, he took the necessary steps to fix it. For a moment he remembered Duyagni's conversation with him from the day before. That he was clueless when it came to a woman's heart.

Taking a deep breath, Kylen nodded. "Alright. But you will report everything you find, immediately."

"Yes, Your Highness." She turned and left the suite.

Her remark caught Kylen off guard. She had just addressed him as if he was Emperor. Kylen knew he was in line for the throne, but the Coalition's emphases had always been on a future son—a natural born profectus that would be accepted by the public. Kylen had never set his sight on becoming a monarch. Too much responsibility. He had presumed that when Duyagni died from old age, his power would be transferred to a profectus grandson. That had always been the Coalition's plans. A golden child raised in the palace that would lead the human race to a new era. *Now they are stuck with me, a computer nerd who secretly prefers gadgets than dealing with people. Who sees individuals as controllable formulas.*

Kylen returned to his wife. She stared without seeing, tears running down her cheeks, hands clenched into fists. For a moment he awkwardly watched her, unsure what to do. Stepping closer, he hugged her. She broke down then, sobbing uncontrollably. For a long time he held her. Gently he led her to the bed where she lay weeping. He brought her tissue, water, anything he could think of. For the rest of the day he stayed near her as servants brought food and aids information. Suson texted regularly. Friends stopped by to offer consolations.

Night had fallen before the head of security visited, reporting what he knew. Someone had evaded cameras and snuck around sentients, then managed to escape unnoticed after the assassination. A ceremony knife of ediethean design was found tossed in a fish pond.

Kylen was suspicious of everything he was told. It was too convenient to blame the edietheans for the murder, especially after Duyagni had just told the Coalition he would not turn against the edietheans. Long after Abarrane had fallen asleep, Kylen poured over security footage on his e-tablet. Suson sat beside him on the couch. She was one of the few he trusted. Suson's loyalty belonged to Abarrane, not the Coalition.

"This had to be an inside job," said Suson when they had replayed all the recordings for a third time, finding nothing.

"Agreed. Many dignitaries have visited the gardens, but few would have knowledge of where all the cameras are. And not a single guard seeing anything?"

"Duyagni often went to the garden to be alone. His bodyguards were posted at the exits of the biome. The murderer must have been hiding in the shrubbery, waiting hours for him to visit. Perhaps he escaped through the ventilation or water system.

"But they are too narrow. It would be hard for anyone to fit through them. I suspect the guards were paid off to ignore anything strange. Perhaps one of them is the murderer."

"They would never betray the Emperor." Suson was offended. She had spent a lifetime in service to the royal family. For a bodyguard to double cross the Emperor was unthinkable to her.

"Depends on where their loyalty lies. Some of the guards are Coalition members. Put them on duty and tell them Duyagni's death is for the good of all."

"Why would the Coalition want to assassinate the Emperor? He was their closest ally."

Kylen glanced down the hall where his wife slept. "Because he was not aggressive enough for them. It's a brilliant move on their part. Kill the Emperor and blame the Ediethean High Council. Then they finally get the war they have been longing centuries for."

Suson turned sharp eyes from the monitor to Kylen. "They will expect you to be their puppet ruler."

Kylen nodded. "If I stand up against them, they will have me killed, just like Duyagni."

"So, sire, will you be the puppet or the master?"

Again Kylen glanced down the hall. "My life is not the only one in danger. If I stand against the Coalition, they will kill me and put enormous pressure on her. She does not need that, especially right now. I will keep playing their game. The alternatives are too costly."

"She will despise you for it."

"Better she hate me than face an assassin's blade or be pressured to marry yet another she distastes. One egotistic husband is enough."

Chapter Thirty

Alexa walked across the living room, brushing her long hair hurriedly. She barely gave the vid her parents were watching a glance. In the bathroom she looked in the mirror, frowning at her bright red hair.

"I'm too visible."

Zara, with toothpaste in her mouth, sputtered. "Nothing is wrong with your hair."

"We are supposed to blend in as human. You do. But look at me. My hair is like a flame shouting, 'Look at me!'"

Zara rinsed her mouth. "We are only going shopping with Nani."

"Yes, our first time out as adults." Only four days ago a small ceremony had been held in Bellus Garden to honor the girls turning eight. If they had been normal males, they would have been giving their first assignments and sent off to begin their fifty years of bonded service to the empire. Instead, they had been given sober speeches by the Five and a fancy meal with their families.

"Not a big deal. We have had outings with our grandparents many times."

"Yes, but we lack detailed training in adolescent human behavior. What do eighteen-year-olds do?"

A slight smile crossed Zara's face. "Perhaps have panic attacks like you are now."

"I am not afraid, only concerned."

Alexa placed her brush on the counter, frowning again at how bright her hair was. Could she not have been designed with more natural auburn? Glancing at her e-band, she hurried back to the living room. Pallavi would be here soon. Her parents were still watching the large vid showing the new Emperor's coronation.

Hennah sat on the edge of a sofa. "He looks so different. The hair, his mannerism. The way he speaks."

In deep concentration, Joseph studied the screen. "From coder to Emperor. Not a typical promotion. The Coalition has intriguing plans for him."

"But what are those plans? Why him?"

Joseph glanced at his two daughters listening silently. "We will discuss this later."

Alexa was used to her parents hiding secrets from them. All her life there had been conversations cut off when she entered a room. She was unconcerned as it was most likely top secret info only Fives and a select few were supposed to know. Darkfern had once told her that it had been the same in her own childhood.

Zara watched the vid showing a young man with a gold crown on his head giving a speech. His wife stood behind him. "Mamma, you met the Emperor?"

"Years ago when he was only a computer programmer. He told me his marriage was to be arranged. I never would have guessed it was to a princess."

The doorbell chimed. Alexa greeted her grandmother. Pallavi talked for a few minutes with her daughter and son-in-law then she headed downstairs with her two granddaughters.

Zara paused before exiting the elevator, double checking the map on her e-band. "No birthmates nearby. We can head straight to the car."

As Pallavi drove, the girls chatted easily with their grandmother. They had visited zoos, museums, aquariums, and many other tourist spots with their grandparents. Today was a shopping day and Kaushal had opted to stay home. To lessen the chance of being seen by friends, Pallavi drove over an hour to a large city with a popular shopping center.

As they explored stores, Alexa observed human teenagers, studying their behavior. How friends joked with each other. Young couples holding hands. Girls giggling over a video ad of a popular popstar. As Zara walked down an aisle containing life-size hologram singers, she paused occasionally to listen, her blank face revealing nothing about what she liked. Alexa could read Zara's slight raise of eyebrows and the faint trace of a smile. She knew her sister's emotions but a stranger would not.

Alexa leaned close to Zara. "I may be concerned that my hair causes me to stand out, but you look like a walking zombie from the movies. You should smile occasionally to look human."

"I am being me. This is a shopping trip, not an undercover investigation."

Pallavi led them to an upscale clothing store. Zara stood on a holopad while clothes were projected onto her body. Mirrors around the chamber allowed her to see the outfits from different angles. Pallavi offered suggestions while using a controller to rotate between different styles.

"Now that you two are grown, you should dress more your age."

"What is wrong with how we dress?" asked Zara, a slight frown indicating she did not like the pink jumper currently being projected onto the white smock she wore over her normal clothes.

"Nothing if you want to always live on a military base. Out in public you need more color, wear current fashions. Look pretty."

"Why would I want to be pretty?"

Pallavi laughed. "There is much your mom has not told you. She is a great scientist but is not the best example for dating or fashion."

Alexa said, "We know about mating, but we are bonded. It will be fifty years before courting will be a concern for us."

Lowing her voice though they were alone in the chamber, Pallavi said, "Do you really think they will force you to wait that long? Rules were broken for your creation. They will not wait half a human's lifetime to see if you can have natural children."

Zara and Alexa shared a glance. In private they had already discussed with birthmates about when they would be allowed to marry, but anytime they brought the topic up with parents, they were brushed off with the warning that bonded quintessences could not pursue romantic relationships.

After Zara selected several floral printed blouses, Alexa took a turn on the holopad. As Pallavi rotated through outfits, Alexa pondered how to balance dressing like a human yet reflect her own personality. Several of her birthmates wore bright clothing, especially Jade and Pearl whose mom was very much into current fashion. After a lot of indecision, Alexa finally settled on three outfits.

A store clerk fetched the real clothes from a backroom. Then Alexa and Zara tried on the outfits in changing rooms. Wearing a close-fitting turquoise blouse with a V-neck, Alexa stared at her refection in a mirror, wondering yet again if her bright red hair made her stand out too much. While she and her sister had been on many outings, their interaction in the *wild* with non-relative humans was very limited. Actually their interaction with quintessences was also sparse. Yes, there was the entire Synod and their families who knew about their existence along with the Shadow Guards. And some psychologists and scientists who regularly questioned them. Yet the circle who know about their existence was kept very tight.

Always they must be on guard to hide their own identities, especially at Essence. They were never permitted interaction with young male quintessences their own age. Whenever they walked about on campus, they had to be always aware where the other pairs of birthmates were and avoid them. Never let anyone suspect there were two sets of quintuplets living at the institution.

Alexa moved closer to the mirror reflecting her hazel eyes and flaming hair. Insecurities hit her yet again. She tried to always appear confident but knew Zara was aware of her conflicts. As far as Alexa knew, male quintessences never stressed over appearances. Or worry about being too emotional. They simply fit in with their countless other clones, never doubting themselves. Zara's model with their quiet demeanor and Asian looks would have no problems one day passing the beta stage.

But what about us? She asked herself yet again, worried about all the CF models. *We are too cocky, too outspoken. No matter how hard we try to act as expected, we fail, especially*

251

me. It was scary knowing her actions affected the future of all CF models—or lack of. If a beta model failed, they become the first and last of their kind.

The only other models who might could relate to her fears were the AS1's and AS2's who were trained to be spies. She personally knew none. Their numbers were kept low on purpose, and the few she had seen were always at a distance. She could not go up to one and say, "Hi, I'm a beta who is too emotional. How do you deal with pretending to be human while keeping true to your quintessence self? I need you to give me a profound answer because my model is in danger of being cancelled."

"Are you done yet?" came Pallavi's voice through the door.

"Yes." Alexa walked out to show off the turquoise blouse and black designer slacks.

"You fill them out well." Pallavi nodded in approval. "Zara, you look lovely too. That red print is beautiful on you. How about you both wear these outfits the rest of the day?"

They walked towards the front of the store, passing headless mannequins in popular body shapes showing off clothes: humanoid, amphibian, even multi-tentacled. After Pallavi had purchased the clothes, they headed to a café to buy frozen coffee drinks. While waiting for the drinks to be fixed, the girls wandered about looking at products on display.

A human clerk cleaning a table smiled at Alexa. The teenager had a tattoo of an animal on his arm. "Your name must be Star because you're hot."

Alexa frowned. Was he referring to her hair? *I need a time machine so I can chew out the two geneticists who designed my body centuries ago. What were they thinking?* Keeping her voice flat, she said, "Actually it's a pleasant day with a cool breeze."

He laughed. "What's your number, cool one?"

"My number?" Why would he wish to contact her?

Zara cut in, "She does not give her number out to strangers."

"My name is Budd. Tell me your name, and we won't be strangers anymore."

"Our drinks are done," called out Pallavi by the counter.

The girls hurried away, relieved to be away from Budd. They walked outside and sat at a table under a large sunshade. As Alexa sipped her dark chocolate accented with chili powder, she decided it was her new favorite flavor. Fire and ice mixed together.

Through the glass windows, Zara studied Budd cleaning another table. "Why did he ask for Alexa's number?"

Pallavi sat her cup down. "He was trying to ask her out on a date."

"Why would he do that?" pondered Alexa. "He has never met me before."

"He was attracted to you. Most likely he asks many girls out. Best to avoid guys like him. They are not looking for long term relationships."

"Do not worry. Zara and I keep to the Code. We know we cannot date for a very long time. But I still do not understand him. What does a human male look for in a possible mate?"

Zara frowned slightly. "We are not supposed to ask such questions, sister."

"I know but our parents are not here. How will we understand if we do not ask?"

"Those are questions for free quintessences only."

Pallavi said, "The Code does not bind me. Besides, it's not against the Code to talk about romance. You just cannot act upon it. I think you quintessences are just so concerned about breaking the rule that you avoid even speaking about it. Ask me anything you wish. I may be old, but little has changed since I was a teenager myself."

"Why was Budd attracted to me?"

"You are well endowed."

"Because of my hair?"

Pallavi laughed. Seeing both girls' puzzlement, she explained, "It is easy for me to forget you are only eight. You have both grown up so fast. You may know a dozen ways to kill a foe but you are naïve about so much else. He was attracted to the size of your chest."

"Why?" *Is this another fault in my design?* Alexa wondered.

"Because some humans place importance on size. Mind you, not all of them. There are many different traits we look for. The more superficial ones like your Budd place emphasis on what they see above all else."

Zara asked, "Why did you marry Grandfather?"

"Ah, we had a common background. Both our families worked at Essence. Mine lived off campus while his lived on campus. We ran into each other a few times in our youth. Then we both happened to get jobs in the Infant Department. We became friends and began hanging out together after work. We fell in love and then married."

"Mamma married her co-worker and so did Firestrike and Darkfern. So is that the proper way to meet future mates?"

Pallavi laughed again. "One of many possible ways. Asking strangers on dates is another method."

"A dangerous one," said Alexa, wishing she had her knife, but it was not normal for humans to bring knives on shopping trips, at least on this planet.

Zara asked, "What traits do male quintessences look for?"

"Hmm." Pallavi sipped her ice coffee for a moment. "I have never heard anyone say. Their wives vary so widely. You will need to ask your father that question."

When Zara and Alexa reached home a few hours later, their parents were in a deep discussion with Jennifer and Skyler. As the girls walked in with bags in hand, the others became quiet.

Hennah said, "I see your shopping was successful."

"Yes," said Zara. "Nani bought us several new outfits."

Joseph turned off the vid screen. "It is your turn to prepare dinner tonight."

"Yes, Papa," both girls replied.

They headed to their bedroom and hung up their new clothing. Then they went to the kitchen. On a monitor Zara pulled up a recipe for a seaweed salad which used three types of seaweeds along with mussels, fish, and crab. The sea lavens their mother worked with had passed along the recipe. Alexa grabbed a knife and made quick work of the fish. Their parents had insisted they develop cooking skills. Hennah had taught them traditional Indian dishes while Joseph explored a wide variety of cruises from many cultures. As the girls worked, they discussed their conversation with Pallavi.

"We should ask Papa," said Alexa.

"You know that topic is forbidden." Zara pureed a purple ribbon of tough seaweed. "We were lucky to get them to talk as much as they did when visiting Shah Luna."

"Still we should try. There are things we should know before it is time for us to seek lifemates."

Jennifer and Skyler left before the meal was ready. As Henna and Joseph ate with their daughters, they discussed the shopping trip and commented on how delicious the food was. Alexa caught Zara's eye, but her sister shook her head. Alexa frown and tapped her fork in irritation.

Looking between his daughters, Joseph said, "What is it that you two are disagreeing on?"

The sisters glanced at each other. Then Alexa blurted, "We were wondering about what traits male quintessences look for in lifemates. And when will we be allowed to marry?"

Joseph sat down his fork and folded his hands, studying his daughters. "What has led you to ask these questions?"

Zara gave a slight shrug. "Nana brought up the topic today. We are just curious."

Alexa added, "We are not in any hurry for marriage. We just wanted to know."

Joseph exchanged a look with his wife. Then he said, "We cannot give you a date for marriage."

"Do we really have to wait fifty years? Mamma will be really, really old by then."

"Most likely you will not have to wait that long, but neither will we give you a timeframe. You may be adults now with mature bodies, but you are still very young. There is much you do not know about yourself, were your talents lay, what you are capable of. You need time to grow up emotionally before you can commit to a lifemate."

"When do we get the chance to do that? Testing ourselves? We have completed all the classes and training you have given us. What is left?"

"A lot. That was what we were discussing with Skyler and Jennifer. It may be time to prepare you for real work in the field."

Eagerly Alexa leaned forward, "We will be spies like the AS models?"

"That is what we hope. Due to the nature of keeping your identity a secret, there are large gaps in your training that your male counterparts would have experienced before turning eight. We are considering addressing that issue. It will involve bringing in more outsiders for you to work with."

"We are ready," said Alexa, her food forgotten.

"I am pleased to see your excitement. It will be the greatest challenge you have yet faced in your young lives."

"Papa," said Zara. "Could you answer our other question? The one about what males look for in lifemates?"

Joseph frowned slightly. "Courtship is not a proper topic for bonded quintessences. Spending too much time pondering this topic when you cannot act on it for years can lead to transgressions. I have seen this happen."

"We are not going to misbehave," reassured Alexa. "We just want to understand. That is all."

"The answer to your question is honesty. We desire wives that are trustworthy, loyalty, and honest. All other traits vary widely."

"Do looks matter? Like hair or sizes of body parts?"

"No. Using the epulo, we look into the minds of others, seeing them for who they really are. The outside is only an illusion. Are not we the masters of illusion ourselves, seemingly human yet alien from them? Quintessences look into the souls of others. Finding a kindred spirit attracts us."

"Is that why you married Mamma?" asked Zara.

"For me, it started with my desire to help her. Overtime that grew into something more. With Desmond, he admired Firestrike's zest for life. Tobias was comforting a widow. Ask any quintessence why he choose to marry and you will get a different answer."

Hennah added, "When your time comes, look for someone who cares about you, someone you enjoy spending time with. Who understands you."

255

Joseph looked at his daughters with stern eyes. "But do not start courting before we say so. Is that clear?"

"Yes, Papa," said both girls in unison.

Chapter Thirty-one

An auto lawnmower chopped grass near a barracks. A sundancer child chasing a ball ran in front of the machine. Quinn looked up from the shrubbery he was trimming, instinct telling him to rush to the child's aid, but the lawnmower paused on its own, waiting until the child was gone before moving again.

For a moment, Quinn remembered the rush of emotions piloting his own fighter in the mist of battle, adrenaline rushing, senses alert. He pushed away the memories as he bent down and picked up limbs he had just cut. Passing other quintessences doing yard maintenance, he tossed the branches into a hopper which chopped them into wood chips to be used on flowerbeds

For nine years this had been his life. Pruning, digging, fertilizing. His punishment for standing up to a tyrannical general. Quinn received regular updates from his birthmates stationed at the edge of the Rim. He knew about their battles, felt their pride in successes and frustration in failures. Mourned the death of six more of his brothers. While they had each other to offer solace, he was alone. He shared a room in a barracks with forty-nine others, all of them being punished for breaking a part of the Code in order to uphold another section of it. Together they formed a loose community calling themselves the Gray Unit, but nothing could replace the agony of separation from birthmates. He should be on the frontlines fighting alongside his brothers.

Quinn picked up his clippers again and began cutting a new bush. Hearing his e-band beep, Quinn glanced at it, expecting it to be his supervisor giving a new location for afternoon duty. Instead, it was a summons by Caden, director of Essence. Shocked, he read the message twice. Why would the director want to see him? *I have done nothing wrong since coming here. Has something terrible happen to my birthmates? Could their entire battleship have been destroyed?*

He looked about, needing someone to speak with. Each of his co-workers were studying their own e-bands or looking about in puzzlement.

"Did you just receive a message from the director?" asked Quinn to the nearest one.

"Yes," said Jason, an IN2. "Right after lunch I am to attend a meeting."

"I have been asked to come too," said Margolis. As a HC4 model, he had a talent for fixing machinery that broke down, including daily issues with the wood chipper.

For lunch, Quinn headed back to his barracks with his co-workers. While eating in the cafeteria, he learned that all the others he shared a dorm room with had received the same message. They debated its meaning. Since so many had been invited, it must mean an important announcement of some kind. But what? Perhaps they had all received pardons and were being sent back to their birthmates. That was their greatest wish, but most doubted such a reality.

After the meal was finished, Quinn joined the forty-nine others heading to Richton Towers. They took elevators up to the fifty floor. Tobias of the Five greeted them and led them through Bellus Garden to a large plaza at its center. The other Fives along with Shadow Guards, several Synod members, and their wives stood near a huge rosa tree.

Quinn stood at attention, arms by his side, face blank. Like his brethren, Quinn felt uneasy. Why here? A lush garden was not a proper location for a military briefing. This same floor held the homes of the elite Five, not a place you invited dishonored soldiers.

"Welcome, brethren," said Caden. The elderly C2 walked down the rows, looking each individual in the eyes.

When Quinn's turn came to be inspected, he kept as stiff as possible, barely breathing. The last time he had been near a Five was at his trial where he had fully expected to be executed.

Inspection finished, Caden moved back to the front. "You have been asked here for a special project. One carrying uttermost secrecy. Breaking that secrecy carries a death sentence. Is there clear?"

"Yes, sir," came fifty voices in unison.

Joseph moved to the front, taking Caden's place. "I am like you, brethren. For eighteen years I was part of the Gray Unit, separated from my birthmates. I understand both the frustrations and shame you feel. You suffer the mark of dishonor for making hard choices. Obeying the Code is not easy. Upholding all of it at all times in all circumstances is nearly impossible. Sometimes one section must be broken to keep true to another part. You each made a decision, knowing it might cost your life, but you did so to protect others. We cannot honor you in public, but we can do so in private."

Skyler replaced Joseph. "Because you understand the quagmire of morality, you can better understand what we have done, and why we have done so."

He gave a brief nod. Ten youths marched out from behind tall bushes. The females lined up, facing the Gray Unit. Dressed in black shirts and camo pants, the ladies stood at attention, faces blank. Several had long hair pinned back, others had short, stylish haircuts. As Quinn studied them, he quickly realized there was only two faces shared by ten individuals. His eyes darted to Jason who looked just as puzzled. Margolis opened his mouth in surprise, but he quickly shut it.

Desmond paced between the two units, a faint smile on his lips. "What have you figured out?"

Members of the Gray Unit continued to glance at each other, but no one spoke. What they were seeing could not be true. From youth there were truths every quintessence knew. The Code was law. Fifty years must be served to recompense for being born. The Five ruled with steel authority. Disobedience meant death. Their species was all male. You did not questions these truths. You simply accepted.

Now suddenly reality was altered.

Desmond stopped in front of Jason. "What do you notice?"

"Ten soldiers, sir, with two faces."

The Five turned to Quinn. "What does logic tell you?"

"That they are quintessences, sir."

"You are correct." Desmond moved back to the front, standing beside the other leaders.

Joseph moved forward. "In a move to save our species, we broke the Purity Law. Some of you may have already been aware of what my wife is."

Quinn, along with everyone else in the plaza turned towards the clone of Layla. He, along with all of Gray Unit, had known of her existence for a while. Henna was never on the official news videos like some of the other wives of the Five, but she could be spotted from time to time walking about Essence. Which quintessence would not recognize the face of their creator? They had seen her countless times in the Canon. Sometimes when communicating by epulo, they pondered about the mysterious clone, but they never said a word out loud. Instinctively they knew her existence was a guarded secret.

"This is the quagmire we Five face. To save our species we broke a galactic law, yet we are the upholders of the law. We did not make this decision lightly. That is why we choose you to help us with this vital project. We trust that you can understand why we have done this and will support us."

Tobias took Joseph's place. "The next phrase is preparing our betas for live field work. You will be working with them in squads of ten, drilling them in urban tactics, hostage recovery, and high-risk environments. They will be put through the same basic training you received. As we learn their strengths and weaknesses, we will adjust the content. You will begin tomorrow."

Caden said, "If I call your name, step forward. Asa, Mitch, Wyatt, Joaquin, and Quinn. Congratulations. You are our squad leaders. Everyone else, dismissed."

Quinn scrutinized the females as they walked away. They were barely adults. At that age, he had been promoted to lieutenant of his unit and sent to his first post on a battleship. A greenhorn in the midst of war. Lessons had been costly. Fortunately, the first couple of years his unit worked closely with two more seasoned units, but then the older units had earned their freedom. After that, Quinn had become the highest ranking pilot on the battleship, overseeing not only his birthmates but the two new units of rookies. He made decisions that sometimes cost his birthmates and other soldiers their lives. Where these young females ready for such responsibility? Could they handle the guilt which came with mistakes?

Joseph led the newly promoted sergeants to a large room which contained dozens of tables and chairs. Quinn guessed it was used for hosting meals for visiting dignitaries. Joseph, Skyler and three Synod members stood in a semicircle.

"We wanted to speak with you in private," said Joseph. "None of you have been involved with a beta training program. For the most part, we will treat the females the same as we do their male counterparts. Already they have had weapons training, hand-to-hand combat, and wilderness drills. Due to the need to hide their identities, they missed out on obstacle courses and urbane drills. Nor have they worked in large squads before. This you will remedy."

Skyler said, "You also need to be aware that we raised them differently than any quintessence before. They grew up in family units. Two sisters with a quintessence father and human mother. We are their fathers."

Quinn looked at the elders. Two Fives and three Synod. To be part of history was exciting, but the realization that he would be working with the daughters of top leaders filled him with dread. "Sir, exactly how realistic do you want their training to be?"

"Extremely realistic," said Joseph. "We will not put them out into the field unless we believe they are ready. They are expected to perform on the same level as you. We may be their fathers, but we are also soldiers. We do not plan to put them into frontline combat, but even undercover agents may find themselves in gunfights. They must be prepared for any situation."

Skyler added, "As their sergeants, you will report how they performed. We want you to be honest. We need to identify and address their weaknesses. Being betas, there are many unknowns."

"Do not worry that we are their fathers. We demand a lot from our daughters and trust you will treat them fairly but firmly. Expect from them the same as you would a male."

"Yes, sir," said Quinn and the other four new sergeants.

Chapter Thirty-two

The sound of bullets hitting a wall came from Alexa's left. In the dim light she winched, reminding herself it was just sound effects. She moved along a concert brick wall, keeping low to the ground. A long hallway with a dozen doors lay before her. Anywhere could be enemy. Behind her three squad members followed. In her ear came Quinn's monotone voice giving commands.

She pulled down her night goggles to cover her eyes, allowing for better vision in the unlit hallway. Quintessence eyes allowed them to see much further than a typical human, but still darkness limited her sight. As she moved, her body felt heavy and clumsy. She was required to wear not only the typical gear of body armor and helmet for a swat team, but also a techno suit which tracked all hits taken from enemy fire.

Through the earpiece, came Quinn's voice. "Team Red, keep searching your wing. Team Brown, permission to pursue your target. Extract information of hostage location."

Alexa grimaced. Why did he have to name her team after her hair? Creeping down the hall to the next door, she pushed it open and rolled inside. Bullets hit the wall where she had been squatting moments before—well, the sound of bullets as no live ammunitions was being used. An IN model was ducked behind a metal desk. Peeking out, he fired again, hitting Margolis's shoulder who was part of Red Team. The techno suit briefly lit bright orange, registering the hit. Margolis would no longer be allowed to use that arm.

Using the distraction, Alexa leaped over the desk, firing as she landed on the other side. Her opponent's entire suit flashed dark red—a kill. But he had been quick enough to fire a shot at her. Alexa's left arm flashed orange, warning she had a flesh wound. The suit around her injured arm stiffened, limiting her use of it. Alexa felt annoyance that only five minutes into the drill she had already been shot.

Keeping focused, she glanced around the room. Decorations and furniture were kept to a minimum. Moonlight could be seen through the windows. The large complex consisted of nine ugly buildings made of concrete and steel. While the structures lacked beauty, they made up in secrets. Everywhere were cameras, sensors, speakers, and traps. From a computer center, technicians could alter walls, even shoot jets of fire. At least that was what Alexa had been told.

Since they were not allowed access to the normal facilities their male counterparts used at Essence, the girls had to endure lots of lectures and videos. In late hours after most were in bed, the girls were given access to the Shooting Center were they practice for hours at a time. In the Recreation Center they played combat simulations games which used real war footage. As much of their training took place at night, they had to become used to a new sleep schedule. All their lessons become more intense, including hand-to-hand combat, giving them little leisure time. Alexa did not mind. She was a quintessence, designed for action.

What she did mind was failure. Ignoring the stiffness of her injured arm, she said, "Room cleared."

Gesturing, she ordered her team to move to the next room. One by one, they cleared each room, taking out two more opponents who were part of the Shadow Guards helping with the drill.

"Blue Leader, the wing is clear," said Alexa into the communicator in her helmet.

"Proceed to atrium. We will meet there."

They walked down the hallway and entered the large central room where a broad stairwell connected to the next floor. Alexa stood at the edge of a doorway, scanning for others. She spotted Zara near the front of the building, her head peeking over the desk in the lobby. Quinn's team appeared at the back through another door.

"Team Brown, secure the stairs."

Constantly searching for enemy, Zara and her three team members moved through the darkness to the stairs. After looking for traps, they climbed up, out of sight. Sounds of gunfire ripped the air.

When Alexa tried to move forward to help, Quinn said, "Team Red, hold position. Report Team Brown."

For a moment there was silence. Then Zara said, "Stairs cleared. One man down. Jason."

"Hold position. Team Red, move in."

With her team following her, Alexa dashed up the stairs. At the top she had to leap over Jason whose suit was highlighted in dark red to mark his death. She glanced at her sister as they passed, but with a visor and helmet on, Alexa could not read any facial expressions. With her team, Alexa explored the hallway, seeking more opponents. Team Blue, led by Quinn, reached the top of the stairs and went in the opposite direction.

Entering a series of connecting offices, Alexa moved slowly. Desks and cubicles were everywhere. Too many places to hide. Seeing movement, she turned right. A round object rolled out from under a desk and stopped by her feet. More concerned about the enemy, she ignored the object as she ducked behind a partition and began weaving through cubicles towards her target. The pulse grenade simulated an explosion by sending out a wave of purple light. The techno suit of anyone caught in the wave turned red. Alexa was protected by a desk, but Margolis was caught off guard. In the darkness, he had not seen the grenade as Alexa had been blocking his view. When the pulse reached him, he dropped to the floor, not moving.

I should have warned him, thought Alexa, flatting herself to the floor as bullets sounded nearby. She crawled in the darkness towards a cubicle. A flash of orange on another of her teammates warned of his leg injury. Alexa clenched her gun tighter. *I need to take down the assailant before we are all dead.*

She rolled across the floor while shooting her laser gun wildly towards the cubicle. A flash of orange told her she had hit him. While she had distracted the opponent, her teammate Fredric had crept closer using a different path. As Alexa ducked into a different cubicle, Fredric fired a killing shoot, ending the firefight.

"Team Red, reporting in. One man down, another with injured leg."

"Proceed with clearing your section."

Alexa frowned. Too bad their foe was dead. Her injured teammate could have feed to heal. The techno suits were designed to reset injuries if a quintessence pretended to use the epulo on another foe. Feeding on teammates was not allowed in drills, but in real life it was a method sometimes used for treating serious injuries when there was no other options. It was best avoided as it weakened the one feed upon. In the midst of battle it could lead to two lives lost instead of one.

After a moment's hesitation, Alexa decided to leave behind injured Draz, hoping to capture a prisoner to bring back to him. She continued through the sea of cubicles with her last teammate Fredric. No more attacks came.

"Section cleared," Alexa reported.

"Hostage located," said Quinn. "Room Seventy-one. Team Red and Brown, meet me there."

Alexa headed down the hallway, eager to finish their main objective. Zara barely beat her to the doorway. Quinn's team had not lost any members, so he sent them in first. Alexa and Fredrik went next. The large room was another sea of partitions. *I hate cubicles,* Alexa decided, ducking down as she moved through the maze. Zara's team took a different route through the cubicles.

Near the far wall was a meeting room with a glass wall. Inside the room was the outline of a human woman dressed in a business suite silhouetted in the moonlight. The hostage. Obviously she would be guarded. Zara's team had to pause to deal with an attacker. As Alexa neared the glass wall, she kept partitions between her and the wall. Passing a snack room, she saw movement just before a laser beam sliced through the air, hitting her already injured left shoulder. Before Alexa could raise her weapon, Fredrik had already brought down the fjouwer with a kill shot. *Cursed techno suit. I should be able to move faster,* thought Alexa.

Quinn was already one cubicle away from the glass wall, near its door. "Team Blue in positon. Report in Team Brown."

"One down. Two injured," said Zara, "including me. Cannot walk."

"Stay put and deal with injuries. Team Red?"

"Near you. I see a hallway and backdoor into the office."

"Get into position."

Alexa and Fredrik moved into the hallway. The walls were concrete but she was certain that one of its doors lead back to the meeting room. "In position."

"My team, move in. Team Red, go now."

Alexa opened the door into a supply closet, its shelves bare. In the distance, she heard shots firing. She raced to another door which opened into a private office. Behind the desk was yet another door. As she opened it, she entered the meeting room, but her view was partly blocked by a wall and large artificial plants. Near the glass wall stood Reanna, Jade and Pearl's mother. Nightstorm pointed one of his guns at her while the other weapon was directed towards Quinn standing with hands up just beyond the open glass door. Several quintessences and fjouwers lay on the floor, their suites dark red or orange.

"Team Red, stand down," came Quinn's voice in the earpiece.

Alexa took in the situation quickly. Nightstorm had two targets to be concerned about. He had yet to notice her. She rushed into the room, firing at the back of his head. She hit, but a purple light pulsed through the room. Her techno suit turned red and stiffened, forcing her to fall to the floor. Behind her, she heard Fredric also hit the floor. The pulse wave filled the room, taking out the hostage. Nightstorm was already dead from her shot. The only survivor was Quinn who ducked behind a cubical wall, just before the purple pulse reached the glass door.

Alexa lay on the floor, shocked by the sudden turn on events. She had been so sure she was about to secure victory. Now she was dead after setting off a booby-trap most likely hidden in the plants.

"Drill completed," said Quinn, standing up. He touched a reset button on his e-band. All the lights on the techno suits turned off. "Objective failed. Everyone, meet back at the atrium for a debriefing."

Overhead lights turned on, brightening the room. Alexa took off her night goggles.

"That was fun," said Nightstorm, rising off the floor. We won."

"Fun?" argued Darkfern, sitting up. "We all died, both the good and bad guys."

"I went out in a blaze of glory. That's the way I want to die in real life."

"My husband with the suicide wish. I can give you death by battle anytime."

264

"How about tonight?"

Reanna smiled at Alexa rising from the floor. "You did well your first time."

"I failed."

"We can't always be successful. Learn from your mistakes."

As Alexa walked with the others, she felt angry at herself. *I should have checked for traps. Why did I not think of that?* When she meet up with Zara, she refused to look her sister in the eyes, still feeling the shame of failure. Meeting in the atrium, humans, fjouwers, and quintessences stood at attention while Quinn gave a brief but concise outline of the events. When he mentioned Alexa setting off the bomb, she flinched, avoiding Zara's probing eyes.

"Our mission was a failure as the hostage died. Causalities were far too high. Zara, Doug, Draz were injured. I was the only other survivor. Now let us talk about our mistakes."

Alexa listened in silence, her frustration growing as he had each of his own team members state their cause of deaths and how it could had been avoided. Two had been injured but would have survived had not Alexa set off the bomb. Next, he focused on Zara's team. By the time it was Alexa's turn, her fists were clenched, her jaw set. *I know I failed. I don't need a lecture about it in front of everyone.*

"Alexa, what was your mistake?"

"I forgot to scan for traps."

"That is not why you failed. Try again."

"I missed the trap. And I caused four to die, including the hostage."

Quinn moved to stand directly in front of her. "You first mistake was not following orders. I told you to stand down but you entered the room."

"The hostile was unaware I was there. Logic dictated that I could take him out before he could kill the hostage."

"But I had spotted the bomb. When I told you to stand down, it was to prevent exactly what happened. If you had waited, we would have won. You could have spoken to him, distracting him and I rush into the room to take him out. Your mistake was not trusting me."

Humiliation flooded Alexa. Everyone was staring at her, knowing she was the cause of failure. Her mind whispered that a simple *"Yes, sir"* was all she needed to say. Instead, she let her anger explode. "You should have told me the bomb was there."

"There was no time. And a leader does not need to explain himself. You should have obeyed immediately." Quinn begin to walk away.

Alexa was furious. "What type of leader are you? Eight dead, three injured. Why were you promoted to sergeant? You are a pilot. Have you ever even faced a situation like this in real life? You fly ships. A C model would have been a better choice as they actually have infantry experience."

The room went deadly quiet. Everyone was staring at Alexa, but she did not care at the moment. She wanted to lash out, to take the blame off herself. It had been her first time doing an urbane drill. *He should have told me the bomb was there. It's really his fault we lost.*

Quinn walked back to her, this time standing only a few inches away, a dangerous look in his eyes. "Soldier, you know nothing about real life combat. You think this little scenario was difficult? Try a space battle with hundreds of ships. Explosions happening all around you. Birthmates dying. But you cannot take time to mourn them. You must shut down your emotions. Focus on the problems before you. Trust your training and instinct. But most importantly, obey instructions. Am I clear?"

This time, Alexa said the expected, "Yes, sir." Still, her body trembled in anger. Quintessences were not supposed to lose their tempers. Yet she was fighting for control. *He will report your behavior. First drill and you doubly failed. Great job, Alexa.*

The group marched out into the night, joining with the others squads and volunteers near the buses that had brought them to the facility which was located on the far side of Essence's vast campus. Alexa continued to avoid Zara's eyes as she boarded a bus. When they entered the penthouse, all was quiet as their parents had went to sleep hours ago. Alexa felt relief she would not have to share the night's events with them yet, but they would hear about it in the morning.

Alexa took a quick shower. As she entered their bedroom, she hoped Zara would not speak with her.

Instead, Zara sat on the bottom bunk of their bed, staring at her. "Sister, why did you behave as you did?"

"I did not see the bomb."

"I am not concerned about us losing. We will learn to do better. I mean why did you challenge him, our sergeant?"

"It was a mistake. I did not mean to. The words just came out."

"You challenged his authority in front of everyone. You know that is against the Code. Do you know how dangerous that was for you?"

"The Code says not to disobey superiors. I did not mean to disobey him. The next time he says not to walk into a room, I will not. Like you said, I must learn from my mistakes."

Zara was still frowning as she headed off for her shower. Alexa lay on the top bunk but sleep was elusive. *Why did I have to open my mouth? I should have just stayed quiet. Be the perfect quintessence girl everyone wants. Be like Zara.* She rolled over on the mattress. *Why did I have to be designed to be emotional?* Anxiety flooded through her.

266

Everything she and the other CF1 models did went into consideration if they would ever pass being betas. *With the way I behaved in my first combat simulation, we may never make it.*

It was almost noon when Alexa woke to the smell of sautéed eggplants. Hungry, Alexa quickly dressed. Zara was in the living room, playing a shooting video game, practicing her combat skills. As Alexa walked into the kitchen, she spotted Hennah stirring vegetables in a steaming pan. Joseph looked up from the roasted chicken he was slicing.

"Alexa, we need to talk."

Those few words from her father filled Alexa with dread. Already he knew about last night. Most likely Quinn had passed on the memory to him. Hennah gave her daughter a sad smile of pity as Alexa followed her father out of the kitchen. As they walked through the living room, Zara glanced up, her face blank, but her eyes showing concern. Entering the study, Joseph closed the door and sternly looked at his daughter.

"Tell me about what happened last night."

"I made a mistake. It won't happen again."

"What mistake did you make?"

Alexa looked towards her father but avoided his eyes. "I accidently set off a bomb, causing the mission to fail."

"I am unconcerned about that. Any rookie could have made that mistake. Why am I disappointed in you?"

"Because…" Alexa clenched her fists, wishing she could be anywhere but here. She had barely slept, fearing facing her father. "I should have obeyed my sergeant and not walked into the room."

"That is still the rookie mistake. What happened in the debriefing?"

"I…I…spoke out of turn to my supervisor."

"To be precise, you said he was unfit for his position. You claimed another could do his job better. You spoke these words in front of your squad and the volunteers. Is that correct?"

"Yes, sir." Again she avoided his eyes. She could not stomach the deep disapproval she would find there.

"Alexa, I personally chose him to be your sergeant. Are you saying my logic was faulty?"

"No, Papa."

"Why did you challenge him?"

"I was angry. At him. At me. I guess I just wanted someone to blame. I made a mistake and will not repeat it again." This time Alexa met her father's eyes.

"Subordination is a serious infraction in any army. For a quintessence to behave inappropriately, doubly so. I do not need to tell you the danger you have put yourself and your model in."

"I am really sorry, Papa. I know I was wrong. Please do not hold the other CF1's responsible for my behavior. It was my first time doing one of these drills. I just got too emotionally involved. I will control my temper next time. I promise."

Joseph studied his daughter, a slight frown on his lips. The silence stretched into minutes. Each second was agony to Alexa. He was a Five. She was young but still an adult. Too well she remembered his warnings of what happened when adults failed to live up to the Code's standards. She did not fear death near as much as disappointing her father.

"Alexa, I do believe you understand the depth of your offense. This time you will not appear in a hearing with the Five but a repeat incident will lead to that."

"Thank you, Papa."

"You will apologize in person to Sergeant Quinn for your behavior."

"Yes, Papa."

"You will do so right now."

Alexa glanced at the door. "Now? It is lunchtime. Can I do so afterwards?"

"No. You will go find him right now. No delays. Is that clear?"

"Yes, Papa." Alexa turned towards the door but paused. "I am sorry again for disappointing you." She saw the hardness in his eyes fade.

Quickly she hurried out of the room. She refused to look at her sister as she passed through the living room and headed out of the apartment. In the hallway she paused to search for Quinn on her e-band. Seeing he was in his barracks, she took an elevator downstairs. Wanting to get the apology over as quickly as possible, she hurried across the campus, passing several huge barracks before reaching his. Entering the lobby, she again checked his location. Following the dot on the map, she passed quintessences who gave her curious glances.

She walked down several hallways before coming to a huge room with fifty bunkbeds. Only half were in use. The occupants looked at her when she entered. Some were relaxing on beds reading e-tablets. Three were engaged in a card game. A few walked into the room, their hair wet from a shower. Alexa recognized her team members from last night. Seeing their stares, she again felt guilt for failing.

Quinn put down the cards in his hand and walked up to her. "Why are you here?"

"Can we talk in private?"

"This is a barracks. There is no privacy."

Alexa glanced at the others watching her. She had fussed at Quinn in public. She might as well apologize in public. Standing at attention, she said, "Sir, I was out of line last night. I accept responsibility for my actions and apologize."

Quinn's face remained expressionless. "Your father sent you."

"Yes, but that does not make my apology any less sincere. I spent the whole night miserable. I barely got any sleep." She paused, hoping for some word from him. When he said nothing, she blathered, "I was upset with myself and took it out on you. It will not happen again."

"I would expect such erratic behave from a human but not from a quintessence."

Alexa winched, feeling like she had been mental slapped. "What can I do, sir, to make up for my poor behavior?"

Quinn glanced at the others listening to the conversation. He turned back to Alexa. "You can start by eating lunch with us. Then help with cleaning duty."

"Yes, sir."

As one, the quintessences rose and filed out the door. Alexa followed behind, feeling out of place. They entered a large cafeteria. Several hundred quintessences eating at tables glanced at her. Alexa kept her eyes on her tray as she took a sandwich, vegetables, and fruit. She sat at a table several seats down from Quinn. Margolis was across from her.

In a low voice, she said, "Sorry, I did not warn you about the grenade."

"We can both be glad it was not real."

At other tables quintessences chatted. They were birthmates who had decided to continue working at Essence after their bond years were completed. The Gray Unit with its wide mix of models was more subdued. Every meal was a reminder that they were separated from their own brothers.

The food was bland flavored. Alexa missed the spicy dishes she had grown up eating. As she looked around the cafeteria, she realized just how different her life was from a normal quintessence. From childhood sharing a dorm room with ninety-nine others. No mother or father. Training hard, not knowing if you would survive the fifty years of servitude to know freedom. During the seven years of their youth, they would not step foot off Essence except for wilderness drills in the nearby national forest. Seven year old AS models would eventually fly jets over the ocean but not even visit New Hope next door.

Alexa and her birthmates had been off campus many times. They enjoyed normal actives of shopping, eating out, visiting attractions, and going to movies. Her parents were a central part of her life. Thinking about losing either of them made her heart ache. She may not have experienced grief herself, but she still remembered its agony from her first epulo bite of a prisoner. As she watched the quintessences eating around her, she understand why birthmates were so important to each other. They were family, the one constant in a bonded quintessence's life of various postings, missions, and dangers.

Meal finished, the Gray Unit put away their trays. Alexa followed them back to their dorm. Quinn handed her a mop. As she cleaned beside the others, she worked without complaint. She had grown up doing light housework, mainly keeping her room clean. Small vacuum bots took care of the carpet and a maid dusted shelves and watered the houseplants.

She learned that Gray Unit rotated major chores with the other units in the barracks. Each week, various groups were assigned bathroom, cafeteria, laundry, or hall duty. Today, besides cleaning their own dorm room, they mopped the entire hallway of their wing.

Eventually Joaquin called everyone together. He was the oldest in the group and served as its unofficial lieutenant. "Time for more training, brethren." He looked at Alexa, quizzing her. "What is on today agenda?"

She stood at attention, "More hand-to-hand in the garden. Followed by another lecture on terrorism by Caden. We will be doing an obstacle course run after dark. Tobias is quizzing us about interrogating prisoners when you cannot use the epulo. And at midnight, we do another urban drill."

Joaquin nodded. "That covers it. Move out."

Alexa jogged with the others across campus towards Richton Tower. Quinn ran beside her, his face blank, his eyes focused in front of him. Alexa tried to look just as expressionless, but she worried about the next drill. She had to do better, be more focused. Most of all, she could not lose her temper again.

They slowed down when reaching the large building and walked cross the Grand Forum. An elevator took up the majority of them. As Alexa stood quietly, waiting for the next elevator, Quinn leaned toward her.

He whispered, "I forgive you." He then walked away and stepped into an elevator that just opened up.

With those few words, Alexa felt huge relief. The tension that had clung to her since last night lifted. She could start over. *This time, I will do much better. Even if my mission fails, I will not take my frustration out on others.* She stepped into the elevator beside Quinn, a faint smile on her face.

Part III

"My rage is unspeakable when I reflect that the murderer, whom I have turned loose upon society, still exists. You refuse my just demand; I have but one resource; and I devote myself, either in my life or death, to his destruction."

—From *Frankenstein* by Mary Shelley

Chapter Thirty-three

Kylen studied the 3D hologram map of a zoomed in section of the capitol city. He leaned closer over the large table, looking at eight city blocks which had been leveled. Around the flatten areas were tall buildings, a few colored red. *Just a few more to knock down,* Kylen thought, smiling as he visualized what the structure might look like that would replace the old, dilapidated buildings.

A golden hair girl of eighteen months wobbled into the study, chasing a cleaning bot. Kylen glanced over at his daughter. "Abigail, you are supposed to be in the playroom."

"Shiny," grinned the toddler, trying to touch the bot half her height. It scooted out of the way, vacuuming the carpet as it moved.

Kylen sighed and picked up the child. "I have work to do. You need to stay in your room with your toys."

Spotting the hologram city, the toddler reached out, trying to touch the transparent buildings. "Zoo. Want to go."

"That is not a map of the zoo."

"Yes, zoo. There." The child pointed to the edge of the map showing trees and the words *Diamond Zoo.*

Despite being annoyed at the interruption, Kylen smiled. Abigail was a profectus. Already she was showing signs of being an advanced reader. "Maybe your mother can take you tomorrow."

He carried his daughter down the hallway to her playroom and set her down among building blocks which she had constructed to look like a life-size cat. She began reshaping the animal to resemble the cleaning bot. The nurse on duty entered, carrying a tray of snacks.

"You lost your charge again," complained Kylen.

"Sorry, Your Majesty. I only stepped out for a moment. I fastened the door."

"She knows how to use those Link-it Sticks to create a lever to unlock the door. Get a digital lock installed."

"Yes, sire."

Kylen headed back to his study, hoping for no more interruptions. His wife and Suson would be gone for a couple more hours. He preferred Abarrane not to be around for his meetings, though this one had nothing to do with the Coalition. Still, she always thought the worst of him. She loved her daughter, but still blamed the

Coalition for the miscarriage of her first child. If she suspected they were responsible for her father's death, she kept the knowledge to herself. Never in public did she say negative comments about the Coalition. In private, she was secretive, telling Kylen little of her personal concerns. Their relationship was rocky. Weeks, sometimes months, would go by without them sharing a bed. Occasionally there were times when she treated him almost like a friend, smiling, teasing him. Then she would turn suddenly cold again, usually when something big was reported in the news dealings with the Coalition.

Back in his study, Kylen pulled up budget estimates. He was still reviewing them when a guard knocked on his door.

"Sire, your guest has arrived."

"Send her in."

Kylen turned off the hologram and glanced in a mirror. His hair was sleeked back, his clothes tailor-made, stylish and elegant. He looked the role of emperor, yet today he wished he could have worn denim pants and a casual shirt. It would have been more fitting for this meeting. Still, throughout the day, he would come in contact with dignitaries who expected him to look the part of a monarch.

The door opened and Amy entered. The moment she saw him, she beamed and started forward, reaching out to hug him. Suddenly she paused, noticing his clothes. "Am I supposed to bow?"

"Not you. Not here." Kylen embraced her in a hug. They had not seen each other since he left New Hope. "You look the same. Well, a little older."

She wore a tan blouse and black pants. "I was unsure what someone wore to a palace."

"You could have worn shorts for all I care." Despite it had been over nine years since he had seen her, he still felt the sibling bond between them. She was one of the few he could feel completely relaxed with. "How is your husband?"

"The same. We both stay busy working on various projects. Rarely do we see each other. We prefer it that way. Still, we do meet up every few months for a short holiday together. No kids yet. The Coalition must be disappointed in us."

"No kids means more time for your projects. I have been impressed with your work so far."

"Thanks. So why the personal invite here? Not that I mind finally seeing the famous Diamond Palace. Remarkable architecture here."

Kylen smiled. "I have a job for you. Your dream project."

"What, pray tell, is my dream project?"

The monarch smiled teasingly. "Combining music with structure."

Amy leaned forward, intrigued. "You know how much I love music. But what job would the Coalition have that deals with music?"

"This has nothing to do with the Coalition. This is my private project. Do you remember those tickets I sent you a few months ago?"

"Yes, the sirens. Excellent concert, by the way. How they combine emotions and music is…well…magical."

"They use telepathy when singing. They are masters of their craft. I have heard many famous singers but none which can control my emotions. Sirens use notes like artists use paint. They take the audience on a journey like no other. Every performance is a treasure to cherish."

"Careful, you almost sound like you are in love."

Kylen laughed. "To bad all of them are married to quintessences. I would love to have one as a concubine. Whenever they visit Basanti on tour, I invite them for a performance here in the palace. My wife enjoys hearing them as much as I do. That brings me back to this project I have for you."

"I have been wondering how this related."

"You will design for them a permanent performance hall. It will be built here in Diamond." He turned on the hologram and pointed towards the flat area in the middle of the 3D buildings.

Amy examined the map. "This is a large area for a concert hall."

"It will be bigger. The buildings in red are scheduled to be knocked down in the next few weeks. I do not want you to design just a concert hall. Think bigger, much bigger. It will double as a homeland for the sirens. As the quintessences have Essence, the sirens will have this."

Amy's eyes widened, her mouth opening in surprise. "You mean living quarters, a school, cafeteria, and offices? The whole works?"

"Yes. It will double as both a performance hall and living area. Most of all, it must be the most beautiful structure on the whole planet. An architecture wonder which will be talked about for millenniums to come. Cost does not matter."

"You are giving me the opportunity to be immortal—to build something for which I will never be forgotten."

"Yes. Every profectus's dream. You can outshine your clone sisters. Will you accept?"

"Of course. How could I turn this down?" Amy bounced in excitement. "The two parts should function separately. Can't have guests wandering around the siren's apartments. There will be a huge glass atrium with an indoor garden. Lots of plants as the sirens are from a jungle world." Amy suddenly paused. "Have you actually talked with the sirens about this? I mean, you are not doing this for free. What is the price they must pay?"

"I have spoken with them, and they are excited. On their homeworld, sirens travel a lot but regularly return to their clan's sacred pools where their elders live.

There they share their adventures through songs which are passed on to future generations. Harmony Complex will serve that function. Sirens can come and go as they please, but it will also serve as a business. Performances will be given non-stop six to nine months a year. There will be a break to give time to design a new show. Each season will be different. This will attract a lot of returnees who will come back year after year to see what is new. The property will be owned by a board of sirens but they will have to pay off the loan for the building's cost which I will provide for low interest. It may be many decades before there is any profit."

"Perhaps a century or more, if you let me build it as I envision. It will cost a fortune."

"The sirens are long-lived. Some of their elders live over three hundred years. They have the patience and drive for this to succeed. All their concerts are sold out no matter which planet they visit."

Amy looked concerned. "I see you have put a lot of thought into this, but what does the Coalition have to say about this? How will this benefit humans?"

Kylen's smile faded. "I have not spoken to any of them about this nor do I care about their opinion. I do this for myself. I want…need to leave a legacy that is not about politics. Something beautiful which benefits everyone." *Something to make amends for the billions who will die by my orders in the coming war.* But he could not tell Amy that. For the last few years, he kept brushing off Bruce and other eager zealots, telling them as a new monarch his power was not yet strong enough. Their patience for his excuses was running out.

"This goes against the Coalition's speciesist views."

"Is that a problem?"

"No. Not at all. This is the project I was destined for my whole life. I will pour my heart and soul into it, making it the most beautiful homeland ever created. It will outshine even Essence." She paused, giving Kylen a serious look. "I am proud of you. Not in just becoming Emperor. You have really matured, seeing there is more in the galaxy than just us humans."

Kylen smiled, hiding guilt. Amy, like the other profectus, knew little of the darkest intend of the Coalition. "I have complete confidence in you. I know I have picked the perfect person for this job."

Chapter Thirty-four

Purple birds flew between trees, catching insects. A large six-wing butterfly landed on a neon green flower and drank nectar. The city skyline was dominated by enormous sleek towers which mushroomed at the top into domes. On the ground in the shadows of the structures grew lush plants. Monorails and sidewalks cut across the peaceful landscape.

Alexa sat on a park bench, pretending to be interested in her e-tablet. Her eyes roamed, carefully watching pedestrians strolling along the sidewalks between flowering bushes. Mansoor was a beautiful planet, but she had little time to explore it. The mission was paramount, at least that was what Alexa told herself. She sighed. *A year of intense training and then two years in the field for what? Low-level missions I could do in my sleep. When will they actually give us a real challenge? Training was more interesting than this.*

"Target coming," came a message across Alexa's e-band.

Glancing along the sidewalk, she saw a slightly chubby human carrying a briefcase. She waited until he was near then she stood, putting on a friendly smile. "Professor Adamson, how wonderful to see you again. I enjoyed several of your guest lectures at my junior college."

The man paused. "Good to see you, miss. What is your major?"

"Journalism. I attend your university now. Just wondering, do you have a few minutes to answer questions for an article I am researching for? It's about alternative theories on ancient history."

"Delighted to help a pretty student like yourself. I'm heading to my office now."

Alexa chatted easily as they passed large ferns being nibbled by fluffy, dark green rodents. Adamson bragged about his latest book which had become a bestseller. Reaching the base of a large skyscroom, Alexa glanced up. The narrow section rose upward for hundreds of feet before ballooning outward, becoming a structure large enough to contain an entire university inside of it. It reminded her of Richton Tower but the base was much thinner and the overall structure taller.

As they entered the lobby, Zara casually fell in step beside Alexa. "How is your article coming?"

"Ah, wonderful. Professor, this is my roommate, a freshman also majoring in journalism. Mind if she watches the interview?"

"No, not at all." Adamson thrived on attention. "I can show you my plaques."

They took an elevator up and exited into a large, open atrium where sunlight streamed in from the glass roof high overhead. Students from many species sat on benches, studying or chatting in small groups. After passing a fountain surrounded by flowers, Adamson led them down a long hallway. At a door, he placed his hand on a panel. It flashed green, unlocking the door.

"Come in. It's a bit messy, but you know how it is. We instructors are always busy."

Alexa took a seat across from Adamson's cluttered desk and turned on a recorder. While she asked the professor about his research, Zara sat quietly for a few minutes. Then she got up and wandered about, looking at the jumbled shelves full of artifacts and books. Slowly she made her way around the room, stopping behind Adamson. With a sudden quickness, she bit him, using the epulo to probe his mind. His eyes glazed over. She ended the bite and continued her peruse of the books. Adamson continued talking without realizing what had happened.

Zara returned to her seat. "Professor, you mentioned that you received your Teacher of the Year award at the same time you claimed in your book to be digging in the desert where you discovered the evidence that proved Mansoor was once occupied by humans a millennium before sundancers first claimed to colonize this planet. Which is correct?"

"Oh, I took a brief break from my dig to accept the award."

"None of your colleagues found human relicts at the site. Can you explain why you are the only one who did so?"

"I have a talent for finding things."

Alexa leaned forward, giving a big smile. "You sure do. Tell me, where did you buy that human skull?"

"From a medical student." The professor froze, suddenly realizing his slip. "I mean, I had a medical student look at it after I found it."

"A brilliant move, planting the skull then pretending to discover it. What method did you use to age it?"

"The skull was already old, just from another planet." Adamson blinked, unsure why he had just said what he did.

"Thank you for the interview." Alexa turned off the recorder and stood up. "You have three days to confess to the media that you faked the evidence or I will release the audio of this interview."

"What? Wait. I don't know why I said that."

"You had the sudden urge to speak the truth. Now you will be honest with the rest of the world. Good day."

Alexa and Zara headed towards the door.

Adamson stood, his face pale. "You can't be students."

"No, private investigators." Alexa flashed him one final smile before leaving.

Once they were outside strolling in the shadow of the skyscroom, Quinn casually joined them. "How did it go?"

"Too easy, like normal." Alexa passed him the recording. "We gave him the standard three days to put his affairs in order before we destroy his life."

"He might actually confess," said Zara.

"They rarely do, despite our warnings. These missions are too much the same. When do we get to see some real action?"

Quinn pocketed the recording. "Betas spend years doing Level One."

"We have already spent two years doing so. Come on, it's time for something more challenging. We are ready. And you must be bored, along with our whole squad. Get us something more engaging, something worthy of our skills."

"You are too impatient."

"Do you honestly want to keep doing Level Ones? You who was once a great major on a battleship? This is far beneath your talents."

"Flattery does not affect me."

"It's worth a shot. Better than me berating you."

"That is my job when you mess up. You two have the next three days off. Try to stay out of trouble this time."

"That fight on the last planet was not my fault. That guy insulted my hair then tried to touch me."

"He was drunk. You should have let it go."

"I did let him go, after I smashed his head against a table."

"And you broke the arm of one of his comrades."

"His buddies should have stayed out of my way."

Quinn exchanged looks with Zara. "This may explain why we are still doing Level Ones while your birthmates are doing Twos. You need to think about the consequences of your actions before you do them."

"I did. And I was okay with the consequences. We walked out of that tavern respected."

"And spoiled the chance to earn the trust of the miner we needed to talk with."

"I got the information we needed, just took a bit longer."

Quinn tapped into his e-band, telling the whole squad about the three day respite. "I will see you two tonight at the ship."

Taking a seat on a bench, Alexa discussed with Zara how to spend their free time. Money was limited. Bonded quintessences were not given a salary. As undercover agents, they did have a small fund for expenses.

"How about the zoo? It is half price today," suggested Zara.

"A zoo? I prefer a gladiator arena."

"There are none on Mansoor or any planet we have been sent."

"Would be nice to be posted to the Rim where the real action is."

"There are dangers on Core planets too, which you have a knack for finding."

"Our missions are so boring, I need to do something to entertain us." Seeing her sister's frown, Alexa said, "Alright, we visit the zoo. Maybe we can see an animal fight."

They spent most of the afternoon roaming about the zoo, though the biggest fight Alexa saw was a flock of birds chasing each other over a bun someone had dropped on the sidewalk. They paused at a crosswalk, debating between the primate or reptile buildings.

Suddenly Zara's eyes lit up. "I have seen this spot before."

"We walked through here a couple of hours ago."

"No, I mean, I have seen this place without being here. There was a large group going into the primate house. And she went to the reptile house to see mutant lizards."

"Who are you talking about?"

"Who else?" Zara leaned close and whispered, "Our creator, Layla."

"Oh." Alexa mentally opened the Canon in her mind and pulled up the memory of young Layla visiting a zoo. "Technically she did not create us. That would be her clone Yashana."

"If not for Layla, there would be no quintessences at all. We exist because of her." Excited, Zara allowed a faint grin on her lips. "Today we walk in her footsteps."

Alexa followed her sister into the large building displaying reptiles. Indoors, it was dark and cool. They peered through the glass at strange beasts from many worlds. The final section still held genetically enhanced creatures spliced from different animals.

"It has been over six hundred years, yet the same buildings are still here in use." Awe was in Zara's voice. "The government has been very stable on Mansoor. No wars."

"A dull history."

"Perhaps there are other places that still exist that she visited. Her home, her school." Zara began searching on her e-band.

"Are you taking this a little too far? Who wants to see an ancient school?"

"Found the address where she lived."

They left the zoo and traveled by monorail a few miles. Zara was excited as they stood in the shadows of the massive structure.

"How do you know it's the same skyscraper? They all look the same," complained Alexa.

"Each skyscroom is unique. Different colors, textures, and embellishments. You have no taste for the arts, only fighting. This is the right one."

They entered the large, airy lobby. Despite the age of the structure, it felt modern and sleek with potted plants and polished floor. Parents holding the hands of their youngsters entered elevators. A couple kissed as they walked out of a mail room, both excitedly holding a large package. Behind an ornate desk, a receptionist barely gave the quintessences a glance.

Zara's eyes gleamed as she slowly wandered around the lobby, imagining young Layla walking cross the same floor. By a doorway was a small plaque saying, "Memorial." Alexa followed her sister down a short hallway that opened up to a large chamber with hundreds of names on the walls. Beside each name was a picture and a list of achievements. Most were local heroes who had retired honorably after serving as teachers, politicians, and other civil focused careers. They found Layla Rangan's picture under her parents' biographies.

"She looks just like Mamma," said Zara, touching the picture. "Our mother is highly esteemed to have such a famous sister clone."

Alexa shrugged, pretending not to care, but even she was feeling reverence for this quiet spot. So many quintessences had died for the Empire to keep Mansoor a peaceful planet. Nice that their creator was still remembered on her birth planet, even if it was only a small token.

They read other names on the wall for a few minutes then turned to leave, almost running into Quinn, Margolis, Jason, and Fredric. For a moment the two groups looked at each other, then Fredric gave a brief smile.

"Glad to see you have not forgotten her either."

"How could we not?" said Zara.

Quinn said, "Most quintessences who happen to be visiting Mansoor stop here."

"A quintessence tourist spot," said Alexa. "I am surprised they do not have a souvenir shop set up."

"They save that for Essence's museum."

Zara led the others over to Layla's picture. Like Zara, each touched the image and read the writing. Silent reflection followed. Finally, Quinn mentioned it was time for dinner. They headed back to the spaceport where their yacht sat on a pad. As it was Doug and Draz's turn to cook, the food was bland mush. Alexa and Zara were the best cooks in the group, but they had to hold back on their favorite spices as the heat was too much for the others.

Near the end of the third day, Quinn gathered all his squad members. "Professor Adamson released an official statement admitting his fraudulence. Good work on another successful mission." He looked towards Alexa. "You will be glad to know our next mission is Level Two."

"About time, sir."

"We head out immediately."

A few days later, Alexa walked along a wet, slippery street on the planet Dieither. As it was the monsoon season, it seemed to always be raining. The buildings were made of concrete or stones, designed with gutters that channeled rainwater into shallow canals along the streets. Eventually the water ran into major arteries leading to a river that cut through the capitol city. Perhaps during the dry season, the city was pretty, but Alexa currently found it dreary and bleak.

A plastic poncho covered Alexa's clothes as she followed her target. Despite the rain, the streets were busy with pedestrians. The target walked into a store. Alexa paused under an awning and looked through a window at a display of expensive handmade clocks. In an age where machines could build objects cheaply, ownership of handcrafted items was considered a status symbol.

Out of the corner of her eye, Alexa saw her target sat at table near a window and pull off his hood. She groaned. *I followed the wrong guy again! I hate Dieither. And I hate raincoats. Why must they be so limited in style?*

She tapped into her e-band, "Lost target again."

Quinn sent back, "Keep searching. Try to pick up trail."

Alexa sighed, knowing it was useless. She could have lost her target one city block ago or twenty.

Fredric sent a message, "Found target. Entering a bar. Closed right now."

"Keep watch."

Following the coordinates Fredric sent, Alexa strolled by the nightclub. In the rain, a huge neon sign displayed animated images of dancers. The door leading in was dark, the lights off in the small lobby.

Zara posted, "Building owned by Dan Millen."

Quinn replied, "Good. We found the link. Fredric keep watch. Everyone else report to base."

Alexa was relieved to head back to the small hotel half a mile away. Normally she did not mind rain, but spending three days trying to track targets in almost constant downpours had made her edgy. Entering the small bedroom she shared with Zara, she took off the rain poncho. The carpet was worn, the paint faded and cracked. Bedsheets had spots that would not wash out. Quinn believed in keeping to a tight budget.

Their room connected to Quinn's which he was using as their temporary base. Alexa tossed her wet poncho onto a nightstand and walked into his room. Already ten of the squad were there, including Zara.

Quinn recapped what they had learned so far. "We now have a clear connection with the mobster Dan Millen. We need to find a way to isolate him and probe his mind. This will not be easy as he is surrounded by bodyguards."

Jason said, "My contact said he will be at the nightclub tonight. Maybe one of us can try to befriend one of his underlings."

"Trying to get into his inner circle will be dangerous. He is very suspicious. Jason, you can claim to be a buyer in need of a large shipment of drugs. That might get his attention. We need to look for an opportunity to separate him from the others. Remember, we have to find hard evidence before the local police can act."

As the meeting broke up, Alexa felt frustrated. Quinn's method may take days or weeks. She wanted to get this mission done with and head off to a drier planet. Back in her room, she sat on the lumpy bed and flipped through hundreds of pictures posted on social media sites taken at the bar which was a popular local hangout.

"We need better clothes."

Zara looked up from her own research. "Our clothes are fine."

"Not for clubbing. We own nothing that fits local styles. Let's go shopping."

"Our expense fund is low."

"We will keep to thrift stores. I saw a few while wandering in the rain."

Within an hour they had visited two stores and bought outfits. After a quick dinner, they dressed in their hotel room. Zara wore a mid-length skirt and a sparkly blue blouse. Alexa put on a black leather miniskirt and red, sleeveless blouse which was low-cut and formfitting. While Zara applied only light makeup, Alexa went all out, not able to recognize herself when she looked in the mirror.

When they finally walked into the room Quinn shared with four others, all the guys stared.

"You are not wearing that," said Quinn, looking directly at Alexa.

"Spies need to blend in. That is what we are doing. You all are dressed for a business meeting, not clubbing. How do you expect to get Dan's attention? The bouncers will not even let you through the door."

"We will get in just fine. You need to change."

Alexa put hands on hips, staring him down. "And wear what? Camos? I did my research. This is what local partyers wear to clubs. You do want this mission to be successful, do you not?"

"Your attire is improper for a quintessence."

"Tonight I am a human who is out to have some fun, and perhaps I can find a way to isolate Dan."

"We already have a plan in place."

"Which may take weeks. Let me give it a shot my way. If I am wrong, then we have Jason to fall back on. But if I am right, I bet I can finish this mission in less than two hours. Let me try."

Quinn kept silent for a long moment before finally giving a slight nod. Everyone donned raincoats and headed out in small groups, taking separate taxis to the bar to arrive at different times. The bouncer let Alexa and Zara in after scanning their fake ID's. In the lobby, a hostess took raincoats from the patrons. In the main room, loud music throbbed and laser lights probed through fog. On the high ceiling, a giant screen displayed colorful morphing images. On a stage a live band performed while a screen behind them flashed images relating to the lyrics. Sentients of many species danced closely together on the rotating dancefloor.

Alexa had visited a few taverns and bars but never seen anything this elaborate. Zara tried to keep a blank face, but a slight frown showed her discomfort.

"Look like you are having fun," said Alexa close to her sister's ear.

"Fun? How can others think this is fun? Getting drunk and acting a fool?"

Leaving her sister's side, Alexa weaved through the throng on the dancefloor. A sundancer began wiggling his body directly in front of her, so she copied him. When the song ended, he grinned as he asked her for a drink.

"Another time," said Alexa before meandering back through the crowd. As she walked, she scanned the room, spotting others of her squad. Three of them including Quinn were seated at a table on the second floor balcony where they could observe the entire room. Others were scattered throughout the crowd. Jason was chatting with a human that worked for Dan. The mobster leader sat at a huge booth partly walled off from the main room.

Wanting to prove herself, Alexa pondered how she could get quick access to Dan. *Think like a criminal human male. What do they want?* She positioned herself so she could peek through the doorway at the booth. Dan was flirting with a waitress taking orders for drinks. *Ah, that is how he thinks.*

She observed Dan and his buddies for a few more minutes. Seeing the waitress heading back to his table, she stepped in front of the woman. "I'll serve those."

The neodite frowned, her blue skin turning slightly orange around her hands. "That is my job."

Alexa pulled out the last of her cash. "Will this do?"

"Sure, if you want to pay me to do my work." The woman pocketed the cash and walked away.

Alexa entered the partition room that was only illumined by blacklights. She carried the drinks to the table and place them randomly in front of the men who were in deep discussion.

"I didn't order this," complained a tattooed human with his arm around a blond woman wearing even less clothes than Alexa.

"Then trade with the one beside you."

"You don't work here," said Dan, studying her. The blacklighting made his shirt glow neon purple and the skull tattoo on his forehead seemed almost alive.

"No. My roommate bet me I could not talk to you. I guess I just won."

Dan laughed, his teeth blue in the eerie light. "How about we make her jealous?" He patted the cushion beside him.

Alexa flashed a smile as she sat down at the booth. Drinks were traded back and forth until the right owners were found. The men chatted about a sports event they had lost bets on. Copying the blonde woman, Alexa leaned against Dan. He placed a muscular arm around her shoulder, slowly sliding it down her body. Alexa stiffened, fighting the instinct to punch him. *You're just pretending. Go with it.*

Forcing herself to relax, Alexa stroked his arm, smiling alluringly like she had seen in movies. *Spies do this stuff all the time.* Through the doorway, she could see Quinn at his table on the balcony, tapping on his e-band. He had chosen that spot to observe Dan.

Her own e-band flashed the word *prim*. He could not say more in case Dan saw the message. Alexa decided to ignore the warning. She whispered into the mobster's ear, "Is there a private place we can go?"

He grinned, "I own this club, sweetheart. Of course there is."

Dan excused himself from his buddies and led her through a backdoor into a dim hallway connected to several offices. As they walked, Dan kept an arm around Alexa's waist. A guard followed a few yards behind. When they reached Dan's office, he waved the guard away. Alexa barely had time to take in the room with its expensive furniture before Dan pushed her against a wall and began kissing her.

Despite having seen such scenes in movies before, Alexa was taking off guard. She kissed back hesitantly, trying to find a polite way to free herself from his hands roaming along her body. When he nudged her towards a leather sofa, she found the opportunity she needed. Smiling, she slid her arms across his chest while she moved behind him. Before he realized what she was doing, she bit, probing his mind. It did not take her long to find what she needed.

She pushed into his thoughts that he was exhausted and needed sleep. She left him unconscious on the sofa as she hacked into his computer using the password she had pulled from his mind. Quickly she copied files onto her e-band. Then she went to the door.

As she stepped out, she complained, "He fell asleep, the drunkard."

The guard barely glanced at her as she walked pass. Casually she backtracked, entering the main room through the same door she had left. She had barely stepped out of the door before Quinn appeared by her side. She meet his eyes and gave a brief nod. Keeping a few yards from her, he followed her through the dancing throng. Zara joined her as they entered the lobby to retrieve their ponchos, and then they hailed a taxi. As they slid into it, Quinn sit beside Alexa. The stiffness of his body and his blank face gave little away, but Alexa sensed he was upset.

I pulled off in a few minutes what he would have taken days to do. She wanted to brag, but knew to keep silent until they were back at the hotel. Impatient, she sent a copy of the files to his e-band. He glanced at them but his expression did not change.

Quinn paid the driver and followed the ladies into the hotel. Once in his room, he exploded—though for him it meant only slightly raising his voice.

"What were you thinking, Alexa? You were flirting with him."

"I happen to be a female spy. That is one of the things we do. I got the information we needed. And I did it far quicker than your method would have."

"I want to see what happen."

"Sure, sergeant."

Alexa turned her back and pulled her long hair away from her neck. He bit, entering her mind. As he watched the memories play out, she felt his outrage. After he broke contact, he stared at her in silence, his hands clenched.

Zara glanced between the two of them, puzzled. "What is wrong?"

"Your sister broke the Code."

"No, I did not. You are upset because I outperformed you."

"You kissed him."

Alexa laughed. "That was not real. I was faking."

"You let him touch you and kiss you—a lot. And you kissed back."

"Only till I could bite him. After that, he was napping while I raided his computer. Human males are so easily manipulated. Mission completed. Now we can move on to another assignment, preferable one not having a monsoon."

Quinn looked at Zara, anger and concern in his eyes. "There may not be another mission."

"What do you mean?" said Alexa. "After you turn over the evidence to the police, we are done."

The sergeant looked back as his charge. "I have to report what you did."

"So they can see how brilliant I am?"

"Are you that blind? All romantic actions including kissing is forbidden for bonded quintessences. It carries a death sentence."

"This was not romance but work. Cannot you understand the difference?"

"The Code does not discern between the two. The Five will have to judge you."

"Report me if you wish, but it will be a waste of time. I was only doing my job. They will understand that."

"Alexa, you still do not comprehend the magnitude of what you have done. As a beta, you need a perfect record and yours is far from that. I do not think having a father who is a Five will protect you this time. Your crime carries a death sentence."

"Protect me?" For the first time Alexa lost her confidence. "I work as hard as you. I may be young and make mistakes sometimes, but I believe what I did tonight was right. I saved us a lot of time and expense. We can leave tomorrow."

The door of the hotel opened, and several squad members entered. Quinn glanced at them before saying to Alexa. "Change your clothes. We will talk tomorrow."

Alexa ignored the eyes of everyone staring at her as she walked back to her room. She shut the door and locked it for good measure. Zara sat on a bed and studied her for a long moment.

"You really kissed Dan Millen?"

"It happened fast. He was kissing me, and I had to do something to keep him distracted until I could use the epulo on him. Spies use seduction all the time in the movies. It is not like what I was doing was real."

"Sister, our Code is very strict, and you broke it."

"For a good reason. They will understand."

"I hope so." Zara began pulling out clothes from her bag.

Hair wet from a shower, Alexa lay in bed, unable to sleep. Over and over she reflected about the conversation with her sergeant. Surely the Five would see the logic of what she did. And Quinn would get over his anger with her. He had forgiven her each time she had messed up in the past, but the way he spoke felt final, like she had passed a line that could not be reversed.

Mid-morning, Quinn called the squad to meet in his room. He avoided looking at Alexa as he spoke. "I turned over the files we gathered. The police will take it from here. We will be heading back to Essence where Alexa will deal with some business with the Five. Grab your gear."

They quickly packed and took a subway to the spaceport their yacht was parked at. Alexa knew the others were casting curious glances at her, wondering what was going on. She refused to say a word. After the ship lifted off, Alexa kept to her cabin for the four days it would take to reach home. Zara said little on the trip, but concern was in her eyes.

On the last day, Quinn called Alexa to the cockpit. The ship was on autopilot, and they were alone

The look in Quinn's eyes had faded from anger to pity. "I am sorry for what you are about to face. Everyone on this squad but your sister has been in your shoes. I did tell the others earlier today the purpose of your hearing with the Five. I felt they needed to know, as we have all worked closely together these last three years."

Alexa felt a tightening of her throat. "You speak as if this is goodbye. The Five will understand what I did was for the mission."

"That still does not excuse you. We are responsible to uphold the Code at all times. We cannot ignore part of it when it is convenient."

"You do not think I am coming back, yet you and the others were given a second chance."

"Over sixty percent of those charged with my crime are put to death. For your offense, the death rate has always been one hundred percent."

Alexa slowly sank into the co-pilot seat. "But it was fake. If I actually kissed him because I felt lust, I would agree with the sentence. But this is different."

"I hope you are right, Alexa. But if you are wrong, I wanted us to part as friends. You are not the easiest quintessence to work with. Challenging, obstinate, unruly."

"I thought you wanted to end this on a positive note."

"I am. You also gave me hope that our species has a great future. That we can adapt and change. Someday be free of imperial control."

"Sorry for ruining that for you."

"I am not sorry for getting to know you. I am honored to have worked with you." While his face stayed blank, his voice was tender.

Alexa gave him a sad smile. "Well, I am not going down without a fight so do not give up on me yet."

When the yacht landed, security officers meet them. Reality hit Alexa full force as she stood on the ramp of the ship, seeing security there to escort her like a criminal. *I was just doing my job.* Keeping her face somber, she walked up to the officers, Quinn beside her. Zara and the rest of the squad watched silently. They had faced dangers together in the past, but there was nothing they could do to help her now.

The officers led Alexa and Quinn into Richton Tower and up to the fortieth floor. They entered the Chamber of Five. Alexa had never seen the white, egg-like room before. Five monitors hung from the ceiling near where each Five stood—except one spot was empty. Joseph was not present. Alexa swallowed. *Why is Papa not here?* Quinn and Alexa moved to the center of the curved room. A few Shadow Guards stood near the wall.

Caden said, "Alexa Kalkar, you are accused of sexual misconduct. What do you have to say about it?"

Alexa glanced towards the empty spot where her father should be. Then she looked across the room. Skyler lived just next door to her family's penthouse and was the father of two of her birthmates. Over the years Skyler, Caden, Desmond, and Tobias had been in her penthouse many times, had taught lessons to her and her birthmates during childhood. Now they were her judges.

"I am innocent. I mean, I sort of kissed a suspect to distract him a bit until I could use the epulo on him. Nothing else happened. I am a spy and acted like one. I used the best course of action to isolate the target and extracted the information needed. That is all I did. I saved us days, perhaps weeks of work."

"Sergeant Quinn, tell us in detail what happened."

Without emotion, Quinn recited their mission timeline, stating facts in a monotone voice. Occasionally one of the Five interrupted with a question.

As he finished, Skyler said, "Alexa was aware there was a different plan that could have been followed."

"Yes, sir."

Tobias said, "Why did you allow her to be put into the position she was in? Where was her squad?"

Not wanting Quinn to get into trouble, Alexa cut in, "That was my decision, not his. I told him I could complete the mission much faster, and I was right about that. The kissing was not real. I was only doing my job. Any spy would have done the same thing."

"Not a quintessence spy," said Desmond. "Never has one used seduction as a method to extract information."

"You only had males before—not that they could not have done so because they are male. I mean…" Alexa blathered.

Caden cut in, "Your birthmates have been doing well without relying on their looks, even your model."

"I…uh…did what I thought was right at the time."

Tobias stepped forward. "I wish to see the memory."

Nervously, Alexa turned her back and moved her hair away. She felt a brief prickle then his mind connected with hers. Quickly he slipped into the memory, reliving it through her eyes. Alexa felt uncomfortable with that. Quinn had only watched, not experienced her emotions.

Breaking contact, Tobias moved back beside his monitor. "At the time of the incident, she thought nothing about the Code, only competing the mission. She wanted to prove herself better than Quinn. She is guilty of sexual misconduct."

Alexa avoided looking at her sergeant. "It was fake kissing. I did not break the spirit of the law."

Caden said, "This is the time we usually vote and the sentence is carried out immediately. Before your birth, we agreed that any trials relating to the betas will be heard in front of the full Synod due to the many that are closely involved with this project. Alexa Kalkar, you will appear for a hearing tomorrow. You have one final night to make peace with yourself and your family."

Trembling, Alexa glanced at the spot her father should be. The director spoke like the verdict had already been decided. As she walked out of the chamber, she tried to keep her face blank but failed.

In the lobby, Quinn said, "I will tell the others. If they allow it, all of us will be there to support you."

"Thank you, for everything. I understand why you had to report my actions. Do not feel guilt for what I did. Zara says I have a talent for messing things up. I was not really trying to show off. I mean, I am competitive. I like to win. That is my nature, but I really thought I was doing the right thing. I would never break the Code intentionally to try to outperform anyone."

"I know, soldier." Quinn walked away towards the elevators.

Alexa wanted until he was gone before she moved to the elevator. Two security guards escorted her home then posted themselves outside the penthouse door. As she walked in, she saw Zara and her mother tensely sitting on a couch.

Hennah's face was pale as she greeted her daughter. "What did they say?"

"That I am to appear tomorrow before the Synod. Mamma, I was only fake kissing for a mission. Spies do that kind of thing. Where is Papa? He was not there."

"He could not vote for he is related to you."

"Still, he should have been there. Have I disappointed him so much that he refuses to see me?"

"I will cook your favorite foods for dinner. Two desserts tonight. You will like that." Hennah's voice nearly broke as a tear trickled down her cheek.

"Yes, two desserts. Do not cry, Mamma. I am fine. My hearing will go better tomorrow. I can explain to all of them that it was not real."

Hennah nodded. "Maybe they will understand. I'll start cooking."

As their mother worked in the kitchen, Alexa sat silently on the couch beside her sister. For a long time neither spoke.

Finally, Alexa lost patience. "Well, say something."

"What can I say?"

"That you do not hate me."

"I do not hate you."

"That is all you have to say? I almost died today. The way both Caden and Quinn talk, tomorrow is my last day."

"I will miss you, sister."

"Miss me? That is all?"

"Do you wish to feel my grief? Then do so." Zara turned her back, inviting.

Alexa hesitated. She had not been trying to goad her sister, yet she wanted to feel connected to her. So she bite, letting their minds touch. She felt Zara's emotions of deep worry, fear, and grief. In the line of duty Zara would have willing step in front of her sister to save her life, but in this situation she was helpless. Her frustration was immense.

"Do not blame yourself," said Alexa through the link.

"I should have been there with you. Together we could have found a way without you kissing him. I failed you, sister."

"No, you did not. You know me, always wanting to challenge myself. This is my fault, not yours. I made this decision. If this is really my last night, then let's make it a happy memory."

Alexa broke the link then found their favorite board game. They played until their mother called them for dinner. Their conversations drifted into silence. Alexa kept glancing at her father's empty chair.

"When will Papa come home?"

"He is working late."

Alexa tasted both desserts her mother placed in front of her, but she had little appetite. Still, she wanted to cheer her mother up. After the dishes were cleaned, they played three board games, Alexa losing them all. Even as she went to take a shower, she glanced at the front door expecting her father to walk in at any moment. She both dreaded and yearned to see him. He would be disappointed in her, but still she wanted to see him, tell him why she had done what she did. But he did not come.

As she lay in bed, she listened to Zara's deep breathing. Her sister had fallen asleep over an hour ago. It must be pass midnight. *What do my birthmates think of me? My fellow sisters who share my body? Their impulses gets them in trouble too, sometimes, but nothing like me. Will our model be discontinued because of me?*

Hearing a sound, Alexa strained her ears, trying to figure out if she had heard the front door open. Like all quintessences, she had good hearing, yet if there was someone, he was being quiet on purpose. *I really have gone too far when my own father will not speak to me.* Perhaps she heard footsteps, perhaps not.

Even if he does not want to see me, I want to see him. She tossed off her bedcovers and opened her door. All was dark. She carefully treaded down the hallway to the living room. The balcony door was open. Outside she could see the silhouette of her father in starlight. For a while she watched. He leaned against the railing looking out over Essence. *Might as well face him now. I may not see him tomorrow.*

Gingerly she moved to the balcony. He did not glance at her as she walked outside. The silence spoke volumes. Vines growing in pots gently waved their leaves in the cool breeze. Far below a monorail carried nightshift workers home.

"Papa, why did you not come today?"

Joseph still did not turn towards his daughter.

291

"Will you speak to me at all? Please, Papa, say something. Anything." Then she noticed in the starlight a tear running down his cheek. "I thought adult quintessences no longer cried."

"They do when the pain is great enough." His voice was raw.

"Papa?" Alexa's own voice quivered.

He reached to her, embracing her in a tight hug. She began sobbing, her whole body shaking. For a long time neither spoke, their grief too intense.

In a whisper, Alexa broke the silence. "I am going to die tomorrow. They won't listen when I say it was not real. I was only doing it for the mission."

"The Code was not written to be flexible, Beti. I am sorry I did not do a better job."

"You are a good father. I am the one who keeps messing up. Please forgive me."

"There is no offense for me to forgive. If you had been human, you would have been commended for a job well done. But we are quintessences living by a strict Code. Over the years I have seen many good quintessences suffer because of it. Yet without it, greater harm could have been done by our species. We must police ourselves, yet we wrote no mercy into the Code. No loopholes. We did the job too well."

"It was not you, Papa, but our founders. I have seen the Canon too. I understand why the Code exist. I really did not think I was breaking it. If I must die then...then so be it. Do not blame yourself. I messed up again. You warned me many times as a child, and now I face the consequences of my actions. Will you at least be there for me? Even if you cannot vote?"

Gently he touched her wet cheek. "Yes, Beti, I will stand beside you."

Alexa went to sleep then, dreaming of being in the forests with her birthmates and their fathers. She was only four but enjoyed the thrill of chasing her father through the woods with a laser gun. Each person in the game wore a device which recorded hits. Darkfern and other fjouwers were there, laughing in excitement. Dodging, running, shooting, climbing. Zara beside her in the underbrush. Together they sprung out of the brushes, shooting where their father had been moments before. But he was gone, knowing their moves before they made them. Grinning, the sisters continued the hunt.

An alarm brought Alexa back to the present. She stared at the clock, marking the minutes she had remaining in life. Reluctantly she rose to dress in camo pants and black shirt. Today she would look the role of a soldier. Zara was quiet, her eyes saying much while her face stayed expressionless. The sisters headed to the kitchen. Joseph was finishing up cooking breakfast. Hennah sat at the dining table, eyes puffy from crying. She tried to carry a conversation, but in the middle of a sentence, she broke down and fled the room. Joseph passed the frying pan over to Alexa and left to console his wife.

Alexa finished cooking while Zara set the table. Eventually all four of them sat down, pretending to eat a normal meal. Few words were spoken. Everything important had already been said.

When it was time, they left the penthouse together. Both security and Shadow Guards fell in step beside them. Miles looked as stern as ever. Darkfern walked in front of her husband, both formidable with their double guns and knives. Alexa tried to keep her face blank, her emotions hidden. If she was to die today, it would be with dignity.

They reached the large lobby on the fortieth floor. Shadow Guards watched silently as they entered the huge chamber. Alexa followed her father to the side of the room. Her mother and sister moved to the visitor section, sitting beside the wives of the Five. A bit higher up, Alexa saw Quinn with the rest of their squad, their expressionless faces watching her. She took comfort in their presence. *They survived this. I can too.*

Her grandparents came through the door. Pallavi broke protocol and walked over to Alexa, giving her a hug. During the brief contact, Alexa lost control of her emotions and a tear escaped. She brushed it away quickly, hoping no one noticed. She must not look weak. Pallavi and Kaushal walked up the steps to sit near Hennah.

Once the last of the Synod members arrived, Caden addressed the crowd. Of all the Five, he was the only one near the end of his lifespan. He was frail with deep wrinkles, yet he still spoke with authority. "We come today to try Alexa Kalkar for the charge of sexual misconduct. If found guilty, she will be executed immediately. Alexa, step forth."

Trying to force her fear away, Alexa walked to the green circle in the middle of the room. She scanned the crowd, noting family and friends. Darkfern and Nightstorm stood on guard duty at the edge of the floor nearest the Five. All the parents of her birthmates were here. When they looked at her, did they think about their own red-haired daughters? Her birthmates and their squads were absent as all were off planet on missions. Had they even heard about her trial yet? What happened today would affect them too.

"How do you plead?" came Caden's strong voice in the quiet room.

"I...uh..."

"She pleads innocent on deliberately breaking the Code." Joseph walked across the room to stand beside his daughter.

Caden slightly frowned. "The accused will speak for herself."

"I am her advocate. I will speak for her."

"We do not use advocates or lawyers at these hearings."

"You do today." Joseph stood in the center of the room, staring boldly at the director. The two quintessences locked eyes, neither backing down.

Desmond broke the silence. "Why does she plead innocent?"

"In the course of fulfilling her mission object, she isolated the target. He kissed her. She briefly kissed him back to keep him distracted. Then she used the epulo to extract the information needed to complete the mission."

Caden said, "So you admit she kissed another."

"Her actions are not worthy of the death penalty."

"The Code clearly states that kissing of a bonded quintessence is a violation."

"I state again, her actions do not warrant the death penalty."

Tobias said, "We understand you care about your daughter, but she is not above the law. You are well aware that all of us must abide by the Code. If we allow one to go unpunished, others will break it."

"We need to look at her motive, not just her actions."

Caden said, "The Code was not written that way."

"It is time for us to amend the Code so that it does."

Shock waves ripped through the crowd. Alexa looked around the room as quintessences glanced at each other. In the visitors section excited whispers broke out. Her father had just made the most controversial statement a quintessence could make. The Code was central to how all quintessences conducted themselves.

Caden's voice took a menacing tone. "You are walking on a thin line, Joseph. Our Code is over six hundred years old. It has not been altered except in the first few decades as the original Five helped our society develop."

Skylar spoke for the first time. "You ask us to change the Code to save your daughter?"

"Yes."

"You do not have that authority," said Caden.

"Yes, I do." Joseph looked at the crowd with steel determination. "Many of you know by what authority I speak. Need I remind you I am a Five, like you, Caden? A vote of three Fives will open up discussion for an amendment by the Synod."

Conversations broke out around the room. Alexa felt her heartbeat quicken. Her father dared to challenge their very Code for her. It was the foundation of their whole society.

"I second Joseph's motion," said Skylar.

Caden turned. "You are also a father of a CF1 model. You are too close emotionally to this subject."

"Nevertheless, I have cast my vote. Am I not also a Five? My vote counts."

"Do not react on emotion but logic. What we do today impacts all of our society."

"It is time for our society to adapt," said Joseph. "We have lived by a rigid Code for over six hundred years. It has protected us while shaping our society, yet we have faced situations it was not written to cover. We have executed good men who failed a section of it. We need the Code to distinguish between good and bad, to define our morality. But we also need a Code that can be flexible enough to deal with gray areas. This is where our original founders failed."

Desmond asked, "What section do you think needs to be altered?"

Joseph glanced at his daughter. "Our hope is that soon there will be freeborn quintessences who live among us. We have not even began to discuss how our laws will affect them. How much of the Code is a freeborn responsible for compared to a bonded quintessence? When is the proper age for marriage? Will a freeborn be required to serve as a soldier? You ask what I believe needs to be altered? A lot. We need understanding and mercy. Less harsh penalties for lesser crimes. Motive should be as important as action."

Caden said, "We will take your words under advisement, but that is a discussion for another time. Today we are dealing with your daughter under our current law."

"I third Joseph's motion," said Desmond. "That is enough to open up discussion today."

The whispers of the crowd became so loud that Caden could not speak for several minutes. Finally, when they had quieted, Caden said, "Amendment discussion can take place after this hearing. We will proceed with one item at a time. There will be a fifteen minute break then we vote."

Loud conversations broke out across the room. Joseph led Alexa towards the visitor section. Hennah leaned over the railing and squeezed her daughter's hand.

"You may make it. Do not give up hope."

"I will not, Mamma." Alexa turned to her father. "You did all this for me? Trying to change our laws. I'm not that important."

"You are to me."

Alexa smiled, feeling the warmth of his love. "I am proud to be your daughter, even if I die today."

Hennah glanced at Amaka. "Is it working? Are their votes changing?"

The kuawazo continued to scan the crowd as she spoke. "The reactions are mixed. Most support alterations to the Code. But it has not been changed yet. They debate if Alexa should be held to the old law or one not yet written."

"They should vote with their hearts."

"Quintessences are led by logic, or should I say bound by logic by their Code." Amaka turned her golden eyes on Joseph. "Leave it to you to take a hearing where the outcome was already known before it started and you turn everything upside down. One would think you had centuries of practice in rhetoric."

"One might think that." A brief smile crossed Joseph's lips.

When the break was over, Caden stood, drawing everyone's attention. Silently Alexa and Joseph walked back to the middle of the chamber.

"Now we will vote if Alexa Kalkar is guilty of sexual misconduct based on our Code—our current Code."

Synod members quietly used screens built into their chairs to vote. Alexa tried to remain calm as she watched. Some of them had taught her lessons as a child. Many were parents themselves. Her life was in their hands. Surely they could understand her intention was not to break the Code. But would they vote against her just because the Code said a bonded quintessence's kiss was a death sentence?

After several minutes, Caden stood again and read the verdict. "Alexa Kalkar, the votes have been counted. Forty-eight percent find you guilty. As that is not the majority, you are exonerated. I will warn you that as a bonded beta your behavior needs to be proper at all times. We expect better of you."

Alexa stood rigidly. "Yes, sir."

"You are dismissed." Caden looked towards the crowd. "As the topic for amendments is not to be taken lightly, we need time to discuss among ourselves the many implications. I move we take a week to reflect. Then we will open the floor for debate."

Alexa heard little else. *I am alive. Papa did it.* She walked beside her father back to the visitor section. As the crowd began to disperse, her family surrounded her. Hugs came from her grandparents and mother. Zara flashed her a real smile.

Quinn walked up to her. "Congrats, soldier. I expect to see you tomorrow ready for our next mission."

"Yes, sir, Sergeant," smiled Alexa.

Chapter Thirty-five

Joseph glanced as his e-band. His brother Gabriel requested a meeting of the Five in an hour. Touching the flat surface of his desk, he pulled up a digital calendar and rearranged a meeting he had with two Synod members. In the three days since Alexa's trial, many had been wanting to have private conversations with him to voice both their excitement and concerns. There were many opinions on how the Code should be altered, and a few who were resolute that it should not be touched at all.

The one certainty all could agree on was that the Code must not be abolished. It was too vital in holding their society together. Take that away and some of their species may become self-indulgent, lascivious, and unstable. Over the centuries Joseph had seen first-hand what happens when a wayward quintessence rejected the Code. Usually they left a trail of victims. While such incidents were rare, it always ended in the culprit being hunting down by the Death Force and executed.

Nearing time for the meeting, Joseph put his desk in sleep mode. Sitting on a couch, Miles looked up from the book he had been reading.

"Another meeting in the Chamber of Five," Joseph explained.

Miles set the book on a table. "I was wondering about your opinion on what was discussed earlier with Rodrick, Kitoka, and Stuart. Do you think the freeborn should be held to different standards?"

"That is a difficult question. They are right to be concerned about their CF1 daughters, as the model is impulsive and highly competitive. What will their grandchildren be like? I think we need the same morality for all quintessences, no matter if freeborn, bonded, or unbonded. But there should be certain rules that affect each group separately. The Code needs to be flexible for each."

Joseph took the elevator down five floors to the Chamber of Five. Miles followed silently behind him. As Joseph entered the room, several of his brothers nodded in greeting. Only Caleb refused to look at him. They had not talked since the trial. Joseph understood that as director, Caleb's duty was to uphold the Code. Still, it was difficult to separate professional and personal emotions when his daughter's life was on the line.

Seeing everyone had arrived, Caleb said, "Good morning, brothers. Alexander, I am surprised that you could find time to attend with all your pressing meetings plotting social reform."

"As you said at the trial, we are reflecting on implications. During a full hearing, we will share with everyone our views."

"You have already stated your view. Change our laws to protect one individual. Your daughter is not more important than the Code."

"She did not break the intent of the Code."

Caleb stepped away from his monitor, the deep wrinkles on his face and arms warned that his body would not last much longer. "She was guilty and you know it. We have executed others for just a kiss."

"They were not undercover agents. Her situation was different."

"If I did not know better, I would be concerned that you are plotting to take my place so you can have full control of altering the society we have built together."

Joseph allowed pain to show on his face. "Caleb, you know me better than that. We may disagree on some things, but I would never challenge your authority. Everything I have done has been to protocol. And when you switch bodies soon, it will be Gabriel who is the next director. We agreed on this long ago."

Caleb held Joseph's glaze for a long moment. His breathing relaxed, and he returned to his monitor. The tension others felt watching the conflict faded.

Gabriel said, "Now that the predicted storm of you two is over, we can turn our attention to why I called this meeting. Last night my daughters brought me disturbing information they learned on a recent mission. I would like to share the memory with you."

He moved around the room, biting each of his brothers and passing along a ziphema. Joseph opened it, seeing into the memories of Khloe.

The ASF1 rested in the sand beside her sister Natalia on a crowded beach. Both were dressed in shorts and tank tops, their shoulder length hair had bright streaks of color. Around them sat four well-fit human males only wearing shorts. Their bodies were sweaty from just finishing a ballgame.

Natalia leaned forward, giving one of the guys a worried look. "What do you mean you won't be here tomorrow? You will miss the tournament we entered together."

"You know how it is with us soldiers. Duty calls. We ship out tomorrow morning."

"What can be so important as to miss the tournament? We make a great team. I am certain we will win."

The young man glanced at the other guys. "It's a secret we are not at liberty to discuss with civilians."

"Well, both our fathers were in the army. We know how to keep secrets. You can tell me, Tim." Natalia gave him a wistful, yearning look.

Tim was about to say something when one of his companions cut him off. "He is just a lieutenant. What does he know? Now a captain like me, we hear things."

Khloe scooted across the sand towards him. "Like what things? About new evils the aliens are committing?" Their assignment had been to investigate reports that off duty soldiers where harassing local non-humans. Over the last couple of weeks they had befriended the soldiers who often spouted off speciesist slurs.

The captain grinned and lowered his voice. "We are about to put an end to their pollution. No more boongs. Soon they won't be able to brag they are the smartest creatures in the galaxy."

"They won't exist at all," added Tim.

Natalia scooted right beside him. "How is that possible? Edietheans live across many worlds."

"Not for long. It's time for the boongs to learn what extinction means." He laughed along with his comrades.

"You are all so brave, facing off against those freaks." Natalia used an alluring smile. "Wish I could join you, but my dad doesn't approve of girls fighting."

"He's right," said Tim. "War is no place for beautiful ladies like you."

Khloe smiled at the captain. "So what is the brilliant plan to finally end the boongs?"

He grinned. "Destroy their home planet while their warships are distracted at the Rim. After that, we will hunt them down, colony by colony."

"But won't you get in trouble? The boongs are part of the empire."

"This is the best part. Minutes before we attack, Emperor Kylen himself will release a public statement that they are responsible for assassinating the former Emperor. He will declare all edietheans enemies of the regime. Then we attack before they even have a chance to know what hit them."

"Wow. My father will be so proud of you, finally getting rid of those pests."

Natalia leaned so she was almost touching Tim. "How long will this take before we see you again? I need my sport partners back."

"The boong homeworld will be rumble by the end of the week. Will take some time, though, to deal with all the colonies. Don't worry, we'll be back, ready for more action."

The memory ended. Joseph looked at his brothers, disturbed. He waited as they reflected on the impact of the memory.

Mason was the first to speak. "I see now, Gabriel, why you were so quick to back Joseph with wanting to amend our Code. Your daughters are also using seduction."

"Flirting only. They needed to get close to the targets. That was the most effective way." Gabriel glanced at Caleb. "They have not kissed anyone. I do agree with Joseph that undercover agents need to be giving more leeway than typical soldiers."

Caleb said nothing, but a slight frown on his face told his opinion.

"The Coalition's plans must be stopped," Joseph directed his brothers' attention back to the purpose of the meeting. "We need to act fast."

"And do what?" said Caleb. "Bonded quintessences have to obey orders. If the Emperor says to attack, our bonded brethren must do so."

"It is morally wrong for us to stand by and do nothing to stop this genocide," said Jacob.

Joseph said, "He is right. We delayed this from happening centuries ago when we arrested Senator Moyers, but the Coalition never let go of those plans."

Gabriel added, "Whatever we do must be quick. We can warn the High Council about the coming attack."

"Not enough time," said Joseph. "Most of their warships are on the Rim. They will not have enough time to get back."

Caleb cut in, "Brothers, none of us wish for another genocide. This is not the first time our brethren have been used in such attacks, but this will, by far, be the worst. Billions will die. Some of our brethren will rebel, and we have to deal with the aftermath."

"How about we give them a way out—a morality clause," said Joseph.

"What do you mean?" asked Jacob.

"We have always held our brethren to keeping the whole Code. But soldiers like me get trapped between the rules about obeying superiors and protecting the innocent. We could add a morality clause which allows a quintessence to excuse himself from an action that would harm an innocent."

"Such a policy would be abused," said Mason. "In every war innocent die. It is impossible to protect everyone."

"True. We can add the requirement that any who uses the clause must report personally to us to judge their actions."

Gabriel and Jacob nodded in agreement.

Mason said, "You are responding to a current problem but ignoring the bigger issue. If we allow quintessences to refuse Coalition orders, then the Coalition will turn against us. They will remove the last of our funding. Within a few centuries, our species will cease to exist."

For a moment all the brothers looked at each other, considering the implications.

Caleb was the first to speak. "You are right. If we do this, we seal our own genocide."

"Doing what is right is worth it," said Joseph. "We have females now. Our species will not go totally extinct."

"We do not know yet if they can have children or what the birthrate will be."

"My wife has ran many genetic tests on computers. She believes there will not be any issues."

"There is Project Void," said Gabriel. "We considered it long ago as a last resort to save ourselves."

Jacob said, "Abandoning Essence to set up a secret cloning laboratory on a Rim planet will only delay the inevitable. Perhaps we will achieve a few more generations, but much smaller. The power we wield now will be lost forever. As our brethren die of old age, only a few will remain. What will stop the Coalition from hunting down the last of us and destroying our base just like they will do with the ediethean?"

A sternness came to Joseph's face. "We need to make a stand now against the Coalition while we are powerful."

Caleb said, "If this stand fails, our whole species is doomed. Having a few females will not be enough to save us long term."

"I am tired of living under the fear of annihilation. From our births this has haunted us—being the first and last of our kind. We grew to become a powerful force in this empire, but if we do not make a stand against the Coalition, they will take full control of what is left of this empire. Will it even be a place we want to live? Do you really believe they will stop with wiping out the Edietheans? How many other species are on their list? If they have their way, they will either destroy or enslave every non-human in the galaxy. That is not a government I wish for my children or grandchildren to live in."

The brothers looked into each other's eyes, weighing the consequences. Slowly Gabriel, Jacob, and Mason nodded. Everyone turned to Caleb.

"This will most likely be the last order I give before I die."

"Then make it worthy for the history books," said Jacob.

Chapter Thirty-six

A dozen C4's walked down a corridor, their hair wet from a shower. Reaching their crew berthing, they separated. Renaldo lay on his narrow mattress and pulled out his e-tablet. Using a password, he logged into his messages. The most recent one was tagged urgent. It was sent by Director Caden. Curious, Renaldo clicked on it. As it was high-level security, Renaldo was required to have his e-tablet scan the chip embedded in his hand then a video of Caden appeared.

"Soldier, this message is vital to the lives of many. A few minutes ago the Synod voted to amend our Code with a Morality Clause which states that a soldier may refuse to obey orders of a superior if those orders conflict with other areas of the Code. Any soldier who does so will report his reason for refusal to Essence and may be required to appear in front of the Five in a hearing to explain such actions."

Caden paused. While his body looked frail, his resolve was firm. "My health is declining. Skyler will soon be taking on the duties of director. During the transition period, the authority of the Five will not waver. My next words will alter our destiny forever.

"We have evidence of the Coalition's plans for genocide against the ediethean. These plans will be carried out within the next few days. Under our new Morality Clause, you have the right to refuse any action which will lead to these deaths. Act as you believe best to protect the innocent, as stated in our Code. Any actions you do will be reported to us at your leisure."

As the video played, several birthmates glanced in Renaldo's direction. He had the volume low, but they had heard enough to know it was something serious.

Renaldo stood and moved to the front of the room. As lieutenant of his unit, it was his duty to keep them informed. "Attention, brothers. Check your messages right now."

As his birthmates began to pull out their e-tablets, Renaldo played the video a second time, making sure he understand the unprecedented message. Essence was giving them permission to disobey imperial orders. Impossible, yet the recording was clear. It was a treasonous act asking bonded quintessences to place their loyalty to Essence over the Empire.

Around him, conversations broke out as his birthmates began to discuss the video. Renaldo rose and headed to the next room. He scanned the rows of bunks stacked three high. Spotting the lieutenant of its unit, he told him about the message.

Then he moved on. The *Warhound* was a Nebula-class battleship with a crew of six thousand. Two thousand where C models used for infantry. Another three hundred were ME's who flew its many Claw fighters and shuttles. Two HC units helped maintain the spacecraft. The rest of the crew came from dozens of species.

As Renaldo visited other crew compartments, some units were already aware of the video. Soon everyone had watched it and was debating its meaning. When Renaldo returned to his quarters, the lieutenant of the unit across the hall met him.

"Do you think that is why they pulled us from the Rim?" Westlen asked.

Renaldo answered carefully. "Could be. We still have not been told our destination, but we are near heavily populated planets."

"If the time comes, will you refuse?"

"I have never disobeyed an order, including those I privately questioned. A good soldier follows orders. Yet neither do I want to take part in a genocide."

For the rest of the day, the quintessences continued to follow their normal schedules. Late the next afternoon a meeting was called for all officers. Renaldo joined the other thirty-two quintessence lieutenants, along with other officers in the briefing room.

As Admiral DeClaire studied the soldiers standing at attention, he scowled at a few arriving behind the others. A human in his fifties, DeClaire was stocky and imposing. "Two late. I expect better. Tomorrow we are about to participate on an historic campaign. We will need to move with lightning speed and precision. Pilots will take our infantry down to the planet Mansoor." The admiral paused to turn on a screen showing a large mushroom-shaped structure. "Our targets are living in clusters inside skycrooms. Infantry will work in squads of five to sweep each skyscroom. All targets are to be eliminated."

"Who are our targets?" asked a C7.

"You will be told that right before the operation begins."

The quintessences glanced at each other. The oldest said, "Sir, we would like to be told now."

"That information will be given to you when it is needed."

"Those skycrooms serve as apartments and businesses. Are we to attack civilians?"

"You will do as told, soldier."

"Sir, you should be aware that I will not purposely fire on an unarmed civilian."

DeClaire marched up to the C2 and leaned close. "Your place is to obey, leech. You will comply."

"If you order us to kill civilians, we will not."

"Do I need to remind you of your own Code?"

"A morality clause was recently added. We have the right to refuse an order if it conflicts with other areas of the Code."

The admiral scowled, glancing at the other quintessences. "I have never heard of such a rule. I am the one in authority here, not your precious Five. Any soldier who does not obey will face serious consequences. Is that clear?"

Beside Renaldo, Westlen spoke up. "If you order us to kill ediethean civilians, we will not."

Fury filled DeClaire. "There has been a leak, I see. Who told you the targets were ediethean?"

"The Five, sir."

The admiral stopped in front of Westlen. "How do they know?"

"You will have to ask them yourself."

DeClaire pulled out a laser gun and pointed it at Westlen's head. "I will ask only once more. How do the Five know about our plans?"

"I was not given that information, sir." Westlen did not flitch.

The admiral stepped back but kept his weapon in hand. "There is a traitor among us. Someone has leaked high-security information. Who was it?"

Officers stood at attention, none moving as DeClaire walked among them, his hand clenching his gun.

A human commander said, "Sir, the leak could have come from many places. No one here may be responsible."

DeClaire stopped near Renaldo. "True. Let us address my other problem." He turned to Westlen. "Will you follow orders to kill all edietheans?"

"No, sir. I will not kill unarmed civilians."

"Wrong answer."

DeClaire pointed his weapon at Westlen's head and pulled the trigger. Renaldo smelt burning flesh as Westlen's face became a mess of smoldering gore. His body fell limp to the floor. Officers winced but none moved.

"Let there be no misunderstanding," said the admiral. "I will kill each and every one of you who disobeys my orders. Then I will start with your birthmates. If I have to eject all of you leeches out airlocks, I will." He pointed his weapon at another quintessence. "Will you obey every order I give?"

"No, I will not, sir," came the quintessence's firm voice.

Enough of this, thought Renaldo. He quickly rushed towards the admiral and grabbed him from behind, biting. Probing through the man's mind, he saw the plans of the Coalition. Eradicating the Ediethean on Mansoor was only a small drop in a huge wave of destruction which would sweep across the empire. Disgusted with the man, Renaldo drained the admiral's life force. When he broke contact, DeClaire's lifeless body fell to the floor.

The admiral was not the only dead human. The moment Renaldo went for the admiral, several top human officers had drawn guns to shoot Renaldo. Immediately other quintessences had responded. Several moved to protect Renaldo while others attacked the officers. Within two minutes, the fight was over. Eight top officers, all part of the Coalition, lay dead. Other non-quintessences, including a couple of humans, looked about nervously, unsure if they were about to be attacked.

Knowing the admiral's plans, Renaldo spoke to calm them. "We will not harm you. Admiral DeClaire was part of the Coalition. They planned a genocide against the edietheans, including destroying their home planet. After that, they will turn against other species they dislike. None of us are safe from them."

"What do we do now?" said a sundancer.

Renaldo glanced at fellow quintessences. "As we have already started a mutiny, I believe we should finish it."

Quickly plans were made. Not all the non-quintessence officers wanted to help, but they agreed to stay out of the way. Renaldo headed back to his birthmates and shared with them the memory leading to the admiral's death. He then led them to a weapons locker where they grabbed guns. They had to wait in turn as other units were also arming themselves. Then the thousands of quintessences spread out across the battleship, congregating in key locations.

Renaldo marched to the bridge. Few on duty glanced at him or the squad following him until he took the admiral's chair. He flipped on an intercom to talk to the whole ship.

"This is Lieutenant Renaldo. The Coalition, with the Emperor's approval, has sent orders for us to attack ediethean civilians on the planet Mansoor. This will happen in conjunction with other attacks on areas of heavy ediethean colonization. A Galactic-class battleship will target their homeworld Edieth, destroying all life on the planet. We quintessences disagree with these orders. Under the Morality Clause of our Code we have taken over this ship. Admiral DeClair is dead along with eight other Coalition officers. We wish for a peaceful transfer of power. I understand if you do not wish to make a stand against the Empire. It is not something I wish for either, but neither will my brethren be willing tools in a genocide. If you wish to not join us, we ask that you peacefully move to the cargo holds where you will remain until we can safely transfer you to a planet. If you attack us, we will fight back."

Renaldo flipped off the intercom and looked around the bridge. Everyone was staring at him. Out of the corner of his eye, he saw a human security officer pull a weapon. Immediately three birthmates rushed towards the human who managed to get one shot off before being tackled to the floor.

The laser cut into Renaldo's shoulder, burning through cloth and flesh. He winched in pain as he walked over to the guard being hauled up. Stepping behind the man, he bit, probing the attacker's mind as his own shoulder healed. He left the man alive, despite being a Coalition member.

"Lock him in the brig." As his brothers marched off with the culprit between them, Renaldo looked around at the others on duty. "Is there anyone else who wants to kill me?" No one moved. "If you do not wish to be part of this mutiny, you may leave your posts and move to the cargo holds. Behave peacefully and no harm will come to you."

Several hesitated then rose from their seats. Renaldo and his birthmates watched but said nothing as they left the bridge. Renaldo returned to the admiral's chair. Reports of fighting came in from several areas of the ship. Within an hour the battlecruiser was firmly under his control. A message came from a HC model that the transponder had been turned off. The empire would no longer be able to track them.

Renaldo walked over to a neodite in charge of communications. "Open a channel to Essence."

"Yes, sir." Her blue skin was tinged with purple in excitement. "May I say, sir, it is about time someone put those bigots in their place."

Chapter Thirty-seven

The war room bustled with activity. It was located deep under the palace in a bunker which no missile could penetrate. Everywhere humans monitored screens and communication channels. A huge display on the front wall showed a close-up map of one sector of the galaxy along with blips where imperial ships were located.

One of the blips disappeared.

"There goes another one," said a red-haired woman named Kathy seated near the display.

"That is the sixth," growled Bruce, gulping scalding coffee. He had not slept all night. "I want to know what is going on, now. We are minutes, people, minutes away from attacking. Get me information!"

Kylen sat in the back of the room with a laptop in front of him, quietly observing the chaos. He was slightly amused. The first ship had disappeared near midnight. Others had slowly followed. *I could tell him, but it's more fun watching him find out the hard way. Honestly, he should have seen this coming. Push any slave too far and they will rebel.*

Bruce turned to retired General McLowary serving as chief military advisor. "Why are we losing contact?"

"As I said before, it could be a malfunction. We did ask for radio silence in case the boong were monitoring our channels. Our people were in the right positions for their missions."

Surely the general has figured it out already, thought Kylen. *After all, he knows firsthand what it is like facing a leech rebellion. Perhaps he is afraid to tell Bruce.*

"Sir," said Kathy, "*Ironhammer* is on approach."

"Give me visual."

The huge display showed a black screen with distant stars. A large green and blue planet slowly grew closer. Edieth, homeworld of the Ediethean. A profitable planet with many spaceports, two orbiting space stations, and a colonized moon terraformed eons ago. Here and there small ships zoomed, some heading off into deep space. The planet had not experienced war in over five thousand years.

Behind the moon a large battlecruiser slowly emerged.

"What the…?" said Bruce, eyes staring in shock. "That can't be one of theirs. We made sure their ships were on the Rim or chasing after one of our fires in other sectors—far, far away."

McLowary peered at a monitor then back at the large screen. "That's one of ours, the *Warhound*. The first to disappear."

"What is it doing here instead of at its post? Open a channel, now." Bruce stepped to the center of the room. "*Warhound*, you will respond. Why are you not following orders?"

On the screen appeared a C4 sitting in the command seat. "This is Captain Renaldo, and I am following orders."

"Whose orders?"

"Essence. I am to tell you that if you proceed as plan, you will be guilty of war crimes as written by our Galactic Senate. You can stand down and prevent this bloodshed."

"Leech, it is I who gives the orders here."

"I thought it was the Emperor sitting behind you."

Bruce's face turned red in rage. "You will be executed very, very slowly."

"To do that, you will need to get pass my many, many eager soldiers who do not look favorably on genocide."

"Close channel." Breathing heavily, Bruce turned to McLowary. "Do we have the manpower to take them?"

"Our ship is larger with a bigger crew. Normally the *Warhound* has five hundred Claws. Only three hundred will be piloted by the leeches. That leaves them two hundred pilots down. Yes, we can take them, but it will be a bloody battle."

"Then we proceed."

"Perhaps I should warn you," said Kylen, speaking for the first time.

Bruce turned angry eyes towards the Emperor. "I have heard more than enough of your warnings. This plan is perfect. We strike fast. We strike quick. We wipe them off their homeworld and eight other planets at the same time. Their ships are too far away to respond in time. We eliminate them before they even have time to put their pants on."

"Good plan, but they have been warned. Your plan relied on the element of surprise. We can still back out before the first shot is fired."

"I have heard enough of your cowardice! We do not back down from our enemies. Now sit there and shut up, Your Highness."

Everyone in the room watched the exchange in shocked silence. No one else would dare speak to the Emperor like that, even if he was just a lackey appointed by the Coalition. Since Duyagni's assassination, Bruce had grown more powerful while carefully replacing key positions at the palace with Coalition members. Everyone in the war room owed their jobs to him.

"As you wish. Enjoy your war." Kylen leaned back and propped his feet up on the table in front of him. He folded his arms behind his head, looking relaxed like he was about to watch a movie.

"Send the message," ordered Bruce. "Let the whole galaxy tremble before us."

On the screen appeared a large image of Kylen which had been recorded several days before. Dressed in an imposing black suit trimmed in gold, he sat in his office with the official tree symbol of the Basanti Empire behind him.

"Greetings, citizens of Basanti. I have disturbing news to share with you. Evidence has come to light of the involvement of the High Council of Edieth in our beloved Emperor Duyagni's death. Supporters of their nation have been hiding evidence on purpose from us while plotting the downfall of myself and my family. They wish to end our great and worthy lineage. Because of their many crimes, I am declaring every ediethean an enemy of the state. They will be shot on sight. Let us come together to rise above their hate. Let us be better than them."

Even as the message faded into blackness, Bruce ordered the attack to begin. The viewpoint on the screen switched back to *Ironhammer* where fighters immediately launched. The *Warhound* responded almost as quickly. Hundreds of ships began firing on each other as they darted back and forth. Quick, brief explosions lit up the screen.

Kylen set up to better see over the shoulder of a technician sitting in the row in front of him who was tracking ship numbers. McLowary had been wrong on his estimates. *Warhound* had launched four hundred fighters. *Looks like more than the leeches have rebelled.* The fighting was vicious, with numbers dropping quickly on both sides.

Bruce barked, "*Ironhammer*, target their capitol city."

As fighters continued to zoom about, the massive Star-class battlecruiser began to position itself to fire on the planet. From the moon and space stations, edietheans launched ships to join the fray. Some were small but fast military fighters. Others were civilian ships equipped with weapons.

Kylen glanced back at the numbers. The Coalition had a third more fighters, but still their number was dropping rapidly.

"We are in position," said an officer on the *Ironhammer*.

"Fire," ordered Bruce. "Let those boong know they are no longer the smartest in the galaxy."

A powerful fission beam shot out of the battlecruiser and hit the planet, creating a massive cloud that slowly began to spread out. Kylen had seen pictures of the city and could imagine the High Council's tall tower swept away along with thousands of other skyscrapers. Millions were dying right before him.

"That ends the reign of their tyrannical council," yelled Bruce, fist-pumping an aide beside him. "Target the next city."

They were warned, you fool, thought Kylen. *Do you really think their council was in that tower when they had hours to evaluate? They will be doing exactly what I am doing right now, sitting safely in a hidden bunker.*

The battlecruiser began moving into a new position, ignoring the fighting of the smaller ships. Kylen glanced back at the numbers. Their opponents had lost over half their force. Many of the fighters, especially the Ediethean craft, were targeting the battlecruiser, leaving themselves exposed. Another beam shot from *Ironhammer*, obliterating a second city.

Kylen leaned close to his laptop and opened up a hacking program. He placed an earbud in one ear to listen to the audio. *I could warn Bruce, but what would be the fun in that? Let him think he is winning. If he thought like an actual soldier, he should have targeted the other battlecruiser first before dealing with the planet.*

More excited shouts came from humans in the room as a third city disappeared under a dark cloud of debris.

"Sir!" yelled Kathy, her face pale as she studied her monitor. "Sir, there are more ships. Big ones. They just arrived behind the *Ironhammer*."

"Impossible. We accounted for all of the boongs' battleships. They are too far away to get back in time."

You fool. A sly smile crossed Kylen's face. *Honestly, even Admiral McLowary could have won this battle if you had listened to him during the pre-planning. Why hire an expert if you then dismiss all his ideas?*

McLowary's face paled as he looked at a monitor. "They're two of our missing battlecruisers. One is Star-class. Sir, you need to retreat now."

"Retreat? We are winning."

"Not anymore. They have more firepower."

Over a link, the admiral of *Ironhammer* asked for permission to withdrawal. Bruce grabbed the earpiece off an aide and yelled into it. "You do not retreat! Do you hear me? We will not cower before those leeches. Now fight like the warriors you are."

Several tense minutes slowly passed as the fighting intensified. Aids glanced at each other, concerned. Bruce ignored them as he continued to bark attack orders.

With a trembling voice, Kathy said, "The Star-class just fired its fission beam at the *Ironhammer*. A direct hit."

The display of the planet flickered then when blank.

"We just lost the *Ironhammer*."

No one spoke as Bruce clenched his fists, murder in his eyes. Over several channels could be heard pilots shrieking as their ships blew up, others pleading for a surrender.

"Turn off all channels," said Bruce.

The sudden silence felt like death itself. The seconds ticked by. Kathy continued to watch her screen, her face almost pale as snow. McLowary directed angry glances at Bruce but said nothing. Others in the room stared at monitors, avoiding Bruce's wrathful eyes.

Only Kylen was unaffected. He turned his laptop around so it faced the humans and tuned up its volume to max. A video played of Caden explaining the Morality Clause. When it stopped playing, everyone stared at Kylen.

"I hacked their communications last night after the first ship vanished." Kylen smiled confidently. "Really great show there, General Bruce. Oh, wait. You never served in any military position, yet you led our historic endeavor. I wonder what the historians will write about you."

Without a word Bruce marched over to a security officer standing by the door and grabbed his gun. He then placed its muzzle against Kylen's head. "And what will the historians write about you, sire?"

Without flinching, Kylen said, "That I was the one that saved our splintered Empire."

Bruce partly pulled the trigger. "You knew the leeches had rebelled and didn't say a word."

"You ordered me, the Emperor, to be silent. So I let you have your little show. Now it's time for you to disappear while I show the Coalition why they put a profectus on the throne in the first place."

"You will never be more than a puppet!" Bruce pulled the trigger but nothing happened. He tried several more times with the same results. Angrily he hit Kylen with the barrel of the gun. Two guards rushed forward and grabbed Bruce.

Kylen stood, all mockery on his face gone now. "The Coalition put you in charge, but they always had backup plans. So do I. Plans within plans. Now I have to deal with this mess you made. I warned you that when you lost the element of surprise, the attack would fail. Now you have stirred up a hive. Their High Council is not dead. And now that you destroyed their capitol city, they will be coming after all of us. Their fleet on the Rim has already begun repositioning."

Bruce tried to pull away from the guards. "You are nothing but a nerd. The Coalition needs me for the coming war."

"A nerd who can hack into any system in the galaxy." Kylen smiled coldly. "I can make the leeches bend to me." Kylen glanced at the guards. "When you fill out the paperwork about his death, make sure you write down that he was a traitor caught in the act of attacking his Emperor."

"Yes, sire."

As Bruce was dragged away, he continued to struggle while yelling rants. The closing of the door silenced him.

Kylen looked around the room at the dozens of faces staring at him. Most of them had only viewed him as a lackey until this moment. *Well, I'm about to prove them wrong.*

Chapter Thirty-eight

Thousands filled the stands of the parade ground. Free quintessences sat beside other species, all somber as they listened to Gabriel speak. On the field itself, young quintessences stood at attention with their birthmates. On a large platform sat the Five and their wives. Only Aurora was alone. The elder sundancer wept, the spikes on her head drooped slightly from both age and grief.

Joseph glanced towards the metal casket covered with a large bouquet of flowers. Caden's body lay in it but Caleb's memories had already been transferred to Vikram, a ME1 now resting in an apartment in Richton Tower.

Gabriel walked back to his seat and squeezed his wife's hand. Aurora moved to the podium and gave a moving speech filled with tearful pauses. As Joseph listened, he knew the greatest sufferer would be Caleb. Like Gabriel and Jacob, he had never told his wife about his past lives. Usually each generation, the brothers outlived their wives, but this time Caleb had died before his. Now as Vikram, he was doomed to watch her final years from a distant. It would be painful, full of second guessing the decision to never tell.

Some wives could not handle the knowledge their husbands were far older and had been married several times before. If Firestrike knew the truth, she would put a dagger in Jacob's heart. She would morn later, but her first reaction would be to kill him. The pride of being a first wife was an important concept in her culture. She would see hidden wives as a betrayal, even if they were centuries dead.

Despite being married to Hennah for twelve years, Joseph still had to deal with her vortex of emotions relating to his many lives. Often they simply avoided speaking about it. She preferred to think of him only as Joseph. If Layla or Yashana were mentioned in a conversation, even by an innocent friend, Hennah's eyes would harden, her pulse quickening. She never spoke about it, but Joseph had peered into her mind many times, knowing she felt both jealousy and intimation. Even after all these years, she believed that she could never measure up to her predecessors. Joseph regularly reminded her of his love for her, giving her heartfelt gifts, taking her places she enjoyed. Overall, she was happy, busy with research preparing for the next generation of betas which would be produced once the others had been approved. She enjoyed being a mother, yet worried about her daughters' safety when they were away on missions.

Aurora finished her speech and moved back to her seat. She bent forward, her body shaking as she sobbed. Jennifer and Firestrike left their seats to comfort her. Hennah and Amaka shared a glance. They both knew the secrets of their husbands. They felt sadness for Aurora but could not share in her deep grief.

A squad of Synod members stepped forward. Moving in formation, they picked up the casket and carried it across the vast grounds. As they passed each unit of young quintessences, the youths saluted. Overhead jets flew by in a missing man formation. Gabriel said a few final remarks as the funeral ended. Aurora left with Jennifer and Firestrike supporting her.

Gabriel said to his brothers, "We meet after lunch."

"No rest for the grieving?" said Jacob, a slight smile on his lips.

"Not during wartime."

Joseph said, "Only you would joke at a funeral."

"It is only his fourth." Jacob lowered his voice to a whisper.

They dropped the subject as Pallavi and Chandresh neared the platform. Hennah stepped down to greet them. She glanced back at her husband. "My mother and I are taking the rest of the day off to shop."

"Great way to deal with stress," said Jacob, ignoring Joseph's reprimanding look.

Joseph stepped down to greet his in-laws. "Our daughters will arrive this afternoon." With a war breaking out, Essence had recalled most of their smaller ships, cancelling all but the most vital of missions. Their space yachts were not equipped for serious battles.

"We should be back by then. Need to finish gift shopping before they get here."

After watching his wife and in-laws disappear in the crowd, Joseph headed towards Richton Tower, taking his time. Miles followed silently a few paces behind. Joseph was in no hurry. He needed time to reflect. Events were moving fast. Two days ago they had thwarted the Coalition's plans for a quick genocide. Six imperial battlecruisers where now under Essence control. Yesterday their director had died. Within hours the Synod had officially announced Skylar as Caden's replacement. Today was the funeral. Tomorrow they would meet with delegates of the Ediethean High Council to from an alliance in the war against the Coalition.

Roobaroo would had loved the irony. Her people have despised us for so long. Now we are the ones who saved them. Well, not everyone. Two battlecruisers who lacked quintessence crews had carried out their plans. On one colony over three thousand edietheans had been rounded up and executed. Thousands of others had fled into hiding. At the second colony, the local government tried to refuse the soldiers from landing, but they came anyway, killing hundreds before police had a standoff with them.

Here and there on other Core planets, small groups of zealots raided homes, slaughtering ediethean families.

Shortly after Kylen's announcement to the galaxy, several planetary governments had condemned the Emperor's words and declared any who killed edietheans on their worlds would be charged with murder. Yet other nations began rounded up their edietheans and put them in hastily formed consecration camps, a few daring to claim it was for the edietheans' own protection. Coalition members tried to keep the darker stories from the media, yet networks were full of personal stories and pictures being sent out to the galaxy.

It would not take long before rebel worlds on the Rim took advantage of the chaos. Worst case scenario would be groups of them forming alliances to attack the Empire while the Empire was at war with itself. *This may be the end of Basanti. We must at least ensure that our species survives in the new regime.*

Reaching Richton Tower, Joseph took off his name badge. He still had an hour before the meeting. Right now he wanted to relax, letting himself be just another quintessence among his brethren. Miles hung back but kept within eyesight.

Joseph walked down a broad glass corridor leading to the Hall of Challenge. He paused in the opening of the basketball courts, missing his birthmates. *When this war is over, I should take a vacation with them again.* He continued on to the Bōjutsu Gym.

He bypassed the beginner mats. Taken a metal bō with sharpened tips from a stand, he sought out a match against an expert. As he stepped up onto the mat, his opponent glanced to where Joseph's nametag should have been. There was no requirement for off duty quintessences to wear one. Joseph nodded and the match began. They dodged and spun, their staffs striking together with enough force to break bones. As his body moved, Joseph became only instinct, pulling from centuries of experience. The records he had set while he was Ariyo had still never been broken.

Joseph soon beat his opponent. He moved on, this time taking two on at once. Here he felt alive, in control. The galaxy was in chaos but he controlled where his bō landed, which foe took a blow. He was a master in his realm. After the fourth match, Joseph put away his bō, ignoring blood dripping from several cuts.

"You are looking quite proper for a meeting." Miles stepped forward, offering himself for healing.

"I've shown up looking worst." Joseph bit, keeping contact brief. When he pulled away, the cuts had vanished. He grabbed a rag and wiped away the blood.

Reaching the Grand Forum, Joseph ate a quick meal with Miles then headed up to the fortieth floor. As they walked across the lobby, a heated discussion between Darkfern and a neodite guard caught their attention. Nightstorm stood beside his wife, nodding with her in agreement.

315

"Your people are cowards declaring yourself neutral."

The neodite's blue skin had splotches of purple. "Our homeworld is staying neutral in the war, not me."

"How long until the Coalition comes after your species?"

"We have never had conflict with the Coalition. It is those species which rise high in power that do so."

"So you admit your race is so cowardly that not even the Coalition thinks they are worthy to fight."

The splotches on the neodite's skin began to be highlighted in red. His hand brushed against his gun. "You speak like a simple-minded fjouwer. From the beginning we neodites have proudly served in the wars of the Empire. Names of our heroes can be found throughout Basanti's bloody history. Our homeworld declares neutrality to protect those who are now serving on imperial ships. It is only the most powerful of nations which can afford to have their own fleets. Your species never developed flight or even writing. You leech many of your technologies off others."

Darkfern drew one of her knives. "So what? We lacked plants that produced fibers which could make paper. But we found a way around that." She pulled up a sleeve revealing a tattooed band which encircled her arm many times, intertwined with various symbols. "We carry our history with us always. We never forget. And we are too smart to get involved in Core politics. What do we care if Core factions blow up each other's homeworlds? Let them come to Shah Luna or Werjouk. The worst they can do is close our spaceports. Our cities are built deep underground. We have self-supporting environments with huge farms and wildlife. We don't need the rest of the galaxy."

Joseph cut in, "You might for those fancy shoes you are wearing. They are imports."

Darkfern looked for Joseph's nametag. Seeing none, she glanced at Miles. Realizing who was addressing her, Darkfern snapped to attention, quickly followed by her husband and the neodite.

Putting her weapon away, Darkfern said, "We were discussing personal opinions."

"I see. Perhaps you should save the debate for when you are off duty. Also, as a security supervisor, you should not pull a weapon on a subordinate unless training."

"Yes, sir." Darkfern looked grave. "It will not happen again, sir."

Joseph continued to the Chamber of Five. The central monitor that had once been Caleb's was now taken by the new director. Gabriel gave his brother a reprimanding glance. "You are late."

"There was a conflict I needed to deal with." Joseph put his nametag back on as he took his place beside Jacob.

"We have many conflicts which need dealing with in here." Gabriel touched his monitor. In the middle of the room appeared a large hologram showing a sector of space. "We have taken out another of the Coalition's battlecruisers used in the genocide. I have ordered two of our new battlecruisers to Essence to enforce our fleet. Two will protect Ediethean's homeworld. The rest are chasing hotspots."

Mason said, "This war has barely begun. We do not yet know which side many worlds will choose."

Joseph said, "I suspect many will try to stay neutral like the neodites. Few smaller civilizations have standing forces of their own, but some of their citizens serve on imperial ships."

Gabriel touched his monitor and the map spread out to show the whole galaxy. "The imperial fleet is vast, spread out across many sectors. The ediethean fleet is already heading back to their homeworld. The question is, what will the other ships do? We have several hundred thousand brethren serving on them. Do we order them to take over their ships or wait until they are given an immoral command?"

Jacob said, "If we give the order for our brethren to rebel, we will triggered a galactic size war instead a local one. We need to be very cautious in how we proceed."

Mason nodded. "We need to keep sending the message to other worlds that we are against the Collation, not the Empire. A full out rebellion will make it seem we are trying to make a bid for galactic power."

"Already several Rim sectors are declaring their independence yet again." Gabriel zoomed in on the map to a sector on the edge. "This has been a hotspot for centuries."

As the four brothers studied the hologram image, it flicked then disappeared, along with every light in the room, leaving them in complete darkness. After a moment, a red emergency light came on. The brothers and Shadow Guards glanced at each other. Power outages were rare here, and at most only lasted a few seconds. Joseph glanced as his e-band, wondering if a major storm had blown in unexpectedly. His small screen warned it had no connection to the network.

"Our satellites are down."

"This is not a normal outage," said Mason.

The quintessences moved to the door but it did not open, as it was a metal security door. Miles pulled off a panel and unlocked the door manually. Two Shadow Guards pushed open the door along its track. Sunlight streamed into the large, quiet lobby. The overhead lights were off. Darkfern and other guards stood by the huge windows looking out over the campus.

"Even the monorails stopped were they were," said Nightstorm, pointing downward.

Darkfern pressed her face against the glass. "I think there is still electricity at New Haven. See, that sign on that office building is still lit up."

"Why has Essence lost power and not New Hope?"

Joseph and his brothers walked up to the glass wall giving a panoramic view of both Essence and the city beyond. Outside the sky was blue with only a few clouds. Traffic still flowed in New Hope, pausing at red lights. Digital billboards rotated through advertisements. Life seemed normal. But Essence had come to a standstill. Monorails were frozen on tracks. No lights were visible from any buildings. Curious crowds were starting to exit. Being in the middle of the summer, the buildings would soon grow hot with no air condition. A few vehicles slowly moved along roads, pausing at every intersection as no traffic lights worked.

"Are we under attack?" asked Nightstorm, looking towards Gabriel.

"There was no indication of one. Our orbiting ships sent no warning."

"What are our orders?" said Darkfern.

"Stay cautious."

"You can stay if you like," said Jacob, "but I am going to where the action is. Our security bunker. Our technicians down there should be able to tell us something. And if we are under attack, it is the safest place to be."

Jacob headed towards the stairwell at the far end of the lobby. Everyone followed. Being trained soldiers, they were in good physical shape. Still, walking down forty flights to reach ground level then another twenty-five to reach the technology hub in the underground bunker was taxing.

The security door to the area had already been manually opened. Red emergency lights revealed a large room with dozens of technicians moving about or hunched over computers monitors. Tension was tight. Nerves flayed. Two coders began yelling at each other while both pointed at different areas of a screen.

"They have power?" asked Darkfern, staring around the room.

Gabriel answered, "Essence has several power sources. Our bunker operates separate from the outside. We should have had full power here." He glanced up at the red lights overhead.

A HC3 model noticed the group. He walked over, a slight frown on his face. "We do not have time for more visitors. Please leave so we can focus better."

"Franco, I am Skylar of the Five. Do you know what is going on?"

"Oh, sir." The technician snapped to attention. "I tried to contact you but even our satellites are being affected. We are being hacked, sir. The worst we have ever seen. The culprit has released dozens of different viruses into our systems. We are working to eliminate each one. Also, we are having difficulty pinpointing how the culprit got access."

"If the electricity is working here, why are we on emergency lighting?"

"He is playing with us, sir. The viruses are working independently of each other, affecting different systems. Each requires a different method for removal."

"We need to reboot," said a tense sea laven, standing up by his monitor. "We need to shut everything down."

Franco turned to his subordinate. "La'Tiek, I said no on that already. Unless we find the source of the infection and shut it down, the culprit can attack again."

Gabriel said, "We will stand out of your way and let you experts work."

Joseph stood against a wall with his brothers and the guards, watching the technicians. Some worked intently on their computers while others dashed about from monitor to monitor. Several arguments broke out about solutions.

"Sir," bubbled a squamiger through his water helmet. "He established an uplink with our mainframe. Ten percent has already been copied."

La'Tiek said, "We need to shut down everything now!"

"Wait," barked Franco. "We must find the source."

"The longer we wait, the more information they steal."

Franco glanced at Gabriel then back at his busy technicians. "Find me the source, now! If he reaches fifty percent, we shut everything down."

"Sir, the longer we wait…"

"Just keep busy."

Suddenly a sundancer leaped up, shouting excitedly, her spikes quivering. "I found him—at least his entry point."

Franco, La'Tiek, and others crowded around the sundancer's monitor.

"Trace the IP," ordered Franco.

After a long moment, the sundancer said, "No location is giving."

"Ping it."

"I have, several times. I can read its model, but I don't recognize it. A Divinus 70. That company uses 3800's now. It would have to be…"

"…ancient," spoke Joseph from across the room. "That computer is in my apartment, and it only responses to my wife. It is impossible that her computer is being used for this hack."

Franco said, "We need to take a look at it quickly."

"Alright," Joseph began moving toward the door.

"Franco," said La'Tiek. "We isolated the source. Now can we do the reboot?"

"Yes. Turn off the mainframe, backups, everything. Give it ten minutes, then we reboot from the latest backup before the attack. Make sure to remove the offending computer from the system."

Franco jogged after Joseph down the hallway and up seventy flights of stairs. Joseph heard the footsteps of others but did not pause to glance back to see who followed. *There is no way someone can be in our apartment right now using that computer.* Joseph continued upward, his breath ragged. He paused briefly on a landing, allowing himself and the others a moment to rest. Then he ran onward, taking the steps quickly.

When they finally reached the penthouse, Franco manually unlocked the door. They walked into the dim living room, the only light coming from the balcony windows. Joseph led the way to the study. The computerized desk remain lifeless when he touched it.

Dropping to the floor, Franco scooted under the desk. Using light from his e-band, he pulled off a panel and poked around. "No electricity. Ancient. Not even connected to the network."

"I know. As you can see, it is impossible that it was used for the hack."

Franco began putting the panel back on. "Who has excess to this unit?"

"Just my wife, myself, and our two daughters. But it only responds to my wife."

Darkfern panted hard in the doorway. "And that tech guy…Hennah brought in…one time."

"What tech guy?" asked Franco, standing up.

"I don't know. Human. Ten, twelve years ago. Never saw him since."

"Kylen." Joseph's face darken as he glanced at Jacob and Miles who had also followed him. "Kylen was in my apartment."

"Why would he be in your apartment? You never told us that," said Jacob.

"It was a personal matter. Hennah invited him in to work on the computer. I thought we would never see him again."

Franco said, "Who is this Kylen? He is not on our staff."

"Emperor Kylen is a profectus clone of Richard Cambridge and Ethan Covey."

The HC3's mouth dropped open for a moment then his eyes hardened. "You allowed a profectus geek who is loyal to the Coalition into our system and did not think to inform my department? Sir, what were you thinking?"

"There was a lot going on at the time. And I thought it was the last time we would hear from Kylen. "

Franco raised his voice slightly. "Richard and Ethan were brilliant coders. Having an evil clone of theirs in our system is the worst possible scenario. Most likely he has set traps, like if the system reboots…" Franco's eyes widen. "I got to go warn my staff." Franco jogged out of the apartment at full speed.

"Does not mean it's going to take longer to get the electricity on?" said Nightstorm, still trying to catch his breath.

Jacob walked over to his brother. "Why did you not tell us Kylen was here?"

"I had thought the matter closed. He was not the Emperor then." Joseph looked away. That was the one secret he wished to never share with his brothers. Kylen, here in his home, trying to seduce his wife. Kissing Hennah on the sofa he now stared at.

"You should have told us nevertheless. We were investigating his involvement with the Coalition. He should never have been allowed inside Essence."

"I did not invite him. Hennah did."

"We need to know why he was here then and how it relates to today."

Joseph clenched his fists. "Motives of the two incidents do not relate. Today, the Coalition wanted access to our files, which they succeeded in getting at least some of them."

"And the other time, why was he here? What are you hiding?"

There was a long pause before Joseph answered, "He wanted my wife. Kylen asked Hennah to run away with him."

"My best friend would never do that," said Darkfern stepping into the room and drawing both knives. "If I had known that was why Kylen was here, I would have ended his life that day."

"I would have too, if he had been present when I found out. Hennah said no to him, and we both thought that was the end of it."

"Obviously not," said Jacob. "Hennah allowed him to have access to our system."

"She is innocent of wrongdoing. She knew nothing of Kylen's plans to hack into our system."

"Where is she?" asked Darkfern. "I have a word or two to say to her about not telling me she almost had an affair with an Emperor. You don't keep juicy stories like that from your best friend."

"She is shopping with her mother. And that topic is not one she or I wish to discuss."

"Well, you ought to talk about things like this. How do you even know if he is over her? Maybe he will try to win her back, now that he is Emperor?"

"Enough of this topic. Kylen is married." Joseph froze, his eyes drifting to the sofa. Kylen had been unhappy about his upcoming arranged marriage. Could he had been after more than data today? Joseph glanced at his e-band. Still no signal. No way to communicate or track Hennah's location. A sinking dread filled Joseph. Hacking into Essence, creating chaos conveniently while Hennah was off campus. Had it all been a diversion? Could Hennah be planning to run away today? *No, I trust her. She was excited about a surprise party she had planned for the girls for making it to Level Two.*

"I need to find my wife, now."

Joseph headed out the door, followed by the others. Seeing he was about to take the stairs again, Darkfern stared enviously at the elevators.

"We could wait until the electricity is back on. Surely it will not take that much longer."

"Stay if you wish. Already too much time has been wasted."

Joseph ran down the stairs, pushing his already tired body. Jacob and Miles kept up with his pace, but the fjouwers fell behind. Reaching the ground floor, Joseph jogged to his car in the parking lot. Jacob took the passenger seat, Miles the back. As he turned onto a main street by Richton Tower, he saw Nightstorm emerge from the building, waving at him. He stopped the car.

The fjouwer gasped, "Your daughters…we saw them…across forum. My wife…getting now."

Moments later Darkfern raced out of the building with Alexa and Zara close behind.

"Papa, what is going on?" asked Zara.

"Is Mamma in danger?" said Alexa.

"Get in the car. I'll explain on the way."

As the girls slid in beside Miles, Darkfern said, "Hubby and I will take my car. But where are we going?"

"The shopping center you regularly visit with Hennah."

Joseph zoomed off, not waiting on the fjouwers. Quickly he reached a gate guarding an exit to the campus. Traffic was backed up, as guards were requiring those leaving to sign their names on clipboards. Normally, computers kept track of that. Joseph weaved through the cars, breaking in line. Workers trying to head home tossed him dark looks.

Reaching the guard booth, Joseph quickly signed his name. Then he zoomed out, dodging around traffic.

"Papa, what is going on?" said Alexa. "Darkfern made no sense. Something about mom and the Emperor having an affair. And he turned off all the lights to get her."

"To distract us." Joseph took a sharp turn. "There was no affair. Just an almost before he became Emperor. Darkfern needs to learn to watch what she says before she starts spreading rumors all over Essence."

"My daughter means well," said Jacob. "She is trying to help you."

"Why would the Emperor want to have an affair with Mamma?" asked Zara. "I thought she only saw him once long ago."

Joseph sped through a red light. "It is a story for another time."

"That is your third violation," said Alexa. "You told me if I every drove like that, you would ban me from driving for five years."

"I still will." Without pausing at an intersection, Joseph zipped across two rows of incoming traffic.

"That was so illegal, Papa. You did that right in front of a cop."

"I know."

Red lights flashed as a police hover car began chasing them. Joseph refused to slow down. By the time he pulled into the parking lot of the shopping center, a second patrol car had joined the chase. Joseph swung the car into an empty spot and jumped out. Both cops stopped their vehicles and rushed out, pointing their weapons at Joseph.

"You are under arrest for reckless driving and intent to flee."

Joseph partly raised his hands. "Only two of you. I had hoped you called for more backup."

"Don't think neodites can take a quintessence? I don't care who you are. You cannot drive around our city like that."

"My name is Joseph of the Five. My wife may be in danger. I need your help to try to locate her. She is supposed to be shopping here."

The two cops glanced at each other, slowly lowering their guns. "If you are a Five, then why did you not call in the problem instead of driving like a maniac?"

"Communications are down at Essence. There was a major hack. Your coms are working, correct?"

"Yes."

"Call your chief and let me talk with him. I know him personally."

The officer talked for a bit into his telecom then handed it over to Joseph. Miles, Jacob, Zara, and Alexa stood by the car watching. By the time Joseph got things settled with the police, Darkfern and Nightstorm had pulled up.

"Do you know where your wife was shopping?" asked one of the cops. "There are over a thousand stores here."

"No, she was buying several presents for my daughters and myself. She was with her elderly mother. They would have wandered into many stores. We need to split up to search. We need your backup telecoms."

The cops reluctantly passed over their two spare. The group split into pairs, with Zara joining Darkfern and Nightstorm. Joseph moved quickly towards the first store he knew Hennah had planned to visit. Jacob kept pace beside him, trying to calm his tense brother. Alexa reported in that she spotted her grandmother's car still in the parking lot.

Ten stores later, Joseph still had found no sign of his wife. He kept telling himself he was overreacting, that any moment Hennah and Pallavi would be spotted, perhaps drinking coffee together. But deep inside, the dread grew. Essence had stolen Coalition warships. The Coalition sought revenge. Stealing Essence's files was not enough. Kylen was making this personal.

Zara's voice came over the telecom. "Found grandmother at Romanware."

Joseph dashed out of the clothing store he was in. Jacob kept by his side as they ran shoulder to shoulder, passing through hologram advertisements competing for their attention. Shoppers glanced in their direction as they sped by. The brothers slowed as they reached the store. Joseph marched down aisles of kitchenware, heart pounded in fear of what Pallavi would say.

Near the back, he spotted his mother-in-law talking with his daughter and the fjouwers. Nightstorm held shopping bags for Pallavi who looked distressed.

"She was right here. I was looking at a dining set. She went around a corner and I never saw her again."

"How long ago was this?" asked Joseph.

"About an hour ago. At first I thought she was still in the store, but when I didn't see her for a while, I tried calling her. My e-band is not working."

"None are. Our systems were hacked. Our satellites are still down."

"I checked stores nearby then came back here. Is my daughter in danger? Who would take her?"

Darkfern lowered her voice. "He thinks the Emperor may be in love with her."

Pallavi's voice become stern. "That is ridiculous."

"It's his theory, not mine. She never told me about the affair."

"What affair?" Pallavi stared flabbergasted.

Joseph glanced at the two cops heading their way. "We found my mother-in-law. My wife has disappeared. I need access to all security cameras."

The cops nodded. "This way."

Alexa and Miles soon joined the group as all tried to squeeze into a small room were the store's security feed was kept. The store manager navigated through the software, soon spotting Hennah and Pallavi entering the store. The manager switched the feed several times as he followed them down aisles. Hennah turned a corner, passing two human men wearing store uniforms, one of them pushing a large cart. Suddenly he turned, placing a medical gas mask over Hennah's mouth and nose. She briefly struggled then passed out. The men quickly placed her body in the cart, covering her with a tarp. Then they preceding out the back of the store, leaving through the warehouse.

"Those are not my employees," said the manager. "I have never seen them before."

One of the cops said, "Send a copy of these files to my department. We will widen our search."

"My poor, poor Hennah," Pallavi wobbled, almost fainting. The manager quickly offered his seat.

Jacob tried to comfort his brother. "We will find her."

"He played us." Joseph clenched his fists, rage in his eyes. "Distracting us. She is probably already off planet."

A cop said, "We will begin searching the spaceport immediately."

The cops and manager left. Joseph remained staring at the last image of his wife on the monitor. "I will hunt him down. And when I find him, I will kill him."

"Ah, good," said Darkfern. "Doing it fjouwer style." Seeing Alexa and Zara's questioning looks, she explained. "In my culture, when there is an affair, the two males fight it out. Whoever lives gets the female."

"What if it is the male who is cheating?" asked Alexa.

"A dagger in the heart ends that problem."

"Enough of your chatter," said Joseph tensely. "Hennah did not have an affair. Kylen tried to seduce her. She said no. End of story. Now I need to find my wife."

Pallavi's slumped in her seat. "The Emperor wants my daughter? Why?"

"I will tell you the story another time. We must hurry now."

"We will go with you anywhere," said Alexa. Zara nodded in agreement.

Jacob stepped in front of his brother, getting his full attention. "You need to think logically right now, not react on emotions. Kylen is the Emperor who we are at war with. It will not be easy to reach him."

"I will go to the ends of the universe if I must. I will get Hennah back, and I will kill him. His title means nothing to me."

Chapter Thirty-nine

A blurry ornament post was the first thing Hennah saw when she opened her eyes. She blinked several times as her vision cleared. The post was part of a frame supporting a lacy canopy covering the large bed she lay in. The sheets were softer than silk. The heavy blanket had intricate patterns of exotic flowers. The air was perfumed with the scent of potpourri.

Where am I? She tried to focus on her last memories. Almost waking, strangers around her, fluids being forced down her throat. Before that, she had been shopping with her mother. Someone had grabbed her.

She turned over in the bed, looking around in confusion. The room was huge with an opulent sofa and table. The walls gilded with gold relief molding. On the ceiling was a mural of a clearing of wildflowers surrounded by a lush forest. In the middle of the clearing was a huge golden tree—the symbol of Basanti.

"Glad to see you are finally awake."

Hennah sat up and looked towards the speaker sitting in a velvet cushion chair. His black clothes were highlighted in bright embellishments. "Kylen? Where am I?"

"You are a profectus. Use your brilliant mind to tell me."

"Your palace on Basanti?"

The monarch smiled. "I am glad to see the drugs are wearing off. I asked that they keep you under on your trip here as I wanted to be the first to greet you when you awoke."

"Why am I here?" Hennah noticed she was wearing a blue silk nightgown. She did not want to think about who dressed her.

"I rescued you, of course, from those leeches."

"Rescued? I…uh." Hennah closed her eyes as dizziness hit.

"You will be hungry as you have not had solid food in days."

Kylen rose and went to the door. He spoke with someone outside. A few minutes later he walked over to her bed carrying a tray of food. As Hennah ate a fancy egg dish she did not recognize, she tried to pull together her thoughts. *I have been kidnapped. Kylen thinks he is helping me. Joseph will try to find me, but how can he reach me here in the palace? We are at war. I need to find a way out of here.*

When the meal was finished, Kylen passed the tray over to a servant. He then pulled his chair up beside her bed.

"I am sure you have many questions."

"Why did you feel you needed to rescue me? We have not seen each other in twelve years."

"The last time we were together, you were miserable, unhappy in your marriage. I wanted to help you then. Over the years I kept thinking about the life we almost had. I never wanted to be a politician. The Coalition shaped me into the tool I am now. Still, I kept seeking a way to rescue you from those mortis elixirs. I forgave you for not leaving the first time. You were scared and barely knew me."

Hennah tried to remember conversations Joseph had at meals with his daughters about their training for hostage negotiation situations. Something about creating a rapport with the enemy. "I appreciate that you actually care about my wellbeing after all these years. I was unhappy at the time you knew me. I was dealing with chronic depression. Eventually I came out of that. I love my husband now."

"Tell me, why did you marry him if you did not love him at first? You claimed it was not an arranged marriage, but it looked like one to me."

"I…uh…" Hennah looked away, uncertain how to answer. "Joseph was a good friend when I was going through a dark time. I wanted him to be happy, even if I was not. The marriage pleased my parents who thought it was a sign I was getting over my depression."

"So you married to please others, not yourself. Just like me." Kylen's eyes studied her face intently.

"Yes." Hennah looked away again, not liking his gaze.

He gently took her hand. "You and I are so much alike. Giving up our dreams, our desires to please our creators, our masters. We are only pawns to them."

Hennah pulled her hand away from him. "That is not true, at least with Joseph. Yes, he used me, but he also cared about me. He changed. I changed. It was difficult at first, but our marriage is real now. I love him and would like to return to him, please."

"Is that what you really want or are you just speaking their words?"

"It is what I want. My family and friends are at Essence. I would like to go home to them."

Kylen pulled back, his face seeming to fall into shadow. "I see. That will be problematic seeing as your husband belongs to an organization that my faction is at war with."

"Just let me walk out. I will find a commercial flight home."

"All space travel is dangerous right now. Also, you cannot simply walk out. We are deep underground in a bunker. Security is high. The elevators will not work for you—got that idea during that tour of Essence you gave me."

"So I am a prisoner?"

"I prefer not to think of it that way. My intentions are to make you my concubine."

"What? Kylen, I am married." Hennah's voice conveyed her shock.

"So am I. Monarchs take concubines all the time. I am actually very conservative compared to some of Abarrane's ancestors who have had large harems down here. You would be my first."

"I do not think your wife will be happy with that decision."

"Abarrane is unhappy with almost every decision I make. Do not worry about her. I gave her the child she wanted. She has no further need of me."

Stay calm, Hennah told herself. "I am flattered you think of me in that way, but I am happy with my husband."

"I know you do not want to hear this now, but you may be a widow soon. Your husband is an enemy of the state." Kylen stood and glanced at his watch. "I am a patience man. I will never force you. This room and everything in it is yours. The closet is full of designer clothes and jewelry."

"I want none of it."

"You can always walk around in that nightgown for the rest of your life. I would not mind." He laughed at Hennah's alarmed expression. "Don't worry. I know you better than you think I do. I made sure they added some normal clothes in there too. Occasionally I take a day off from playing Emperor and don't leave my room. Spend all day tinkering with gadgets while wearing only boxers. I will invite you over the next time I do so."

"No, thank you."

Kylen glanced at his watch again. "Sadly, today is one of those days I must work. And you have a part to play in it. Takes funds to organize a rescue in enemy territory—or kidnapping, as you might call it. I needed to give the Coalition a reason for taking you, so your presence is required at the meeting. I will leave you to get dressed. Wear whatever you like."

He left, leaving Hennah alone in the ostentatious room. She sat in the bed for a while, wondering if she should refuse to go to his meeting. *As a hostage, I am most likely safer playing along. Try to be his friend.* Hennah opened the closet door. The room was three times as large as the bedroom she had shared with her sister growing up. Besides rows of clothes were shelves for shoes, hats, jewelry, and other accessories. She bypassed the fancy clothes, grabbing brown slacks and a peach blouse. The brush she used to untangle her hair was made of silver. She skipped putting on makeup.

When Kylen returned, he nodded in approval. "Classic without the need of showing off. I knew this is what you preferred. I must offer an apology for what is to come. During the meeting, I must appear as a dignified ruler intent on completing

Coalition goals. I am sure you will disagree on our policies. I highly suggest you remain quiet unless directly spoken to. When discussing you with them, I will treat you as a pawn. Please do not be offended. What I say in the meeting will not reflect what I really feel for you. It is dangerous for me to show emotional attachment for anything as my many opponents will try to use that to manipulate me."

"Don't take anything you say personally. Got it." Hennah felt a tightening of her chest. What was she about to walk into? She still got panic attacks when addressing the Synod about her research.

She followed him down the hallway, passing doors with vine patterns craved onto the frames. The carpet was thick, looking pleasant enough to take a nap on. A golden haired child ran from one room to another, followed by a nanny. The child dashed back into the hallway, holding up a paper flower.

"Daddy, I make for you."

Kylen bent down and took the flower. "Thank you, Abigail. It is beautiful."

"Beautiful as me?"

"No, you are more beautiful than the most beautiful flower in our garden."

The toddler giggled. "I make Mommy one now."

The nurse led the child away. Hennah studied the smile on Kylen's face. *He likes being a father. He ordered a genocide, yet he cares for his daughter.*

Kylen noticed Hennah staring at him. His face sobered. "Abigail gets her brains from me, and her looks from her mother. She is a profectus like us."

As they left the residential suite, guards followed closely behind. They took an elevator up several floors. Kylen easily navigated the labyrinth of passageways, arriving at a conference room with a long table. He sat in a ziricote chair with images carved into the dark and light wood. With a wave of his hand, he indicated for Hennah to sit beside him in a less embellished chair.

Hennah looked at the others coming into the room. All human, a mix of different races and ages. Mostly male, but there were two females. She recognized General McLowary's face. Too well she remembered the trial of Quinn when it should have been the general facing judgement.

"Welcome," said Kylen. "What conclusions have you reached from analyzing the data I stole from Essence?"

Hennah glanced at him in surprise. What else had he done besides kidnap her? She wanted to ask but remembered his warning to be quiet. The room was full of Coalition enemies. She had no idea how they would react to her. Most had given her curious glances when they walked into the room then ignored her.

McLowary said, "We now know the size of their fleet and current location of all ships."

"Except that ships move," said a tall man with a mustache that curled at the ends. "What good is this information when it becomes irrelevant in just days?"

Kylen said, "Peterkin, by knowing where their ships start helps us to predict where they might go. Go ahead, General."

"Besides our six battlecruisers they stole, the leeches own five light cruisers, eight frigates, three destroyers, six transports, plus a wide assignment of yachts, fighters, shuttles, and even jets."

"Nothing close to our massive fleet," said a red hair woman wearing a business suite. On her name badge was the words *Kathy Moyers*.

"True, but the leeches are joining forces with the boongs who have nearly twice as much firepower. Together they make a dangerous armada."

Peterkin said, "But we still vastly outnumber them. Why do we not just bring our own armada from the Rim and wipe out both the leeches and boongs in one glorious battle?"

Kylen gave a loud sigh, drawing everyone's attention. "Peterkin, leave the tactical discussion to those who actually understand it. General, please explain to the laymen in the room why we have not done so before now."

The imposing soldier with the scar frowned. "The moment we pull all our forces from the Rim, all hell will break loose. And not just against us. Many of those barbarians have ancient grudges against each other. Our forces are the peacemakers there."

"Who cares if a bunch of aliens kill each other?" Peterkin leaned forward, eagerness in his eyes.

Kylen cut in, "We import rare elements from the Rim which are used in constructing weapons for our fleet. Those regions and their trade routes must be protected."

Kathy said, "Surely we can bring back half of our forces do deal with our current problem."

"That was a possible consideration before our first attack. But repositioning such a massive amount of ships would have drawn too many questions, so it was decided to use a small strike force to quickly eradicate the boog. But as you know, that attempt failed."

"Then we bring them back now."

"Ah, now we have reached the stalemate we find ourselves in. The majority of our ships have bonded quintessences serving on them. The moment any realize they will be used for our objectives, they will rebel."

Peterkin said, "Send those foeditas horribilis out the nearest airlock."

The general gave Peterkin a cold stare. "Have you tried to kill a leech before? We bought them for our military in the first place because they are so damnably hard to kill. You can't simply throw thousands of leeches out airlocks. Instead, they will come after you, sucking the life from you. So go ahead, sonny, order half the crew to be slaughtered and see who controls the ship afterwards."

Peterkin fell silent, angry at being belittled.

Kathy said, "Can we gas them?"

"Not easily, not without killing almost everyone on board. The ships' air ducts were not designed to cut off certain cabins from others."

"Then how do we take control?" She looked towards Kylen. "My ancestor Steven Moyers put much faith in you to lead us into the promised Golden Era for humans. You stated after dealing with Bruce that you had a plan which would control the leeches. I backed you. Now how do we defeat them?"

Despite the tension in the room, Kylen appeared relaxed. "Actually Steven predicted this grand hero to be my daughter, as she is the first natural born profectus of royal linage. I am just filling in for now. Of course, we will need to change that ancient, outdated law that the ruling monarch can only be male. I'm sure I have your backing on that issue, Kathy."

"Yes, of course, sire."

"I plan to leave a strong empire for my daughter to inherit, albeit a bit smaller with a few less sentients species. The best way to deal with the leeches is not by destroying them but by controlling them."

"That has not been working out so far," complained Peterkin.

"It worked quite well for us for six hundred years." Kylen turned to Hennah. "She is the key we needed."

"What? Her? I've known dogs which looked prettier than her."

Kylen gave the man a sharp look. "I am beginning to question why Bruce appointed you to this cabinet. Just because your father is a prime minister does not give you the right to be an idiot. Now can anyone besides Peterkin tell me who she is?"

Hennah sat as still as possible, barely breathing as the others in the room studied her face. Suddenly several of them took on shocked expressions.

Kathy was the first to speak. "She is a clone of Layla Rangan. But our version died young due to a virus outbreak."

"This is Hennah Kalkar, wife of Joseph of the Five. While we were busy breaking the Purity Act, the leeches were doing the same thing." Kylen leaned closer to Hennah. "By the way, yesterday I signed a law ending the Purity Act. No one involved in creating me or my fellow profectus can be prosecuted. By accident, that new law protects those who made you also."

"Oh." Hennah felt her heart quicken. "I no longer have to hide what I am?"

"No cloned profectus will need to fear their true identity again. See, the Coalition has helped you."

Kathy asked, "Why would the leeches clone her?"

"Why else but to design new models. The most important thing to be learned from her existence is that the leeches are willing to break laws if they see it benefits them. So we find out what they want most and use that against them."

"How is she a key?" asked the general. "The leeches have a hive mind. Their loyalty is to each other. Their precious Code puts the wellbeing of the whole race over the individual. If you threaten to kill her, they still will not change their plans."

Hennah's face paled. "My husband cares for me."

McLowary pulled out an old-fashioned revolver and laid in on the table. He tenderly placed a hand on it. "I can bet my life that if I put this gun to your head, he still would not change his position on this war. She is useless to us, sire."

Trembling, Hennah tried to calm herself. *He is right. I am useless. I already gave the quintessences what they wanted. Others can continue the research without me. I am no longer needed.* Still, she knew her family would mourn her, but her death would make no waves in the politics of this war.

"From the angle you speak, she is," said Kylen. "But I did not steal her under the noses of the leeches so she can be used as leverage. What I did show them was that they are vulnerable. Even on their home turf they can be hurt. I have something better for them. And now it is time for me to send them my message. If you will come with me to my office, everyone?"

Kylen stood and walked out. Not knowing what else to do, Hennah followed. The rest came behind, speculating among themselves what he was up to. They entered a large room with a huge embellished desk. Behind it was large wooden craving of a tree overlaid with gold. A camera was set up in the middle of the room along with a small crew to operate it. Kylen sat behind the desk and indicated for Hennah to stand behind him. The others watched outside the camera's view.

Kylen looked straight into the camera. "Hello, my rebellious friends. Do you like the surprises I left for your technicians? They will spend weeks trying to eliminate all my little presents and still not be able to remove them all. You will continue to experience random glitches, especially during critical times like when you are relying on communications in the midst of battle. At any moment you may lose all contact or the information lies to you. Perhaps there are three battlecruiser coming your direction. Or maybe twenty."

Kylen turned towards Hennah and slowly swept a gaze along her body. "I accept, Joseph, this gift from you. I am glad you have come to realize her talents were not being utilized to their fullest with you. Your seed cannot give her children while mine can. Our beautiful profectus offspring will be in the position to change the galaxy in whatever way their unique talents lie."

Hennah trembled, turning her face away from the camera. *Joseph will see this. Our children. It will hurt them so much. Kylen told me not to take this personally, but how can I not?*

"Now that I have your attention, I would like to discuss our future. Either one of us can easily turn our skirmishes into a massive war, the likes of which no one has seen before. It will tear this galaxy apart, leaving thousands of civilizations in smoking ruins. Not billions but trillions will die. Personally, I believe you do not want that on your conscience. Despite what you think about the Coalition, neither do we. Our wish is to get rid of a few pests, not destroy other sentients who understand their place. Now, being the benevolent ruler that I am, I offer you a compromise.

"I will give you what you desire most in return for your complete loyalty. Nationhood. Essence will make its own laws governing its civilians. You will have a seat in the Galactic Senate. In turn, you will provide soldiers who will serve until their bond years are completed. Yes, you will be used in a few genocides. Not many. The rest of our foes will quickly fall in line. Again, the Coalition wants a strong, united empire. You can be a part of that or a tool in its destruction. And as an added bonus, I will eradicate those viruses creating hectic in your computer systems."

As the camera crew packed up, Kylen walked around the equipment to address his advisors. Hennah moved against a wall, standing by a bookshelf. She wanted to run but where could she go? The bunker was a maze with guards everywhere. Even if she found the elevators, she could not operate them. *Joseph, please don't do anything stupid because of me. Protect those civilizations in trouble.*

The cabinet debated for nearly another hour, wondering if the quintessences would take the deal. If they did, could they really be trusted again? As Hennah listened, she felt queasy. *How can they speak so lightly of genocide? Of taking so many lives like they do not matter?*

Eventually Kylen dismissed his advisors. Hennah followed him back down to the royal suite. He entered the parlor, inviting Hennah to sit on a thick cushion beside him. She sat on the far end of the sofa away from him, wrapping her arms around her body in defense.

"You are upset. I asked for you to not take anything I said in the meeting personally."

"How can I not take it personally? The way you addressed my husband? I will never have your kids."

"I will settle for your friendship."

"I believe nothing you say."

Kylen looked at her in earnest. "Hennah, I have never lied to you, not once. There are extremely few people I trust and you are one of them. There is a connection between us."

"Kidnapping is not the way to treat a friend."

"To be fair, I believed I was helping you. You said yourself that you were a slave to the leeches."

Hennah tried to force herself to relax. *Remember, you are pretending to be his friend until you can escape.* "If you want to earn my friendship, send me back home."

"I cannot do that. If the Five do not take the offer, we will have to destroy Essence to end our disagreement. I will not send you into a danger zone."

Forgetting what she had just told herself, Hennah leaned forward, eyes ablaze. "My family is there, Kylen. You will kill my parents, my friends. There are many families at Essence. Children, like your daughter." Her own brother lived in New Hope with his wife and kids. Her sister's family was located several cities away. Perhaps they would be spared, or an attack might destroy much of the planet.

"War is never pretty."

"How can you live with yourself? Millions have already died on Edieth because of you."

"Because of the Coalition."

"You gave the orders!"

"Actually, I never gave the order to attack, only permission to do so. Bruce Higgins gave the attack order, and I killed him soon afterwards. So your welcome."

Hennah stared at him for a long moment. "Is all of this a game to you? Do you feel anything at all when people die because of you?"

Kylen took several deep breaths before responding. "The Coalition forged me to be exactly what I am. A tool hardened through fire. Someone has to lead. That is my job, and I cannot afford the luxury of emotions. You can hate me for what I am. Before this war is over, most in the galaxy will. I have accepted my role long ago. I gave you the chance twelve years ago to change that, but you refused."

"Don't do that. You cannot blame me for your decisions. You could have refused to obey the Coalition."

"Then I would be dead and another chosen in my place. This war was destined to take place. The Coalition is vast, with members on every planet where there is a large human population. There are many voices with different views inside our organization. Over the centuries it was those who spoke the loudest that swayed the others. The zealots eventually won. I am their spokesman to the galaxy."

"Then just stop doing what they say. You are the Emperor."

"Hennah, they assassinated Emperor Duyagni. They have no qualms doing so to me if I fail to complete their agenda. Then they will try to control my wife. And

I can promise you they will quickly loss patience with Abarrane who will not bend to them. Her limit was marrying me, and she has despised me for it ever since. They will kill her, leaving my young daughter in their care. You think wiping out the ediethcans is horrible? The zealots are capable of doing far worst in my child's name. I force a balance on them, pulling them back from their darkest whims. Without me, their reckless decisions will destroy the Empire, leaving most of the galaxy in ruins. You may see me as a monster, but I am trying to help by lessening the collateral damage."

Hennah stared at a painting on the wall commemorating the birth of the Empire. It showed the first Emperor and several edietheans sitting under a tall tree, signing a parchment. Surrounding them in the forest clearing were their soldiers, celebrating the alliance. "There should be peace and not war between all species."

"Agreed. If your husband would join me, I can soon restore order."

"But you would still kill the edietheans?"

"Yes, I cannot prevent that. Their High Council is guilty of many crimes which they have covered up for thousands of years. Surely, you are aware of some of it, like enslaving the lower castes."

"You don't wipe out a whole species because a few are committing crimes."

"There are tens of thousands in the uppercastes who are guilty. Bringing them to justice when they control the whole society is difficult. Many Collation members only wanted to target them, but in the end, the zealots won out."

Hennah heard the suite's door open. A moment later, Abarrane walked into the room. Behind her followed an elder lady carrying several bags.

The empress fixed cold eyes on Hennah. "Is this what you were hiding last night?"

Kylen stood up, his body rigid. "I hid nothing, only saying I would introduce you when she awoke. Hennah, this is my wife Abarrane. Abarrane, this is my new concubine, Hennah."

For a long moment neither woman spoke. Finally Abarrane icily said, "Kylen, you moved up in the universe. Usually your playthings are electronic."

Hennah sputtered, "I am not his concubine. I am married."

"So you are having a fling with my husband?" Contempt was in Abarrane's voice.

"No, he kidnapped me. I want to return to my own husband."

Abarrane studied Hennah's pale face then turned condemning eyes on Kylen. "This is a new low even for you. I never thought you capable of taking an unwilling woman."

"Hennah will be well-treated. Her husband is a Five, and unless he allies with me, she will soon be a widow."

The empress looked back at Hennah, the coldness in her eyes replaced with pity. "Enjoy your stay. We women are but playthings in imperial politics. Now I will see to my child. I have new toys for her that do not relate to electronics or politics."

Chapter Forty

In broad daylight the massive diamond shape dome of the palace seemed less impressive. *Just another glass roof,* thought Joseph, looking through a high hotel window. Behind him Miles and his daughters were strapping on weapons hidden under clothing. There had been no lack of volunteers who wanted to come, but Joseph kept the strike force small. Better for getting in and out.

Joseph had been uncertain where Hennah was being kept. Diamond was one of the top possibilities, but there were half a dozen key military bases that would have served just as well. Then Kylen had sent his egotist message. Over the centuries, Joseph had been in that office several times where the video was shot. Thinking now about how Kylen had gazed at Hennah in the video made Joseph's heart race in rage. Only once before had he known such anger—the day he learned that Lashana had broken her vows to him by marrying Seth Lanneret. At that time, he would have killed Seth, despite the man had been innocent of wrong doing. Seth never knew his bride had promised herself to another.

This time I am justified. Kylen is not innocent.

There was a knock, and Zara opened the door. Todd and his siren wife walked in. Todd was dressed casually but Dyjuna wore a see-through veil over a flowery layered dress. Her exotic, striking looks and curvy body drew looks wherever she went.

Todd said, "My wife is second-guessing this, sir."

Dyjuna pulled the veil off her head and spoke in a singsong voice. "The Emperor has been kind to us. He is building a homeland for my wandering clan sisters. Must you kill him?"

Joseph glanced at Todd. The C2 was loyal to Essence, but he also cared deeply about his wife. Every few years they traveled back to Yunikinniah with a squad of quintessences who married eager sirens wanting adventure away from their primitive homeworld. As Dyjuna was the first to leave their world, she was seen as the group's leader. She was also vital for Joseph's mission to succeed today.

"I understand your loyalty to your clan sisters. You must remember that the Emperor has ordered a genocide and will order more in the future. He must be stopped. He also has my wife."

"But to kill him? He is generous, at least to us."

Todd took Dyjuna's hands. "His wife has been kidnapped. If anyone took you, I would stop at nothing to save you. We must help him."

Reluctantly, the siren nodded. "It will end all our plans, our dreams."

"We will make new dreams."

Dyjuna looked towards Joseph. "You promise we will be safe? Our families will not be hunted?"

"I promise to give you time to rejoin your families. By the time the investigation of his death occurs, you will be off planet. Essence will put out a public statement of my involvement so attention will not be directed your way."

The frown did not leave Dyjuna's face, but she nodded.

Joseph hid a knife under his jacket. As it was autumn on this planet, the quintessences were using that to their advantage to conceal weapons under long clothing. Ready, they walked into the hallway. Several sirens were rounding up children who were leaving for the spaceport.

Mirja glanced at her mother then boldly walked up to Joseph. "Your plan is endangering us, Five." Unlike her mother Dyjuna, Mirja talked in a normal voice. She was the first natural child fathered by a quintessence. While she had her mother's beautiful looks, she had grown up in an urban culture and dressed in popular fashions for adolescents. At thirteen, she was only two years from adulthood.

"Your parents will be safe."

"They better. We are giving up a lot because of you."

"Mirja," reprimanded Todd, "That is no way to talk to a Five."

Joseph looked soberly at the girl. "At the hospital on the day you were born, I kissed my future wife for the first time while your clan sisters celebrated your birth. I care about the wellbeing of your clan."

Mirja relaxed somewhat. "I hope you get your wife back." As she walked away, she still shot Joseph a warning that he better keep his promise.

Other sirens and their spouses left hotel rooms. A fourth of the group headed to the spaceport with the younglings. The rest traveled with Joseph and his comrades across the street to the palace. The troop was scheduled to give a performance in a few days and had been practicing daily. They soon arrived at a side entrance to the palace.

Dyjuna smiled at the guard on duty and placed her hand on a pad. It turned green. "Will your kids be at our performance?"

The man entered data into an e-tablet. "Of course. They still have not stopped talking about your last concert. My wife will be taking off work to come this time."

"Good, I would like to meet her afterwards."

While Dyjuna chatted with the guard, sirens and quintessences walked through the gate. Most of them went through the metal detector. Joseph and Todd, carrying a heavy crate of props, skipped the detector. Zara and Alexa wore hooded cloaks to shadow their faces. They held in front of themselves large boxes that had artificial plants sticking out in all directions. Miles carried a large plastic tree. The guard took no notice as they passed.

Joseph walked with the group deep into the palace, passing more guards and checkpoints. Those on duty were friendly with the sirens. A senator stopped Todd to ask when the next performance would take place. Two finely dressed women burst into song when they spotted the sirens. Several sirens paused to sing with the beaming ladies.

When they reached the theater, several of the husbands began unpacking props and moving scenery around on the stage. The sirens put on costumes making themselves look like forest spirits. Joseph positioned himself behind the stage curtains where he could look out at the empty seats. Two entrances on the bottom floor. Two more to the balcony rows.

The sirens ran through several numbers. Dyjuna paused the group often to address mistakes. She appeared calm except for constantly glancing at the doors. As time crawled on, Joseph looked at his e-band for the hundredth time. There was no certainty that Kylen would come today. Dyjuna had sent him a personal invitation last night. If Kylen did not show, then Joseph, along with Miles and his daughters, would try to work their way into the underground bunker where security would be much tighter.

Movement in the back caught Joseph's attention. Abarrane and Suson walked in. Behind them came Kylen arm-in-arm with Hennah. Joseph's body immediately tensed. Two guards stood beside the main entrances. Another four guards appeared on the balcony where they could observe the whole room.

Joseph focused on Hennah, noting her slight frown when Kylen touched her shoulder as she took a seat beside him. She looked healthy. No starvation or physical abuse. He studied her face. Tense and worry. But not fear. He wanted to go to her immediately but the guards needed to be dealt with first.

He pulled back from the curtain and hand signaled directions to his daughters and Miles. They nodded. All three quietly left through backstage doors.

The sirens finished the song they were preforming. Dyjuna gave a polite bow to the arrivals. "Good afternoon, Emperor, Empress, and lady friends. I thank you for coming. Your insight has been very helpful in the past as we do not always know which songs will be liked by your culture. We are trying a few numbers which rely on costumes more than we usually do. Empress suggested more drama last time."

From the front row, Abarrane said, "Yes, along with a story which connects all your pieces. Your songs are beautiful, but it helps to have them relate to each other instead of being random."

"We will show you a few and see what you think."

Sirens in tree spirit costumes walked onto the stage. They began humming. Their voices grew louder, stronger. Dressed in all black, two quintessences with exaggerated monster masks covering their faces slowly moved among the spirits. A siren dressed as a young girl sung sadly as she moved through the forests of spirits. Whenever one of the masked quintessences neared her, she acted frightened. The tree spirts' voices increased in tempo, adding to the suspense.

Joseph kept watch from behind the curtain. Abarrane observed the scene with a critical eye, intently studying the performers. While Kylen watched the actors, he moved a hand to touch Hennah's fingers. She pulled her hand back and placed it in her lap while keeping her eyes on the stage. Joseph felt a rush of rage. *Keep focused,* he reminded himself.

Joseph looked at the guards. Their attention was on the performance. *Good, keep looking this direction.*

The song ended and another started, this one with a fast beat. The girl actor had found her way home. Sirens pretending to be her mom and aunts swirled around her in a happy dance, their feet pounding the stage in rhythm.

The thumping covered up sounds of Miles attacking the guards near one of the main entrances. Miles quickly took out the first one by grabbing him from behind and using the epulo to put him into a deep sleep. The second guard was so entranced by the sirens that he was slow in noticing the attack. By the time he had his gun pulled, Miles was almost to him. The guard tried to shoot, but Miles kicked the gun from his hand then twirled around the man, biting him from behind. Miles pulled both guards' bodies out of view of the main entrances, hiding them in the last row of seats.

Zara and Alexa were just as busy. Each entered the theater through a different balcony entrance. The sirens poured their telepathic skills into the fast-pace music, their rhythmic melody captivating the guards. Zara and Alexa took out the guards quickly and quietly, biting each from behind while they watched the performance.

The song ended. Dyjuna stepped out onto the stage. "We have one more unique one for you to see then we discuss. This one we wanted to pull lovers on stage. May we?" She beckoned to Kylen.

The monarch smiled. "This should be fun." He stood and held out a hand to Hennah. She frowned, looking towards Abarrane for help, but the empress refused to look in her direction. Reluctantly Hennah stood. She refused Kylen's hand but followed him onto the stage.

"Stand here." Dyjuna directed them to the center of the stage.

Sirens begun a love ballad as they danced in a large circle around the couple. As the music built, Kylen reached out and took Hennah's hand. Her body stiffen, and she looked away towards backstage. In the deep shadows cast by the curtains, she spotted a C5, the only one in the group. Todd and his birthmates where C2's. Another squad of husbands were C1's.

Hennah stared, her heart quickening. Silently, she mouthed her husband's name. Joseph nodded.

A small gasp escaped her, and she took a step towards him before freezing. Kylen looked at her, the relaxed smile on his face fading. He studied her expression then followed her line of sight back to Joseph. Kylen's eyes hardened.

The song ended. The sirens and their husbands vanished behind stage curtains. Abarrane gave a brief clap of approval. "You have outdone yourself this time."

Joseph stepped out onto the stage, locking eyes with Kylen. "You have something that is mine."

"So good to finally meet you in person, Joseph. I have been wanting to speak with you."

"So have I."

Hennah tried to move to her husband, but Kylen tightened his grip on her hand. From the front row, Abarrane and Suson realized what was going on. Both stood, looking about for guards but none were to be found. From her purse, Suson pulled out a knife.

"No need to threaten our guest," said Kylen, not taking his eyes off Joseph. "We have an alliance to discuss."

"There will be no compromise. I will take my wife and your life."

"Ah, you rhymed. You should try singing that line. You have been spending time with my sirens, I see. A pity they sided with you. I have really enjoyed their singing."

"This is between you and me. No one else needs to be hurt."

"Agreed. Do not touch my family, and I will not touch the sirens. Now about this alliance. I have already stated my terms."

"Tell them to me again, in detail." Joseph wanted to give Dyjuna's group enough time to leave the palace. As soon as an assassination was discovered, the palace would go into shutdown.

As Kylen talked, Abarrane and Suson began slowly walking backwards towards the exit. Miles had remained hidden in the last row, but now he rose and moved to block their path. They could not be allowed to sound the alarm. Suson, with knife out, turned to confront Miles. Abarrane dashed towards the other exit. Reacting quickly, Zara leaped off the balcony above and landed on her feet. She pulled out

341

her own knife. Abarrane backed towards Suson. Both ladies were trapped between the armed quintessences.

Kylen had stopped talking the moment he saw his wife run. For the first time, he looked worried. "You said you would not harm my wife."

"I will not."

"The terms include no one else hurting her."

"I will not promise that. You still have my wife."

Kylen looked at Hennah, her body taut, her hands shaking slightly. "I have never threatened harm to her. I do realize that the moment I let her go, you plan to kill me."

"Yes."

Kylen gave an ironic laugh. "Are all leeches this polite when they kill?"

"Usually there is less talking. I would like my wife back now."

"Killing me will be a big mistake on your part. My assassination will end any attempts of peace between our factions and trigger the galactic-level war we both wish to avoid."

"You should have thought about that before kidnapping my wife."

"Joseph, he is right," said Hennah. "Can we just leave him?"

A suddenly movement caused Kylen to turn. Alexa had jumped off the balcony and began marching towards the stage, karambit blade in hand. Kylen watched her for a moment then looked towards Zara. Puzzlement crossed his face. When Alexa walked onto the stage, Kylen took a step towards her, studying her face intensely.

"Hi, Mamma," said the warrior with hair of flames. "How are you?"

"Well." Hennah's voice was strained.

Alexa turned her fierce eyes towards the monarch. "Take your hand off my mother or I will take your hand off you."

Kylen did not react to the threat. Instead, he gave Hennah a slight bow. "Congratulations. Your creations are well-designed. I knew you were created for something special. This I would never have guessed." Kylen looked towards Joseph. "Now that you have females, nationhood is more important than ever to you. One of the points written by a critic long ago was that your species was synthetic, unable to produce naturally. Now that you can, it will be much easier getting your nationhood accepted by the Galactic Senate."

"We cannot accept the price you ask."

Alexa cut in. "I grow tired of all this talk." Her body was taut, ready for action.

Her father met her eyes, giving a slight nod. Alexa smiled and charged forward, flipping the blade outward. Kylen reacted by stepping sideways, partly in front of Hennah. Joseph had been waiting for this distraction. He rushed forward, grabbing Kylen from behind. Alexa pulled her mother safely away as Joseph bit the monarch.

Joseph could have killed Kylen immediately, but his wrath was so great he now sought revenge. He poured his own emotions of rage, contempt, and helplessness into the monarch. When he regained a bit of self-control, he formed a mental image and allowed Kylen's consciousness to appear in a flat, endless plain. Only a few stars were visible in the night sky.

Kylen looked about in confusion. "This cannot be real. Is this death?"

"Not quite yet." Joseph appeared a few yards away. "You will not live through this experience. I am inside your mind, seeing every thought as they form, every emotion you feel."

Briefly Kylen felt panic, but he forced himself to calm down, focusing on logic. "If we are talking, then there is yet hope that we can form an alliance."

"You kidnap my wife and think I wish to join you?"

"It was not personal. She did not love you the last time I was with her. I believed I was rescuing her from a slave master."

Anger filled Joseph and he wielded it like a weapon, throwing it at Kylen. He gathered memories of pain he had felt over the centuries and forced Kylen to experience each one. Burning, flesh ripped by bullets, broken bones, deep gashes. Falling, falling until hitting the ground. A fiery explosion ripping the body, searing the lungs. As waves of pain whipped through Kylen, he screamed. Dimly, Joseph was aware that in the real world on the stage, the Emperor also screamed, his body contorting.

Joseph allowed the memories to fade. He was aware he was going too far. During training, he had repeatedly told young quintessences that the epulo should never be used to torture the host, yet here he was doing so. *You must calm yourself. Hennah is safe now.*

Kylen lay in a fetal positon on the ground under the endless night sky. Slowly he sat up and turned angry eyes at Joseph. "I do not understand how she can claim to now love you. You are nothing but a beast, a brute soldier."

"What do you know of love?"

Joseph probed Kylen's thoughts, first seeking his treatment of Hennah. He had tried to flirt with her, hoping she would return the affection he felt for her. Joseph looked deeper. Kylen had kidnaped Hennah, believing he was freeing her from cruel slave masters. A face of Amy appeared. Kylen cared for her, seeing her as a sister. He felt warmth for his wife and child, a protectiveness, yet the relationship with Abarrane was complicated. The empress spurned his attempts of friendship, accusing him of being behind Coalition plots to harm her family. Kylen returned her coldness with his own contempt, hiding his hurt and loneness. Yet he had a secret contingency plan to protect her and the child in case Diamond ever faced siege. Already he had in place money, new IDs, and a fast ship that would take them and Hennah far away from hot combat zones. As his face would be too well-known, he would stay behind to face the enemy.

This was what Joseph had not wanted to see—Kylen as human, faulty but with redeemable traits. Over the centuries, Joseph had killed many. In war deaths came quickly. Others he had condemned at trials. Sometimes it was he who probed their thoughts, at times one of his brothers. Never had he wanted to kill, but it was necessary at times. Except now. He desired very much to kill Kylen.

The monarch stood and looked defiantly at Joseph. "No wonder you will not accept my offer. Animals act on basic instincts, unable to plan long term. You destroy me, you destroy the galaxy."

"You know little about predators. We plan, we strategize. We can be patient for months, even years. When we strike, we know exactly what we are doing."

"You sound like the Coalition."

"We are nothing like you. We defend the weak, not commit genocides. You are a shame to your office. The Emperor is supposed to fairly represent all sentients who are a part of his government. I have known many Emperors. Some I highly respected. Some I felt contempt for, but still I respected their position. You are the first that has completely dishonored the title. I find you unfit to complete your duties and condemn you to death."

"Just like that. Who are you to judge me, the Emperor? How would you even begin to understand my responsibilities? I am the force which restrains the Coalition from doing their worst. Kill me and you will unleash a monster you cannot control."

"Who am I? I will show you."

Joseph allowed images of his other selves to appear around him. He now stood before Kylen looking like a muscular Middle Eastern human. To his right was Ariyo who appeared as a slim, athletic Asian man. Ace was of Native American lineage with piercing eyes. Alec shared the same identical body as Alexander but appeared older. Joseph was a burly Caucasian.

Perplexed, Kylen looked at the five men in front of him. "What is this?"

"I am Alexander, first born of all quintessences. Known for my long term strategic planning. I am one of the writers of our Code and husband to Layla Rangan."

"I am Ariyo. Emotional and sometimes hasty. I also killed more than any of my other selves. I knew deeply both love and hate, marrying Yashana after she betrayed me."

"I am Ace. Wise and benevolent. I ended decades old wars, turning enemies into comrades."

"I am Alec. Master manipulator. Willing to break the Purity Law to save my species. From my planning Hennah was born."

"I am Joseph. Willing to stand up against those in authority when it is clear they are in the wrong. I take great offense to any who tries to seduce my wife."

All five men spoke at once. "We five are part of the bigger Five. The original Five who are the guardians of our species. We were there in the beginning. We are still here. And we will be here, long after you child and grandchildren have died."

Kylen stood before the quintessences, his mind reeling. "You are more than what you seem. You are far, far older than I. How is this possible?"

"The how I will not tell you. Only know I have the experience to judge you, Emperor."

Even as Joseph spoke the words, he remembered what it was like to be a peacemaker. As Ace, he had walked into many volatile situations, looking for common ground among enemies. With great patience, he used understanding as a tool to forge friendships. Now he faced Kylen with the intent to kill him after showing off. Was he truly being fair? Kylen grew up with no parents, the Coalition feeding him on propaganda from infancy. There was so much life experience Kylen had missed while growing up.

"I am about to try an experiment with you. It may make no difference, but it might change everything."

Instantly Kylen was wary. "What experiment?"

"I personally knew Richard Cambridge and Ethan Covey. Both were good men I respected. I am going to allow you to experience their lives."

Joseph pulled the many memories he had of meeting Richard who had developed New Hope at the same time Essence was being built next door. Kylen saw a man with his same face smiling as he greeted construction workers, asking their opinions about where the new school should be built. He walked beside Layla as the first beams were placed in what would become Richton Tower. Beside them was a chirpy Diane Richton—who shared Amy's face—bragging about what the tower would someday look like. Richard stood in front of a cheering crowd as he gave his inauguration speech for becoming mayor. Beside him was his beautiful wife Alana. Their kids cheered from the front row.

More images of Richard's life swirled by. Joseph had visited his home several times with Layla. He had listened to every inauguration speech Richard made when he won elections. Richard grew older but kept busy. Always he seemed a beloved leader, reaching out to his town's citizens, no matter their jobs. His software company won prestigious awards. While he had a large, talented group working for him, he continued to code until the last weeks of his life when he died at one hundred and ten, surrendered by children and grandchildren.

Richard's memories where shown through Joseph's eyes of what he had seen himself. A different approach was used with Ethen. As a youth, Ethen had had a crush on Yashana. Decades later when she had moved back to Essence, she and Ethen would meet up from time to time. Just to be certain that Ethen's intentions stayed honorable, Joseph had occasionally probed his mind. He now shared Ethen's personal memories with Kylen.

A happy childhood with supportive parents. Writing his first program when he was five. Hacking into a local network when seven. His mother slowly becoming sicker and sicker. Intense grief at his mother's funeral. Turning down attending Luncaster University because he was worried about his father. Using silly hacks to cheer up his father. Finally heading to Luncaster where he became best friends with Yashana and Gauge. Adventures, an arrest, more hacking. Heartbreak when Yashana choose Ariyo over him. Graduation. First job. Attempts at dating. Falling in love. Meeting her grandmother. Recoding his robotic dog to help the invalid grandmother. Seeing the elderly woman smile the first time the dog brought her a plate of food. Marriage. Starting a robotics company. Laugher of children. Eventually winning awards. Lots more hacking—but getting paid for it by top companies to evaluate their security. A happy life. A productive life.

When the memories stopped, Kylen dropped to his knees, breathing hard. The emotions of the memories raw and overpowering. Joseph knew Kylen's thoughts as they came to him. For the first time, Kylen felt deep love for family, of comradeship with others. The joys of successes, of being praised by others for work he did himself, of support from a wife when dealing with failures. Friendships given in trust.

"Your life could had been similar to theirs," said Joseph, "but the Coalition never gave you the opportunity. It is not too late to change the path you are on."

Kylen slowly stood. "You said you were going to kill me."

"That depends on what you decide in the next few moments. I believe you deserve a second chance. My brothers and I will never agree to an alliance with the Coalition, but we can agree on one with you. The one condition being you must forsake the Coalition."

"Even if I wanted to, that is impossible. They control much. Even my guards."

"Within hours I can have two thousand quintessences here. They can weed out every employee in the palace who belongs to the Coalition. Serve as your personal body guards. They will follow you loyally as long as you do not ask them to break our Code. Change will not be easy. You will have to earn the edietheans' trust back, and that will be challenging. You will need to be Emperor to all sentients, not just humans. That is the deal I can offer you."

Kylen was quiet for a long moment, reflecting. "You will know if I lie to you."

"Yes."

"If I do not agree with you proposal, you will kill me."

"Yes."

"Then logically I must agree."

"You could agree then try to betray us later. There is a high chance we will figure out your plans before that happens and still kill you."

Kylen gave a brief laugh. "You claim I have a choice but I do not feel like it."

"I am providing you with the opportunity to change your fate. You have felt trapped by the Coalition your whole life. I offer you freedom from them. Other than the few conditions I mentioned, you are free to do as you please. It is your life. I have seen good in you. Wanting to give the sirens a homeland. Protecting your wife though she despises you. Wanting to give your daughter the right to rule though it goes against tradition. You want others to admire you for your own achievements. For gifts like the Harmony Complex. You want history to remember you as a benevolent ruler. It is not too late to rewrite what historians will say about you."

"I stand naked before you, nothing hidden from your sight." Kylen felt both awe and trepidation. "Alright. I agree to your terms."

Joseph broke contact and stepped back. Kylen blinked several times, getting his bearings.

"You left him alive," said Alexa, disappointed.

"The plan has changed," replied her father.

Chapter Forty-One

Hennah stared as Kylen twisting in pain, his body only remained standing because Joseph held him so tightly. Never has she seen an execution with her own eyes. Over the years she had been bitten with the epulo many times, but it was painless except the brief prick at the beginning.

"Is it supposed to be like this?" she asked her daughter.

Alexa frowned. "No, Papa is torturing him. Which is forbidden."

Kylen's screams became louder. Nervously Hennah looked towards Abarrane who stared at her contorting husband. Zara shifted her position slightly. Her knife out in warning. Suson stood back to back with the empress, her eyes shifting back and forth from Miles to Zara.

The screams abruptly stopped. Then nothing happened for a very long time. They must be talking, thought Hennah. *If Joseph didn't kill him immediately, maybe there is hope he will change his mind.*

It had been nearly two weeks since Hennah had been kidnapped. During that time, she had many conversations with Kylen. They usually avoided speaking about politics. Instead, Kylen showed off his gadgets he had been working on, including an organic computer he was especially proud of. They played a video game he was in the process of designing for his daughter. What she soon realized was that Kylen really did want a friend who he could share things he liked with. When he was off duty from playing politician, he was relaxed, funny, with a wide variety of interests in many things. They talked for hours about random things. Hennah ignored his occasional flirtatious remarks, finding that her fake friendship was becoming genuine. What was hard for her to reconcile was that this nerd who beamed when discussing gaming theory was the same who so casually chatted with Coalition members about slaughtering millions.

Suddenly Joseph broke contact and stepped back. Dazed, Kylen blinked, wobbling slightly as he slowly got his bearings.

"You left him alive," said Alexa, disappointed. Knife in hand, she took a step forward.

"The plan has changed," said Joseph. "The Emperor and I have formed an alliance."

"Papa, he cannot be trusted."

Turning to Joseph, Kylen raised his hands, touching his arms together while spreading out his fingers to create the symbol for the tree of Basanti. Joseph returned the gesture.

Hennah smiled. Seeing her daughter's puzzled look, she explained. "The first Emperor of Basanti gave this gesture after signing the alliance with the edietheans. The gesture is only given by an emperor to those he considers his equal."

"We need to move to a more secure location," said Joseph.

"Our suite will do," said Kylen. "You and that other male should borrow costumes here. Cover your heads. I cannot be seen walking with leeches...quintessences." He walked off the stage towards his wife.

Joseph grabbed two cloaks, putting one on. Hennah and Alexa followed Joseph towards the main entrance. Joseph tossed Miles the other cloak.

As Kylen neared his wife, Suson positioned herself to protect the empress, her knife clutched tightly. Over her guardian's shoulder, Abarrane said, "I do not understand. One moment he was killing you. Now you are friends?"

Kylen glanced back at Joseph. "There are somethings I cannot explain to you."

"I thought the leeches would never bow to the Coalition. How did you change his mind while he was trying to kill you?"

Joseph said, "My alliance is with the royal family, not with the Coalition. You are part of this treaty, Your Highness. I know you have hated the Coalition from childhood. We can work together to end their reign."

"How do you know what I think?" Abarrane looked between Kylen and Joseph, pondering what secret was being shared between them.

"You and I fight on the same side now, along with your husband. Perhaps I can explain more to you later, but we need to move to a better location."

Reluctantly Abarrane nodded, and Suson put away her knife. The group walked out of the theater, the royal couple leading. They walked down gilded corridors, passing statues and portraits. Guards standing at attention glanced at them but said nothing. Hennah walked arm-in-arm with her husband, trying to appear this was a normal stroll. She had thought a rescue meant leaving the palace, not staying. An elevator took them deep underground.

Once they were in the royal suite, the quintessences took off their cloaks. Abarrane glared at the intruders in her home but remained silent.

Joseph said, "Can you get me a secure outside line?"

"Sure," said Kylen, leading the group to his study which had half a dozen computers around the room, along with a huge digital desk. Kylen woke an e-tablet. After tapping in a long password, he handed it to Joseph. "Untraceable. Unhackable. Say anything you like."

"The password to remove the viruses? We would like to use our normal communication channels."

Kylen grinned. "Like my presents to Essence? Wrote the coding years ago but had no reason to use it—until now."

"We would appreciate their removal." Joseph said politely, but sternly.

"The password is easy. Tell your programmers to use the first one thousand digits of pi. That will deactivate them all. When can you get your troops here?"

"Four hours." Joseph begin tapping a message to Essence.

"You had a ship that close?"

"Battlecruiser. Thanks for the loan. It was backup in case I needed it."

"So if your strike force did not work, you were going to send a full army into my palace? Knowing we have strong planetary defense? At least half your shuttles would not had made it to the ground."

Joseph locked eyes with the monarch. "I would do whatever was necessary to get my wife back."

For a moment Kylen said nothing. Then he gave a light smile. "Sorry about that misunderstanding. At least it has worked out well for both of us, after all."

As the two men continued to plan, Zara and Alexa took up guard duty in the hallway. Suson and Miles wandered about, eyes alert for danger. Abarrane left to check on her daughter. When she returned, she sat beside Hennah on a coach, watching the Five and the Emperor at the digital table studying a hologram 3D map of the palace.

Abarrane frowned. "I never thought I would see today. Kylen really is breaking away from the Coalition."

"My husband believes so."

"I still do not understand why your husband did not kill mine. Kylen was helpless. Then your husband just let him go. Suddenly they are buddies. It was like they were talking to each other during that bite." Abarrane studied Hennah's face, looking for an answer.

"There are things we do not tell outsiders."

"But I am right. Leeches can communicate through the bite."

"It would be best if you stopped calling them leeches—at least to their faces. It's considered offensive."

"I apologize. I am...grateful that my husband's life was spared."

Hennah decided to offer a token of friendship. "I know being married to Kylen has not been easy. Sorry that he was giving me so much attention lately."

"You do not need to apology for his behavior. We have never gotten along well. I have loathed him for being the Coalition's lapdog. It is a miracle we managed to have a child at all."

"Maybe when all this is over, you might could give him a second chance. He is not so bad, well, besides the kidnaping."

Abarrane gave a bitter laugh. "Oh, he had many faults. Like turning this once beautiful study into a lab for his gadgets. And his bedroom is even worst. Have you seen that hideous computer that is actually alive? If I did not stop him, he would turn this entire suite into a workshop."

Imagining piles of scrape metal beside fancy statures caused Hennah to laugh. Abarrane grinned then suddenly let out a loud chuckle. The men stopped in the middle of their discussion to look at the giggling ladies.

"Um, I think that is a good sign," said Kylen.

"Yes, that enemies can become friends," said Joseph. "Now about the security feed, can we monitor all cameras from here?"

"Of course. I will show you how to operate it. Rewrote a lot of the palace software myself to make our system more effective."

Kylen moved to a table where he had six monitors hooked up to one computer. He showed Joseph, Alexa, and Zara how to maneuver between the many cameras by pulling up the theater and zooming in on the sleeping guards.

"How long will they stay under?"

Zara said, "Perhaps a few hours if there are no loud sounds near them. We put them into heavy sleep."

Hennah sat on the couch, talking with Abarrane or listening to the tactical debates of others. She knew Joseph had a lot of experience in these type of situations, but still she worried. They were planning to round up all Coalition officials in the palace and arrest those living in nearby apartments in the city. Every worker at the palace would be probed. Any that might be dangerous would need to be dealt with. Kylen was certain that many of palace guards would have be replace permanently by quintessences.

With the battlecruiser half an hour away, Hennah decided she needed a few minutes alone with her husband. While he was in the middle of talking with Kylen, she walked up to him and brushed his arm. When he glanced at her, she gave him a look and walked away. Without stopping, she walked out of the room and headed to her bedroom. Joseph excused himself and followed after her.

The moment they were alone, she embraced him in a tight hug. For a long moment they stood with arms around each other.

"I was so afraid you were going to kill him."

Joseph stroked her face gently. "I wanted to. On the trip here I planned a hundred ways to do so."

"But you didn't."

"No. I saw good in him. And he had not bedded you. If he had, I would not have spared his life."

Hennah smiled and tilted her head. Joseph kissed her. The contact ignited a fire. The kissing became passionate. Soon they tumbled onto the bed, aware of only each other.

Knocking stole their attention. Alexa yelled through the door, "In ten minutes *Warhound* will be in orbit."

Joseph pulled away from Hennah. "You and Abarrane need to stay here where you will be safe."

"Be careful." Hennah gave her husband a final deep kiss before they left the bedroom.

Miles, Zara, and Alexa were standing at attention, ready for orders.

"You three will stay here and guard the royal family," Joseph said.

"Papa, we are ready for combat," Alexa protested.

Joseph fixed her with a stern glare. "Soldier, I know you are. That is why I want you here guarding the royal family and your mother. This is a Level Ten mission and they are vital. Do not let me down."

"Yes, sir."

Standing by the door, Kylen flashed a confident smile. "Time to lead a coup to take over my own palace. How many monarchs have done that?"

"A few," said Joseph putting on one of the cloaks. Then he walked out the suite with Kylen.

"Level Ten." Alexa beamed at her sister. "We bet our birthmates."

"He also wants to protect our identity. The other quintessences do not know we exist."

"Do you have to be a buzzkill? I want to enjoy this moment. And I am tired of hiding what I am. It would be nice to finally be able to walk as equals among our own kind."

The sisters used the cameras to follow their father and Kylen as they walked across the palace with half a dozen guards following them. Hennah, Abarrane, and Suson stood near, watching the monitors. Miles used a different computer to keep watch on the main hallway right outside the suite.

Abarrane said, "Normally my nanny goes home about this time, but I asked her to work overtime. I do not want her out in the hallways while this is happening."

"Good idea," said Hennah.

"By the way," said Alexa, adjusting a screen, "your nanny passed my questioning."

"Did you bite my nanny?" horror filled Abarrane.

"We have to test everyone. Your nanny is a Coalition member but not a zealot. She loves kids and is proud to be caring for a princess. I think you can keep her. She does steal chocolate from your private cache sometimes. I was tempted to grab a piece myself."

Abarrane gave Alexa a long stare but said nothing.

"Don't worry. I'm not a thief. Your gourmet chocolate is safe."

Reaching the far side of the palace, Kylen and Joseph stepped outside to the large launchpads. Nearby was a hanger holding private craft for the royal family.

"Is the ship in orbit?" came Joseph's voice through a hidden comlink he wore in his ear.

"Yes," said Zara. "Kylen's trick worked. They think it is one of theirs. *Warhound* is already launching shuttles. Should be landing in a few minutes."

"Technically *Warhound* is one of my ships," said Kylen. "You only have it on loan."

Joseph replied, "I am thinking about keeping it. You owe me."

"I will take your request into consideration when this is over with."

Two shuttles flew over the palace and landed on the pads. As quintessence infantry, dressed in full battle gear, began to unload, the guards around Kylen became uneasy.

Kylen turned to his guards. "Men, I am conducting a training exercise. You will put down your weapons and follow these soldiers' directions."

Hennah watched tensely. The guards sensed something was wrong. They looked towards Joseph whose head was covered by the cloak. Most likely they were trying to figure out if the stranger was somehow controlling the Emperor.

"That is an order," barked Kylen.

Reluctantly, the guards put down their guns and backed up. Several quintessences stepped forward and picked up the weapons. Joseph pulled off his hood and begin giving the two units directions. The shuttles lifted into the air. Almost as soon as they were out of sight, two more approached for landing. Another two hundred quintessences marched out.

"Did you remember to turn off palace communications?" said Kylen through the link.

"Yes," said Zara.

"Patch me in for a moment." Kylen waited until she gave him the go-ahead. "This is Emperor Kylen. We are currently practicing drills. You will see an increase number of soldiers in the hallways. Please do not be alarmed. Follow the directions given to you by them."

There were now six units on the ground. Alexa sent palace blueprints to their e-bands, each squad with different areas marked in red for them to target. Joseph signaled, and the units begin marching into the palace. Two squads were assigned to watch the guards that had surrendered. Joseph and Kylen remained by the landing pads as shuttles brought more soldiers.

Using the cameras, Alexa and Zara monitored the progress of squads, reporting back to their father information. The units quickly spread out across the upper levels of the huge palace. Guards were confused, but most complied with Kylen's directions which were broadcasted every five minutes. A few guards panicked and fired weapons, but they were quickly taken out. Various guests, workers, and palace residents scurried out of the way of the marching soldiers. Guards were rounded up and sent to a holding area.

The last of the two thousands infantry unloaded. Now came the difficult part. Dealing with Coalition officials. Joseph sent three companies down into the bunker while sending half of the remaining units into the city to hunt down key officials. Many cabinet members had already become alarmed and hid in the bunker. Bypassing the elevators, squads marched down emergency stairs that Kylen had already overridden the security for.

Hennah watched nervously as squads searched room from room in the lower levels, ordering everyone they found to come with them. Cabinet members headed deeper down, with General McLowary leading them.

Alexa warned, "McLowary is heading to a weapons stash. Squad B12, head to your left to cut them off." She beamed at her sister. "This is actually fun being in the communications hub. Here I was thinking Quinn must be miserable. I think I will ask about doing his duty sometimes."

Zara said, "I do not think Quinn will turn over his job to you."

"It is worth a shot. Surely he misses being in the field more."

"He is in the field a lot—to keep you out of trouble."

Gun fire sounded in the distance. "That is on this level," said Abarrane, face pale.

Miles said, "You are safe, Highness. There is a squad of our men directly in front of your suite."

Hennah's nails bit into the flesh of her palms as she watched on the monitors guards having shootouts with soldiers. Dead bodies lying on the marble floors. Spooked maids trying to barricade themselves in the laundry room. Panicked kids being shoved into closets by frighten parents. War was terrifying.

The cabinet members became trapped in a series of connected offices as several squads approached from different directions. The general pulled out his pistol and pointed it at the soldiers. The cameras did not provide sound but Hennah could guess what was being said. Soldiers ordering everyone to the floor. The general waved his gun while ranting. Suddenly he pointed the muzzle at his own head and pulled the trigger. Blood and brain matter spattered against the wall. His body dropped to the floor.

Abarrane screamed and looked away from the monitors. She covered her mouth and ran out of the room. Hennah felt queasy herself and had to sit down for a moment until the room stopped spinning. Joseph had told her some of the things he had experienced as a soldier, but she had never actually seen it with her own eyes. How did bonded quintessences keep their sanity when working in such intense environments for fifty years?

Feeling a bit better, she went to find Abarrane. The empress sat on the bathroom floor, wiping her mouth with tissue.

Hennah sat down beside her. "My first time seeing something like this too. I grew up on a military base, surrounded by soldiers. Married one. Yet I never really understood what it was like to be them until now."

Abarrane tossed the tissue into the trash. "This is not my first time to see death. My mother was assassinated right in front of me with I was fourteen. My father was murdered in the same garden I have been in a thousand times. It used to be our one safe spot where we would go to get away from stress. But now I cannot even walk into the garden without wanting to break down into tears. I have lived my whole life in a gilded cage. The Coalition dictating who I would marry, who my best friends were supposed to me. What politically views I was supposed to support in public."

"My life was similar—though not as bad as yours. You, me, Kylen. All feeling trapped. It is a curse being a profectus. An illegal clone who must hide your face from cameras. Always fearful of being discovered by the public. But we are both free now."

Abarrane stood up. "You are just as surprising as your husband. You could be seeking revenge. Instead, you are befriending your kidnapper's wife."

"We need friends. I mean, I do have other friends, but they cannot understand what it is like to be us. We can support each other."

"Friends. I like that." Abarrane gave a small smile.

The last of the fighting ended. The soldiers shifted through the many captives. Most palace workers were sent home, some told to never return. Others were promised a normal workday tomorrow. Three guards involved in Emperor Duyagni's murder were arrested along with cabinet members still alive. Other top Coalition members were jailed. As prominent politicians in the city were arrested, the media began buzzing that something unusual was going on at the palace.

Shortly after midnight, Kylen made an official statement. Exhausted and emotional drained, Hennah sat on a sofa with Abarrane in the living room to watch the news release.

Kylen appeared in his office, looking composed. "Greetings, citizens. A few hours ago I withdrew my membership from the Coalition of Human Advancement. I disbanded my entire cabinet. Members of my new one will be chosen from qualified candidates from any sentient species. I retract an earlier statement I made accusing the Ediethean High Council of assassinating Emperor Duyagni. I was aware at the time I said the words that the Coalition was actually responsible for my father-in-law's murder. My family and I have basically been prisoners to the Coalition for many years. Today I successfully, with the help of quintessences, lead a coup against the Coalition. From now henceforth, no Coalition member will hold power in my regime.

"I offer deep consolations to the edietheans who have suffered greatly during this time. I cannot bring back those who have died. I can offer peace and aid. Also, I commend those governments who stood up to protected edietheans living on their planets. Some time back the Ediethean High Council sent a list of crimes they believed the Coalition was responsible for, but that list was ignored. I will open up a full investigation into every item on that list. I know healing will be difficult. I would like to offer my hand in friendship. Together, we can overcome hate."

Another hour passed before Kylen and Joseph returned to the suite. On a monitor, Hennah watched both men sitting in Kylen's office chatting, but she could hear no words. They had turned off their links just before the news release.

Hennah was half asleep on a sofa when they entered. She smiled at her husband, glad to see he was uninjured.

Joseph looked at his daughters and Miles still in alert mode. "You have done an excellent job. Now get some needed rest."

Zara nodded, and Alexa beamed.

Kylen said, "There is a lot for us to do tomorrow—today. I can gratefully say thanks for not assassinating me."

"Your welcome," said Alexa. "Just don't go kidnapping our mother again."

"That is a mistake I will never make again." Kylen moved towards his bedroom. As he neared his wife, he said in a quiet voice. "I apologize how I have treated you over the years. I should have been more understanding."

Abarrane studied him for a long moment. "I could have been…well…less harsh. I am proud of you for finally standing up to the Coalition."

Kylen gave a brief smile and turned towards his room. Abarrane reached out and took his hand, guiding him towards her bedroom.

When Hennah reached her own room, Joseph pulled her close, both needing the physical contact after the stressful separation. He stroked her chin then kissed her gently on the lips. Hennah smiled and drew him towards the bed.

"Shouldn't you be tired?" she teased between kisses. "Rescuing your wife, almost assassinating an emperor, and staging a coup."

"All in a day's work for a Five." Joseph pulled back the thick bedcovers.

"What were you talking about for the last hour?" Hennah tightly held her husband's hand as she pulled him down onto the silky sheets.

"He wanted marital advice."

"And what did you say?" Hennah wrapped her arms around his muscular body.

"Tip One was to never touch another's wife."

"Tip Two?"

"Always treat your wife like a queen."

"Excellent advice. What else?"

Joseph gave a faint smile. "Always, always let your wife drive when she asks."

Hennah rewarded him with a passionate kiss that lasted quite a while.

As Joseph begin taking off his shirt, he said, "When we head back to Essence, we will be taking my new battlecruiser."

"Is that what I am worth? A battlecruiser?"

"No, you are worth an empire."

Chapter Forty-two

The Grand Forum was busy. Essence employees stood in line buying meals. A couple headed into the museum with their kids in tow. Newsfeed played on large screens located at key spots around the huge room. Alexa pointed to a pot of soup and a worker dipped the steaming liquid into a bowl. While the food was good here, she could have eaten better in her family's penthouse. Still, today was special.

As Alexa walked across the huge room with her tray of food, she ignored stares of those she passed. It had only been three weeks since the CF1 and ASF1's faces had been televised at the Galactic Senate. All ten birthmates had stood shoulder to shoulder in front of the galaxy as witnesses that quintessences had become capable of normal reproduction. It had been a proud but scary moment for Alexa. No longer did she have to hide what she was, but it ended her spy missions—at least for now. The ploy had been successful. Essence had been granted nationhood a few days later. It did help their cause having the backing of the Emperor. Even the Edietheans has voted on their behalf.

Natalia and Khloe, carrying their own food trays, joined Alexa as she walked towards a table large enough to hold all ten birthmates. Alexa gave Quinn a brief smile as she passed where he sat with the rest of their squad. He gave her a curious glance as she kept walking. Yesterday she had sent him an invitation saying that Gray Unit should eat today in the Grand Forum instead of their barracks cafeteria. They had come, but none of the females where eating with their squads. Instead, the birthmates were sitting together several tables away.

Zara was already eating sushi with the others when Alexa sat down. "Are you really going to do it?"

"Of course." Alexa stirred her soup, pretending she was not nervous.

Jade said, "I will not believe it until I see it."

Pearl defended, "Alexa has never backed down from a challenge, just like the rest of us CF1's."

Khloe said, "I suggest it would be wiser if you did refuse a few challenges. That way you could avoid unneeded trouble."

"What is the fun in that?" asked Natalia.

Alexa glanced at her e-band. A few minutes yet. She quickly ate her soup, keeping her meal light. Today she could not afford to have her reflexes slowed down from a heavy meal. Out of the corner of her eye, she kept watching Gray Unit while pretending not to.

Zara whispered, "You should stop staring."

"Quinn keeps looking my way," said Alexa.

"That is your imagination. He is busy talking with the others."

"They must be wondering why we invited them then did not sit with them."

"It is almost time," said Natalia, eagerness in her voice.

On all the screens across the room flashed the words "Breaking news." Skylar appeared on camera with the other Five standing behind him.

Pearl complained, "I hope your dad will not be so longwinded this time."

Natalia said, "He has a lot to explain. Be patient."

"Shush. I can't hear." Khloe shot her birthmates warning looks.

"Greetings," said Skylar. "As you are aware, since our nationhood had been approved, the Synod has been in meetings discussing our new government laws. This is not an easy task, and I predict debates will go on for years to come. Still, there are key pieces we have agreed upon which I will share with you now.

"First of all, the Code will continue to be our primary law. Amendments will be added to it, a few already. We will recognize three groups of citizens in our government: bonded, unbonded, and free-born. There will be a set of laws all quintessences are expected to follow which includes our Code of Ethics, then specific laws for each group.

"In the far future, it is our dream that the majority of quintessences will be free-born. They will lack birthmates which has always been our primary family unit. We are a collected society whose strength has always been our unity. To keep that unity, we will require all free-born at the age of seven to train at Essence or a similar facility for a year. Then they will serve in our military for a set number of years. After which they will receive full-level citizenship.

"To speed up the growth for this group, the beta models CF1 and ASF1 have been commissioned. Their models will now be in rotation with others for cloning. Also, the current batch of ten have been given full citizenship, which includes the right to marry. Future versions of their models will have to serve their complete bond years before receiving full citizenship."

Around Alexa, her birthmates smiled, a few poking each other in excitement. Alexa keep her face blank, knowing what else was coming in the speech.

"This brings us to the most important change in our law. Bond years. We in the Synod believe all quintessences, including free-born, need this time to mature and form strong friendships with other quintessences which will last a lifetime. Therefore, we will continue to require military service for a set number of years before any quintessence can receive full citizenship into our nation. No quintessence will belong to the Basanti government. Bonded quintessences will be under the authority of Essence who decides where their postings will be. Many will still work for the Basanti Empire, with payment for their services being sent to Essence. We are still in the process of amending laws dealing with the bonded. Secret agents will have a few more liberties. Some punishments will be lessened for minor offensives."

Pearl sighed loudly. "I knew he was going to be longwinded."

"Quiet," warned Khloe. "Show my father respect."

"While the debate will continue, what we did unanimously agreed upon was the length of service. From this moment onward, all bonded will be required to serve twenty years. Free-born will be required ten years of service. If you have already served your twenty years, you are now a full citizen of Essence. You should shortly receive a message confirming your status."

A great ripple of surprise swept through the room. Besides Gray Unit, most of the quintessences eating in the Great Forum were already free. Alexa tried to image being on a battleship with decades left of bondage to look forward to when suddenly you are told you are free. It would be a moment those quintessences would talk about the rest of their lives.

Skylar continued, "Now I need you to carefully listen. Many of you are positioned in vital areas, some at military bases, some on ships, some in the midst of battle. Though you are now free, we ask that you do not walk away from your postings. Many lives are still counting on you. Instead, we ask that your unit lieutenants put in requests for transfer. We will begin moving you as we can, but we must have bonded quintessences to replace you. Currently, we will not have enough for that. We will be increasing our cloning back to full capacity, but as you know, it will be eight years before the new cadets will be ready.

"During this time of transition, we ask that you patiently work with us. Free quintessences will receive wages for their services. The Basanti Empire has already agreed to begin paying all free quintessences who remain in their current positions. Some planetary governments will wish to employ you. We appreciate your dedication, service, and patience."

Skylar's image faded from the monitor. Immediately excited conversations broke out around the room, meals forgotten. Quintessence society had just been altered dramatically.

"Finally, the speech is over," said Pearl. "So are you really going to do it, Alexa?"

"Of course, she is," said Jade.

Alexa looked over at Gray Unit. They talked animatedly, a few glancing at their e-bands. "They need a few minutes to take it in."

"She is chickening out," said Khloe.

"No, she is not," defended Zara. "Give my sister a moment."

Quinn read a message on at his e-band then showed it to those around him. Others began showing off their own messages. *They are free citizens now*, thought Alexa. *Now is the time.*

She rose and began walking towards their tables. The distance was only thirty feet but it felt far, far longer. Behind her, she heard the chairs of her birthmates scraping the floor as they rose to follow her. Around the Grand Forum, eyes turned her direction. Scientists, soldiers, janitors, food servers, and caregivers were all staring at her and her tagalong gang of clones. Members of the Gray Unit watched the ladies, curiosity in their eyes. Then Quinn looked directly at Alexa.

Panic hit. *Why would he say yes? I have been quarrelsome, obstinate, and reckless. He has lectured me too many times. No way will he take me serious.*

Alexa would have turned and walked out of the Grand Forum, but her birthmates were right behind her. She had spent the last five days bragging to them about this plan, and now all she wanted to do was run away. *Stop, Alexa. You are the firstborn, the example for the others. If you don't at least try, you will be ashamed of yourself forever.*

She forced her feet to keep moving until only a yard from Quinn. "Hello, Sergeant. I formally request…" She froze as she looked into his brown eyes. *I'm only twelve. He is eighteen years older. Does he even like me at all? He did turn me in to the Synod. I have been nothing but trouble for him.*

Zara whispered in a low voice, "You can do this, sister."

Alexa took a deep breath and tried again. "I request a battle for marriage."

Quinn looked at her, puzzled. "A what?"

"Um, my birthmates and I have discussed for a long time what a proper marriage for quintessences should be like. Usually males just follow the customs of their wives. Well, my birthmates and I are setting the custom for quintessences." Alexa held herself rigidly, speaking as properly as she could. "We decided that to become engaged a male must defeat a female in an epic duel. No holding back. If a male cannot beat the female, there will be no marriage. The marriage itself will follow a more romantic human tradition of exchanging vows." Alexa glanced at her sister. "The ASF1's insisted on that."

"So you are asking to marry me?"

"No, I am asking for you to fight me to see if you qualify for marriage. I will not go easy on you."

For a long moment Quinn said nothing. Around him, others of the Gray Unit glanced at each other, a few faintly smiling. *They are finding this amusing. At least Quinn did not laugh.*

"Alright, I accept this challenge." Quinn stood. "Where do we duel?"

"Uh…" Alexa had doubted the conversation would even get this far. "As I offered the challenge, then you choose what type."

"How about bōjutsu?"

During the four years Alexa had known Quinn, bōjutsu was never a sport they had practiced together. She had trained intensely under his leadership, but twirling a stick was not usually helpful in a shootout. "Sure. Right now?"

"Alright."

As Alexa turned towards the corridor leading to the Hall of Challenge, she noticed a flying drone pointed in her direction. *Had someone recorded our conversation?* Quinn kept in step beside her, his face expressionless. Behind the couple came all of Alexa's birthmates and the Gray Unit—along with almost everyone who had been in the Grand Forum. They were curious to see the outcome of this new battle marriage.

The camera drone followed them down the hallway and into the bōjutsu gym. As Alexa walked in, she was surprised to see a crowd far larger than what was typical for this time of day. As she glanced curiously around, she spotted her parents, grandparents, the Five, and their wives.

"How did they know we would be here?" asked Alexa.

Zara said, "We did tell Mamma who must have told Papa."

Pearl added, "My sister and I did discuss this with our parents."

"I know we told our parents. I mean, how did they know to be here, now? Even I did not know that."

"I may have had something to do with that," said Quinn. "Two days ago your father asked me to refresh my bōjutsu skills. He did not explain why."

Alexa noticed a second camera drone had joined the first one. "Did everyone know but us?"

Quinn shrugged. "No one in my unit knew."

Darkfern and Nightstorm stepped forward, each holding out metal bō's. Alexa took one and Quinn the other.

Leaning forward, Darkfern whispered, "Make him bleed double for every wound you get."

"I will try my best."

Alexa moved to a central platform and climbed up. Looking around the packed gym, she saw many familiar faces. Dread filled her. She was certain the whole Synod must be here. *At most, only my birthmates were to be witnesses. I was not trying to make a historical statement—at least not a big one. What if Quinn is highly skilled and beats me quickly? I will look like a fool. What if I beat him easily? How will this affect us working together?* Suddenly, she really wished she had thought things out more before bragging to her birthmates about this plan.

Taking a deep breath, she faced Quinn who stood on the other side of the mat. He stood poised and confident. She had trained often with her father and knew she was pretty good, but Quinn was almost two decades older than her. What was his skill level? How often did pilots practice bōjutsu? Alexa forced her fears away, letting her instincts take over. *I am a warrior.*

She nodded to Quinn and stepped forward. They began to circle, moving into different stances as they tested each other. Quinn matched her step by step. After several minutes, Alexa became more serious, pressing the attack. Quinn dodged while quickly shifting hand positions on his bō. He swung, its end cutting across her arm, its sharp tip slicing into flesh. Alexa winched then leaped over his bō aimed for her feet.

Their deadly dance continued. Ducking and twirling, feinting and rushing, spinning and striking. Quinn landed solid blows, but so did Alexa. Soon both bled from shallow cuts. Quinn jabbed a tip of his bō under her elbow, attempting to disarm her. She managed to recover, but pain in her fingers told her one might be broken. Still, she pressed the attack. He sidestepped, dodging her thrust. She felt pain as his bō smashed against her side.

Stumbling, she feigned to the right. As he moved to intercept, she quickly shifted to the left, doing a sweep. He fell and rolled away from her strike. Quickly he was back on his feet. They circled, looking for an opening. Their metal bōs clanged loudly as they smash together. Alexa dodged to the right, only to feel her feet knocked out from under her. She tried to roll away from his next strike, but he anticipated her action. Quinn pressed a sharp tip against her throat. A kill move.

"You win." For a brief moment, Alexa felt anger at losing, but she pushed the emotion away. The fight had been fair with both contestants equally skilled.

Quinn removed the bō tip and held out a hand, helping Alexa stand. For a moment both stood looking at each other, uncertain what to do now. Clapping broke out in the crowd, with cheers coming from non-quintessences. Quinn gave her a bow and Alexa returned it. Then she hopped off the platform's edge. The moment she landed, she wished she had taken a more gentle way down. Pain throbbed through her body. Cuts, a broken finger, a possible fractured ankle. If she was not quintessence, tomorrow she would have a lot of ugly bruises.

Friends surrounded her, giving congratulations. Zara stepped forward, offering herself for healing, but Hennah cut her off, turning her own back. Alexa had never used the epulo on either of her parents. It felt weird connecting to her own mother until she felt Hennah's warm, motherly pride.

"You have done well, Beti."

"Thanks, Mamma."

"You will make a great wife and mother."

"I hope so. You have been an excellent example for me."

Alexa broke the link, her injuries healed. She embraced her mother in a hug. When she let go, she realized her blood had smeared onto her mother's clothes, but Hennah was not upset. Alexa tried to move to the rag stand to clean up, but it was difficult because so many wanted to speak with her. Never had she been so popular—in a good way. Memories of her trial flashed by. Some Synod members congratulating her now had voted for her death nearly a year ago.

Finally she was able to clean up. As she tossed a bloody rag into a bin, Quinn managed to reach the rag stand. Like her, he was surrounded by friends—and her father. As Joseph had sort of given Quinn a warning about today, Alexa was certain he approved of the match.

Joseph gave his daughter a faint smile. "You fought well."

"I learned from the best."

Feeling emotional, she hugged him, this time not getting blood on her parent's clothes. Quinn took a rag to clean his healed cuts. Alexa secretly felt pride that she had gotten in some good licks. It was a worthy battle.

Across the gym, the crowd became electrified again. Natalia had challenged her own sergeant to a battle marriage. Bystanders surged forward to the platform to see the new fight. Alexa was relieved that attention was being turned off her. She stood beside Quinn, both silently watching the combatants. Natalia was talented, but so was the C5 she battled. The couple weaved and lunged, striking with bone-breaking blows. By the time the lieutenant managed to win, both were bloody. Still, Natalia beamed as she gave a bow to her new fiancé.

Quinn asked, "Are all your birthmates going to battle today?"

"No, at least I don't think so."

When no new fights broke out, the crowd begin to disperse. Alexa walked with Quinn down the broad corridor of the Hall of Challenge, passing many other gyms. They spoke little. Finally, they stepped outside into bright sunshine. Awkward silence came between them as they wandered across the sprawling campus.

Alexa felt uncertainty. She had long thought about an engagement battle, but not what happened afterwards. What did you do with a fiancé? She had known Quinn for four years, but always in the role as her superior. Never had they been alone before.

As they walked pass the huge ball-shaped Recreation Center, Quinn said, "When is our wedding?"

"Well, most likely all of my birthmates will be engaged within a few weeks, so we thought about having one big wedding in Bellus Garden. It was where all our parents were married."

"Who does Zara plan to ask?"

"No one. She prefers to be asked, but she is worried no one will. Several of the other ASF1's feel the same—that is about waiting to be asked."

"They will have no lack of wooers, if the males knew they had a chance. Is there anyone in particular she is interested in?"

"Actually, she likes Fredric but does not know what he thinks about her."

"I can give him a hint when I see him tonight. I suspect it will not take him long to challenge her."

"Thanks. Most likely she will want to duel on the shooting range. See who can get the best score."

"She is one of the best marksman on our squad. Fredric will need to practice before asking her."

The awkward silence returned again as they walked. They paused to watch young ME2's practicing basic bōjutsu stances. The four-year-olds trained in a large plaza as an instructor walked among the group, giving advice.

"Why did you ask me?" said Quinn.

Alexa began walking again, avoiding his eyes. "Logic, I guess."

"Logic?"

"Well, I respect your leadership skills. You taught me well. Did not ask to have me transferred despite my many mistakes. Only reported me once—though I almost died because of that. If I had been found guilty, that would have been a deal breaker."

"Being dead does have that effect," Quinn spoke with a faint smile.

"Since you put up with me this long, I thought maybe you would like to put up with me a lot longer."

They reached the barracks section. Slowly they wandered through small plazas separating the buildings. The courtyards were hedged by bushes and flowerbeds.

Quinn paused in the middle of an empty plaza. "I am honored you choose me."

"I was not sure if you liked me…well, any type of like. We don't always get along."

"Now that I am unbonded, I can confess I was jealous that night you kissed that mobster."

Alexa looked at him in surprise. "You were furious. I thought it was because I broke the Code."

"It was because you broke the Code. But later when I was trying to sleep, I kept thinking about you being executed. I realized my anger came from more than just your carelessness of our law. I admitted to myself my jealousy and tried to be more understanding of your actions. I was afraid you were really going to die, and I could do nothing to prevent it."

"You were supportive, even if you were the one who reported me. Still, I know it was your duty. You had to. But that is behind us now. No grudges?"

"None."

He took her hand while studying her face. Alexa felt a flutter in her stomach. *He is not going to kiss me, is he?* Nervously, she wondered if she should stay still or walk again. Quinn stepped closer until only inches separated them. Alexa's heartbeat quickened.

"I think I am permitted to do this now." Quinn bent forward and kissed Alexa, his lips barely touching hers.

Alexa opened her eyes. "That is it?" Having made out with a criminal, she had expected more. Before Quinn could respond, she wrapped her arms around his neck, pulling him to her. She kissed him firmly, not letting go. His arms tightened around her body as the kiss deepened.

When they finally pulled about, Alexa smiled. "Now that is a proper kiss for a fiancé."

"Yes, ma'am." Quinn faintly grinned, keeping his arms around her. "Good thing your undercover missions are over. I will not need to kill anyone else you try seducing."

"Who said my spy days are over? You think because my face has been in the newsfeed lately that I can't disguise myself?"

"Perhaps we can do diplomatic missions for a while, but I will do the talking."

"Do not take this personally, but you are not that charismatic. I know how to show emotions."

"You will start wars."

"Hey. Well, maybe you are right. Zara might be the best speaker for our diplomatic missions. But we are still doing spy ones also." Seeing Quinn's slight frown, Alexa said, "Don't tell me no. I am about to be your wife."

"We are going to fight a lot, aren't we?"

"Most likely."

"Good, I like a challenge."

Alexa grinned. "So do I."

Epilogue

Five years later

In the observation room, Joseph stood by the large window looking out into the second section of the Fetus Department. For decades the five thousand incubators had sat unused. Now every one of them held growing fetuses. Joseph looked at the nearest rows. There four hundred tiny females slept peaceful in their synthetic wombs. The CF1's and ASF1's would be adopted in pairs. With their existence no longer needing to be kept secret, the requirement that one parent must be human was dropped. As long as the other parent was quintessence, any couple could apply for adoption. The list of eager couples was long.

"Nice to be up to full production again," said Miles, leaning against a wall.

"I have wondered when you would settle down and get married," said Joseph.

"Me? Nah. I like being single. Besides, someone has to put up with your dry humor."

"I have a wife for that."

"Does she even notice when you try to be funny?"

The door opened and Jacob walked in followed by his Shadow Guard. "A meeting here, brother?"

"I have something I needed to share."

They waited as Mason, Gabriel, and Caleb arrived. For a few minutes, they watched through the window as workers birthed a unit of fetuses. The workers drained fluids and expertly removed the squirming infants from their placentas.

Gabriel turned to his older brother. "Why have you asked to meet us here?"

"I have some profound thoughts to share and this seemed a good location." Joseph looked from brother to brother. They had gone through much together over the centuries. Sometimes they bickered, but always they forgave. This would be the hardest thing he would ever tell them. "I have decided to die."

The brothers looked between each other then back to Joseph.

"Hopefully not today," said Jacob.

"No, not soon. But I do believe no one should be immortal. We are not gods. We choose to be reborn so we could guide our species over the generations. We have done that, sometimes at a heavy cost to ourselves." He glanced at Caleb, knowing his brother's struggle of not being with his wife Aurora. "Together, our species made it through a crucible, hopefully the worst we will ever face."

Gabriel said, "There are still problems needing to be dealt with. So many questions unanswered about the freeborn. How will they fit into our society?"

"True. I plan to be around for a few more generations, but when I feel certain that our species has stabilized and is safe, then I will not pass on my memories. I will allow myself to die."

"You miss her," said Mason.

"I always miss Layla, but Hennah brings me great happiness. Someday death will take her from me too. And still I must live on. We all have experienced this grief of losing those we love. Family members living out their lives while we watch from a distance. I now have faith there is life beyond death. I am at peace and am ready when it is my time."

For a long moment no one spoke. Then Caleb said, "I am with your, brother. This burden is heavy that we carry, sometimes unbearable yet we somehow suffer through it. I see Aurora almost every day. She looks at me but cannot see the real me. To not be able to hold her, talk with her like we used to—that is my burden. Still, we are needed here. You are right that in a few more generations, our society should stabilize. Then it is time for us to fade away."

"Fade?" said Mason. "We are legends. Long after we are gone, our memories will live on in every quintessence. You have my blessing, Joseph. I, too, will join you when it is time."

"I also," said Gabriel. "We are talking many centuries yet. There is much that needs to be done until then. I plan to enjoy living."

Jacob said, "This talk is too morbid, especially today of all days. I have a lot to live for, a fourth grandchild on the way. Still, you have my agreement on this matter. Now, how about a game of rugby? My son is visiting with his two younglings. I can round up enough for two teams."

While his brothers made plans, Joseph excused himself. Today, he wanted to reflect. He took an elevator up to the top floor of Richton Tower and strolled along the paths of Bellus Garden. Miles followed several paces behind.

As Joseph rounded a bend, the path opened up to reveal the huge rosa tree growing beside the central plaza. Under the shadow of the tree sat two girls. The young HCF1 had taken apart a telecom and had the pieces scattered around her on the flagstone.

Her sister said, "Do you think you can fix it? Dad will be pleased."

"Yes, I think so. Just needed a new chip."

As Joseph stepped out from the bushes, both girls glanced at him. The HCF1 returned to her work, but the AFF1 gave Joseph a piercing stare which seemed to look into his very soul. She did not have her mother's telepathic abilities, but at a young age, she had begun to copy Amaka's stare when the kuawazo was reading minds. The girl looked very much like her father Mason, with dark skin and braided hair. She, like the other beta AFF1's, showed strong signs of being gifted with the epulo, just like their male counterparts. Someday, she would make an excellent integrator, just like her father.

Joseph gave her a brief smile. She relaxed and flashed him one in return. Then she returned to talking with her sister who had begun putting the device back together.

After checking his e-band, Joseph headed towards his penthouse, barely arriving after Hennah. His wife sat on a sofa, checking messages on her e-tablet. Sitting down beside her, he pulled her legs across his lap and begin massage her feet. Slightly ticklish, she giggled and gave him a light kick.

"How was work?" asked Joseph.

"The newest prototypes are coming along well. Ready for live testing once the current betas are approved."

"That will be some years yet."

"We move too slowly. I think we should go ahead and birth them."

"Normally, we only have one active beta at a time. We are doing two now."

"And that is why you have so few models after all these centuries. I am writing a proposal for the next Synod meeting that we need to speed up the process."

"You will have to speak before a live audience."

"I know, but Lark'ukva and Fran'ukva will be there helping me." She pointed to a message on her screen. "Dyjuna sent us tickets to the first performance of the upcoming season at Harmony Complex. We can also visit Abarrane and Kylen while on Basanti."

"As long as Kylen behaves himself."

"Must you always give him a hard time? He has been a perfect gentleman since the…incident."

"I know, as the quintessences posted as his personal guards give me regular reports. Still, everyone needs balance. I am his."

Hennah sighed. "I know he can be a bit egotistic, but he is putting that brain of his to good use now. Be nice to him this trip."

"I am always polite."

Both Joseph and Hennah's e-bands beeped at the same time. Hennah's eyes glowed with excitement as she read the message. "It's time."

They quickly headed to the elevator and went down many floors to where the Medical Ward was located. The small hospital had beds for only sixteen patients, but rarely were more than half in use. Quintessences were seldom sick, and with their ability for quick healing, almost never did they have a use for the ward—until now. Other sentients at Essence did make use of the ward's services. Anyone needing long-term care was transferred to the large hospital at New Hope.

As they walked into the small lobby, it had already begun to fill with friends and family. Hennah sought out Fredric. "How is Zara?"

"She just went into labor. The doctor says it could be hours. Excuse me. I need to be with her now."

Joseph took a seat beside Hennah. He remained calm, but she was full of nervous energy. All the chairs in the lobby were soon full, yet more came. All of the Five and their relatives. Zara's birthmates and their spouses. Synod members. Even Aurora. Caleb slowly wandered over to her, chatting with her about the documentary about Layla she worked on using video footage transferred from Layla's old computer. Though retired, Aurora kept busy.

The head nurse became upset with so many filling the small lobby. She took on the bustling air of a drill sergeant and began sending visitors away—a difficult thing to do as many held high titles which outranked her. She managed to clear out all but close relatives and those related directly to the Five.

Alexa sat beside Quinn, a furious look in her eyes. "She beat me by two months—two months."

"It was not for lack of trying." Quinn glanced proudly as his wife swollen abdomen. "You cannot win every contest."

"As I was firstborn, I should have had the first child."

"You will give birth to the first male freeborn."

Alexa relaxed. "Yes, at least I can claim that title."

Giggling from a young fjouwer drew Joseph's attention. The three-year-old sat on the floor playing with two dull blades. Nightstorm knelt beside his daughter, showing her how to swing the blades. Darkfern sat on a chair beside her family, her own slightly enlarged abdomen hinting a second child was a few months away.

The head nurse patrolled through the lobby. Seeing the knives, she yelled, "No combat training! This is a hospital. Put those away now." She glared until Nightstorm tucked them away. His child pouted sadly.

"Feels like we are back in school," complained Darkfern.

The nurse took several deep breaths then marched over to Gabriel. "Director Skyler, may I suggest for the next celebrity birth the use of New Hope Hospital. They have a much larger faculty for dealing with this."

Gabriel gave a faint smile. "I have complete confidence in your staff. This is just the first freeborn birth. Soon enough it will become a common event."

"Perhaps then, you will consider moving us to a larger area? Maybe build a proper hospital with a lot more space."

"I will look into that matter."

Satisfied, the head nurse left to check on her only patient. Seeing that she was gone, Rockgem moved to sit on the floor beside his niece. He pulled out his karambits and rapidly switched the blades' positions. His niece clapped her four hands in delight.

Mistdawn smiled. "I remember when our two sons where that young. They grow up so fast."

"Not as fast as quintessences," said Skylar. "I am looking forward to being a grandfather myself soon."

Several hours later Joseph and Hennah were permitted to see their daughter. Zara lay in bed, tired but with a tender smile as she held her new daughter. Fredric kept by his wife's side, his attempts of keeping a stoic face failing miserably. Everyone wanted to hold the new infant.

Alexa cuddled the infant gingerly, a motherly smile on her face as she thought about her own coming son. Hennah cooed over her grandchild, reluctant to give anyone else a turn. Pallavi and Kaushal could not stop beaming. Aashi held the infant low so her two young children could get a good look. Dhruvi had his wife take pictures of him holding his new niece.

It was sometime before Joseph got his chance. He tenderly held his small granddaughter—the first quintessence without a genetic twin. She was unique, her abilities unknown.

"What is her name?" he asked her parents.

Zara glanced at her husband before answering. "We named her Hope."

Joseph studied the sleepy infant with a frizz of black hair. "That is a good name."

Author's Message

Books have fascinated me since I was a small child sitting beside my mother, listening to her read books I had selected from the library. Soon I was reading on my own, and I never stopped. Over the years my interests have varied wildly from stories about animals to the classics to science fiction, and much in between.

In sixth grade my English teacher assigned us to write a short story. I got a tad carried away, writing a VERY long story about the adventures of a cat. Part of the way through the writing process, I realized this is what I wanted to do the rest of my life.

So I began writing short stories and eventually novels. I also became an English teacher because I wanted to share my love of literature with others. I later branched into teaching technology, another one of my passions.

The results you hold in your hands is from years of exploring my imagination and the intensive but exciting labor of writing.

I would appreciate, if you have a moment, giving my book a rating at Amazon, Goodreads, and other sites that interest you. In the limited free time I now have, the books I choose to read are usually recommended to me by friends, so I know the power of word-of-mouth.

I hope you enjoyed reading this book as much as I enjoyed writing it.

Sincerely,

Vista Townsend

Updates for new projects can be found at:
Website: vistatownsend.net
Facebook: Vista.townsend
Twitter: Vista_Townsend

www.ingramcontent.com/pod-product-compliance
Lightning Source LLC
Chambersburg PA
CBHW060155260626
47160CB00001B/273